Touch

Okay, so I gave this book 5 Stars, only because I seriously could not put it down. It captivated me. The story was told beautifully.. I also found myself having to reread certain parts just so I could understand things correctly. The story has a few twists and turns you won't see coming. You will understand Beth's desperate attempt to save her husband. You just may not understand why, until the end.

This will be like no other love story you have ever read.

~ Two Ordinary Girls and Their Books

I've just finished my third reading of TouchStone for ever, and it gets better every time. I cry in the same places, I lose hope, hope returns; I fight for them both, as the author intended. However, most of all I TRUST that Sydney Jamesson will deliver an unforgettable story - the likes of which you will never read again. Yes, it's that good. It's "movie-worthy-good" - transcending the ordinary in a spectacular way! This is what you get with TouchStone for ever: two incredible characters whose love is so powerful, so destined, it surpasses what we accept as the human experience and becomes something truly metaphysical - the kind of love we would ALL like to believe is possible. It is the theme upon which every fairy tale is based - and we remember them all for that reason.

~ Lady Loves Books Blog

An Opera of a Novel

I often criticize books for being too stereotypical or using too many cliches, and I have to compliment Sydney Jamesson for doing something completely different. It was creative and I had no idea what was going to happen next. This was absolutely a stunning conclusion to The Story of Us Trilogy. Feels less like a conclusion to a trilogy and more like an adventure of its own. Lots of spirituality, fate, and introspection on the true nature of love.

Margo's Red Light Fiction District

Blown away, does not even cover how I feel about this book. In all honesty, I don't think that whatever I say in my review will EVER begin to relay just how much this story affected me. I think I experienced every single emotion on the spectrum. The conclusion to this beautiful trilogy has left me with a story that will be enjoyed time and time again. Sydney has captured my heart and imagination with these characters

~ A Goddess and Her Books

Unlike the first two TouchStone books, this takes a completely different turn down the road of fantasy. I honestly was not expecting this twist at all. It definitely is very beautiful, full of love and lust and a richness I could never even imagine. It is a very interesting and unique read and trust me… it's not what you'd expect at all. Just throw away everything you ever thought you knew about Ayden and Beth and pick up TouchStone for ever today!!

~Eryn La Plant: author of Beneath the Wall, The Blue Lute, Falling for Shock.

To Sylvia,

TouchStone

for ever

A love like this is beyond ordinary... it's extraordinary!

Sydney Jamesson

Regards

Jamesson
xo

First Published by S. J. Publishing, 2014
Copyright © Sydney Jamesson, 2014

A CIP catalogue record for this book is available
from the British National Bibliography (BNB)
S. J. Publishing

sjpublishing@virginmedia.com

ISBN 978-0-9575850-2-7

To the people in my life who mean the most to me, I thank you for your love and support: Barry, Jenna, Mum & Dad

Time is too slow for those who wait,
too swift for those who fear,
too long for those who grieve,
too short for those who rejoice,
But for those who love,
time is eternity.

Henry Van Dyke

This is no ordinary love ... it's extraordinary.
Read with an open heart and mind
and ... believe in Beth.

The Story of Us ...

T hese past few months, I feel as if I have lived several lifetimes. I have fallen in love, travelled the world and changed my name; I have been face to face with Evil and come through the experience battle weary but alive.

Ayden Stone and I wear our scars like medals of honour; matching mementoes of a time when we did what had to be done and lived to tell the tale; each new chapter bringing us closer to this point when our love transcends even the powers of the universe. He is and always will be my saviour and my soul mate.

Our bond cannot and will not be broken.

Some days are better than others; the ghosts remain hidden, afraid to appear in the light but, when darkness falls and I dream, that which I fear most rises as if from the dead to haunt me, possess me and steal me away.

I cannot outrun it, defeat it or deny my destiny.

Self-sacrifice is my only weapon; I must wield it with care, for every deadly blow to the heart strikes deep, deeper than an ocean, wider than the sky.

Only my knight in shining armour can save me... or, perhaps, we will have to save each other once again.

So, as I prepare to embark upon this magical adventure in search of my happy ever after, I invite you to look and listen, and let me conclude the story of us ...

1

In a single thrust he enters me, swallowing up my moans as the sweet agony of his penetration has me convulsing. He rocks back and forth, widening the gap, making the outward movement infinitesimally longer each time until he is ready, once again, to slide into me in one stomach clenching thrust.

He growls with contentment. "Look at me, Beth."

I open my eyes and see my husband's features. All my senses combined serve only to seduce me into total submission.

Through heated breath he whispers, "I love you. You're mine."

W hat's buzzing? Is it in the room? Is it in my head? I feel as if I've been caught between two radio stations; I'm trying to tune in but only hearing white noise.

With absolute concentration I engage my senses until the distorted sounds disperse and reform into the beeping of a machine and gentle snoring.

Where am I?

My head is resting heavily on a pillow and turning to the right feels like a major feat, requiring actual mental effort to do so.

My body appears to be glowing with warmth; the balmy air in this hospital room is suffocating and the body heat radiating off Ayden's hands around mine has me close to igniting. A centimeter at a time I release my fingers and raise my hand as you would a lead weight until it comes to rest on his left cheek. I linger on the bristles before weaving my fingers into his hair, gasping in horror when I see the extent to which his face has been battered and bruised. My chest hurts and tears form. I try to contain them as you might a pint pot overflowing with froth but ...

My beautiful boy...

He stirs and I still my hand, following the line of his silhouette with my eyes. He's wearing crumpled clothes and a white shirt that has been roughly rolled back to the elbows. His wedding ring is the only object to draw the light. It's a reminder, if any were needed, that we are connected; that we have always been connected.

I leave him to sleep, letting myself settle to the sound of his slow, even breaths then open my eyes suddenly when I hear movement at the other side of the room. Fearful of what I might see in the shadows, I turn my head to the right, squinting until my eyes make sense of the shape sleeping in the chair by the window. It's Jake.

Relieved, I allow my head to fall backwards into the pillow and return to that dark space devoid of sensory stimulus; the place where there is only warmth and the reassuring clutch of his hand as it reaches for mine.

As the haze of half sleep is diffused by the glow of early morning light, I hear hushed voices...

"... I know you're worried about her Ayd but she's gonna be alright. Now stop with the fucking moping around."

"Fuck you, Jake! You don't know what she's been through. I should've made sure she had protection. That bastard was about to rape her. He would have killed her. I know it."

I picture Ayden's hand across the back of his neck, massaging muscles that have become knotted with anxiety and lack of sleep. I listen in, letting them think I'm still sedated.

"Look, if she wanted to go off on her own after you told her not to, you can't blame yourself for what happened. Lester recognised the guy from her apartment block. He was dead set on getting her. Even that Bowker guy said he'd been stalking her. What a fucking psycho!" He pauses, thinking through what he's about to say. "The last thing she needs is you on a guilt trip. For fuck's sake have you gotten a look at yourself lately?"

I'd only had a glimpse of him and that was bad enough. I squeeze my eyes shut and focus on silent breathing.

"Once she's up and about you can take her off somewhere. She mentioned going on your honeymoon on the flight back."

There is a thoughtful pause ...

"She did? What else did you two talk about?"

"This and that."

"Don't play games, Jay, tell me."

"She knew about Alenka and ... Elise."

Ayden huffs. "Yeah. We spoke about Elise. Beth got hold of the video, you know, the one with you in the basement..."

"Fucking hell!"

"Yes. That's what it was alright," he states plainly.

"How did she get hold of that?"

"Elise paid me a visit while we were in Vegas and left the SD card where she knew Beth would find it."

Jake is horrified. "What a bitch! And Beth watched it?"

"She watched enough ..."

"Jeez! And did she think ..."

"... Oh yeah. She assumed it was me ..."

"And you told her it wasn't, right?" He waits expectantly for Ayden to answer.

"I had to. It scared the shit out of her, thinking I wanted to be like *that* with her."

"I'm not surprised. She's not some twisted fuck who gets a kick out of being treated like that. Have you heard from her?"

"I told her not to call me but she does, around ten times a day. I don't think she's one to take rejection in her stride. She'll be trouble."

"I've got your back. I'll have a word with her."

"Watch your step, she's a loose cannon. Why do you think I've played along for so long?"

"Beats me! It's none of my business but why you even got involved with that bitch in the first place is a mystery to me. She's got some major issues."

Ayden sniggers. "I just hope she never finds out who Beth *really* is or that will be one almighty mind-fuck"

"What do you mean?"

"Those pictures of the three of us at Bright Hill, remember, I showed you once?"

"Yeah. Now that *would* rattle her cage."

"I won't let her get to Beth. I have to keep her safe, or die trying."

"You almost did that already, remember?"

"I tell you Jay, when I saw that bastard with her over a table ..." He can barely bring himself to utter the words.

Jake is disgusted at the thought. "I'd have carved him up."

"Yes. Well ... he might have had something to say about that ..."

"What do you mean?"

"He was a big bastard, you know. And turns out he was a boxer, heavy weight I'd say. He could box. He had me."

"Fuck!"

"I watched as Beth played for time while I caught my breath." He pauses. "She was like a rag doll in his hands and she still took him on. You had to see it to believe it, Jay."

"She is something, Ayd."

"Always was ..."

There's movement and I visualize a hand on a shoulder. "Well, you've found her and she's safe now. The last thing she needs to see is you in yesterday's clothes. Go take a shower, have a shave and I'll keep watch. Don't want her coming face to face with some fucking hobo when she wakes up."

Ayden sighs at the thought. "You're right, especially as I have to break the news to her."

The news ...

"What will you tell her about the baby?"

No ...

"What *can* I say? He must have used her as a punching bag before I got there."

"Right now she needs to get over the operation and recuperate, Ayd. She needs you to be strong."

Operation?

"Look, Lester's brought your overnight bag." He moves across the room. "Here take it and go make yourself presentable. If she wakes, I'll come get you."

The door of what I assume is an en-suite bathroom closes and the sound of running water tells me I am alone with Jake. I hear him approaching and sense him looking down at me.

A gentle hand pushes back a strand of hair from my brow. "I don't know if you can hear me, Beth but ... I apologise for the way I've treated you, as if you were just another one of Ayd's ... friends. You're more than that. I see it now. Get well beautiful." I feel warm lips on my forehead a single second before I fade into oblivion.

***

A black Golf GTI crawls along the curb, crushing fallen leaves in the gutter, before coming to a deliberate stop outside 4 Milton Avenue. That's the address Elise Richards has scrawled on a scrap of paper; it belonged to Dan Rizler.

Earlier in the day, she called Human Resources at Cambridge University pretending to be a Police Detective confirming the address they had on file for their recently deceased employee. They had been eager to assist with her investigation and in less than ten minutes had provided her with what she needed to check out his primary residence.

Anticipating it would not be a desirable place in which to live, she has dressed down; slipped into a pair of jeans and a white blouse, even tied her hair back, intending to freshen up and put her work clothes back on before returning to her office in town.

Leaving the sound of the car alarm ringing out behind her, she approaches no. 4; a two-story, seedy-looking block of apartments that would benefit from being knocked down and rebuilt; better still turned into a car park or a supermarket.

Next to the door there are four buzzers; 4a has the name Rizler next to it but she presses them all: 4d answers.

"Yeah."

"Delivery for 4a," she says. To her delight, it clicks open; she steps inside, taking care not to touch anything, even though she's wearing a pair of black leather gloves.

Stepping into the dark and dingy entrance she becomes aware of the smell of dampness and neglect. The first door on the right is 4a. The lock has been broken and it is slightly ajar. It creaks as she pushes it open, one inch at a time.

All she can do is shake her head when she enters. "What a shit hole," she remarks. "So this is where you lived is it, Dan?"

Stepping over broken pieces of chairs and shredded cushions she makes her way to the far end of the room, spotting the clean rectangular patch of wallpaper about the size of a noticeboard on the far wall. "I wonder what you had pinned to that wall, Dan? Pictures of little Miss Perfect I should think." She sneers at the thought.

In the bedroom there is more evidence that someone once lived there. Tattered clothes, an unmade bed and ... on the floor she spots an old mobile phone. It must be around ten years old. She picks it up and turns it over, detecting the missing battery by its light weight, hoping to find something else in it that could prove useful. She slides off the back and shakes her head. The SIM card has been removed. "Oh, well."

She dismisses the remaining contents of the room and returns to the kitchen area, scanning the corners and crevices for any clues that might help to unravel the mystery of Dan Rizler. She marches over to the rubbish bin and, with one hesitant hand, lifts off the plastic lid that is carelessly balanced on top. Inside she sees a plastic bag. The bag seems full of paper but, when she drags it out, she sees it's full of torn photographs. Tipped out onto the kitchen table the photographs scatter like jigsaw pieces, leaving her to match faces to bodies. She soon recognises that it's the same girl in every photo.

"What have you been up to, Dan?" she sneers. The tell-tale pin prick holes on the corners of each photograph are all the clues she needs. "You have been stalking Miss Parker for some time, it seems. You naughty man."

She prepares to step away from the spread of mismatched images, but one of them catches her eye. It's yellowing around the edges but Elizabeth Parker is in perfect focus, posing shyly. Her dark hair is blowing around her and her right hand is lifted to her mouth as she leans into the group sheltering from the wind.

She holds the two halves of the photo in front of her and scowls. "What the fuck!"

2

Awakened by the thirst of a desert rat, I wrestle with the light. When I blink my way back into the present, I'm confronted by a clean-shaven, deliciously fragrant husband whose smile is so profoundly intimate I could weep.

"Hello, Mrs. Stone. Welcome back. Don't try to speak. Take your time." He caresses my face with a warm hand and I lean into it and close my eyes, without the need for words. Seconds come and go and I lick my parched lips, in an attempt to coat them with moisture, but there is none.

"Wait a minute, I'll get you some water."

He returns with a glass of chilled water and a straw. When the liquid hits my throat, it does so with the force of an avalanche, making me cough.

"Slowly..." He places down the glass and takes hold of my right hand. "You had me worried. I thought you'd hibernated again."

I shake my head and mutter words that scarcely sound like my own. "No, just sitting out a cold spell," I answer, recalling one of our earlier conversations.

"That's good to hear. And are you ready to come back to me?" he asks tentatively, his tired eyes overflowing with devotion.

"I never left you, Ayden," I reply, smiling lovingly. "I've been right here all the time." Lifting a weighty arm I outstretch my fingers until they come to rest on his heart.

He weaves his fingers into mine and keeps my hand in place. "You were so brave." He's shaking his head and holding back an outpouring of emotion that threatens to smother us both. "But it's over now. All you have to do is get better."

I lift my hand as before, gently stroking his bruised jaw, caressing the skin beneath his left eyes that's still tinged with grey. "You fought so hard." I blink away tears.

"I had everything to lose."

I slide my hand around his neck and pull him to me, feeling his breath brushing against my left cheek. "Tell me what's happened to me."

Pulling slowly backward, he takes a galvanizing breath. Unable to meet my anxious stare he looks down and strokes my hand. "You were beaten up pretty bad and ... and they had to operate on you straight away."

I wrinkle my nose, "Operate?"

"Yes. But you're perfectly fine now."

"I have a heart monitor attached to my body and a cannula in my hand attached to an IV, so it must have been something serious. What did they have to operate on?"

He hesitates. "You were bleeding internally. I assume he punched you before I got there ..."

"He did ... I was stalling and he punished me for having a smart mouth."

He squeezes his eyes shut tight at the thought. "Well his punishment was brutal, Beth. He caused a serious trauma to your abdomen ..."

I'm shaking my head, trying to make sense of it but his explanation is cloaked in medical jargon.

"What does that mean?"

"It means he perforated the wall of your uterus with a single blow. You were hemorrhaging internally. They performed an ultrasound scan, saw what had happened, and got you into surgery within thirty minutes." He reaches out and strokes my hair, patiently waiting for some kind of response.

My mind is in a whirl. "What about our baby?"

He shakes his head, slowly, feeling the agony of loss with each millimeter.

I nod. It's not like I didn't know.

"Try not to worry about that now. There will be plenty of time for baby-making when you're fit and well." He tries to lessen the blow with a flat smile. "I'm upset about it too." He edges closer and wraps his arms around me. "You're all that matters now."

With my one free hand I stroke his back, feeling tense muscles beneath my fingers.

His soft thumb brushes away my tears. "Now. This is what we're going to do. I'm going to call the nurse and have her come and freshen you up. And, while she does, I'll go and get you something to eat. What would you like?"

"I'm not hungry, Ayden."

"You must be. It's been two days since you ate. Today's Thursday."

I'm shocked. "Thursday!"

"Yes. You've been out of it for a couple of days. It's ..." He glances at his watch. "It's 5p.m. What shall we have to eat?" He's trying so hard to be brave but the way his eyes are darting from left to right, I know it's all bravado.

"Anything. But only a small portion."

"Leave it with me. I have special training in patient care, remember." He kisses my forehead. "I'll be right back."

Alone for the first time, I feel the weight of a heavy heart. I have a scar on my stomach, which I have yet to see, and a feeling of emptiness that is sucking my energy with the force of a black hole. I remember falling into this dark place and now, clawing my way out of it will take every ounce of willpower I have.

The door opens and a smartly dressed nurse of around forty enters, pushing a silver trolley. On the top of it is a bowl of steaming water fragranced with something flowery. Beside it is a white, fluffy towel and a flannel; next to that an assortment of toiletries and a mirror. I assume I'm to have a bed bath.

"Good afternoon, Elizabeth. It's good to see you're awake. My name is Lorna. Now let's get you feeling a little fresher, shall we?"

Silently, I nod and prepare to be bathed.

I'm feeling a little better when Ayden returns laden down with brown paper bags, brimming over with food. I assume he has invited guests as there's surely enough for a party of four. He proceeds to empty the contents onto the side table, whispering something about knives and forks. I take my eyes off the food and give him a lengthy appraisal from head to toe, noticing his roughly dried hair and the four o'clock shadow on his chin that fails to conceal the bruises. I look at his hands and how they are bruised and grazed on the knuckles, the result of bare-fisted brawling with my monster. But, most of all, I focus on the clouds of sadness extinguishing the fire in his eyes. He is a man exhibiting the emotional and physical scars of a life and death struggle. He's my savior. He's the man I adore.

"Ayden," I call, drawing his eyes from the food to me. "Help me sit up and tell me what you've brought for dinner." A person can only wallow in self-pity for so long.

One handed, I eat what I can of the delicious pasta and vegetables and sample the meat dish, trying to appear willing but, in truth, forcing it down. He's doing the same and we both pick at gourmet food that finds its way into our mouths only to stick in our throats. It's a kind of weight-watchers waltz that involves pushing food around a plate and feigning consumption. We're both too full of sorrow to eat.

I pat my mouth with a napkin and marvel at the swiftness with which he clears away the food, refilling the bags until they are once again brimming over. With that distraction out of the way he fluffs up my pillow and perches on the side of the bed, preparing to make idle gossip, but he has absolutely no idea how to do that and I come to his rescue.

"Have you spoken to Charlie?"

He nods, thankful for my conversation starter. "Yes. She was one of the first people I called. She's been here three times while you were sleeping."

"Is she alright?"

"You're the one in the hospital bed, Beth," he reminds me.

"I know but she worries about me."

"As well she might, you've been to hell and back."

I force an amiable smile. "I'd like to see her later. Just to let her know I'm okay."

"I'll call her, don't worry. Do you feel tired?" He pulls up the bedding around my waist.

"No. Just worn out, but I'll be alright."

"You will. The consultant Gynecologist should be along soon. He has the results of some tests and of the ultrasound scan you had this morning."

"This morning? Why don't I remember that?"

"You've been sedated. I told them I didn't want you to suffer, so they thought it best you rested while your body healed."

"Oh. I suppose I should thank you for that."

"No need. I was happy to watch you sleep." His hand finds my face. "You're so beautiful, Beth"

I huff away the compliment. "I don't feel beautiful and the nurse wouldn't let me see myself in the mirror. She said maybe tomorrow as if I was a two year old. Why don't you pass me a mirror so I can see *just* how beautiful I am?"

He's shaking his head. "There's no rush. Just take my word for it, for now."

"You're a terrible liar, Ayden. I can imagine what I must look like. I can feel my lips are swollen and my face is puffy. I remember what he did to me, and what he did to you."

"Don't worry about me. Just a couple of cuts and bruises. It's nothing to write home about."

I lift his left hand to my lips and kiss his knuckles. "There. All better."

Unable to contain powerful emotions, his voice cracking, he wraps me in his arms. "Beth, I love you so much."

I bury my nose in his hair. "I love you more, Ayden."

The door opens and a tall gentleman enters wearing a golfing sweater and slacks. Unselfconsciously, Ayden releases me, wipes his eyes and turns to face him, "Good evening, Mr. Roper. This is my wife, Elizabeth Stone. She's wide awake and looking lovely." His face creases into an exaggerated smile.

"And so she is. Good evening, Elizabeth. I'm the consultant Gynecologist. How are you feeling tonight?"

I shrug my shoulders. "Fine."

"I do hope your husband has been taking good care of you." Ayden steps aside, allowing him to take up his position by my side. He takes my hand in his, resting experienced fingers on my wrist to feel my pulse, and checking the monitor beeping to my left. "You have a good colour. Have you eaten anything?"

"Yes, we've had a picnic dinner," I answer, glancing over at Ayden who, for some reason is beginning to pace anxiously.

"Very nice." He looks into my eyes and I sense some kind of announcement is coming. "I assume Ayden has told you that we had to operate?"

I nod.

"You're doing very well now, but the baby you had growing inside you is no longer there. Thankfully it was early days, but I know that's no consolation."

"We've spoke about it. I understand. We have plenty of time to make babies." I force a smile and look over to Ayden who's nodding in agreement.

He slides off the bed. "Good. Now I must continue with my rounds. If you need anything or want to chat about anything at all, you have my number. Goodnight, Elizabeth." He turns to Ayden, "Mr. Stone…"

I watch him leave and wonder why Ayden is so quick to follow him out. I feel perfectly fine, a little sore but not in any pain or discomfort.

When Ayden returns, he has the weight of the world on his shoulders; he's pacing, rubbing his neck, looking across at me then turning away.

"Ayden? What's wrong?"

With a thud he rests uncomfortably on the edge of the bed, contemplating his words. He begins to speak then stops.

I can't stand the waiting. "Tell me!"

"They analysed the results of the ultrasound scan this morning and it's … it's …" He looks at me through eyes that are swimming in tears. " … it's not good."

My heart is racing. "What do you mean?"

"There was a lot of internal bleeding. They fear you may not be able to conceive again after what he did to you … baby, I'm so, so sorry."

He leans in to embrace me but I push him away. "What! You're telling me I can't conceive. We may never be able to make another baby?" The seriousness of his declaration causes tears to roll down my cheeks like a flood. Between sobs I'm pleading, "That can't be true. Please tell me that's not true."

He lifts my hand to his mouth and his tears trickle over my fingers. He can't speak. He simply nods.

"How can this be happening? Ayden! How? That bastard has haunted me forever and even in death he still tortures me." I shake my hand free of Ayden's and sob into my palms until my cries fuse into a gut-wrenching howl.

Forcefully, he pulls my hands from my tear soaked face and places his own inches in front of me. "We'll travel the world looking for a cure. There are things we can do." He's trying to offer me a lifeline but, in my emotional state, his words are lost in the whirlwind of realization. He can offer me no hope. Nothing.

"Beth," he whispers, this is another hurdle for us to get over, baby. It's just that. We still have each other. I love you more than life itself. You remember that, right?"

I'm shaking my head; too distraught to hear anything.

"I know you wanted our baby so much, but it wasn't meant to be."

I can't accept what he's saying. "But it's what *you* wanted. You said so; to finally have a family. You won't have that, not if you stay with me."

"Beth, I don't give a fuck about what I said. This is about us now. We'll get through this, together."

I pull my hands free of his. "No. I can't let you do it. You deserve better. I can't give you what you want most. I've been nothing but trouble since the day we met. Leave! Just leave!"

He looks at me with undiluted horror. "No! Why would I want to leave you?"

"Because I don't want you here." I slip down under the bedding and turn away from him. I can't allow him to settle for me. I have always been damaged goods. I've been soiled and now ...

His hands are in his hair. "You're upset. I get that, but you're doing what you always do. You're taking the fall for me; trying to let me off lightly when it's *all* my fault." He's shaking his head, massaging his neck and so fueled with rage I think he may explode. "I should have organised 24 hour security for you. I should have kept you safe and I'm the one responsible for this not you! I'll leave so you can rest but, no matter what, I will *always* come back to you." He storms out of the room, leaving me open-mouthed and speechless.

Left alone to reflect on my unreasonable behavior I struggle to hold onto a rational thought. The drugs have dampened my senses, I'm not thinking straight. I didn't mean what I said. He's not responsible. I sit bolt upright and call out his name. "Ayden."

No one comes.

"Ayden!"

Nurse Lorna appears, leaving the door ajar. I catch sight of him sitting on the floor, his back against the far wall; his head in his hands. Jake towers over him, placing a sympathetic hand on his shoulder.

"Lorna, please get Ayden."

She senses my agitated state. "Now, Elizabeth, please settle down. Are you feeling any pain?"

"No. Please get Ayden."

"Can I get you a drink or anything?"

"No! Just get me my husband," I yell at the top of my voice.

Looking startled she returns to the door and opens it. I see Ayden snatching the keys out of Jake's hand. His fists are clenched and he is visibly shaking and yelling. "Give me the fucking keys!"

Before I can form a sentence, he's gone. I call out his name, "Ayden!" But no one hears; only Jake turns and glares at me, stunned, realizing what just happened.

What have I done?

***

Too incensed to return to work, Elise storms out of Dan Rizler's apartment and dives into her car. She heads home harnessing her thoughts long enough to call her office, claiming to be laid-up with a migraine.

Once inside her top floor apartment she makes straight for the tray of spirits neatly arranged on a wooden cabinet and pours herself a very large whiskey. She gulps it down and smashes the glass onto the tray with a noisy clatter.

Kicking off her shoes as she goes, she drags a dining chair beneath the loft opening and begins lowering dust-coated boxes one at a time until three of them litter her tidy lounge. They were once labelled but the letters have long since faded and the occasional streak of a marker pen is not enough to distinguish one set of contents from another.

With hands covered in a layer of black soot, she tears open the first box; a plume of dust scatters across a cream rug, speckling it with black polka-dots until it resembles a snow leopard.

Unconcerned, she rifles through the contents, lifting out estate agency paraphernalia: brochures, a Contract of Employment, old wage slips. Realising it's not what she's looking for she pushes it aside and tears off the tape from the top of the second box. Inside are old exercise books, a Certificate for taking part in a Tennis Tournament and a small winner's cup for an under 16's Netball Competition. All these things are worthless in her eyes. The one thing she is looking for must be in the third box.

She scratches off the tape with her fingernails and lifts back the flaps. Inside are multi-coloured pouches from an assortment of photo processing companies; odd photos are bundled together in years or holidays. Right at the bottom are a selection of photos that have faded and yellowed over time. At least two of them are 22 years old but no less important for the passage of time.

She takes hold of them, one in each hand. The first, on the left, is of her with an older boy. He has waves of black hair and eyes that sparkle like the Caribbean Sea. He has his arm around her shoulders as if protecting her from all the horrors of a cruel world. She rubs her thumb across his image and smiles at the recollection; days spent in summer sunshine, hours spent in the library, just the two of them; him reading aloud, her dozing under his arm, listening to the gentle beating of his heart. She holds the photo to her breast and closes her eyes, as if it will magically take her back to a time when she felt safe and loved.

When she opens her eyes she's still a woman sitting alone, surrounded by an assortment of memories that pale into insignificance compared to the photo she has in her right hand. She holds it so tightly her thumbnail turns a ghostly white, chilled by the ice that has leaked into her bloodstream.

Like an injured animal she whimpers at the sight of the three of them together; her with Saffi and *that* girl who came to stay for a week. The one he watched over, took under his wing and married beneath swathes of dust-sheets and ladders they had transformed into a Cathedral. She played the part of the priest; made up something or other about being in love forever and gave them her blessing. This little speck of a girl was the princess and Saffi, well, they both adored him so much he could be whoever he wanted: a lord, a king, even a prince.

Pushing everything aside, she places the photo down onto the parquet floor and takes the torn image from Dan's apartment out of her bag. Just to make sure, she places it beneath hers. Recognising the stance, the hair and the emerging beauty of the dark haired girl, she comes to only one conclusion. Ayden has married Frances; he must have looked high and low for her. That one realisation cuts through clothes, flesh and bone and pierces her heart.

She voices her desolation with an agonising cry. "You looked for her but never looked for me." She beats her fists onto the floor and sobs while her tears fall and crash around her like hailstones.

Still hoping she's wrong she drags herself across the floor and opens a drawer, taking out a newspaper cutting of the recently married Mr. Stone.

She spreads it out beneath the university photo and makes comparisons. The hair colour has changed but it's the same girl. There's no mistaking her childlike stance and gentle smile.

Elise's body appears to crumple beneath her; she visibly wilts like a flower on the verge of blossoming but starved of attention and left out in the midday sun to die. Of all the disappointments in her life this is by far the worst.

She rocks back and forth and wails mournfully for the love she thought she once had; out of a long line of painful disappointments, that was the single sliver of goodness she could look back on and retain in her memory as one might a precious particle of hope in a vacuous empty space.

With that gone, she is left with nothing.

She tries to stand but the combined effects of grief and neat whiskey have affected her balance. Instead she crawls on all fours over to the cabinet and uses the knobs and frame to stand. With one trembling hand she holds the glass and with the other, starts to pour the whiskey until all her fingers are covered. She sips at the golden liquid and staggers over to the dining table. In front of her is a notepad and pen but she won't be jotting down the names of prospective homeowners or addresses for viewings, this will be the last thing she ever writes. Thinking only of Ayden, she puts pen to paper and begins ...

To S.

When there was nothing but dark shadows in my life, I had you. Your radiance was so bright I was happy to kneel at your feet and lift my gaze to catch some of that light on my innocent face.

When the dark shadows took me away I called for you every night until I realised you wouldn't come. I was alone ...

Having completed it, she throws back the dregs from the glass and folds the notepaper in two, her dirty fingerprints serving as a seal of sorts. She places it in her bag and stumbles as she steps over the tattered pieces of meaningless flotsam; all that remains of a world now in pieces.

She grabs one of the sharpest knives out of the kitchen drawer and drops it into her bag, taking a lingering look at herself before she reaches the front door. Her brown eyes are framed in mascara that has become smudged and runs like grey scratches down her cheeks. Even her blouse is spattered with dusty black patches from lifting boxes down from the loft.

"What a fucking mess," she exclaims, throwing down her bag. "I can't face you looking like this."

She makes her way across the corridor in the direction of her bedroom, dragging herself along one step at a time, through a drunken fog that clouds her vision and numbs her senses; smearing the wall with dirty fingerprint. Not stopping to close the curtains, she tears off her clothes and sorts through her wardrobe for something suitable for the occasion. She finds a figure hugging black dress just above the knee with a neckline that shows off her ample bustline. She sniggers, "You'll love this."

She ties back her hair and washes the smudged make-up from around her eyes and from her cheeks with a flannel until only the palest of canvases remains. As per her routine she applies moisturizer, foundation, blusher and eyeliner with trembling hands and a body that sways like a boat lost at sea. The crimson-coloured lipstick is the final touch.

She smiles into the mirror, having intentionally transformed herself, incorporating everything Ayden despises in a woman. She knows what men want; she worked that out at an early age, too early. He'll see her as she is: flirtatious and brazen to the core. High heels and a couple of squirts of heady perfume and she's done.

She grabs her bag and car keys and leaves the apartment, wobbling on black stilettos as she descends three flights of stairs. She flings back the exit door, leans into the icy wind and prepares to right all wrongs.

3

No matter which way I turn I cannot sleep. I'm haunted by the memory of Ayden's panic-stricken face. I had no right to say the things I did. It was a knee-jerk reaction that I should have thought through, considered with a level head and a less troubled heart. I've hurt him badly with my flippant disregard for his feelings. Why must I continue to be plagued by my own insecurities and subject him to them? What possessed me to send him away?

I'm attached to these tubes and electrodes like a woman on her deathbed but I have to get them removed. I press the buzzer by my bed and wait for the nurse to arrive.

When she does, she instantly recognises my unease and begins to fuss with my bedding.

I draw her attention. "Will you get me my phone, please? I need to make a call."

"I think you should be resting, Elizabeth. We don't want you worrying about making phone calls."

I'm shaking my head. "I really do need to call my husband, right now." I'm becoming more distressed with each word; my breathing is becoming jagged and uneven.

She takes my hand. "Elizabeth, your husband is very worried about you. He has probably gone home to collect clothes and toiletries." She starts to pat my hand. "Now can I get you a cup of tea or anything?"

I feel helpless but I'm too physically and emotionally exhausted to put up a fight. "A cup of tea would be very nice. Thank you."

Ayden will be back soon ...

Sedated by hot tea and a nurse's affirmation that all's well, I'm listening to the radio, allowing myself to paint pictures in my mind. A fifties classic by the Flamingos voices my thoughts. *I Only Have Eyes for You.*

From beneath grey clouds, hanging like dirty laundry obscuring a clear blue sky appears a terracotta landscape and a technicolour slide show of our Vegas trip; images that comfort me and help to reshape my bruised face into a smile. I hear Ayden's voice and feel his lips on mine but then ... my artistic endeavours are abruptly halted by the sound of irate female voices outside my door, increasing in volume.

"I know what bloody time it is. This is important ..."

"I'm sure it is, Miss Miller, but Mrs. Stone is sleeping."

No I'm not

"Believe me, she'll want to know what I have to tell her. Get out of my bloody way!"

Only Charlie would cause such a commotion and unsettle the still evening air with the velocity of a tornado.

The door opens.

"Move out of my way!"

I turn to face them both. "It's alright nurse, I'm not asleep. Let her come in."

She closes the door behind her. "They're like the friggin' Gestapo in here!"

I see something in her eyes that worries me. She is the bearer of bad news, I just know it. "What's up Char? What's got you so fired up?"

She flops herself down on the bed on my right side and reaches for my free hand. "I've been here a few times while you've been out of it and you're looking better every time I see you."

She's stalling.

"And you caused such a fuss to come here and tell me that?"

There's more ...

Her eyes evade mine, momentarily. Then she faces me square on. "There's been an accident and I don't want you finding out off some friggin' nurse."

What little colour I have on my cheeks begins to fade as I am gripped by fear. "What do you mean, accident?"

"It's Ayden."

Air fills my lungs in a gasp and a whimper leaves my open mouth. "What!"

"He was driving Jake's car too fast on the motorway and it hit the central reservation and then careened off onto the hard shoulder. It came to rest in a ditch."

"Oh my God!" I'm clenching my fists, trying to hold onto the desperate thought that he's okay. "Please tell me he's alright!" I grip her hand much too tightly.

She glances at the heart monitor that is beeping, recording my anguished state. "Beth, you've got to calm down."

"Just tell me he's alright," I plead, seeing her through eyes that are bubbling with tears.

"He's alright but ..."

"But what? Tell me!" I'm shouting.

"He's concussed and appears to have an injury to his face from the windscreen when it smashed. Also a couple of bruised ribs from the seat belt ..."

"But he's not in any danger?" I'm thinking of the word fatal but I can't bring myself to say it.

She shakes her head and tries to reassure me with a flat smile. "He's not in intensive care or anything, but he's pretty shaken up."

I'm beginning to sob, torn apart by both relief and guilt. "It's *all* my fault!" I mutter, weakly.

Charlie grips my hand. "No it isn't your fault. How could it be? He was driving recklessly. Too fast. Why the hell was he driving Jake's car, anyway?"

I know why.

"I made him leave. I said some horrible things to him and he was so distraught. I tried to call him back but he rushed off and took the car keys." I shake my head despondently. "I was so worried that something like this might happen."

"Even so, you shouldn't blame yourself. That's just not right."

"But I do. He wanted to stay. Oh Char, what am I going to do?" I look into her eyes in search of an answer but I see only compassion.

She reaches around me and I rest my head on her breast, only for a moment before she leans back and strokes my hair. "The first thing you're going to do is get some rest and get yourself better. He won't want you worrying about him. He's physically fit and he'll bounce back. You'll see."

"I pray you're right. He doesn't deserve to suffer like this, not after all he's done for me."

"He's not suffering. They have him here in the hospital and they've done every test known to man. Jake's had them running around like ants."

I'm suddenly alert. "He's here, in this hospital?"

She nods. "Jake had them bring him here. The Cromwell Hospital is recognised as one of the best in London."

"I didn't think to ask what hospital this is." I feel like such a fool.

"Well now you know." She's smiling, affectionately.

I have an idea. "Then I want to see him now."

She's shaking her head. "You can't. It's late. You're all wired up."

"Then go and get someone to unwire me!"

"Beth ..."

"I mean it Charlie. I have to see him." I lift my left hand, watching the tubes to the IV bag sway and jiggle around.

"Whoa! Be careful. I'm going, I'm going. Jeez!"

When she returns she isn't alone. A rather disgruntled nurse is pushing her aside to check the cannula inserted into the top of my left hand is intact.

"Mrs. Stone, you really should calm yourself."

"As you can see from the machine I am calm. Now I want you to disconnect me from it so I can go and see my husband. He's been involved in a car accident."

She prepares to speak but recognising my dogged determination, reconsiders. "I can't do that without authorisation from a doctor, I'm afraid."

"Then go can get the doctor," I instruct, unwavering in my stare.

She's shaking her head. "I don't think that's a good idea."

"I didn't ask you for your opinion. I just need to be disconnected, now, so I can leave this room."

She leaves the room in a flurry or disapproving sighs.

"Charlie. Get my bathrobe and slippers from the wardrobe please."

She places the fluffy robe on the bed.

"Go see if you can get a wheelchair from somewhere."

Now she's blowing a strand of hair off her face. "For someone who's supposed to be sick, you're friggin' bossy."

All I can do is shrug my shoulders.

After a ten-minute conversation between the Head Nurse and my consultant, Mr. Roper, I'm separated from the heart monitor, but the cannula must remain.

With extreme care, the IV bag is pulled through my left sleeve and in 30 minutes I am dressed in my nightie and bathrobe, ready to be wheeled across the hospital to Ayden's bedside.

The night nurse leads the way and Charlie pushes me down empty corridors smelling of disinfectant and floor polish, taking long strides to keep up. We take the lift up two floors and, when the doors open, we are greeted by the duty nurse.

"This way, Mrs. Stone. Your husband is comfortable but unconscious at the moment. Sometimes this can happen after a serious accident."

Fearful of her answer, I ask one question, "When will he wake up?"

"It's difficult to tell." She smiles apologetically.

"I have to see him."

She stretches out her hand to open the first door on my right. "This is his room."

Before entering I close my eyes, saying a silent prayer. I feel Charlie's hand on my left shoulder, squeezing it gently. Instinctively I hold onto it with my right hand. Ayden's words resonate in my head like a song.

"Be bold, baby."

He is lying beneath a single light, looking like a sleeping prince in a fairy-tale; his hands by his side, fingers outstretched, motionless. The familiar beep, beep of the heart monitor is reassuring. At least he's alive.

Silently, Charlie wheels me over to his bedside. Across his forehead are small scratches like splashes of red paint, but most shocking of all is the pad of white lint covering his right cheek. The last time I looked upon him like this was in Rome, when I awoke and observed him sleeping, dreaming. We watched the sunrise over the rooftops and met the new day with confessions; we made love and conceived our first and probably only child. And now, here we are, all that shot to hell.

There are things I need to say to him, alone. "Will you give me a minute please?" I whisper, not really asking at all.

Charlie kisses the top of my head. "We'll be right outside."

I nod silently.

Ever the professional my nurse leans into me. "Please don't stand, Elizabeth. I don't want you to fall."

I nod again.

Once the door clicks shut behind me I crumple like a pack of cards. Quietly sobbing, I wheel myself nearer to him. I take his right hand between mine, comforted by the warmth of his fingers against my cheek. But it's a dead weight and I must hold it in place, wrapping my thumb around his, folding his fingers around my hand in a tender embrace.

After a hard swallow I begin. "Ayden, I'm so sorry for sending you away. I don't know why I said the things I did. I love you so much and I want you to have everything. That includes a family. But we *are* a family, I realise than now. You're my family, you're the family I've never had but only dreamed about, waited for. And I'm yours. I have always been yours."

His eyes flicker. There's a slight increase in the heart rate displayed on the monitor, or maybe it's just wishful thinking.

I wipe my tears on my sleeve. "We created life and it was the best of both of us, and it's gone. But I'm still here, you're still here and the best is yet to come. I just know it." In a faltering voice I prepare to address my promise; the promise I made on our first date. The one I have broken.

"I promised to take care of you, to always be here for you however you needed me. Please forgive me for forgetting my promise and come back to me. I can't live my life without you."

I bow my head and reach out to brush the left side of his face with my fingertips but I can't reach and settle for bristles masking purple coloured bruises. "You're still my beautiful Saffi, my husband, and the only man I will ever love."

In an act of contrition I bow my head, resting it on his bed and cry so woefully I think I may drown in my own tears. Like a miracle, I feel his fingers against my hair, the gentle caress of a lover raised from the dead.

Yet, when I lift my head, he's motionless, statuesque in his gentle repose. His right hand rests on the covers, in the same place. Did I imagine it?

Having regained a little composure, I run my fingers under my eyes. "I know you can hear me and I know that, when you're ready, you'll come back to me. Because what we have, Ayden is bigger than both of us. We have to get through this ... together."

I pull up the covers around his chin and wheel myself backward. "I can hear you saying I love you, Beth so I'll say I love you more. Goodnight sweet prince. I'll come back tomorrow and awaken you with a kiss. You'll see."

The door opens behind me and I signal my desire to leave.

"Ready to go back?" Charlie asks, resting both hands on my shoulders, offering her support and understanding.

"Yes. I'm tired." I have one last look and lean back into the chair. "Let's go."

***

In no fit state to drive, Elise Richard starts up the engine and heads in the direction of Cromwell Hospital. She plans on visiting a patient there who may be less than pleased to see her but, 'What the fuck,' she muses. 'It's about time we had a little chat about a couple of things.'

She parks carelessly in a disabled parking spot and flips down the mirror. Pleased with her appearance she ruffles her hair to give herself a ravaged look and licks her lips, hungry for physical contact of the sexual or the painful kind, preferably both at the same time.

Not bothering to lock the car or turn off the engine, she staggers in the direction of reception, steadying herself as she reaches the doorway.

Like a man possessed Ayden pushes past her, looking once then twice before recognising her. "What the fuck are you doing here?" He storms off, not waiting for a reply.

Regaining her balance she trots after him. "Ayden, wait!"

"I'm not in any mood for your fucking mind games, Elise." He shakes off her hand as she makes a grab for him.

"Slow down. Where are you going?" she calls out, breathlessly.

"That's none of your business." He turns to face her. "I told you we're through. You won't be getting anything more off me so you may as well get on with your life and I'll do the same." He inserts the key in the Shelby Mustang GT 500, Jake's prized possession. Before he can start up the engine Elise slides into the passenger seat and slams the door shut.

"Why are you driving? Where's Lester?"

He flips over the key and the engine begins to purr. "I gave him the day off," he answers harshly. "Now, get out of the car."

She shakes her head. "Not until I've said my peace."

He inhales deeply and catches the odour of hard liquor. "You stink of whiskey. You're pissed!"

"I might have had a couple of drinks, so what do you care?" She tries to fasten her seat belt but gives up after a couple of bad-tempered tugs. She reaches for the radio, instead.

He's shaking his head. "Have you driven here in that state? It's a wonder you weren't arrested." He shifts into reverse, pushing her hand away from the dash. "Leave the fucking radio. I'm taking you home."

Feeling suddenly unsure of herself, she flattens her hair and sits back in her seat. "That's kind of you," she says, sarcasm dripping from her lips. "Aren't you the gentleman?"

Ayden gives her a sideways glance. "Just shut the fuck up, Elise, and enjoy the ride."

She begins to giggle, the way a deranged woman might on the verge of something catastrophic. "I always do, Ayden. You know that. In fact I have the video to prove it!" She begins to laugh hysterically and runs her hand along his collar.

He shakes his head free. "For fuck's sake. Just sit down and behave yourself."

She turns to face him. "You'd like that wouldn't you, for me to bend over and take it like a good little girl? Like Elizabeth Parker - or should I call her Frances? What name does she go by these days?"

Shocked by her outburst, Ayden fights to compose himself, tensing the muscles in his jaw, containing his rage. "Look, I don't know what you think you're playing at, but forget it and don't mention Beth, again."

She's not intimidated by the harshness of his tone or even the way his jaw is flexing as he concentrates on the flow of traffic. Nothing he can say or do can hurt her now.

"I stumbled across some old photographs and there we were the three of us at Bright Hill. We spent days together when *she* came and then, when she left, it was just the two of us. We were like two peas in a pod: Saffi and Elise. You fought all my battles and read to me. You even hid me in your bed until they came for me." Roughly, she wipes a tear from her eye, "She was only a visitor Ayden; we were residents. We only had each other."

His eyes dart from left to right but he says nothing.

"It just struck me as odd. How you managed to find her but you never came looking for me." She feigns nonchalance but Ayden picks up on the hurt in her voice.

"I did try to find you. Once I got my shit together and started making some decent money, I paid a private investigator to look for you, but it was a waste of time. You'd married and changed your name, moved around and there was no trace of you once they took you away."

Her head falls. "They took me away to another residential care home."

He speaks quietly. "I asked everyone, but no one knew - and if they did, they wouldn't tell me. I didn't know what happened to you."

"How could you?" She pushes back her hair from her face. "I waited and waited for you but you never came, and the years just came and went. I did what I had to do to get by."

"I realise that."

She raises her head like a cobra about to strike. "No you don't realise anything. They still abused me. Those two bastards from Bright Hill used to come and visit. One would hold me down and the other would hurt me. Month after month they raped me, Ayden."

He reaches out a hand and places it on her arm. "I'm sorry, Elise." He punches in the button on the radio, hoping a ballad will sooth her. Buddy Holly sings *True Love Ways*.

He's wrong.

Her bottom lip begins to quiver. "I loved you. I still love you and I found out today you never loved me. You only loved *her*. She was your princess then and she's that now. She has her prince and I have ..." She begins to sob.

He's searching for the right words. "Look, I did love you, Elise, but not the same way. I loved you like a ... brother."

"A brother! But you fucked me," she roars, her face contorting into an unrecognisable snarl.

He shakes his head. "No I didn't, Elise."

She will have none of it. "Yes you did, Ayden!"

He keeps his eyes fixed on the road ahead. "When you were in the basement, that one time, I couldn't do it. That was Jake." He turns to face her. "I'm sorry."

Open mouthed she falls backwards into her seat and begins sobbing and shaking uncontrollably. "No! You're lying! It *was* you!"

He can't find the words and simply shakes his head.

"Then *everything* has been a lie. My whole fucking, miserable life has been based on a lie." She reaches for her bag and takes out the knife. "Turn around and go back to the hospital."

Startled by her irrational behaviour, Ayden swerves the car. "Put the knife down, Elise," he whispers showing the upmost restraint.

She takes hold of it with two trembling hands and puts it against his left side. "I mean it. There's someone I want you to introduce me to."

He feels the sharp edge of the blade against his left side. In response, his eyes flash in her direction. "I'm not going back to the hospital. I'm not letting you get within ten feet of Beth. I'm taking you home." He accelerates and moves into the outside lane of the motorway.

Elise rocks back into her seat and yells, "I mean it, Ayden. Turn around."

"No fucking way!" He tugs at his seat belt, ensuring it's securely fastened. "Put your seatbelt on and put the knife away. You'll hurt yourself." He glances over to her as fresh tears begin to swamp her eyes. "Now stop this craziness and let's get you home."

For some reason that single word, *home*, seems to strike a discordant note with her; she plays with the knife, running her finger along the blade, passing it from one hand to the other, deciding what to do next. She lets the knife fall but, rather than follow his instructions, she lunges at him with bare hands.

He leans back. "What the fuck!" Thinking she's trying to claw at his face he raises his arm defensively, but she has other ideas.

"I won't let you go back to her," she screams, taking hold of the steering wheel with both hands and pulling it towards her.

Ayden calls out at the top of his voice. "What are you doing, you crazy bitch? You'll kill us both!"

He holds her off with one hand and fights to right the car, but the metal fencing on the central reservation is on his right side and other vehicles on his left. There is nowhere to go.

Single-handedly he tries to straighten the wheel but over-compensates. The car hits the barrier and a crunching sound signals the folding of metal and the shattering of a headlight. By way of a rebound, the car veers off to the left and spins as if on polished ice, throwing them both backwards in their seats. He slams on the brakes and they jolt forward. The screeching sound of burning tyres is deafening but Elise is too unhinged to hear it. Her screams ring out, not out of a fear of dying but of living *without* him.

"Elise, Elise!" Ayden shrieks as the car slows to a grinding halt but, before he can regain his bearings and take control, an enormous four wheel drive vehicle ploughs into the side of the car on the passenger's side, sending them careening off the motorway, flipping over twice before coming to rest in a deep ditch.

Two spinning rear wheels and one flickering brake light appear out of shroud of dust. All that can be heard is the sound of screeching brakes coming from passing cars and a ghostly rendition of *True Love Ways*. Two passengers are motionless: one slumped in their seat and the other spread eagle out across the bonnet.

4

F eeling more like myself than I have for days, I skirt the room with my eyes. It's more like a hotel suite really: teak wardrobes and easy chairs, a dressing table and a view. Who could ask for a better place to rest and recuperate?

Thankfully, the cannula was removed from my hand last night. I even accepted a sleeping tablet, knowing I would simply lie here tossing and turning until breakfast; left alone to torment myself with self-deprecating thoughts and numbing fear. Instead I slept.

As the November sun edges its way between the blinds, I'm reminded of the days I have missed, lying here apart from the world outside my window. So much has happened: most of it memorable for all the wrong reasons. Ayden and I have to start over; pick up the pieces and re-shape them like hot dough; then watch them rise and transform into something wholesome and good.

One day at a time ...

When the door opens and Nurse Lorna enters, I'm relieved to have my reflections halted by the prospect of hot food. I'm hungry. I settle for toast and cereal with a cup of tea, which goes some way towards grounding me. It's a taste of home.

No sooner have I eaten than my first visitor of the day arrives. Charlie appears around the door carrying a bunch of my favourite flowers. The fragrance from the freesias fills the room with memories of summer and I'm taken back to happier times. She knows what I like. Yet, she's gazing out of the window, onto what I have no idea, playing with the buckle on her suit skirt, biding her time.

"It's only 9.30 a.m., Char, I expected you later."

"Yeah, I was going to come this afternoon but I got a call from Jake and thought I should drop by." She's shrugging her shoulders, intentionally lengthening her sentences, unwilling to meet my eyes.

"And ..."

"He told me what happened last night." Now she's biting her lip. That's never a good sign.

"What about last night? Do you mean with Ayden and his accident?"

She's nodding her head.

"And are you going to tell me? Or should I get the nurse to inject you with something; a truth serum, perhaps."

She sniggers. "No, I'll tell you. You'll find out soon enough anyway." She sits down on my bed with a heavy thump. "First, let me say I'm so sorry, Beth, about the baby and, you know ..." Through pursed lips she tries to smile. "Keep your chin up."

"I will. So, tell me ..."

"About last night ... Ayden was driving, but he wasn't alone in the car." She gives me time to take in the implications of her words.

"He wasn't?"

"No. Someone called Elise was in the car with him."

Elise! I just knew that bitch would crawl out of the woodwork again.

"And is she in this hospital too?" I enquire, brusquely.

She's shaking her head, slowly.

"Stop with the head shaking, Charlie and just tell me. Where is she?"

"What do you care? She's in the morgue." She scrutinises my face for a reaction.

Her news hits me like a shockwave, making me shudder. "What! Are you sure?"

"Yes. Jake said she was dead at the scene. Ayden was unconscious so they cut him free of the wreckage and air-ambulanced him to the nearest hospital. When he was stable, he was brought here. They said it was a miracle he wasn't killed outright with the force of the collision." She takes my hand. "He must have had a guardian angel watching over him, Beth."

Instinctively, I wrap my hands around my cheeks and cover my eyes. "Thank God for that. Did Jake say what she was doing in the car?"

"Who?"

"Elise!"

"No. Anyone would think you knew her," she huffs. "They looked through her bag and got her name off her bank cards. They asked Jake if he could identify the body, and he said yes. He must have known her too."

Oh he knew her all right ...

"I can't believe it. It's just too shocking to get my head around. Thanks for telling me." I reach out to her and we hug, allowing any remedial healing to diffuse through our clothes.

She strokes my hair and pulls away. "So who was she, anyway?"

"A friend of Ayden's," I lie.

"Friggin' hell. He'll be cut up about her being killed, especially as he was driving."

I nod silently, lost in a myriad of thoughts.

She tucks a strand of red hair behind her ear. "Anyway, that's all I know. I suppose you'll be taking another trip to see him later, so I'll let you get some rest. I've got an 11 o'clock meeting I have to prep."

"I understand. I'm going to be up and about. I can't lie around here all day." I smile affectionately. "I'm going to wake him with a kiss."

She nods and fashions a sympathetic look that has no need of words. "You know what? Nothing would surprise me right now. Just don't push yourself too hard, that's all." She offers a farewell hug and scoots off; bag in one hand, phone in the other.

"I'll take it easy. Bye."

She leaves my scented room quietly and, once again, I'm left alone to devise some kind of plan, having been rocked to the core by her news.

Elise is dead!

I have to get out of this bed and on my feet. Ayden will need nursing once he's discharged. I press the call button and my friendly nurse appears.

"I want to get out of bed and walk across the room," I state, throwing back the covers.

"Oh! Slow down there, Elizabeth, you'll need to practise standing before you can walk. You'll feel a little dizzy at first. Let's take it very slowly, shall we?"

I swivel around to my right side and edge my feet off the bed in search of terra firma. Lorna slides a pair of slippers onto my feet and I gradually lift myself up and off the mattress, swaying with the after-effects of sedatives and anaesthetic. Breathing deeply I take a single step, feeling the weight of my own body pressing down upon me like a sack of rocks. Gradually, I regain my balance, my coordination returns and, between deep breaths, I take lengthening strides. I turn when the door opens and the shock of seeing an apparition causes me to wobble and tumble into the arms of Nurse Lorna.

Ayden comes to my rescue and lifts me off my feet. With the broadest of smiles, I rest my head on his chest and wrap my arms around his neck, in no hurry to be put to bed.

"What were you thinking ..." he chides, finding it difficult to conceal a smile.

I caress his face with my hand, stopping short when I feel the ragged line of fine sutures an inch in length across his right cheekbone. "I was thinking of you."

He's shaking his head and lowering me onto my bed. "I might have known. Let's get you back to bed before you fall and hurt yourself." He glances over to Lorna who seems rather taken with my delectable husband - and so she might. He's a vision in charcoal grey. He turns to her and presents one of his hard to resist smiles. "Would you excuse us?" As she leaves he continues to fuss with my covers.

I try to meet his elusive gaze. "Ayden! Leave the covers and look at me." I take hold of his hand firmly.

Reluctantly he lifts his head until it's level with mine. Fixing him with a magnetic stare, I see how those blue, green hucs have mingled into a kind of speckled pallet of cerulean light. Even with apologetic eyes he's beautiful.

"I'm sorry for behaving so irrationally yesterday and causing you to crash." I feel my lips beginning to quiver. "I didn't mean what I said. I need you. I want you here with me, forever. Nothing will change that." I rest my cheek in his upturned palm.

"You didn't cause me to crash. Elise was in the car with me. She became incensed and grabbed the steering wheel. We veered off the road and ended up in a ditch because of her psychotic sense of injustice. It had nothing to do with you."

"But if I hadn't sent you away, you wouldn't have been driving the car. And ..."

"... And nothing. I would simply have driven around for a while and returned, unscathed."

"You say that but ..."

"No. I say that because it's true. We both needed time to process what we'd learned. It was distressing but we're both stronger for it and we'll get through this together."

Through happy tears I am nodding. "I can't believe that Elsie is dead. You must feel terrible."

He clears his throat and blows out a gust of air. "I feel for her but I'm not grieving; for the girl I knew perhaps, but not for the woman she had become. She was damaged, through no fault of her own. Yet she chose to take the path she did and to behave as she did of her own free will."

"She did. But any loss of life is tragic in its own way. She's been so badly treated. She didn't learn how to love."

"That's a very charitable way of describing her failings."

"No it's not, Ayden. It's the truth."

He's nodding and swept away, lost in his thoughts.

"Are you thinking about your childhood, your time at Bright Hill, your marbles?"

He shakes his head and smiles softly.

"Maybe you should leave them with her when you attend her funeral."

He's startled by my assumption that he would even consider making an appearance. "Why would I attend her funeral?"

"Because you loved her, once."

"Be that as it may ..."

"You have to go."

He gives me a reproving look. "I don't have to do anything of the sort."

"You're right, you don't. But at least think about it."

He pats my knees beneath the blanket. "I will."

I grasp at his hands. "I came to visit you last night when you were concussed. I was so worried about you. Do you feel okay? "

"I'll be fine." He offers a reassuring smile. "I heard you but I couldn't respond. I came around in the early hours and paid you a visit but you were sleeping."

"You did!"

He nods. "But enough about me, how are you feeling? Ready to come home?"

I'm nodding my head and the bed is shaking.

He's laughing at my overly animated response. "It feels good to be here, with you."

"That's because it's where you belong," I state smartly.

He offers a tight-lipped smile. "Yes. It is."

Nurse Lorna makes her presence felt with a cough. "Excuse me Mr. Stone, but I would like to take Elizabeth's blood pressure and temperature now."

He pulls a disgruntled face and takes a backwards step. "Go right ahead. She's all yours for the next ten minutes."

I watch him head off into the bathroom; the door is ajar and I make a point of observing him. I'm tracing the line of his broad shoulders and muscular back; the way he fills his jeans front and rear. No wonder my heart rate is a little high, suddenly. He winks at me and it skips a beat. Oh, how I've missed this husband of mine.

Lorna inflates the cuff at the top of my left arm and catches me looking. She leans in to whisper. "He came here last night in the early hours and stayed for half an hour, just watching you sleep."

"He told me." I smile and continue my visual inspection, a little unsettled by the fact he is looking at himself in the mirror. There's nothing strange about that, except for the intensity of his look and the time elapsing; it smacks of narcissism. Perhaps it has something to do with the cut to his cheekbone and the likelihood of a scar. But that wouldn't have bothered him before. He's not a vain man; he has simply been blessed with good looks and a generous helping of charm. Yet, I look at him now and I wonder ...

For a minute longer he practises his movie star smile and turns this way and that, playing with his fringe ...

"There, all done. Everything is perfectly normal, Elizabeth but, if you take my advice, you'll try and calm yourself down and resist any ... urges for the next couple of days." She tips her head in Ayden's direction and smiles shrewdly.

All I can do is smile innocently in response to her observation. She's right of course. I still have to recuperate from my stomach operation. That's just one of my battle scars I have yet to inspect.

"All done?" Ayden asks, returning to my side.

"Yes. All your wife needs now is rest and lots of attention, Mr. Stone."

"Oh, I think I can arrange that," he states humorously. "I'll call Lester and have him bring the car around."

"Please wait until I can arrange for a wheelchair." She turns to me. "Would you like me to help you get dressed?"

I shake my head. "No thanks. I think I can manage." Once again, I slide my legs out of bed and cautiously place my feet on the floor, mentally counting the number of steps it will take to reach the bathroom.

"Here, take my arm."

I hold onto his right arm, leaning into him as I move gingerly towards the illuminated mirror and my big reveal.

"What do you want to do?" he asks, unsure of my intentions.

"I want to freshen up and get dressed." I straighten my back and try to balance myself unaided.

"Here, sit down. I'll get your clothes."

He leaves me to sit and catch my breath, but the pale and bruised woman I see reflected back at me steals the breath from my lungs.

On returning he stops dead. "Don't worry about the bruises. They'll heal quicker than you think."

His words seem hollow and lacking in compassion. "I know the bruises will heal." I look up at him. "I'm more concerned about you ..."

He tips his head to the right. "Me? I'm perfectly fine."

"Are you? You seem a little ... distant; as if you're scared to touch me." I wait to be reassured.

"I'm sorry. Seeing you like this ... it's ..." He looks about the room for an answer. "It's distressing. I'm afraid to touch you in case I hurt you. You've been through such a lot and your body is still healing."

"This is true," I answer almost as a reflex action but he doesn't react. I can't help but wrinkle my nose. What's happened to him? Where's my playful Ayden? I need him to raise my spirits before I fall backwards again into that dark abyss.

"Leave my clothes. I'll dress myself." Feeling just the right amount of tenacity to stand, I reach for my underwear.

"If you're sure?"

"I am."

He exits quietly, leaving me to struggle with my clothing and face my hideous twin. I dress as quickly as I can, running my fingers over fading bruises on my arms and my face. I remove the padding from my stomach and I'm pleasantly surprised to see a small discreet scar just below my belly button. It's not as bad as I had imagined, but it's the invisible damage concealed in the cavity beneath it that causes tears to prick my eyes.

I reposition the padding and cover myself with a plain black dress; somewhat fitting under the circumstances. I clip back my hair and splash my face with cold water in the hope of encouraging cream coloured cheeks to blush. My tinted moisturiser helps but does little to conceal the tinge of blue beneath my left eye.

Holding onto the counter top, I trace the worry lines forming between my eyes and apply lip-gloss to lips that are still a little swollen and, then it hits me … I haven't kissed him for over four days. He's not even made any attempt to hold me. Has his concussion taken away his ability to feel anything for me?

I've heard of people changing after accidents; not being themselves…

There's a knock on the door. "I'll be right out." I pull myself together and prepare to face the music, terrified my own imaginings might actually be true.

I'm met with a warm smile. "All set?" He pulls the wheelchair out for me to sit down. "Take a seat while I pack your things."

Obediently, I sit, monitoring his movements as he hurriedly collects toiletries and bits of clothing. As is my way, I am silent and pensive.

Lorna hands Ayden a bag of tablets and creams for me; he places them on top of everything else and zips up the leather case. We're ready to leave.

Lorna bids me farewell. "It's been nice meeting you, Elizabeth. You're well on the road to recovery. Just make sure you don't do too much too soon."

"Thank you Lorna." I look up at him. "Let's go home."

Lester is waiting outside the main entrance. He quickly opens the door to the Rolls. I catch his sympathetic smile and acknowledge it with a nod. After some careful manoeuvring, I seat myself on the back seat and Ayden joins me. Instinctively I reach for his hand and he takes hold of mine gently, offering reassurance but nothing more.

"I've asked Bernie to set up the bed in the guest bedroom for you until you feel a little stronger. I don't want to roll over in the night and hurt you."

I knew that was coming.

"That's a good idea. I'll feel right at home there."

Why make a fuss?

"It's only temporary, until ..."

"... Until, we both feel more like ourselves".

"Exactly."

I try to settle my misgivings about his remoteness and attribute it to concussion and his need to take care of me; depriving him of my affections in the process, it seems. But, all I want to do is curl up in his arms, to feel the warmth of his body next to mine; to have him whisper sweet nothings in my ear. To be healed by his love.

***

Detective Constable Sheridan is struggling to carry a large box of items relating to the Richards case. He moves towards a glass door with the initials CID – Criminal Investigation Division - neatly engraved in a gold font, and pushes his weight against it. Grateful to be relieved of his burden, he places it on a side desk and begins to remove its contents.

Once they are laid out, he finds the appropriate form on his laptop and begins to list them in no particular order. He reaches for his camera out of the drawer, clicking away until every single item has been listed and accounted for; this includes a knife in a sealed plastic bag and a hand-written note that he reads through then slides into a plastic wallet, recognising its significance to the case.

He adds the case reference number to the file and prints it out complete with the photos from the attached SD card, including those taken at the scene and his seemingly relevant array of items. All this will await the attention of a senior offer. He was told to record, but can't help reading through the report written up by the officers on the scene.

It makes for a gruesome read but he presses on, reading two witness accounts. One says how the car spun out of control and the other makes reference to a passenger who seemed to be leaning over to the driver, causing him to lose control of the car. Two eyewitnesses have given an account of a four-wheel drive vehicle that appeared to slow and then speed up, purposely charging into the sports car.

The fatal injuries sustained by the passenger would support that, indicating the driver, Mr. Ayden Stone, was merely a victim in this crazy woman's suicidal scheme to kill them both; but ... what does he know?

With the job done, he places the file on the in tray, turns off the light and leaves the premises, thinking no more about it.

5

Ayden places my case on the guest bed and I sit myself down beside it, kicking off my shoes. "Thanks, I can take it from here."

"Would you like me to run you a bath?" he asks hesitantly, watching my face for signs of discomfort.

"Yes, that would be nice."

"I'll organise something to eat; a salad of some sort with a selection of cold meats. How does that sound?"

"Delicious." I smile weakly at his attempt to move things along. Maybe this is how he deals with such a traumatic series of incidents? Just to get on with things; act as if nothing of any significance has happened?

But it has ...

I stifle a whimper with my right hand. He's standing a foot away from me but there's an ocean between us. One of us has to reach out before we are swamped in sadness so deep we may drown in it.

"Ayden, look at me." I rest my hands on my thighs and lift my head so our eyes are locked: misty aquamarine and blue topaz bonded together. I see the tell-tale marks that bear witness to our encounter with a madman, but those scars run deeper than the bruises on his face.

"I understand why you want to wrap me in cotton wool; to lock me away where you know I'll be safe and well looked after, but that's not what I need." I reach out my hand to him. "I need you."

He takes my hand and edges closer. "I know."

"I don't think you do. I think you're grieving or you're in shock or something, because you're not yourself, not with me." I tighten my grip on his hand and tug at it to prompt a response. "Talk to me. Tell me how you feel because I don't think I can take much more of your coldness." I wipe away my tears with my free hand before they dampen my cheeks.

He bows his head. "I'm sorry. It's a coping mechanism, I suppose ..."

"But you don't have to cope alone. We've both been close to death and the dead, there's no denying that, but ... by some miracle we're alive. Fate has taken us by the hand, Ayden, and led us to this point and ..."

He lowers his head and smiles ruefully. "Is that how you see it?"

I stand before him, caressing his scarred cheekbone with my fingertips. "It is. I won't cease to exist if you say my name. The name you whisper when you're teasing me; that same name you call out when we make love. I need to hear my name leave your lips, if only to be reassured that you still love me; that you remember me and what we had."

"I want to remember, but for that I need your permission." He fixes me with a serious stare.

"Permission?"

"Yes."

I flop down heavily on the bed and fiddle with my wedding ring. "I don't understand."

"You will, in time ..."

Our conversation is ended abruptly by a knock on the bedroom door. "Excuse me, Mr. Stone, I have a selection of your wife's clothes from the master bedroom as you requested."

He points Bernie in the direction of the wardrobe. "Thank you. Please place them in there."

Ending our conversation he exits the room and I am left watching my clothes slot one piece at a time into an empty wardrobe. Bernie closes the door and turns to face me, trying unsuccessfully to conceal her surprise as my ghostly pallor. "Can I get you anything, Mrs. Stone?"

I shake my head. "No thank you Bernie, and please call me Beth."

"Thank you. You can reach me by pressing zero on the phone by the bed at any time. Please don't hesitate. I've prepared a selection of food for you in the fridge, so when you're ready ..."

"That's kind of you, thank you."

She turns and walks quietly out. I lick at the gloss on my lips, feeling the plumpness of tender flesh. As I breathe, the scar on my stomach stretches and contracts, leaving me with a painless feeling of tightness. All in all I am visibly healing, but the fact I may not be able to conceive is a crushing reminder of my brutal attack. An unwelcome shiver of fear runs the length of my body; fear at what might have happened and fear of what is to come. I can't begin to even contemplate living my life like this; a married couple under one roof with nothing to connect them other than a surname.

I pour some expensive bubble bath into the bubbling water and watch it fill with scented froth. The room folds in around me as the steam rises from the bubbles. When I turn to my left I flinch slightly, seeing Ayden standing by the door, leaning on the frame.

"You'll feel much better after a bath," he states. "Let me help you."

I don't resist.

He begins by unbuttoning my dress and folding it over my shoulders, around my elbows, holding it while I step out of it. He falters.

"What's the matter?" I ask. "Can't you bear to look my bruised body?"

He's shaking his head. "Of course no, it isn't that."

As I wait to be rejected, I'm transfixed by his penetrating stare. His features appear to soften; that faraway look in his eyes morphs into something else...

Sadness.

A single tears falls from his right eye and trickles over the fine row of sutures before descending onto his cheek. I stand on my toes and catch it with my lips when it reaches his chin. As my tears fall, he does the same and kisses away my pain, until my sobs become no more than a hard swallow.

"You've been very brave but there is one more trial for you to face before you can be truly free of all this. My only concern is that you're in no shape mentally or physically to process what I have to tell you."

Feeling restored by the closeness of his body I offer a reply, "There's nothing I can't handle if we're together." I take a step back. "Why do you mention a trial? You mean for having killed my attacker?"

"No. That's being taken care of and you won't be charged with anything. My legal team is handling all that and there's enough evidence against him to forgo any charges that may be levelled at you." He takes a deep breath. "No. This is more of a personal sacrifice ..."

"It is?"

He's nodding. "Take your bath, and once you're refreshed and we've eaten, I'll explain."

We're sitting across from each other. The glass table is highly polished and the crystal wine glasses reflect in it as I did not so long ago. Thankfully, there are no traces of my fingerprints or smears left over from my naked body; everything is pristine and untouched.

Between mouthfuls I look up and he catches my eye but I refuse to respond to the midnight blue hues of flickering light emanating from those bewitching orbs. I need to think straight and I must not let myself become caught up in his silent seduction.

"You've found your appetite," he observes, watching the last morsel of carpaccio leave my plate. "Are you feeling revived after your soak?"

Still unsettled by the tone of his voice I nod slowly. Both timbre and phrasing are recognisable as Ayden's, but the playfulness I love so much is missing, and no amount of wine will restore this man to his roguish self tonight.

"So, you mentioned a trial." I align my knife and fork neatly. "What am I to be put on trial for?"

He pushes back his chair. "This isn't the place to discuss that. Come and sit down." He reaches for our glasses of wine and moves gracefully in the direction of the sofa. Once seated, he taps the cushion for me to join him.

I join him on the sumptuous leather sofa and turn to face him. He looks calm and composed, perfectly at home.

"Do you recall your first meeting with Alenka?"

Alenka!

I simply nod, still hearing her name whirring in my ears several seconds after he has spoken.

"Something surprising happened in the washroom, didn't it? Something that has puzzled you since then. What was it?"

The washroom?

"I don't recall ..."

He raises a disbelieving brow. "Think carefully. It isn't a trick question."

I think back. "There was something."

"Yes."

"I was shocked to find out that she knew me; who I was before, you know...?"

He nods. "Yes I know. And how did you think she acquired that information?"

"From you, of course." I lower my shoulders. "Look, Ayden, why are you asking me this? What has Alenka got to do with us?"

"Very little to do with us, more to do with me, actually."

What!

"Aren't you forgetting something?" I hold up the impressive band of platinum sitting next to my engagement ring and flick it with my thumbnail. "We're married, remember?"

"I haven't forgotten."

"Well there's a surprise. Seems like you've forgotten everything else; like my name for instance. Why can't you bear to even utter it? Is it because it's not Alenka? Are you missing the fantasy fucking already? Is that it?"

He's shaking his head vigorously. "No! Absolutely not!"

"Then what?"

He leans into me and faces me squarely, I notice how the scratches on his forehead have disappeared, and the sutures on his cheekbone have melted into his skin like leftover ice cream.

"Tell me, what do you see?"

I can't help but reach out to touch his flawless skin, absent of bruises and swelling.

"I see a handsome man who looks remarkably well, considering what he's been through."

I wait for a jovial 'this is true' but I'm left wanting.

"There's a reason for that and it's not one you will be prepared for or want to hear, I'm afraid."

"I don't understand."

"I have had you in my sights for some time, most of your life in fact. Only now have I come face to face with you, like this." He glances down but, sensing I'm about to speak, puts a broad finger against his lips. "Shhh ...you must try to listen. Don't speak until I have said what I must. Please try, Frances."

Frances?

"I first met you when your grandmother passed away. It was a warm summer's evening and you were eight years old. You were sobbing by her bedside and she spoke to you of fairies and Neverland. Do you remember?"

Wide-eyed, I nod and dissolve into the sofa.

"She was a very sweet lady and her passing was filled with sorrow but you grew and your sorrow eased." He reaches for our glasses of wine; I take hold of mine and throw back two large mouthfuls before handing him the glass.

"As I recall, your mother's passing was a tragic affair, and there was much sadness in your home, but ... she was suffering unnecessarily and she welcomed me with open arms, fearing only for your welfare." He pauses for a moment but I am so mesmerized by him that I cannot speak.

He inhales deeply. "Your father left you with a grieving heart that simply would not mend." He searches for the right words ...

"To die, to sleep—
No more, and by a sleep to say we end
The heartache and the thousand natural shocks
That flesh is heir to—'tis a consummation
Devoutly to be wished. To die, to sleep.
To sleep, perchance to dream. Ay, there's the rub,
For in that sleep of death what dreams may come
When we have shuffled off this mortal coil
Must give us pause."

He can't be serious ...

"You're forcing me to relive some of the saddest moments of my life, quoting Hamlet's soliloquy and you expect me to be quiet. What's going on? You review my life as if it's some kind of soap opera."

He looks down dejectedly. "If only it was that simple."

"Simple! Let me simplify it for you. The truth is I've had two stalkers; one's dead and then there's *you*. Why now? After everything we've been through. Tell me ... why now?"

"You need to listen, Frances. What I'm going to say will be hard to grasp, initially." He takes my right hand between his and rests it on the cushion between us. "Our fourth meeting was by far the most traumatic for you. Taking the life of another human being is never easy, even in self–defence." He pats my hand softly. "Mr. Rizler left without fanfare or a farewell. His dark and deadly soul left this earth in a rush with no one to mourn his passing. But I suspect you knew that."

With his free hand he tips up my chin. "Listen closely with an open heart and mind. Our two destinies have been interwoven for decades, and the window I've had into your world has allowed me to see your vulnerability but, more importantly, the strength of character you have to see this through."

I'm bewildered. "To see what through ..."

"When I came across your husband, he was close to death ..."

I lose control of my jaw and my mouth opens and stays that way.

"I prepared to take him, but did not. I was arrested by his frantic determination to hold on. You see, I recognised him from your battle three days earlier. To my surprise, he did not ask to be saved; he addressed his God and asked him to watch over you. Such a selfless act, I thought."

As if telling a story to an attentive child, he settles into the back of the sofa and continues in a steady, no-nonsense tone.

I'm dumbstruck.

"You see, most people fear me; they hate the thought of meeting me because they know the life they have taken for granted is about to end. Your husband was different in that respect. His thoughts were not of himself, but of you. So earnest was he in his plea, I sought you out, recalled your past. I knew you as sweet Frances, so the name Beth meant little to me until then."

Unable to contain my agony for a second longer, I begin to sob and try to contain the sounds of my sorrow in my hands. I can hold back the noise of a breaking heart, but not the tide of bubbling tears trickling down my cheeks, coming to rest on my lap like two unsightly ink stains.

"You're lying. If this is one of your games, Ayden, you've gone too far; conjuring up this elaborate story to terrify me, to get me to imagine what my life would be like without you." I'm shaking my head. "You're doing it to make me forget about the baby or the fact we may never make a child again." I'm sitting upright, carelessly wiping away tears with heavy fingertips. "Just stop it! We should be grateful for having each other; I get that. No need to carry on with this charade."

I feel his hand caressing my cheek, so I lean into it and close my eyes, allowing the heat from it to permeate my skin.

"Frances, I have known you most of your life and I have no reason to lie. I have nothing but affection for you."

I open my eyes and shake free of him. "Ayden! It's time to stop. You're scaring me." I edge over to him and take his face in my sweating palms. "Kiss me. Tell me you love me." I rest my mouth on his. The plumpness of his lips feels unnatural but that's to be expected; we haven't kissed for four days and my lips are still tender. I close my eyes, anticipating a prize-winning kiss, good enough to curl the trickiest of toes, but in its place is a lack-lustre peck so unrecognisable it has me edging away backwards.

"Who are you?"

He smiles affectionately. "You know who I am."

I'm shaking my head left and right. "No! I don't know you. I don't want to know you." I scuttle backwards, out of his reach.

"Take a breath and let it out slowly ..."

"I don't want to take a breath. I want my husband back. Who the fuck are you?" I cry. "And why have you stolen Ayden's body?"

"Stolen? Hardly. Under the circumstances, I believe the word *rescued* to be more fitting."

"Rescued? From what?"

"Why, from death, Frances."

Like a torn parachute, I fall down to earth, with any hope of happiness ripped from my heart. Here I sit in pieces, feeling more alone than I have ever felt before.

From somewhere I find the strength to speak. "Why? Why did you rescue him?" I snarl, breath leaving my mouth in a feverish gust.

He glances around the room. "Believe me Frances, I am beginning to ask myself the same question." He manifests a serious stare. "Would you rather I had not?"

Horrified by the thought, I shake my head.

"Well then, we have reached an impasse." He rubs his hands together. "I'm not in the habit of claiming bodies; souls yes, but not the physical, human aspect of being. The human body is much too fragile a form to occupy."

What the hell ...

"Yes it is," I huff. "We feel everything and suffer as a result." I'll leave him to work that out for himself. "We take risks with life and with love ..."

"I realise that."

With nothing to lose, I prepare to claim back what is mine. "But you stealing ... *rescuing* Ayden's body is too big a pain to endure, even for me." I rise from the sofa and tiptoe slowly back to the guest bedroom, feeling the weight of grief bearing down upon me like a crucifix. "Goodnight."

***

In a side office away from the hustle and bustle of police life, Detective Inspector Bowker is flicking through the details of a fatal car crash on the A40 the previous evening. He should have finished his shift half an hour ago, but the name Stone has all kinds of bells ringing. He's curious to see why someone like Ayden Stone would be driving like a lunatic on a busy highway on a Friday evening when his wife is still recovering in hospital.

The more he reads the more curious he becomes, realising Mr. Stone was not alone in the vehicle. With only an ageing Golden Retriever to go home to, he removes his coat and sits down.

On the pad he uses for personal notes and references, he jots down the name, 'Elise Richards,' the co-passenger and the only fatality. He taps his pen against his bottom teeth and wracks his brain. "Richards ... why does that name sound familiar?"

He leans back in his chair, pushes his iPad aside and turns over pages in his notebook from previous days. Every page is full of notes relating to Dan Rizler, pieces of a puzzle that he had logged for another day, even though it was a cut and dried case of self-defence.

Be that as it may, he likes to think he has a sixth sense, and that sixth sense is telling him there is more to this case than some crazy bastard breaking into a school and attempting to rape a school teacher. For now though ... he has nothing but fragmented pieces of information to go on.

He contacts the duty Sergeant to check a few things: times, details, and so forth - for no particular reason other than to satisfy his curiosity and his need to make sure everything is above-board.

"Hi Rick, it's Mack. I'm just casting an eye over last night's log and notice there was a smash-up on the A40..."

"Yeah, that was a nasty one. Some woman was thrown through the windscreen."

Mack taps his pen on the open pad. "Right. And what about the guy? He wasn't seriously injured, right?"

"They had to cut him out and airlift him to hospital. I haven't heard any more."

"OK. I'll see who did the clear up. I'll be interested to see who the lady was," Mack says, still intrigued. "I'll have a chat with a couple of CID mates and see what happened."

"Is there something dodgy going on?" Rick asks curiously.

"Not that I know of. I gave evidence in the Rizler case – the assault at the school - and I've met this Stone guy a couple of times. Didn't strike me as the type to go joyriding."

Rick laughs down the phone. "They never do until they're caught."

"Yeah, you're probably right, shame about the passenger though."

"Right, but I heard she was the one who caused the crash."

Mack stops tapping his pen to listen. "What makes you say that?"

"There was a knife on the floor by her seat; it looked like she was threatening him or something."

In big letters Mack writes *knife under her seat*. "That should take some explaining."

"Looks like your instincts were right, Mack," Rick acknowledges with a chuckle.

"Oh, we'll have to see about that, but thanks, Rick." He pauses, thinking through the information. "How's the wife doing?"

"You know what she's like. Never sits still. It's like living with a bloody ferret."

Mack laughs out loud. "You poor sod. No wonder you volunteer for overtime."

"Tell me about it. I'd move in here and set up a bivouac behind the counter if they'd let me." He's laughing out loud.

"Ah, but you'd miss the home cooking."

"Maybe you're right. I'll try and stick it out for another couple of months." He composes himself. "How's your daughter doing?"

"Not too bad. Kate's away at University, studying law of all things. Think she would have seen enough from me to be put her off it for life, but no." His eyes soften at the thought of her. "She takes after her mother, God rest her soul. She's a do-gooder."

"There's nothing wrong with that, Mack. You should be proud."

He nods his head in response. "Yeah, I am."

"Catch you later. They just brought in a couple of comedians; looks like they've been drinking for England."

"Go to it. Thanks for the info, Rick."

"Anytime, Mack."

Mackenzie Bowker draws an enormous circle around two words: Elise Richards. "Now, let's find out who you are Miss. Richards."

6

My clothes lie in a heap on the bathroom floor. The fine silk straps of my pyjama top sit comfortably on my bare shoulders. The last time I dressed in white was my wedding day. Was it only a week ago that we were married in front of friends, family and God Almighty?

Now look what we have become. My baggage has been the death of us; our relationship, our baby and now ... I replay our conversation over and over but the fact remains. I'm here with a stranger. There's a knock at the door.

"Yes?"

"Come out here. I want to speak with you," he commands. I picture him folding his arms as Ayden would; standing tall, looking impatient.

"I'm going to bed. It's been a traumatic day, one way or another."

The knob turns and he steps into the doorway. "Yes, it has." He passes me my bathrobe. "Put this on."

I slip it on and pull the belt tightly, wincing a little with the pressure on my stomach.

"You're in no condition to be up this late. You need to rest. Are you in any pain?"

Wearily, I confront him. "No."

In a split second he's positioned behind me. There we stand like a human landscape; white foam against an impregnable cliff of charcoal grey. Our eyes meet in the mirror.

"Close your eyes."

Another command.

I do, lowering my head, defeated.

"Open them."

I do so with a gasp. Every mark, graze and bruise has vanished from my face. I am myself again. I hurriedly untie my bathrobe and lift up my top. Where there was a healing scar only minutes ago on my stomach, there's a faint line of an inch or so. I can't conceal my astonishment. I lean forward, tracing the clear skin beneath my left eye and drawing circles across my jaw with my fingertips.

"Now do you believe me?" he asks, standing high and mighty behind me.

"Yes," I concede, fastening my bathrobe snugly around my body. "But I don't understand. Even though you look like Ayden, you're a stranger. I don't know you."

"I can appreciate that, but in time ..."

"Time? What do you mean? *You're staying?*" I can't conceal my horror.

He turns me around to face him, forcing me to lift my eyes to meet his. "I can leave anytime."

"And if you do, will I wake up next to a corpse? Is that the way this thing works?"

"You think so little of me, Frances. I would not do that. I have taken a great interest in your plight over the years and watched you grow..."

"Then that was you at the book launch, speaking through Alenka? Is that why you asked me earlier?"

"Yes. It was the first time I had seen you so ... resplendent."

"So that's why you turned up, to see me in a fancy dress and heels?"

He shakes his head, picking up on my irreverence. "No. Your involvement with your future husband was about to put you in danger. It was a warning."

"It worked. We broke up."

"I know that."

"But we got back together because we couldn't bear to be apart. We're soul mates, since we were children ..."

"I felt it. The pull between you was irrefutable; another reason for my intervention."

"Then if you know that, why are you doing this?"

"Because I can."

Fearing I might actually reach out for him, I stuff my hands into my pockets and confront him. "You know what you are, don't you?"

"Enlighten me ..." He folds his arms and tips his head in a very Stone-like way.

"You're a universal stalker. You've watched me suffering from afar all these years and now you're intensifying my suffering by doing this."

As Ayden would, he licks his lips before speaking, forcing me to look away. "If that were the case, sweet Frances, I wouldn't be here and neither would your husband. We would not be having this conversation and you would be alone."

What a stark statement of the truth that is.

I lean back, against the counter top, letting the room fill with silence. He turns to leave.

I stop him in his tracks with two words. "Thank you."

He answers my words with a smile that has been so long in coming it touches my heart like a ray of sunshine; the light from it brings much needed warmth to my bones. I offer a weak smile in return.

"You have seen and survived many things, Frances. You have an inner strength that few possess."

I tip my head to one side, disbelieving his admission. "Oh, I don't know about that."

"I do. It comes as no surprise to me that your husband's last thought was of you and your safekeeping. I have often had similar thoughts."

"What do you mean?" I ask, with a frown.

"The light coming on in the alley, the movable furniture, the close proximity of the knife ... need I go on?"

I shake my head and lower my eyes to the floor. "You're an Angel?"

"Of sorts ..."

"Without wings."

"Wings are so last century, Frances," he says with a wry smile.

"So is Frances. I haven't been *her* for over seven years."

"Ah yes, but you were *her* for over twenty."

"I was. But I left her behind and I don't want to go back there. Can't you call me, Beth?"

He's shaking his head. "I prefer Elizabeth."

I sneer at the associations with that name. "But I'll feel more comfortable around you if you call me Beth."

"Very well ... Beth. Come and sit with me and tell me what we're going to do tomorrow." He heads off in the direction of the lounge, assuming I'll follow.

I glance one last time in the mirror at my rejuvenated image and across at the bath behind me, smiling with the memory of bath time and Ayden's words ...

Come back to me, baby ...

I switch off the light and claim those words as my own, whispering into the darkness, "Come back to me, baby."

The door clicks shut and I lock that memory away for safe keeping; it will be mine to cling onto as I walk into this living nightmare, one step at a time.

***

Mackenzie Bowker is not one to be put off by the prospect of hard work, or by what appears to be unrelated incidents. It didn't take him long to discover the identity of the deceased passenger. Once he found out where Miss. Richards worked and where she lived, the rest was easy.

She arranged the rental of apartment 53c at Elm Garden for Mr. Rizler, and her number was on his phone. Knowing that satisfies his curiosity about where he had heard her name before. What it doesn't explain is what she was doing in that car with Mr. Stone - with a knife under her seat.

He's returned home to the comfort of his three bedroom, semi-detached house in Bromley. What remaining light there is from the watery sun is leaking through the enormous bay window, making it unnecessary to turn on a lamp.

Mack has digested a man-sized helping of lasagne; he is now sitting back with a large glass of good quality Claret and a fine cigar. Laid out on the sofa is a copy of the report on the car crash. He's called in half a dozen favours to get this report completed by the boys in forensics and he intends to give it his full attention. It makes for interesting reading, not because of the seriousness of the accident, but because of the involvement of Mr. Stone; a pillar in the community and a self-made man; a man with everything to lose from something which could potentially damage his reputation.

As it stands, the accident has been dealt with and remained under the radar. Mr. Stone's media contacts have gone to great lengths to suppress it and the reporting of the accident has been relegated to page three in national newspapers. Being one to defend the under-dog, Mack wonders who will fight for Miss. Richards in her absence. Doesn't she deserve more than having her tragic death swept under the carpet?

He leaves the cigar to extinguish itself in the ashtray; a column of smoke weaves its way skywards, carrying with it the aroma of tobacco, but he's too engrossed in paperwork to notice.

First he spreads out the photographs of the crash site on the coffee table. An unsightly table cloth of mangled metal and broken bones covers every inch of it. The angle of the vehicle is such that Miss. Richards has been propelled through the windscreen and sprawled across the bonnet like a broken mannequin; a mop of blond hair is splayed out across twisted metal, making the scene look very macabre.

Inside the vehicle, Mr. Stone is slumped over the steering wheel, still wearing his seatbelt but clearly concussed. The time frame on the photographs is no more than five minutes, but it was ten more minutes before the ambulance and fire brigade appeared to cut him free of the wreckage; and another fifteen minutes before he could be airlifted to hospital. Removing Miss Richards's body took much longer - she had not survived the fatal accident and there was no urgency.

With a visual reminder of the event, Mack shifts his attention to the written report, seeking out the specifics about the knife. He wonders if, by any chance, it was the same as Mr. Rizler's. He's disappointed to find it was merely an everyday kitchen knife - a woman's weapon of choice - usually associated with a crime of passion or self-defence. Either way, he's intrigued.

After being dusted it for prints, he notes the knife only had her fingerprints on it. Mack nods and purses his lips, trying to make sense of the clues. The black markings across the left side of the steering wheel were the strangest finding of all, as if it had been grabbed by the passenger.

His curiosity piqued, he flips through the pages to the pre-autopsy report and confirms his suspicions. Her hands were covered in dust or a kind of black powdery compound like soot. It was embedded in her cuticles and had settled under her manicured nails.

In death she looks grotesque: her pale face, soulless eyes darkened like hard caramel and smudged red lipstick make it hard to believe she had ever been attractive.

He takes a deep cleansing breath, two swigs of wine, and gazes around the room. The light is fading and the photographs are beginning to blend into a jumbled up jigsaw.

"What were you doing in that car with him, Elise?" he asks. "This was no joy ride."

7

I'm standing by the kitchen counter top waiting for the kettle to boil, regarding him out of the corner of my eye. He's never looked better. I can't begin to imagine what wickedness has been employed to transform bruises into baby soft skin and facial scars back into flawless features. He is restored to his old self, physically at least.

"I'm making tea. Would you like a cup?" I ask out of politeness.

"Is it Darjeeling?"

"No."

"Then I'll pass."

He stands bolt upright, looking out of the enormous floor-to-ceiling sheet of reinforced glass. The darkness has seen to it that the only things reflected in the glass are lamps and furniture but it's his reflection that takes centre stage.

I sit quietly, observing the self-absorbed way in which he tips his head to the left and then the right; how he lifts his chin, discovering a chiselled profile polished to perfection by magical powers as old as time itself.

"Enjoying the view?" I ask, breaking his concentration.

He laughs, at himself. "Yes, very much so."

I want to say "me too" but I don't. I blow the steam from my tea and sip it slowly, savouring precious seconds of normality before having to face more of his revelations.

"Go ahead," he says, picking up on my quizzical expression.

"With what?"

"Your questions. You can ask me anything." He's straightening the fine denim material on his knees and repositioning his cuffs as if preparing for a photo shoot.

I settle my cup down in its saucer. "I don't know where to begin."

"Then I will explain my expectations until such time as a question occurs to you."

Expectations...

Before he can continue, I interrupt. "I've seen what you're capable of. How can you assume someone like me will be able to meet your *expectations*? It's laughable."

"Your husband saw something in you when you were a child. You spoke to his heart, and the memory of you stayed with him all his life. To the very end."

I look away, wounded by his words. "How can you expect me to look at you when you say something like that? It's like a dagger piercing my soul, don't you realise?"

"I didn't, not until this very moment."

"And if I ask you a question, will you answer me truthfully?"

"Yes. I will never lie to you; it isn't in my nature."

For some inexplicable reason I believe him. "Then tell me what it is you want from me and what I can expect from you in return."

"It's very simple. I want your love."

I begin to chuckle. "Oh, that's all!"

"It is."

"By love you mean sex, I assume?"

"Well, that usually goes hand in hand with a loving relationship, does it not?"

"Yes it does, but we don't have a loving relationship. You're an imposter, a ... a body snatcher."

He's laughing at me.

"What's so funny?" I ask, a little shocked by my indignation.

"Your turn of phrase. I find it amusing." He folds his arms as if settling in for the night. "You really are quite charming, Beth."

"I can assure you, I'm not trying to be," I declare, shaking my head, and sighing.

"Nevertheless ... do continue."

We're face to face, but now he's massaging his chin with his thumb the way Ayden does. Feeling the pull of sexual attraction, I have to look away. I reach for my tea and sip it quietly, fearing that my newly-renovated body will betray me. I feel my cheeks flushing and hope he hasn't noticed.

"Your husband is a handsome man, Beth. It's natural that you still have feelings for him of a sexual nature."

Shit, he knows what I'm thinking!

I turn to face him. "Is that another one of your party tricks? You can read people's thoughts?"

"Yes, when I choose to. But I don't have to read your thoughts to know what you're feeling. Your arousal is detectable in your blushing cheeks, the heat radiating from your skin and the darkness of your pupils." He rests his hands on his thighs and I wonder if he's directing my gaze to his body.

My eyes make the climb from his hands, across his thighs, skim his groin and ascend languidly before coming to rest on his handsome face.

Ayden's words come to me and I smile.

So responsive but so little self-control ...

My expression softens, cold, hard edges melted by a memory. "Did you hear that?" I ask, facing him squarely.

He nods. "That's a very endearing quality. It's refreshing to meet someone with this level of transparency."

"You think?" I huff.

"I know."

"You might know about the universe and God knows what else, but don't presume to know me. And don't think you can step into his shoes so easily. People will be able to tell you're not him; one conversation with Jake and your cover will be blown. And what then? What of Ayden? Will you leave, move on? Find another handsome body to inhabit and admire through mirrors and sheets of glass?"

He considers my words but does not venture to speak.

"You say you want to be loved by me, yet offer me nothing in return. If I'm as transparent as you say I am, then you should know I'll need some kind of reassurance from you."

He arches a brow. "What kind of reassurance do you want?"

I place my overheated right hand on his arm. "That you'll bring Ayden back to me."

He pats my hand. "You are in no position to negotiate, Beth. It is indicative of my good will that I'm here at all."

"You might see it that way, but try to look at it from my point of view, please. For years I had nothing but my dreams of Ayden finding me to keep me warm at night. It was the promise of him that helped me survive my encounter with a demon. He woke me from a great sleep, and we discovered each other. So profound was our love, it brought you here."

Out of the blue, a line from Sense and Sensibility comes to mind.

To Love is to Burn, to Be on Fire!

"Ms. Austen's words do seem to be quite apt at this juncture."

What!

He strokes his chin again, contemplating a resolution. I look on, wide-eyed.

"I will make no promises. What I will offer you is an arrangement of sorts. I will consider returning your husband to this somewhat fragile body on one condition." I attempt to speak but he holds up a single finger and I desist. "That condition being, we live as man and wife for a period of six months, or until such time as I decide to terminate this arrangement. It is non-negotiable and absolute."

"Six months! You're offering me nothing? No compromise?"

"Why would I? For me to truly immerse myself in the Stone experience, I will need your help, naturally. But it's in your interest to make my replication utterly convincing."

"You're holding all the cards ..."

"I am indeed." He pauses to smile assuredly. "But I am hopeful that we'll be able to play them together."

"That could be problematic for me."

"How so?"

"I can't conceal my feelings. 'So responsive, no self-control,' remember? I'll find it hard to lie, especially to those I care about."

He shrugs his shoulder dismissively. "Then you must learn, Beth, and quickly. You are forbidden to tell anyone."

I finish off my tea and stand. "Who would believe me, anyway?"

"Precisely."

I check my watch. "It's 10 p.m. I'm going to bed. I'll see you in the morning." I take a lingering look at my "husband" sitting self-assuredly on the sofa, his right leg across his left knee and his hands resting on his lap. This 'arrangement' seems so unfair. I spin around, determined to make it as painless as possible, but dying a little inside with each step. "Okay. I agree."

"Good." He stands and approaches me, seeming larger than life, statuesque in his majestic beauty. "Take my hand."

I raise my right hand and he lifts it to his lips. A perfectly plump V shape presses against my skin, making every muscle in my stomach clench and tighten.

"You are my wife, Beth, and I will try to be the perfect husband; but, rest assured, I will not be toyed with, taken advantage of or played for a fool. Do you understand?"

Realising the implications of those three special words, I instinctively suck air into my lungs; recollections of soft cord, blindfolds and Ayden's hands move through me like the aftershock of an atomic bomb, causing an involuntary moan to leave my mouth. Embarrassed, I look away.

"Beth, look at me," he urges softly. "You cannot conceal anything from me. What I cannot hear I can feel and what I cannot feel I can see. I can read you as one might a child, and your innocence is a powerful aphrodisiac to me."

In his eyes I see the colour of the night sky, minus starlight or clouds; the tell-tale indicator of his arousal. Any other time I would succumb to my desire for intimacy, but not now.

"You can't expect me to fall at your feet. I didn't do that for Ayden and I sure as hell won't do it for you." I look away. "I'm a human being, not a robot. I can't turn my emotions on and off at the flick of a switch."

"I realise that. Nevertheless, we have an arrangement, do we not?"

"And that involves you fucking me whenever the mood suits you, I suppose?"

He tips his head and thinks through his words before speaking. "I will not put any pressure on you to ... perform. If that were my intention I would be elsewhere. It is my desire to experience love, not sex. You may be surprised to know that I do, in fact, know the difference." He releases my hand. "Go to bed and rest. You've a lot to consider. Then tomorrow, we will begin our adventure."

"Adventure! You think this will be an adventure?" I'm shaking my head in disbelief.

"How would *you* describe it, Beth?"

I lift my head confidently, considering my response. The last thing I want to do is to offend him; he holds all the cards. "It'll be an ordeal, but nothing I can't handle."

A smile graces his lips. "That's what I thought."

"Where will you be sleeping?" I ask.

He sniggers, anticipating his response. "In the master bedroom - where else?"

"I should have guessed."

He smirks, finding my response amusing no doubt. "Although I will not be sleeping, as such. Life goes on for me."

"That's a rather insensitive turn of phrase isn't it, taking into account your job."

His smirk widens as he laughs gleefully. "My job? Yes, of course. Forgive my insensitivity. I see your point."

Shaking my head I turn to leave. "By the way, what will you do with Ayden while you're off doing your job?"

"I will simply leave his body..."

Taken aback, I swivel around. "Where?"

"In bed."

"Will he be alright?"

"Yes"

This I have to hear. "So you never sleep?"

He raises a brow and shakes his head. "You find that surprising?"

"Not really, just another thing to add to my list of surprises. I think I may be getting to the point that I'm totally un-shockable."

He huffs away that idea. "I very much doubt that. The universe holds many secrets, the least of which is my requirement for actual sleep."

"How do you function, then?"

"I exist. That is enough."

I begin to laugh nervously. "Is it? I'll take your word for it."

"That would be wise," he states with a glint in his eye. "Ask me no questions and I will tell you no lies."

"I thought you said you never lie?" I ask mischievously.

"I did, and I don't. I was merely being playful."

I tip my head over and hit him with a wide stare. "Being playful ... and who taught you that?" He smirks in such a sexy way I swear I can feel my pupils dilating.

"Why you, Beth," he declares. "Every minute I spend with you is an education."

I turn on my heels and walk away. "Oh please ... goodnight."

"Goodnight, Beth."

***

An exhausted Golden Retriever waits to be released from her leash, then trundles into the kitchen in search of refreshment. She had only been on a fifteen minute walk but, from her gait, anyone would think she had doggy-paddled across the channel.

Mack refills her bowl with fresh water and hangs up his coat under the stairs, eager to continue examining the documents. "Don't drink too fast, Judy, or you'll make yourself sick," he calls out, slipping off his shoes before entering the lounge.

He flips open the file to discover:

"ITEMS RECOVERED FROM THE DECEASED."

It's a long list, consisting of the items usually found in a lady's oversized handbag, with one exception: a hand-written note.

To S,

When there was nothing but dark shadows in my life, I had you. Your radiance was so bright I was happy to kneel at your feet and lift my face to catch some of that light.

When the dark shadows took me away I called for you every night until I realised you wouldn't come. I was alone ...

I have done things in my life I'm not proud of. The years have not been kind to me, and what I've done has come from a need for survival. Finding you again after all these years was like winning the lottery; not for the money, but for the feeling that I deserved to win something.

Even then you kept me hidden, concealed like a dirty secret locked away in your basement, but I understood. I know I'll never be your equal but to find out now that I never meant anything to you is a truth too painful to bear. No one knows better than me how hard it is to come face to face with the truth. For me, the truth has been something that exists in fairy-tales. It's out there with true love and happy endings, and not meant for the likes of me. I was never worthy of you or your love. I see that now. You have found your princess ...

I have loved only you and I will do so with my dying breath.

Goodbye.

Yours always.

Elise.

He takes no delight from the document and what can be inferred from her words. It's a suicide note. Little can be gleaned from her words as far as clues are concerned; not yet, anyway. He flips through the pages for her address. Hatch End is only an hour or so away and something tells him he'll discover more clues there, but it's 7 o'clock on a Saturday night and he has a couple of reports to type up. The Richards case will have to wait.

For his own peace of mind, he prepares to call Cromwell Hospital to enquire as to the condition of Mr. and Mrs. Stone; a star-crossed twosome who seem to have been saddled with some bad luck lately. He knows only too well the path of destruction left in Mr. Rizler's wake, but to have lightning strike twice in the same week seems suspicious.

Finding out they were both discharged yesterday comes as a surprise, especially considering the state they were in last Tuesday. He glances at the photo tablecloth and is reminded of Ayden's unconscious state. He rubs his chin clearly agitated. That sixth sense of his has his brain doing somersaults.

"Something's not right here..."

8

S tanding before the bathroom mirror after brushing my teeth, I scrutinise my face, lifting my hair from my forehead and holding it back. Anyone would think I had just returned from a weekend at a spa resort. Who would believe I had lost a tiny baby and a husband in the space of five days? Only me.

Yet, here I am glowing; irises the colour of a summer sky, glossy and bright. I've become a counterfeit wife; an actress. I might as well be standing in my dressing room, waiting for my cue.

"Final call, Mrs. Stone," shouts the stagehand, and I dutifully prepare to make my entrance recalling a line from As You Like It:

All the world's a stage,

And all the men and women merely players ...

That's me ...

I climb between the sheets, willing myself to sleep but the ear-splitting silence is too much to bear. I toss and turn, feeling fragile and forsaken but refusing to cry. I have no residual tears; every teardrop has been shed or dried up throughout the day like morning dew. Maybe a glass of milk will help?

All the lights are off in the lounge and only a luminescent glow is coming from the lights along the cupboard bases. On opening the fridge door I'm blinded and, turning to pour out the milk, spot a pile of unopened mail.

Most of it is addressed to Ayden; the thought of him not being here to read it smarts like a hard slap, so I toss it aside and see what else there is to be sorted and thrown away. A heavy brown envelope, A4 size, holds my attention. It's addressed to Mr. & Mrs. A. Stone. I can do no more than gaze at it, feeling utterly despondent when I see the postmark: Las Vegas.

I know what it is.

I pull back the tab and carefully tip out the leather-bound folder containing the DVD and a pen drive of our wedding. On the DVD is a photo of us. As I rotate it in my hand, round and round we go; a magical moment in time re-created and captured on brittle plastic.

With no desire to sleep, I head for the lift, quietly close the door and descend, coming to rest at the basement level.

Instantly the lights spark into life, showing me the way to the cinema room. Only when I flick on the lights am I reminded of just how plush it is; eight rows of Pullman chairs to choose from, each one a reminder that I must mourn alone. I whisper words I know no one will hear. "I miss you, Ayden."

The instrument deck is simple enough to operate. Switch it on, slot the DVD in place and press insert. I hurry to the front row and take my seat, reminded of Ayden's comments about discarded tissues and popcorn. Instantly my recollection fades when the enormous screen bursts into life.

Unbeknown to me his arrival at the Wedding Chapel had been filmed. I'm smiling behind my hand at his eagerness to get inside; the bounce in his step and the way he is grinning into the camera like an excited school-boy. Fresh tears begin to blur my vision and so I blink them away not wanting to miss a single frame.

I come face to face with myself. I barely recognise the woman dressed in white, flanked by Charlie and Celine. She's the princess I'd envisioned I would be someday, on her way to meet her Prince Charming at the altar. That day now seems like a half forgotten fairy-tale.

The service gets underway. I'm walking down the aisle on Patrick's arm, faltering at the sight of billowing sheets and enormous wooden stepladders, handmade for the sole purpose of triggering a childhood memory we shared.

I hear the sincerity in our voices as we recite our vows; unified promises of devotion, love and protection; all that Ayden held sacred for over two decades being sanctified in front of God and the congregation.

" ... and I solemnly promise to cherish you and to keep you safe from harm; to love you from this moment on as I always have, for as long as we both shall live."

And then ... as the music fades, I close my eyes and he places a tattered pink ribbon in my hand.

"Wake up, baby," he pleads.

And I do ...

I remember that boy I 'married' 22 years ago beneath my father's stepladders; the promise he made to always love me, to find me - and my innocent vow to wait for him.

We both kept our promises.

Thankfully, the emotional turmoil that followed was not recorded, but our stirring farewell was. My stampede through the paparazzi to reach him does not go unrecorded. Like a heat-seeking missile I launch myself at him, forging my way through an invisible force field only to be swept up in his arms and disarmed in the process.

The cameraman shifts position and zooms in to capture the overpowering magnetism between us. It may be invisible but it's no less tangible; eyes locked, a timeless attachment, compelling in its intensity and broken only by his forced departure.

I whisper to no one, "Enjoying. Always enjoying, Mr. Stone," knowing somewhere out there in the cosmos he's merely sleeping, sitting out a cold spell.

The video comes to a silent finale, and so does my session of self-absorption. Strangely, I see things more clearly; I *did* contribute to his untimely departure. Elise may have turned the steering wheel, but it was my words that put him in the car. Of that I am guilty and no one can persuade me otherwise.

I slip the DVD back into its sleeve for safe-keeping, turn off the lights and head back to the lift, steadfast in my purpose. I will serve my sentence willingly; I will love and be loved without reservation, and damned be the unearthly being in my bed if he should deny me my soul mate at the end of my term.

Ayden Stone has been my saviour on two occasions. Now, the tables are about to be turned. I'll rescue him right back and do whatever it takes to awaken him from his eternal rest or, God help me, I'll die trying.

I'm tiptoeing, trying not to make a sound. The last thing I want to do is draw attention to myself. I'm on the first floor, being led to the master bedroom by my nose like a bloodhound following a scent.

The bedroom door is open but I can't enter; I'm propelled backwards by the memory of our last night here in this very room. Moonlight sears through a gap in the curtains and settles on that chair, triggering a barrage of recollections that floor me, one sweet kiss at a time. I close my eyes and focus on steady breathing, listening to how air enters Ayden's lungs in life affirming breaths and leaves them in a wheeze. My husband is sleeping peacefully, untroubled by talk of near death experiences and arrangements; knowing that makes me smile into the darkness.

"Ayden," I whisper, nearing the bed. "Ayden?" There is no reply. I have him to myself, it seems.

Without a second thought I throw off my bathrobe and slip between the sheets, wearing only a flimsy set of pyjamas. On my side of the bed the sheets are crisp and cool against my bare arms but, as I edge closer to him, I'm becoming aware of body heat and expensive cologne - a heady mixture for someone who has not been touched for five days.

I nestle into his back and slide my hand across his chest so I can open my palm and pull him into me; like that missing piece of sky in a jigsaw puzzle, we slot together perfectly.

Secretly, I'm praying the closeness of my body will rouse him from his sleep, but it's a silent prayer that goes unanswered.

He may be breathing, but that's an unconditioned reflex; even a new-born baby gasps for air. I nuzzle into his neck and whisper softly, "I know you're only sleeping, but I'm here, Ayden, I'm not going anywhere. Can you feel me holding you?" I screw up my eyes to stem the flood and pull him into me. "I'll never let you go." I kiss his right shoulder. "Now you rest, baby. I've got this."

Lulled by that thought, I doze off, comforted by the closeness and warmth of his body.

***

It's 2 a.m. Mack is stepping out of bed and dragging his feet along a worn-out carpet in search of slippers. He's been tossing and turning for the last hour, troubled by the three-ring circus into which Elise Richards has tumbled. From what he has seen and read it seems unlikely she would fall for Mr. Stone's unquestionable charm or Mr. Rizler's fiendish fascination. And yet, she appears to have come into contact with them both. Unable to even contemplate sleep, he sits on the edge of the bed, flicks on the lamp and begins to assemble theories until they are stacked as high as breakfast pancakes. Their inconclusive nature only troubles him more.

He snatches his paisley bathrobe and pulls the belt tightly around him, taking cautious steps across the landing and down the stairs. Hearing him descend, Judy is there to meet him at the bottom of the stairs, her tail wagging as a token gesture.

"Go back to bed, girl. There's no reason why we should both be wide awake."

Seeming to understand every word, she returns to her basket in the kitchen and winds herself into a cosy capital C.

Before returning to the carnage, he switches on wall lights and reaches for the bottle of whiskey his daughter bought for him when she was last home. It's a familiar nightcap, an old friend. Before his wife passed away he wouldn't dare touch the amber nectar for fear of receiving a lecture on the dangers of becoming an alcoholic. Now, with no one to remind him of the errors of his ways, he is free to do as he pleases, although, he knows only too well that it's no fun drinking alone. Even so, he pours a generous measure into a tumbler and holds it against his chest like a medallion, hoping it will bring him luck in his pursuit of the truth.

He creates four untidy piles for his character study and lays them out on his lounge carpet like portfolios for an audition. The difference is that two of the leading players are dead, and the other two just as silent and too well-connected to be dragged into the limelight.

Elise Richards's driving licence holds his attention. There's something about the way her eyes are staring straight ahead, piercing his soul; the way her lips are tightly shut as if she's stifling a secret …

"Maybe if I listen carefully enough, you'll tell me what I need to know to help you, Elise," he says, licking the whiskey from his lips. "But for now, we both need to sleep. Tomorrow's another day and we'll see what clues you've left for me at your apartment."

He returns the glass to the tray of spirits and turns off the lights. As he climbs the stairs he thinks he hears the sound of rustling papers coming from the lounge. He stops and tips his head to listen, but hears nothing more.

Anesthetised a little by the whiskey he crawls into bed and drifts off to sleep, still troubled by theories based on suppositions. He needs hard evidence of Stone's complicity in the death of Elise Richards and he won't rest until he has it.

9

I feel familiar fingers, a masculine palm and a thumb encasing my hand as it rests across Ayden's chest. My first thought is to pull away. But I reconsider and relax my hand, allowing the stranger in my bed to caress it and savour the sensation of my body melded to his.

And so our *adventure* begins ...

When I feel able to face the day, I open my eyes slowly, with some trepidation, unsure of what I'll see. I retrieve my hand and roll onto my back, preparing to slither out of bed.

"Good morning, Beth."

Hearing Ayden's voice, causes me to flinch a little, knowing the words are not his own.

He rolls over and props his head on his right palm, looking every bit the man I adore; eyes alight with morning glory.

"Morning. Did you sleep well?" I sense my cue and manufacture a smile.

"Yes, I did. You kept me warm." He smiles cheekily and, unprepared for an early morning assault upon my senses, I reach out and cup his face in my right hand.

"You kept me warm too. We have a busy day ahead, so I'll leave you to shower while I rustle up some breakfast." I edge away to my right.

He takes my right hand and returns it to his face, closes his eyes and draws it across his mouth sensually. My heart is beginning to flutter. This is something Ayden would do ...

When he opens his eyes, I see a familiar colour; deep, dark sapphire.

Oh shit!

"What do you have planned for us, darling?"

Darling? Ayden, doesn't call me darling...

"Erm ... I thought you should go and see your parents: Sylvia and Patrick. They'll be worried about you."

He raises an inquisitive brow. "Is that necessary?"

I nod. "Yes. They're your family. You should reassure them you're all right after your accident. Elise was *killed*, you know!"

He glares at me with wide eyes. "I am perfectly aware of that."

"Then ... you should know how worried they'll be."

"That really isn't necessary. They were at the hospital when I ... when your husband awoke. We exchanged embraces and I had Lester drive them back to Hove."

"Oh! I didn't know that."

"And now you do." He manufactures a 'gotcha' smile. "That being the case, I assume a family outing is unnecessary?"

I'm shaking my head. "You make it sound like a chore. If you want to ... fit in, you should try to be more human."

He pushes an erect penis into my hip. "I am."

I swallow deeply, unable to suppress the kind of visceral response that has me blushing. "Tell me. Do you know what it's like to have a family and to be loved, unconditionally?"

He looks to the side to consider his answer; turns back and pins me to the pillow with an intense stare. "Not as such."

"And yet you said you wanted to be loved ... by me? Love takes many forms, you know, and physical love isn't the be all and end all. For all your universal greatness, I would have thought you'd know that."

His mouth twitches. "Who better than you to teach me?"

"Ask me about punctuation and poetry and I'm your girl. Ask me about love and I ... I only know what Ayden has taught me. Consider the irony in that!"

"I am. It's poetic in a paradoxical kind of way."

"It's crazy! In a fucked up kind of way."

He chuckles and shakes his head. "And that is precisely why you are perfect for the job. You recognise the significance of the moment but aren't overwhelmed by it."

"You think!" I guffaw. "You must have done this before? Taken a body and claimed it?"

He's nodding.

"When was the last time?"

"Over 30 years ago."

What!

"Thirty years ago! Bloody hell! No wonder you have a hard-on!"

He falls backwards onto the bed in a fit of laughter. I can't help but laugh too.

I step from the bed. "This is too crazy to even contemplate. I'm going to make tea."

"Beth!" he calls, making me turn to face him, his eyes still full of laughter. "Thank you."

"For what?"

"For reassuring me I had not misjudged you."

"You didn't." I leave the room, a little relieved but under no illusions; six months is going to be a long time.

By 11.30 a.m. we are stepping from the Rolls. Lester seems eager to speak to Ayden about something but he seems oblivious to the clues.

"I'll leave you two to chat for a couple of minutes."

Ayden gives me a strange look.

"Thank you, Mrs. Stone," Lester replies, with a half-smile.

I turn to my right and walk a couple of feet away to check my phone for texts off Charlie. I read it and listen in, catching the occasional word.

"The Inspector ... funeral ... the press ... Mr. Harrison ..."

I read Charlie's text:

I rang the hospital! They said Ayden had discharged you! Are you really OK? So he woke up? He's a resilient bastard, I'll give him that! As long as you're OK & resting up. I'll call round later and make a house call. Love ya. C x

I reply with a reassuring text, wondering what the hell she will make of my appearance minus scratches and bruises. I've never looked so good! I'll put it down to modern medicine, knowing full well it won't satisfy her curiosity.

Ayden returns to my side. "So what was all that about?"

"Apparently our D.I. Bowker has been sniffing around and has taken it upon himself to investigate my private life."

"Is that bad?"

"Not necessarily, but he may unearth a few things that are better left unseen."

I nod in agreement." You mean about Bright Hill and the incident with Elise?"

"I believe so. But I won't let it get out of hand." He's smiling and taking my arm. "Shall we?"

"What do you mean, 'you won't let it get out of hand,' What can *you* do?"

He shrugs his shoulders nonchalantly. "Why anything, Beth."

I stand perfectly still, unable to move. "What do you mean 'anything'?"

He lifts my hand, kisses it and takes a step forward. "You'll see."

We're standing on the north bank of The Thames, looking up at The Tower of London. The Tower is a complex of several buildings dating as far back as 1066, set within two concentric rings of defensive walls and a moat; once a palace, but better known as a prison with a dismal reputation.

The Beefeater clad in black and red begins our tour, using voice and gestures to recount the troubled history of the Tower. Every so often Ayden turns to me to offer a correction, which begins,

"That's not how it happened. She did not resist or, in the case of Anne Boleyn, she was very beautiful."

The Crown Jewels glisten in glass cases, every crown and sceptre a relic of past monarchies - most of who failed to keep their heads.

I'm not sure who is more entertaining, the tour guide or my escort who appears to have first-hand accounts of every historical event. I test his knowledge further. "So tell me about Elizabeth I. She was mentioned a lot."

He shrugs his shoulders, the way someone does when faced with tedium. "What would you like to know?"

"What was she like?"

"The Virgin Queen was born 7th September 1533 and died 4th March 1603. She was the daughter of Henry VIII and the fifth and last monarch of the Tudor dynasty..."

" ... I can Google that." I'm folding my arms, looking impatient. "Tell me about the woman. Did you meet her? How did she die?"

"She had a melancholic disposition that resulted from being abused as a child ..."

I'm taken aback. "How do you know that?"

"Because I know everything," he replies, assuredly.

"Do you know who abused her?"

"Of course."

"Was he ever punished?" I enquire further.

"I would say *they* were."

Now he has my attention. "They?"

"Yes. Catherine and Thomas Seymour came to rather unpleasant ends, as I recall."

"What happened?"

"She died in childbirth, and he was beheaded," he states, glancing at his watch, wearied by my questions.

I offer a smile. "Well, I didn't know that."

"I'm sure it's well documented." He takes my hand. "Shall we find a less depressing location?"

I pick up the pace to match his stride, then stop abruptly. "Where? Where can I take you in this historical city that you don't already know more about than the tour guide?"

He takes a moment to consider. "That's a very good question."

"And ..."

"I really can't say. I have visited every part of the globe at some time or another." He looks positively dejected.

I'm wracking my brain. "I know somewhere you haven't been. Come with me."

A smile forms slowly. "Lead on, Macduff ..."

The Macbeth quote has me rolling my eyes.

Our taxi takes fifteen minutes to make the two mile journey across the city to Covent Garden. It's bustling with activity; there's nothing unusual about that, but what I want him to experience is the street performers. Directly in front of us is a man wearing no more than purple shorts; he's juggling and telling jokes at the same time. People are laughing.

"Have you been here before?" I ask.

He nods slowly.

"But I bet you weren't laughing then."

He smiles and shakes his head. "No. I wasn't laughing. As I recall, it was a red-light district in 1800's, and didn't regain some of its dignity until the beginning of twentieth century." He looks around. "There are people here from around the world."

"Yes, it's a tourist attraction now. Let's walk around." I take his hand and lead him through the jostling crowd. I sense female heads turning and wonder if he can read their thoughts. I stretch up to speak into his ear. "You're getting a lot of attention from the ladies," I point out.

"You're getting a lot of attention from the men," he states.

I screw up my face into a grimace. "I think you're imagining things."

I lead him towards the red canopy advertising Balthazar Boulangerie and keep walking past the row of motorbikes to the restaurant next door. This is an all-day brasserie I have visited before with Charlie. It has a cosy atmosphere that I think he'll like. "Let's go eat something."

He follows me inside and we are quickly seated by the waiter at a small table slotted into a row, partially concealed behind a glass divider. It's a little noisy, but if we concentrate we'll be able to hear each other speak.

"What do you think?" I ask, watching him scanning the room.

"It's tastefully decorated but much too noisy. I can barely hear ..."

I wrinkle my nose, not catching the last part of his sentence. "Pardon?"

Seeming perturbed by the rowdiness, he beckons me over. "I think we need a little quiet, don't you?" He raises his left hand a clicks his fingers. Instantly the deafening chatter becomes a distant hum. He unfolds his napkin and lays it across his lap as if he's done nothing at all.

I simply stare and look around the room; I'm watching a movie with the sound turned down. People are laughing and waving their hands about, but there is no sound.

"Another one of your party tricks?" I enquire, opening the menu. "You should join the street performers out there. You'd make a fortune."

"I prefer to keep my tricks to ourselves, Beth." He looks down checking the list of hors d'oeuvres but I can see a smirk forming. "After all, we don't want to draw a crowd, do we?"

"No we don't." I look up. "You'll have to try to fit in or people will notice the change. I'll be able to help, but I can only do so much."

His eyes meet mine. "I'm aware of that. But I'll be able to modify my behaviour when necessary."

"How?"

"By reading their thoughts and acting accordingly."

"Oh yes. There's always that." I sigh resignedly.

"Does that bother you?"

"What? The fact I have no privacy around you? That I'm having to edit what I'm thinking, knowing you're listening in? No, that doesn't bother me."

An eyebrow lifts disparagingly. "Do I detect sarcasm?"

"You do."

He places down the menu. "Then I won't read your thoughts. It will be more of challenge for me that way."

I snicker to myself.

"I'm beginning to wish I hadn't agreed to it now. What does that response signify?" he asks.

"It signifies nothing. Merely the unlikely idea that anything I say or do could be a challenge for you." I fiddle with my knife. "A single click of your fingers and voila. You get exactly what you want."

He clicks his fingers and the sound returns. It makes me squint.

"Would you prefer I didn't?"

"No!" I shout. "Turn it off!"

Silence is restored.

"Now. What shall we eat?"

"What do you like?" I ask, making my own selection.

He places down the menu. "I don't know."

"What do you mean you don't know?"

"The last time I was here was some time ago. The food selection was much more ... rustic."

"Really?"

"Yes. I will trust you to choose for me." He scans the room for a waiter. "You make the selection and I will select a bottle of suitable wine."

I look on, surprised. "You don't know about food but you know about wine?"

"I'm using the prices on this wine list as an indicator of quality."

I'm shaking my head. "That's not a good idea."

"No?"

"No. Some wines are overpriced, and some wines are better than you might think for the price."

"Then I'll select a wine somewhere in the middle and we'll hope for the best."

I begin to laugh.

"Clearly you are finding my ineptitude in this matter amusing, Mrs. Stone?"

There's no denying it. I am. "If Ayden were here he'd be fussing around with food options and selecting wine like a connoisseur. But ..."I look down, unable to conceal my sadness. "But he isn't, so we'll hope for the best."

"I think not." He turns his head to his right and scopes the room until his eyes come level with mine. He casts a knowing eye over the wine list again. "If you choose the fish we'll have the Pavillon Blanc du Château Margaux and if you select a meat dish, we'll have the Château Branaire-Ducru '05."

I'm astonished. "So what did you do, read through a set of wine reviews in record time?"

"No, I accessed Ayden's knowledge about wines to inform my selection."

"You did what?!" I fall back into my chair. "How can you do that?" I don't give him time to reply. "No, let me guess. Because you can?"

He smirks ever so slightly. "Yes."

"Please don't do that. It's bad enough you have his body. Please don't take his memories too," I implore, taking hold of his hand across the table. "I've told you I'll do this, as best I can. It's my love you want, and the whole experience of love in its many forms. You don't need Ayden's recollections for that. You have to discover it for yourself."

"I may need his knowledge on occasions with regard to his business. How else will I be able to operate without prior knowledge?" He's totally serious.

"Business knowledge and personal knowledge are two different things entirely. You're forgetting we are man and wife, we have said and done things that are not meant to be shared, especially not with you."

He grips my hand. "Are you asking me not to read *his* thoughts too?"

Slowly I nod, but say nothing.

"In that case we must create our own set of memories of a public, personal and private nature. Don't you agree?"

He has me boxed in. "Yes."

"Still hungry?" he asks, like a swimmer testing the water.

"Starving," I reply. "I think we should both have the Fillet De Boeuf Au Poivre, don't you?"

"The perfect choice. The Château Branaire-Ducru '05 it is then."

With my lesson learned, I make lively conversation. As delicious as the beef is, it sticks in my throat and requires a hard swallow to force it down; the pomme frites go untouched on my plate. Knowing my thoughts are my own, I'm listening attentively, but my mind is drifting to better days. To an afternoon meal in Rome; the castagnaccioa, chestnut cake for dessert, and "due cucchiai." Just one solitary memory taken from so many that led to even more *happy days*.

We toast to the creating of new memories and I smile, taking his cheek in the palm of my hand as I have done so many times before. "Cin cin, Ayden."

"Cin cin, Beth"

***

Mack has dressed quickly. He's slipped into a comfortable pair of Sunday slacks and a grey sweater that has become a little frayed at the cuffs. He has seen to his chores and is setting up his Sat Nav. It's a straightforward route; north on the M25 until he reaches the Harrow turnoff.

Even though it's a Sunday the motorway is still packed with cars and a caravan of haulage vehicles advertising well-known supermarkets and delivery services. Mack sticks to the speed limit and cruises at 70 miles per hour, forcing impatient drivers to overtake him in the outside lane.

It's 10.15 a.m. He's listening to the Archers, enjoying the watery sunlight and the scenery; it makes a pleasant change from crime scene stills and paperwork. It's good to be out of the office.

Feeling a little envious of the neighbourhood, he looks up a Miss. Richard's third floor apartment. It looks much like any other from the outside, but it's the inside that interests him.

Using the key from her possessions box he enters, closes the door behind him and looks around; he's in no rush. He steps inside the lounge and remains motionless just inside the door, taking it all in: the furniture, the boxes, the photographs scattered on the floor like autumn leaves, crisp and curling around the edges.

His eyes are drawn to the Whiskey bottle minus a top, the glass covered in lipstick and dirty fingerprints. He makes an instant deduction. "Something upset you, Elise. I'm here. Show me what it was."

He takes a long look at the three boxes in turn, drawing his finger along the open tops and running it against his thumb until the black soot coats his skin like fingerprint powder. He closes his eyes and sees her gripping the wheel of the modified Shelby Mustang GT 500, threatening the life of the driver and herself; the act of a desperate woman.

Moving on, he rummages around in each box but finds nothing of value. Each one appears to be storing up memories of no particular significance; none more so than the one ripped open. It's full of photographs. He pieces clues together, taking his time, massaging his chin between his finger and thumb. As his eyes dart from left to right he is drawn to the photos on the floor, wondering why such a woman would become so distraught over a photograph. Upon a closer inspection, he thinks he may have found out why. One of the photographs is a newspaper cutting of Mr. and Mrs. Stone. It documents their engagement: two beautiful people in evening dress, obviously in love.

Weaving his way through the debris, he stands above the photograph torn from the newspaper, looking down upon it like a scientist through a microscope. But, as with every scientific investigation, his must reorganise his focus and zoom out if he is to make sense of it. "Come on, Elise. Talk to me," he mumbles. "Show me what brought you to your knees."

He closes his eyes and waits to hear her voice. It comes to him slowly, making him smile for the first time in quite a while. He follows the line of sight immediately above the engagement photograph and sees a torn photograph of group of people, University types. To the left of the group stands a shy, dark haired young woman. She looks familiar. It's cold and she is turning into her male companion; her hand is positioned close to her mouth, coquettishly. There's nothing strange about that.

Sensing there is more to this than meets the eye, he takes out his notebook and begins jotting things down excitedly, spurred on by the prospect of having stumbled upon something meaningful. But there is more ...

Directly above the group photograph is a picture of three children. In the middle is a tall, handsome boy; to his left is a blond girl with a fierce stare that he has seen before. To his right is a little girl with a dark hair and an oversized pink bow. As in the photo below it, she has her hand to her mouth and is turning into him for protection. Mack balances his weight on the balls of his feet and bends to inspect the photograph close-up.

All it takes is a minute for the pieces to fall into place. The three of them have a history together. He's shaking his head. "Well, fancy that. I think we may have stumbled across a secret you might not be able to sweep under the carpet, Mr. Stone."

Mack takes a clear plastic bag from his pocket and placed the three photographs into it; seals it up and slips it back into his pocket. Dusting himself off, he stands and tiptoes back towards the door. He presses a familiar number into his phone, clears his throat and prepares to issue an order.

"Yeah, Sam, it's Mack. I'm at the Richards's place in Hatch End. Tell forensics to come over here and give it a sweep. I'd like to know who's been here and what we're dealing with." He doesn't wait for a reply.

"Good. I want them here today." He nods "That's right. The full Monty. I think we've got some investigating to do with this one." He returns his mobile to his inside pocket, taking a preparatory breath. "Alright Elise, let's see what else you've left for me. You've got my attention."

10

We are home by 4.30 p.m. As it turns out, the red Bordeaux was an excellent choice; the zing of pepper tickles my tongue and the cherry aftertaste lingers on my taste buds, adding to a feeling of intoxication. In my nervous state I must have consumed over half the bottle and, even though it was soaked up with steak and crème brûlée, it has numbed my natural instinct to bolt.

"Coffee?" I call out flouncing over to the kitchen. "Or do you want more wine?" When I turn to observe his response, he's is by my side.

"Wine would be good but I think coffee would be the more sensible option at the moment." He smiles and eyes me as a teacher might a pupil. "Is this how you spend your Sundays? Eating rich food and drinking overpriced wine?"

"It's only overpriced when you can't afford it!" I remind him happily, snapping a cupboard door shut. "My husband signed everything over to me in Vegas, so I can afford the occasional bottle of overpriced wine."

He folds his arms and leans back against the counter, looking more like my husband by the second.

"Is that so? And there I was thinking that had run its course and you only had Power of Attorney until yesterday." He tips his head to the side, anticipating a tirade of insults.

Refusing to look at him I pour coffee into two cups. "I suppose you knew that and never thought to tell me?"

He shrugs. "What would have been the point? I'm better equipped to handle your husband's affairs than you, surely?"

I meet him head-on. "At home and at work it would seem."

"Precisely."

Without a single sip of coffee, I feel the effects of the wine diminishing; him taking control of Ayden's business interests is a very sobering thought. I push past him on my way over to the sofa. "I hope you know more about business than you know about wine or we're fucked."

He holds up his hand and I am stopped in my tracks. I cannot physically move. "Stop it! Release me." My body jerks forward. "I get it. You're in charge. You can do whatever you want, whenever you want. You're omnipotent, and I'm scared of you." Jerking forward, released from his grip, I place down my coffee cup and turn to face him. "Isn't that what you want to hear?"

He takes a lingering look at me, his eyes softening. "Not at all."

I flop down into the leather sofa, at a loss, cornered. "You talk of love and yet you haven't the faintest idea what it is. Everything you do is for yourself and that's not what love is about."

"Then tell me. Paint me a picture of love that I might see it for myself."

I smile mockingly. "You see, you want me to spell it out for you, as if the answer lies in a sonnet; to paint you a picture ... assuming the answer can be found in colours on canvas." I reach for my coffee. "Love is more complex than that."

"Forgive me but you fell in love quickly. You met and made love and married in a month; is that not what is referred to as a whirlwind romance?"

Affronted, I stand. "You don't know me. You've visited me four times in my whole life and yet you presume to know me and make judgements about my love life. I don't care who or what you are. You don't have the right to do that!"

I'm about to walk away and he raises his hand.

"Go ahead, stop me. Make me stay. We both know you can."

He lowers his hand and I'm able to keep walking. Before I reach the lift I turn to him. "You should never raise your hand to those you love. You know that, right?"

He says nothing.

Close to tears, I come face to face with myself in the mirror in the en-suite bathroom, enveloped in Ayden's cologne; my eyes are drawn to our bed. Bernie has made it and every surface is gleaming. She must wait for us to vacate the premises and slip in covertly like an undercover agent. I must thank her.

As I return to the bedroom, feeling in a better frame of mind, he is standing by the window looking out over a tidy stretch of green. He turns when I approach.

"Forgive my insensitivity, Beth. I have been alone for too long. One forgets what it is to consider others when there is so much to do."

I find a resting place on the edge of the bed. "You weren't doing it intentionally. It's just your way." I look down and play with my rings. "When I met Ayden five weeks ago, almost to the day, my life changed forever. Somewhere out there in your universe, two worlds collided; it was a fateful connection, written in the stars as we say ..." I stifle laughter.

"From the moment he touched my hand and I looked into his eyes, I saw forever. I knew and so did he. He'd kept the childhood memory of me alive, nurtured it. But I'd banished it into the realms of my subconscious. He was my wish come true."

He draws up the chair and crosses his right leg over his left knee, rests his chin on his right hand and invites me to continue with no more than a smile.

"You see, I'd been hiding myself away. Like you I thought I didn't need love; I kept busy with my job and night classes and my music. I thought I was happy but, truth be told, I wasn't. I was simply biding my time; waiting to be found – by Ayden." I settle my eyes on my wedding ring. "Read my mind." I close my eyes ...

I take Patrick's arm and walk toward Ayden, standing expectant and stunningly handsome. I see the love in his eyes, I hear his words, I feel the pink ribbon in my hand, and I am transported back to my childhood ...

When I turn to face him it's through eyes that are swimming in tears. "So you see, the love I have for my husband cannot be feigned or given easily, not even to you; we're soul mates - and that's the one piece of him you cannot conjure up or command, only possess."

"So you cannot love me," he asks mournfully.

I shake my head. "I'm saying that I want you to understand how difficult it is for me to exist between a rock and a hard place. I want to give myself to you in the hope you'll show mercy and return my husband to me. I've seen what you can do. You healed us both with no more than a click of your fingers. And yet … it's like committing adultery." I stretch out my left hand, allowing my engagement ring to catch the light. The heart of stone is a constant reminder of the love I've had and lost.

"You have no concept of it, but I belong to Ayden – I always have and always will. He carried me out of the shadows and showed me what life could be like; he kissed me, woke me from a great sleep, and allowed me to live again. That's miraculous, in itself. As Ms. Bronte would say, *"He is more myself than I am. Whatever our souls are made of, his and mine are the same."*

He smiles and contemplates the literary allusion.

"So … what I'm saying is I need time; time to grieve the loss of our baby, and the loss of the only man I have ever loved. Your party tricks are wondrous, but can never compare to that."

He bows his head. "Yes, I see that now. Thank you for explaining it so eloquently." He's rubbing his chin the way Ayden does when he's thinking. "Will you allow me to read his thoughts? To see how he wooed you?"

The turn of phrase makes me smile. "Wooed me?" My mouth twitches at the thought. "Oh, I think he did more than that. He seduced the hell out of me." My declaration makes me laugh. "Alright."

He's smiling pensively. "I like to see you laughing."

"Well, keep talking like that and you'll see me laughing a whole lot more."

"Then I shall." His smile dissolves. In its place is a thoughtful frown. We sit in silence, waiting to be united once again through shared memories. I roll my rings around on my slender finger unaware of the change befalling him.

I glance up, witnessing the transformation. Gone is that self-serving arrogance I've come to expect; in its place I see a mixture of humility and uncertainty.

"Are you alright? What did you see?"

He clears his throat. "Unadulterated love in its purest form."

His announcement pierces my heart like a shard of broken glass. I conceal a quivering mouth behind my hand. "So now you know?"

"I do." He stands and approaches me.

Unsure of his intentions I lean back, fearful and apprehensive.

He reaches out. "Give me your hand."

My palm in moist but he takes it anyway. "What are you doing?"

"Offering you a lifeline, Beth."

I take hold of his hand and stand before him, my tear-stained face inches away from his. "I belong to Ayden."

"This is true," he says calculatedly, knowing exactly what he's doing.

I gasp. "Don't! Don't take the words from his mouth too. You have his body and his memories. Leave him something."

He raises his chin, seemingly fighting his life-long habit of taking without regard for the feelings of others. "Very well. I will lay him to rest and we shall continue with our adventure, both better informed as to how we can move forward."

I stand on my tiptoes and kiss his left cheek. "Thank you."

"You may be thanking me prematurely, Beth."

"Why?"

"Because you should prepared yourself to be wooed, darling."

I smile weakly. "Ayden wouldn't call me that."

He kisses my right cheek. "Then that's precisely why I shall. Now go and tidy yourself up. Your friend is parking her car outside."

I roll my eyes and head for the door. "I'll see you in the lounge. Will you make sure there is white wine in the fridge?"

"Any particular vintage?" he asks for his own amusement.

"No," I call out, entering the lift. "Ayden's made the choice for us both; you don't need to go pilfering his memory anymore tonight."

With some serious decisions made and our differences reconciled, I feel a little more settled. He won't pressure me to perform or drag me to his bed. All I must learn to do is pretend everything is as it was, but doing that with Charlie around won't be easy.

Ayden stretches out his arm and ushers Charlie out of the lift. She steps out in a flurry of cheerful laughter, stripping off her winter coat, causing me to wonder what he's said in response to her thoughts.

She sprints over towards me. "Holy fuck! Look at you!"

I hold out my hands and glance down at my black skirt and crisp white blouse.

"You look amazing. What did they give you at that friggin' hospital, and where can I get some?" Her arms tighten around me in a fierce bear hug. "I thought you'd still be in bed resting, and here you are."

"I feel fine, Char, just glad to be home. Come and sit down, Ayden will gets us a drink."

Picking up on my signal, he strolls in the direction of the kitchen. I sit and watch him opening and closing cupboard doors in search of glasses.

"I couldn't believe it when they said you'd been discharged. I thought you'd be in there for at least another week," she says.

"I wanted to get out and sleep in my own bed, wear my own clothes, you know?"

"Sure. Well, you look like a new woman, Beth." She takes my hand and whispers, "How's Nurse Stone coping?"

I see his head turn, ears pricking up at the mention of his name. "Nurse Stone is becoming very skilled in the nursing department." I laugh at the thought.

He turns and shakes his head at the likelihood of that ever being the case, making me laugh even more.

"Did you hear that, Ayden? You might be in line for a first-class reference if you can keep it up."

Realising Charlie's comment is laced with sexual innuendo, he replies, "Rest assured, I will not have a problem keeping it *up*, Charlie." He hands us a glass of wine and winks at me, leading me to believe, momentarily, I have my husband back.

With total confidence, he states, "I make it my mission in life to exercise good practice in all areas." He positions himself next to me on the right and takes hold of my free hand. As I listen to Charlie relaying her news, I feel his fingers sliding between mine; he's gently caressing my hand with his thumb as Ayden would. My need for close contact with him ignites, making it impossible for me to pull my hand away. This less than innocent gesture has gone unnoticed by Charlie, but not by me.

"So how long are you staying in Brussels for?" I ask, excitedly.

"Four days. Why don't you come along? It'll be a break for you." She taps my glass with hers.

You can't go ...

Hearing his voice I turn to him sharply only to be met with a carefree smile.

"Have you been to Brussels before, Charlie," he asks, not saying a word to me.

I continue to stare at him.

It's rude to stare ...

I hear his voice but his lips remain fixed in a roguish grin.

I asked you not to read my thoughts ...

I wasn't. I'm allowing you to hear mine.

Discretely, I release my hand from his, marvelling at his capacity to communicate silently. I focus on Charlie. "I think I need to take things easy. Maybe see who's looking after my classes at school."

"What?!" She places down her glass. "Tell me you're not seriously thinking of going back there!"

"Well ..."

"Why would you even bother?"

Ayden senses his cue. "For once we're in agreement, Charlie. I promised Beth a honeymoon and I have yet to deliver on it."

She's nodding frantically. "See. You could be lying on a beach sipping cocktails. What the hell! Ask me nicely and I'll come with you." She laughs out loud, her flaming hair bouncing on her shoulders in an exaggerated display of enthusiasm. "Better still, bring Jake along and we'll make it a foursome."

"You're shameless, Char," I declare, giving her hand a squeeze. "I do like the idea of a honeymoon, though."

The sofa dips. I feel a warm hand resting on my shoulder, sliding beneath my hairline, fingers caressing, a thumb delicately stroking the skin beneath my right ear in a kind of sensual torture.

I start to fidget and tip my head into his embrace, trying desperately to quell desire pooling beneath my navel.

Oh God!

What can I do? I'm beginning to overheat. I gulp back my wine. "I'll get you a top-up, Char," I say, attempting to stand.

"No need, Beth, I have the bottle right here." he kisses my right cheek and reaches down to the bottle of Chardonnay that magically appears by his feet. "This is turning into quite a celebration." His seductive smile is a sucker punch, leaving me with no alternative other than to remove his hand and take it in mine. There it rests, encased in two slender hands, fanning out and positioning itself on my knee.

Better?

No!

He exhales loudly seeking attention. "It was going to be a surprise, but never mind. I've arranged to take you to Hong Kong and then onto The Great Barrier Reef for our honeymoon. How does that sound?"

All I can do is stare into his eyes, glowing with delight. "It sounds ... spontaneous," I reply, shaking my head.

"Not at all. It's all part of my devious plan to spend time alone with you." He smiles in such a way I could slap him, but this is him taking charge with captivating charm; more like Ayden than I dare to admit.

"Wow!" Charlie announces. "Now that's what I call a honeymoon." She turns to him and enquires, "When were you thinking of going?"

"Tuesday."

"Tuesday!" I cry, tightening my grip on his hand. "Why so soon?"

"Soon? We were married over a week ago, darling. I know you've slept through most of it but ..." He laughs at his attempt at humour. "But I did promise."

I feel his lips against my cheek and his hand ascending northwards on my knee. I offer a retort. "You did and I love you for it, but you have ASMI to think about. What with me being in the hospital, *sleeping*, you must have so much to catch up with ..."

He's smiling contentedly. "No, everything's ticking along nicely. For the next couple of weeks, I'm all yours."

Charlie calls out, "Friggin' hell! Just go pack, Beth! Quick, before he changes his mind." To the left and right of me, the air fills with excited laughter. "Anyone would think you didn't want to go."

I'm quick to respond. "I do. But I don't want Ayden to be put under any pressure."

He removes his hand from my knee and strokes my hair, gently. "There's no chance of that, Beth. But thank you for caring." He pulls me to him and kisses my head, letting his lips linger on my hair.

Instinctively I rest my hand on his chest, savouring a rich cocktail of cologne in my nostrils and muscles under my palm. All I can do is close my eyes and lean into him, forgetting, for a moment, the who and the why, focusing only on the here and now.

Charlie throws back the last drop of wine in her glass. "Look, I can see you two have some packing to do and so have I. I'll leave you to it." She stands and reaches for her coat.

"You don't have to leave, Char, stop and have something to eat with us."

"I can't. I'm meeting a Broker friend for drinks in Knightsbridge in thirty minutes. But thanks for asking. When you get back from your honeymoon we'll get together." She eases my disappointment with an affectionate smile.

I help her put on her coat and step into the lift with her. I sense she is holding back, but whatever it is she wants to say is bubbling behind her smile.

"Beth, I know you love Ayden and he loves you; I can see that. But remember who *you* are. Even before he found you, you were beautiful in your own right – you still are." Her hands take mine. "All I'm saying is be careful you don't lose sight of who you are and become his creation." Her words are well-intentioned.

I pull her close to me. The lie that my life has become is one I dare not share. All I can do is pretend. "Don't worry, Char, I know what you mean. I'll be forever Beth and you'll always be my big sister looking out for me. I know what I'm doing."

She sniffs away a tear. "That's all I need to know as you go gallivanting off around the world with Mr. P." She slams me against her chest for a farewell hug.

"A girl's got to have her honeymoon," I state gleefully.

"I hope it never ends for you. Bye."

"Bye, Char. Drive safely."

I wave her off and step back to close the door. At that precise moment a van pulls up a couple of yards from me. Out steps a young man with spiky hair and a beaming smile. "Are you Mrs. Stone?" he asks, consulting a piece of paper.

"Yes," I answer, a little bemused.

"Then these are for you." From the rear of the van he lifts out an enormous bouquet of red roses. "Would you sign here, please?"

I press down lightly on his clipboard and sign my name, writing the word *Stone* for the first time, pausing to look at the signature, unconvinced that the name actually belongs to me. The 'S' looks back at me like a note off a sheet of music that simply does not resonate.

I fumble around in the lift, reaching around petals and stems for the number two. When I step from the lift, Ayden is nowhere to be seen. I want to call his name but the 'A' is leaving my mouth in an exaggerated stutter. "Ayyy ...den."

No answer.

I place the flowers on the kitchen countertop and expectantly make my way to the guest bedroom.

He's lying there on the bed, facing away from me, resting. "Did Charlie tire you out?" I ask, leaning against the doorframe. "The flowers are beautiful, by the way. I haven't read the card yet, but I assume they're from you. Thank you."

He doesn't answer.

I sit on the edge of the bed, trying to make sense of things. I touch his shoulder and he doesn't move. This can mean only one thing: "he's" left, and I'm alone with my husband. Making the most of the moment I scramble around to the other side of the bed, kneeling so we're face to face. I push back a stray curl from his forehead, caress his cheek with my thumb and relay the events of my day.

"We made plans today for our honeymoon. You have everything sorted out: Hong Kong, then on to The Great

Barrier Reef. I'm really looking forward to it, Ayden." I try to smile, but my smile dissolves into a quivering slant. "I miss you so much." I lean in and place a feather-light kiss on his cheek, but when I pull away his eyes are open causing me to tumble backwards onto the carpet with an almighty jolt.

"It's always nice to be missed," Ayden whispers, mockingly. "Shall we pick up where we left off?" He raises himself off the bed and offers me his hand.

I take it and regain my balance. "You scared me."

"I'm sorry. It was only a brief departure. I'm back now." Keeping hold of my hand, he leads me back into the lounge. "Your flowers have arrived, I see."

"Yes and they're beautiful. I love red roses."

"I'm glad. Would you like to tell me how you're feeling?"

"Why bother asking? You can tune into my thoughts anytime, can't you?"

"Yes. But I said I wouldn't."

"But you did."

"No, I merely spoke to you. I made a point of not listening to your reply, although I think it would have been quite amusing to have done so."

I'm not convinced, and merely answer with a carefree shrug.

"What does that mean? You think I'm lying?" He raises an incredulous brow.

"I think you say and do whatever you want," I confess, briskly.

"If that were the case I would have voiced my thoughts long ago."

I fold my arms and wait for his thunderous reply. "And what thoughts might those be?"

"Thoughts of you, naked and splayed across my bed, waiting, aching for my touch, predominantly."

The words explode from his mouth, leaving a crackle of something sexual in the air that ripples over me. I feel my cheeks glowing and turn away. "I see."

He cocks his head to one side. "Well, you *did* ask ..."

"I did. Thank you for sharing. I feel so much better knowing that." I reach for the bottle of Chardonnay and slam the fridge door shut.

"Why are you offended? Doesn't every woman want to be desired?"

"Desired?" I huff and walk away. Out of the side of my eye I see him raise his hand and then think better of it.

"I ask the question again, and for the last time. Why are you offended?" He follows me across the room and stands over me like a handsome shadow.

I look into his eyes. "Because ..." I think through my reply. "Because you treat this as a game with no regard for me." I sip at the wine. "I thought you said we would find a way to approach this *adventure* that would suit us both?"

"I did."

"And yet ..."

"Have I hurt you? Demeaned you, forced you to do anything you haven't wanted to do?"

"No, but ..."

Finding it difficult to control the tone of his voice, he prepares to explain the finer points highlighted in our earlier discussion. "There are no 'ifs' or 'buts', Beth. Don't you realise I could have fucked you and fled like a thief in the night, and that would have been the end of the matter? I have revealed myself to you and offered you honesty and yet here you are, taking every opportunity to profess your love to your husband, reneging on our agreement."

Thoroughly chastised, I lower my head. "I thought you were off somewhere doing what you do. I didn't do it to offend you."

He positions himself besides me, tilting up my chin and holding me in place with a fierce stare which reminds me, if I needed to be reminded, that Ayden is not here.

"This is not a game." He leans in and kisses me softly, leaving my lips tingling; brushes his lips over my moist eyelids until I ache with a longing for my husband that tears at my soul. "Be my wife or be bereft. The choice is yours, Beth."

When I open my eyes again he's gone. Feeling dazed by his decree, I wobble to my feet. My thumbnail finds its way to my mouth and I'm quick to remove it, not wanting to appear too shaken by his declaration.

Arranging the flowers gives me time to collect my thoughts. A lemon envelope falls from the bouquet and I open it tentatively, unfolding the flap like the petals on a daffodil.

Inside there is a crumpled piece of paper, yellowed and tattered around the edges. On it is neat, slanted handwriting; some words have been crossed out and replaced but there is a legible signature at the bottom. It reads: *S.T. Coleridge*.

Wow!

This is an early draft of Desire. My prospective husband sent me the poem and now I've been gifted the original. I can scarcely believe my eyes. It's priceless. I can't even begin to think where he got it from ... a museum? Or, maybe he retrieved it from the man himself?

Just thinking this through makes my head spin; it's an irreplaceable piece of history, if somewhat ironic. I imagine what Ayden would be feeling right now; my Romantics man would be smiling from ear to ear, and so would I.

11

T aking energising breaths and long strides, I enter the lift and descend one floor. The hallway is illuminated and the door to the master bedroom is ajar. I approach it with my head held high. One single thought is on repeat in my head like the chorus in a song.

Be bold, baby.

Feeling fearless, I push open the door, catching sight of Ayden bathed in lamplight, undressing for bed; his grey T-shirt has been carelessly discarded and thrown onto the chair. His belt buckle is undone and he's sitting on the bed removing his socks. He turns to acknowledge my arrival with a half-smile, given more out of politeness than any need to be forgiven for his blunt proposal. Unselfconsciously, he lowers his jeans and they land on top of the T-shirt. There he stands before me, a perfect specimen.

"You've chosen the perfect man to possess," I comment. "I'd forgotten how beautiful you are, Ayden." I use his name purposely, feeling something sharp penetrating my chest as the final consonant leaves my mouth. "I've missed you."

"And I you, Beth." He outstretches his hand and I will myself to move forward even though my feet appear to be glued to the carpet. I take one step and then another until I'm standing before him, looking up into the dark indigo eyes of the man I love.

With the gracefulness of a magician he moves his hand to my face, slipping it beneath my hairline as I tilt my head; I feel the strength of his palm on my cheek and close my eyes to absorb it.

Keeping my eyes closed, I lick my lips in anticipation of what's to follow. He doesn't disappoint. I taste the lips I have come to love and claim as mine in this exploratory kiss. I open my mouth in response, feeling the need to take in more air as

I succumb to the lush wetness coating my lips as the kiss deepens. His hands are framing my face and I'm being devoured. No one kisses like Ayden.

I'm rocking back and forth, being slowly unravelled one limb at a time; my fists are unclenching and my feet are gradually moving toward him. He's doing very little, but his perfect nakedness and kissing prowess is enough to have me in a hypnotic spin.

"Open your eyes, Beth," he whispers.

I do, feeling intoxicated by physical longing and his oh-so-familiar cologne.

He tilts my chin up to focus my attention on his words. "I want you to do something for me."

I blink, knowing what's coming next.

"I want you to relive your first encounter with you husband. Do you remember it?"

I do. I have visions of Ayden stretched out across my bed, attached to the headrest by my stockings. It's not what I expected him to say. "Why?"

"Because I want us to start over. I think you need that, don't you?"

"Yes. I do."

"I will be totally compliant. I am yours to do whatever you wish tonight."

"And tomorrow night?" I ask.

He tilts his head to the right. "I hadn't thought that far ahead ..."

Liar.

"Alright." I agree. "But you're already undressed."

"Close your eyes."

I do.

"Open."

When I open my eyes he's dressed in the same clothes Ayden wore that night at the theatre. Even the shirt looks crisp and freshly ironed. "Another party trick?"

He nods. "One of many."

"I like it. All we need now is the music and we're back in the moment."

"I think we may have very different tastes but I have a song in mind. May I?" He reaches around and selects Aqualung's *Strange and Beautiful*. "Do you approve?"

"Does it matter one way or the other?"

"No, but I like it."

I return his smile. "Then so do I."

The buttons on his shirt are fiddly just as I remember them. This role-play isn't so bad. The only difference is that it's undertaken in silence. I feel like I'm starring in a silent movie. Surely there must be subtitles to go with this? That thought makes me smile.

"What made you smile?"

"This is not how I remember it. I was jabbering on about nothing to hide my nervousness, taking my time ..."

He takes hold of my hand, making me jump. "Then take your time ... please."

I take a step back and close my eyes, remembering how it was - the pretence. Ayden already knew who I was, and was already in love with me. The way he gave himself to me like a gift I had to unwrap. I feel tears leaking from my eyes, and wipe them quickly with my fingertips. I can't back out now.

I straighten my back and begin unbuttoning my blouse. "This is bullshit! I can't relive a moment like that. Just because it's lodged in Ayden's memory doesn't mean it can be re-enacted like some blockbuster movie." I fling my blouse onto the chair. "Get undressed and get into bed." Covertly, I watch him remove his trousers for the second time, pull back the bedding and stretch out beneath the sheet. Just as I remember it, his erection holds my attention as it creates a ridge in the bedding; but, rather than lying perfectly flat, he turns towards me, planting his chin on his left palm. I'm the leading lady now and I don't like it one bit.

This is beyond embarrassing. I've never undressed in front of any man other than my husband. Now look! I have a stranger in my bed. I'm rolling my eyes, feeling hesitant again.

Instantly he wriggles a hand out of the sheets and switches off the bedside lamp.

I'm grateful for that. "Thank you."

"I'm not totally oblivious to your bashfulness, Beth; although why you would be shy when you are so beautiful, mystifies me."

I begin to unhook my bra. "It's because of who you are. You must have seen so many beautiful women. I can't compete with them." I peel off my bra and place it on the chair then settle my eyes on a spot on the carpet, bending my knees and covering my breasts with my arms.

"Beth, I have travelled through space and time to be here. Do you seriously think you could disappoint me?"

I raise my head. "Travelled? I thought you were brought here by Ayden crashing the car?"

He corrects himself. "Yes, of course I was but we are not strangers. I have been aware of you for some time. I explained that."

I'm standing in my panties, feeling as if I have nowhere to hide. "Yes, but you've not seen me naked."

"Oh ... please. Come, you'll catch cold standing there looking like a quivering figurine." He pulls back the sheets.

Shivering, I clamber over him. "My mother had one of those."

"A quivering figurine?"

My teeth are chattering. "No. A Lladro figurine."

"Did she?" he chuckles. "Is this the way you usually embark upon a romantic liaison with your husband? Discussing Spanish pottery?"

"No, we usually begin with wine and music, then move onto literature and take it from there."

He wraps his arms around me and I fold my forearms to my chest, hoping to absorb some of his body heat.

"Why are you so cold" He rubs his left hand up and down my arm.

"I'm frightened."

He tilts back and frowns. "Of me?"

I nod, knowing he can just see the outline of my features.

"What can I do to reassure you?"

"Just hold me and let me fall asleep in your arms. It's been a while since I felt safe and I always felt safe in Ayden's arms."

"I understand." He kisses my hair. "Go to sleep. You're perfectly safe now. No one will ever hurt you again."

Wrapped in his arms, I know that to be true. Nothing in heaven or earth can touch me now.

When I awake, I'm still encased in a kind of human force field, warm and untroubled by fearful thoughts. I lift up my right hand and stroke Ayden's left cheek.

Out of the darkness a voice materialises. "I'm still here."

At first I'm startled but I settle quickly. "I know. You breathe differently." I continue to caress his cheek. "Can I ask you something?" He nods. "Have you had many lovers?"

"Define 'many'."

"More than ten, fifty, a hundred, two hundred?" His silence causes me to raise myself and to look down at him. "*More* than two hundred?"

He's shaking his head. "I think it's best I don't answer."

"Why? Are you afraid I'll think you sleep around?"

He begins to laugh out loud. "Why would I care about that?"

"If you want me to fall out of love with my husband and in love with you, you'll want me to respect you and not to think of you as ... promiscuous."

"I hardly think you're in a position to judge."

"I think I am. Why won't you answer? Are you ashamed?"

"Ashamed?"

I detect indignation in his voice. "Yes."

"I have nothing to be ashamed of, Beth"

"How can I know that?" I enquire further.

"Because I say so, and I never lie!"

"Never?"

"Never."

I lower myself onto the mattress. "Tell me about your last lover. Was she stunning and voluptuous or one of your kind?"

"No and no. There is only me."

I turn to face him. "Only you? You're one of a kind?"

"I am."

"Can't be much fun being you, then. No wonder you possess handsome men's bodies."

He raises himself up off the bed and stretches out his left arm until it's across my body. "Beth, tell me. Were you like this with your husband?"

"Like what?"

"Utterly delightful."

"I don't know. I was myself."

"Then no wonder he never stopped looking for you. I would have done the same."

Without thinking my answer through, I reply, "I think I would have gotten lost in the stampede ..."

"The stampede?" He looks quizzically at me.

"Yes, from all those lovers you've had pursuing you to the ends of the earth."

He's laughing. "I have outlived them all. They're all sleeping peacefully."

"Like Ayden?"

"Yes. But he has not experienced eternal rest. It's more of a ... nap."

"And what would happen if you chose to wake him from his *nap*? Would he remember everything you'd done or would it all be a blur?"

"He would have recollections, if I allowed him to retain some memories, but it would be like a dream."

My face contorts into a frown. "What a terrible dream; sharing your wife with another. I wouldn't want him to ever have a dream like that."

"It wouldn't be like that. He would be the one in the dream, with you," he states frankly.

"He wouldn't know anything about you?"

"No. Does that put your mind at rest?"

I sigh resignedly. "A little. It eases my conscience."

His flat smile says it all. "Is that why you tremble when I touch you?"

"Not just that. I'm afraid I may actually enjoy spending time with you. That's the thought that terrifies me the most."

"Would that be so bad?"

I turn away. "It would be betrayal. He doesn't deserve that."

"Betrayal would involve deception and disloyalty. Surely you can't find yourself guilty of that?"

"No but I'd be sleeping with the enemy."

His eyes flash with surprise. "You consider me your enemy?"

"No. It's just a phrase that came to mind. I don't mean it literally."

"Metaphorically then?"

"Sort of ..."

"And is this the part where we discuss literature?" He's smiling and I see the kind of glint in his eyes that signals trouble.

"I suppose so. Thank you for the Samuel Taylor Coleridge draft. That was the first poem Ayden sent me."

"I know. That's why I sent it."

"But you've given me the first draft."

"Yes."

"Why?"

"Because I can."

I lick my lips. "That was the first time we kissed. Can you kiss me like that too?"

"I think I could be persuaded to try." He raises a curious brow. "In fact it wouldn't take very much persuasion at all. You're a brave and beautiful woman, Beth. I have put you in a difficult position, but this is not the body of a stranger." He places my hand on his heart. "Can you feel a heart beating?" I nod. "This is your husband's heart, as is every other part of this body. I possess it, but it belongs to you. I will make no demands, other than insisting on total commitment on both our parts to love, without boundaries." He moves in for a kiss.

I hold him off with my hand on his shoulder. "Do you think you can love me like that?" I ask, hesitantly.

"Yes. I can."

"And why should I trust you?"

"Because it's true. I never ..."

"... Lie," I call out, completing his sentence, lowering my hand from his shoulder and placing it on a firm pectoral muscle. "Then I trust you to take care of me."

"It would be my pleasure. Although I fear six months may pass much too quickly."

"Six months is a long time."

He shakes his head. "If time were an ocean, Beth, our six months together would be no more than a ripple on an endless sea."

"Would it be that insignificant?" I ask, slighted by his analogy.

"Not insignificant at all; merely imperceptible to humanity, but attested to by me."

"And that's all that matters, right?"

He lowers his head, preparing to conclude our discussion. "You know the answer to that question."

"Yes. But I won't change for you; I can't be someone I'm not." I draw my forefinger across the chest hair that I have longed to touch for the past hour. "You'll have to take me as you find me." The second the words leave my mouth I regret them.

He smiles broadly and it's so contagious, I find my giggle. It had become lost; I'd slipped it into a back pocket never expecting to rediscover it. Yet ... here it is.

"I don't have an issue with that," he replies, charming me further with a wide stare that only complements the roguish smirk.

"You didn't really want to be tied up did you?" I venture to ask.

"No. It would have been a first, I must admit."

"But you were prepared to do that, to put me at ease?"

"Yes."

"That's what Ayden did." I turn away, reliving the memory.

Gently, he turns my face to him. "Don't go there. Stay here, with me. I want you. I want to make love to you, and I want to know what it is to be inside you, Beth; so deep you're too breathless to even call my name."

Fuck!

All I can do is tremble, either with fear or anticipation, or a hot fusion of both. Without saying a word, I slip my hand around his neck, weaving my fingers through soft curls; I pull him to me until I am cloaked in his lethal shadow, drawn to his beauty and craving his love.

His mouth finds mine. It's moist and as I remember it - the texture, the shape, the hunger. With everything to fight for, I will myself to relax, to touch familiar ripples of muscles and skin; commanding trembling hands to still and feel without hesitation, while being kissed and caressed in such a way I can't help but respond.

His right hand is snaking down my body, coming to rest on my panties, positioning me beneath him, locking me in place. A hard and unyielding erection presses into my groin and I clinch involuntarily, feeling the friction of hard flesh brushing against me. His knees sink to the mattress, parting me and I endure the heat of his muscular torso radiating through my fingertips as his breathing quickens, sending waves of masculine scent over my face and into my hair. He's fanning the smouldering embers of passion inside me, those my husband so skilfully ignited a month ago: I am his.

There's a sense of urgency in his movements; I feel it. We will not be engaging in lengthy foreplay tonight. He lacks Ayden's patient caress, his finesse, but that's okay. I can donate my body; it's for a good cause. I'll keep my mind and my heart under lock and key, out of reach and hidden in a place so deep and dark, even he won't be able to reach it. Consoled by that thought, I prepare to gift myself to him, taking my first tentative step into that endless ocean that stretches out before me for miles and miles …

He makes his move, rocking and dipping his body into mine in a rhythmic embrace; his mouth finding my breasts and his fingers feathering my thighs. Wet kisses and hard pulls on my nipples have me groaning with pleasure and then … I become aware of something ancient and unbidden: it's music unlike anything I have heard before.

From somewhere and everywhere in the room there is choral music; harmonic voices blending and floating about my head, wrapping themselves around me like a fog.

My senses are heightened, super-charged; I'm tingling from head to toe. I hear my own voice and it's like the whisper of a helpless child. "What are you doing to me?" Before I lose myself completely, I ask again, "What's happening to me?"

"You are becoming…" he growls, from just below my navel.

Through heavy breathing I ask, "Becoming what?"

He raises his head until our eyes are locked like glistening orbs. "Becoming mine."

His stare is so intense it makes me shudder. Unable to turn away, I watch him descend; scraping his noise against my inner thigh, following through with a moist tongue, lapping at heated flesh like a primordial cat.

I call out between his groans and arch my back, wanting him to stop, yet urging him on, my hands fisting in his hair as his mouth seeks out the most sensitive part of my body.

Forgetting myself, I call out, "Ayden!"

He stops, acknowledges my cry with a devilish grin and dips his head, using his hands and tongue to take me to the point of orgasm. Without seeking permission, he shoulders my legs apart and proceeds to lick and suck at my clitoris until I am writhing with need.

The music increases in tempo, the thumping rhythm matching my heartbeat, propelling me until I am teetering on the edge. Without warning, two forceful fingers penetrate me, bending, teasing my sensitive internal flesh until I can take no more.

My orgasm hits me like a flash of lightening; a roll of thunder ripples through my stomach and explodes against his fingers making me jerk and spasm. I call out "Ayden!" loud enough to raise the dead; then simmer down one breathless gasp at a time. The earth-shattering brilliance fades like a comet and I hit the sheets hard, trembling and tearful.

But this is just the beginning ...

He drags my limp and wasted body to the edge of the bed until my legs are bent at the knees.

Barely conscious I tip up my weary head and observe his mighty frame. He seems to have grown in stature; muscles are flexing and glistening in the half-light of a full moon. He's inspecting my naked body, splayed out before him. Isn't this what he said he wanted, me like this?

"Now you're ready," he snarls, more animal than human; alien eyes finding the light and flashing malevolently, filling me with terror.

He takes hold of my hips with both hands, fastening me in place, and then proceeds to raise my body off the bed until my groin is level with his. I feel the tip of his cock like bone against my saturated skin; he spreads me wider with his hips, taking his time to steady himself, building anticipation before lunging into me in one long, spearing intrusion.

I cry out.

I try to pull back but I am ensnared, overpowered, exposed. All I can do is count the seconds and pray they rush to form minutes ...

When I look up at him the veins in his neck are bulging and his face is contorted, unrecognisable. Still gripped by fear I allow my body to fall limply until I am no more than an inanimate object in his hands - a fuck doll or a corpse.

His guttural groans lessen. Has he finished with me?

No.

"You're not participating, Beth," he reminds me, as if I needed to be reminded. "If you do not, we'll have to keep at this for hours. You do realise that, don't you?"

His menacing tone causes the air in the room to chill. As heat leaves my body, so does my belief I have the physical and emotional strength to handle this kind of humiliation.

"You're inside me. Isn't that what you wanted?" I whimper, managing to hold onto some fragments of my dignity by my fingernails.

"But that's not true is it?" he pushes more deeply into me. "I have your body but your mind is elsewhere. This is a contact sport, Beth, but it should involve cerebral engagement, darling."

His final word leaves me icy cold. "You do what you want with me, Ayden." I spit out my husband's name, knowing I'm inflaming him further.

"A courageous invitation, but one I can't accept." He pulls from me roughly and takes a step backwards, still eyeing my trembling torso. "You are beautiful in your nakedness, you always have been."

Always have been ...

His knowing smile is that of a man who has seen everything, but learned nothing. He places his right hand between my legs. "Giving me this is only the start of our adventure, Beth. I want your body, of course, but as I explained, I insist on total compliance."

"You mean obedience?"

He tips his head to one side. "Call it what you will. It's your mind and your heart that escapes me, as yet."

I snigger at my naivety. "Is there a single thought of mine you haven't pilfered since our paths crossed?"

"I have heard everything."

"So you lied ..."

"I had no choice."

I throw back his words. "You always have a choice, and you chose to lie."

He laughs softly. "Touché. As your husband would say."

I hate you so much right now.

"You really are a piece of work."

"I'll take that as a compliment." He grins, menacingly. "But I do have very particular tastes and demands which have to be met or ..." He shrugs his shoulders. "Or this adventure may end quickly and tragically."

I tell him with my thoughts. *I hate you, you fucking bastard.*

"Now, now. There's no need for profanity," he chides, tutting and shaking his head. "A sweet young woman like you has no need of that kind of language." He places a coated finger against his mouth and spreads my seeping moisture across his lips, making me cringe. I watch as his tongue drags across glistening skin and turn away, repulsed.

"As I said, you are very sweet."

Leaving me naked and chilled to the bone, he makes his way into the bathroom. I hear the sound of water and assume he's showering.

I retrieve my clothes and dress hurriedly. When he enters the bedroom I'm standing in my underwear, illuminated by the fluorescent light shining from the bathroom. He stops in his tracks when he sees me. I'm not sure why.

With a muted voice he asked, "Are you going to shower?"

"Yes. I feel dirty." I bundle my clothes together and attempt to walk around him into the bathroom, but, as I pass, he grabs my arm.

"I'm sorry," he mutters.

"It's a little late for that." Freeing my arm, I push past him.

I place my clothes down onto the counter top and turn to inspect myself. My hair is a tangled mess; my eyes are lifeless, encircled with mascara. My throat bears the marks of his teeth and my breasts are tender and sore. If that were not enough, through clouded vision I settle my eyes on my hips; around them are bruises that start at the bone and keep going until they form the shape of two powerful thumbs at the front and fingers around the side like shackles. I lower my head and allow gravity to take charge of my tears. One thought is on repeat in my mind...

What did I do to deserve this?

In an instant, he appears behind me. I flinch when I feel his hand on my shoulder and try to shake it off. It won't budge.

I spin around. "Look what you did!" I gaze up into his eyes, seething breath leaving my nose in a snort. "You think that possessing my husband's body allows you to do whatever you want with me? You'll never be Ayden. He would never hurt me like this."

He bows his head. "Turn around and close your eyes."

"No! You can't magic this away." I try to reach around him for the shower controls. "Would you mind? I'd like to take a shower and cleanse myself of your stench."

He takes hold of my hands and puts them together into a double-handed fist. "Don't toy with me. Let me explain."

"Don't bother. "

"I insist." He tightens his grip on my hands. "The fault is mine. I had forgotten how fragile the human body is. It's been a while since I made love to ..."

"Fucked!"

"What?" He frowns, his eyes turning into slits that are unresponsive to light.

"You didn't make love to me. You fucked me."

"But you climaxed, didn't you?"

"I'm not completely without feelings. I haven't been intimate with my husband for six days. I missed his touch."

"I sensed it."

"You took advantage of it." I confront him head on. "Why didn't I feel you hurting me then? I hurt everywhere now?"

"I put you in a kind of trance so your senses were heightened but you felt no pain. Now I realise that was wrong."

"It was shameful. You could have seriously hurt me."

"I can heal you ..."

"No. Take a long look at your handy work. You got off on hurting me."

"That's not true. I got off, as you say, on the intimacy we shared. If I'd wanted to hurt you, you would not be standing here asking me about it."

"Is that a threat?"

"Of course not." He's shaking his head. "A simple explanation."

"There's nothing simple about it." I wriggle my hands free. "You only know how to take. Anyone would think you had never loved ..."

He snaps back, "I have not."

"But surely you ..."

He's shaking his head. "No."

I grab my bathrobe off the hook. "So what's this? Another lie?"

"I wish it were."

"I don't trust you. You said you would take care of me, and here I am looking like I've been raped."

He leans back to absorb the magnitude of my declaration. "But you have not."

"No, but if I were to walk into a hospital right now and say I had been, they would believe me," I state frankly.

"That would be a very foolish thing to do, Beth."

I rest my hands on my hips petulantly. "I didn't say I was going to, just *if* I did."

"That's not necessary. Let me heal you and we can begin again."

"No. I want you to see what you've done and reflect on how long it takes for these bites and bruises to fade."

"Are you attempting to punish me?" He finds the thought quite amusing.

"Not punish. Teach." I pull my hair back into a rough ponytail. "I said I would go through with this, and I will. But I won't let you spend six months with me and leave having not learned anything about love." I hold my hand against my neck, drawing his attention to the bite marks. "What emotion is this? Can you tell me?"

He tips his head to the side, baffled by my question.

"Just so you know, this is cruelty." I push him aside. "Now if you'd excuse me, I'd like to shower."

He steps to his right. Only now can I see my husband in all his glory, naked and covered in perspiration, his hair untidy, his chin darkening with stubble. This is the man I love, and no amount of bruising will change that.

I toss my bathrobe to one side, unhook my bra and step out of my panties immodestly. My mottled skin begins to glow under the steaming spray. I tip back my head, close my eyes, feeling its full force on my face and the sting of it on my neck and breasts. In less than five minutes all evidence of my infidelity is washed away.

When I have towelled myself dry, and some of the steam has cleared from the mirror, I inspect myself. The bite marks have disappeared; my breasts are untouched and my hips are smooth to the touch and the colour of tinted alabaster. I am healed and, if I'm honest, very relieved. Surely I've endured more physical and emotional pain than any one person deserves in a lifetime, haven't I? To be able to rectify the former is miraculous but ... the latter? That's a different kind of hurt. Only I can repair those scars and that process will begin tomorrow.

***

Mack is standing by a stray dining chair, looking up into a loft opening, assessing whether a woman of Elise's size could reach up into it to retrieve three boxes. He climbs onto the chair and reaches up. The low ceiling makes it possible for him to rest his elbows on the edge and peer inside. To the right, poking out of a black bin bag is a large Christmas tree, beside it a box labelled decorations, to the left he sees two suitcases and nothing more. He sighs, realising Elise had few mementos. Her past would appear to be contained in three small boxes that have been hidden away, out of sight. He wonders if that's a reflection of her life.

Lying around on the bedroom carpet are discarded clothes - jeans and a white blouse - covered in more black dust. Wardrobe doors have been flung open and cosmetics thrown into the sink.

This was a woman in a hurry, he surmises. 'But what woman would be in such a hurry to die? Maybe one who had nothing, or no one left worth living for?'

He leaves her apartment, slamming the door behind him, more determined than ever to find answers to questions he has yet to devise.

12

S till stinging from the emotional and physical savaging that was tonight's encounter, I resist the temptation to speak softly to Ayden as he sleeps peacefully by my side. I turn off the bedside lamp, run my fingers through his hair, say nothing, and leave the room. It's only 10.30p.m. and there's something I must do while left "unsupervised."

Settling on the sofa, I boot up my laptop, seeking a private place to hide my heart and to keep my love alive for my husband.

I download the software for a digital scrapbook, planning to record the events of the next six months. If and when he - in all his infinite wisdom - returns Ayden to me I don't want him grappling with out-of-focus memories of our first year of marriage. The thought of being no more than a ghost scares the hell out of me. I'll help him to re-live this time; to see it with my eyes through a camera lens, and through my words and music. It will seem to him that we were never apart. I listen to Daughter singing *Still*, picturing the night's events and reliving the nightmare. Through tears I type and relive our day ...

NOVEMBER #1

"Boldness be my friend."
Shakespeare: Cymbeline

Today we took a stroll around The Tower of London. The tour guide tried so hard to entertain us, but had you rolling your eyes and checking your watch after 30 minutes. Ha!

I dragged you away to Balthazar's in Covent Garden and we had a delicious meal. Of course, you intimidated the hell out of the waiter and took seven long minutes to choose the wine. But I was happy to wait and watch.

In a couple of days, you'll be whisking us off on our honeymoon to Hong Kong, and The Great Barrier Reef. I can't wait!! (Pictures to follow!) Having you all to myself for a week will make up for all the craziness we've had to deal with.

I love you, Ayden.

Beth. X

To this first entry I attach a stock photo of the Tower and upload a photo of a menu from Balthazar's to add context. I save and shut down; close the laptop lid and lean back, contemplating my next move.

I'm not accustomed to duplicity, but that doesn't mean I can't exhibit it in one form or another. I must play my part to perfection and count down the days until my body and my thoughts become my own. Hopefully, this scrapbook will make serving my time a little easier. Doing what I must will be the biggest challenge of my life, but it's not insurmountable. To save Ayden's life, I must give the performance of *my* life.

Last night passed without incident. I'm awake early: it's only 6 a.m. As I turn, I notice Ayden is lying on his back. I have my chin propped up on my left palm, caressing him with my eyes; dark wisps of eyelashes sit motionless on smooth sweeps of skin beneath his eyes. Sculptured cheekbones catch the light and his mouth ... oh how I long to trace the shape of that perfect pout. I lick my lips reflexively and close my eyes. When I open them he's awake, looking back at me quizzically.

I'm no longer startled by his presence; I half expect it now. "You're back?"

"I am indeed. Why are you awake so early?" he asks yawning widely.

"To wake you up. You have to go to work today," I remind him.

He huffs, rolling his eyes with incredulity. "I don't have to do anything," he reminds me.

"If you want to be accepted as Ayden, you have to be him in every sense of the word. That means running his business, and attending functions – all of it. You've picked yourself a handsome guy who is a media mogul and a well-known face in the press. You need to keep up appearances or people will think something is wrong."

"I don't see why I should have to burden myself with that. I'm sure there are better ways to amuse myself - and you too for, that matter."

"You mean like visiting more tourist attractions?" I ask sarcastically.

He gives me a disapproving look. "Distain does not become you, Beth."

"I'll keep that in mind the next time you try to complicate things more than they already are." I jump out of bed, naked, and reach for my bathrobe. "Look. I'll come with you if you like, to help out." I turn to face him. "I can't say fairer than that."

"It's a tempting offer." He's grinning. "On one condition..."

I tighten the belt around my waist. "And that would be?"

"You wear a business suit ..."

"OK. I can do that ..."

"... but no underwear."

I feel my face folding into a frown. "What? Are you serious?"

He's licking his lips in such a sensual way I know I'll have to leave soon, before my neck turns the colour of steak tatare.

"Absolutely!"

I'm shaking my head. "Why would you insist on such a thing?" I hold up my hand and beat him to his answer. "Let me guess. Because you can."

He laughs quietly. "That's correct."

"If you don't mind I would rather not attend a high-powered meeting of media men in suits minus my panties, thank you very much."

He turns over and pulls up the cover to his chin with an exaggerated sigh.

"So that's it. You're going to stay in bed all day because I won't go and face the world in a state of undress?" I fold my arms in front of me and tap my foot. "Don't you think that's a little petty? You'll be bored senseless."

"Not at all. I won't be here," he mutters.

"Of course you won't. You'll be off gallivanting around the globe with your scythe counting the dead and collecting souls, while I'll be making up some implausible excuse about you having the flu." I storm out of the bedroom in a huff.

Fifty minutes later I'm stomping in high heels across a marble floor, throwing my phone into my handbag, quietly simmering. When I glance up, Ayden is lounging on the white leather sofa, looking like he's just stepped out of a photo shoot; his arms are outstretched into a 'Titanic' pose across the headrest, with his right leg across his left knee. His signature Armani suit clings to his muscular body like a second skin. Before I can self-edit, I'm thinking, *Wow!*

He looks across at me, supressing his delight but unable to hold back on a wry smile. "You look sensational too, darling," he announces. "Are we ready to go?"

I say nothing and simply nod.

As we descend to street level, the closeness of his body and the invisible cloud of expensive cologne works like a charm. "Here, hold this." I hand him my bag, raise my skirt and wiggle out of my panties. I swap them for my bag. "There. You've got what you wanted, haven't you?"

He's shaking his head. "Not entirely."

"What do you mean?"

He peels back my navy jacket, to reveal a sheer white blouse. "Aren't we forgetting something?"

"This blouse is see-through," I say, indignation plastered across my face.

"And ..."

"And ... and I don't think ..."

"You don't have to think, Beth. That's what I'm here for." He's spinning my panties around the forefinger of his left hand like a gunslinger with a lingerie fetish.

As hard as I try I can't prevent a giggle from escaping my mouth. "I don't see what difference it makes whether I'm wearing a bra or not." I slip off my jacket and fold it over his arm. I unhook my bra, slip out of the straps, and pull it down my left arm until it appears like bunting from a magician's sleeve.

"Ta da!" With his arms full I wrap the bra around his neck. "Happy now?"

"Ecstatic."

Before leaving the house I quickly don my jacket and fix my skirt; take my lingerie from his hands, and shove it into my bag. The cold air nips at my cheeks and my nipples as we make a dash for the Rolls.

"Morning, Lester." I give him my sweetest smile.

"Good morning, Mrs. Stone. It's good to have you back home."

"Thank you."

He gives Ayden the customary nod and slams the rear door. Within the minute he is weaving through traffic and we're on our seven-mile journey from Belgravia to Canary Wharf. There is just enough time to develop an action plan.

I turn to face him, "Does everyone know we're coming? Will they be assembled?"

"Yes. I contacted Charlotte yesterday and asked her to arrange a formal Board meeting at 9 a.m."

"How will you know who they are or what to say?" I ask, uncertain about his ability to pull it off.

Charlotte will be putting name plates out, for your benefit, and I'm hoping you will be able to assist me as well."

"Me? What do I know? I'll be the one sitting there without underwear. I'll be more concerned about keeping my legs crossed and my jacket fastened," I remind him in a sulk.

He begins to chuckle and I catch him smirking.

"I know what you're doing!" I shake my head and trace the droplets of rain that are now running down the window.

"You do?"

"Yes. You're sifting through Ayden's memories again, finding ones that are playful; when he was amused, when we had fun." I turn to face him. "That's what you're doing isn't it?" I straighten an already smooth skirt. "The underwear thing; you would never have thought of that. After last night's assault on my senses, I have a good idea of what you're like. Your ability to heal my bruises doesn't detract from the fact you were more animal than human. I would have been screaming if you hadn't numbed my perception of pain."

"I have apologised for that." He takes my hand. "It will not happen again."

"How can I be sure?" I wait for a reply but none is forthcoming. "I can't live in fear of you." Having said my piece, I look away.

"You won't have to. I will not touch you unless you want me to. Is that assurance enough for you?"

When I face him, he's gazing straight ahead. "Ayden?"

He offers me a smile. "Yes, Beth."

"I can do this. I can show you love but not if you treat me like that. I will begin to despise you and fear you. Neither of us wants that." I take his right hand. "Now about this meeting. Are you nervous?"

He's a little surprised by my question. "Nervous? About what?"

"Facing all these strangers and faking it."

"Not at all. I think it was a good idea. I'm feeling rather excited at the prospect of it."

"Have you done this kind of thing before?"

"Never. But I'm not unfamiliar with the concept of role-play."

I snatch my hand away. "This is more than just role play. This is someone's business you're talking about. You don't want to appear different or confused."

His quiet laughter draws my attention. "I can say with total certainty that in all my years I have never appeared *confused*."

"I'll have to take your word for that. But, like you've said, you've never had to pretend to be a successful man with his finger on the pulse of a billion pound media empire, have you? It's not like throwing half a dozen souls into a sack and carrying them off to God knows where."

He's laughing out loud. "Your description of my other job is closer to the mark than you might think." His laughter subsides and he places a soft kiss on my left cheek. "Nevertheless, I will do my very best to keep in character, Beth, if only to please you."

"Thank you."

He checks his watch. "Are you ready for your performance?"

"Why? What do I have to do other than pretend you're my husband?" I'm shrugging my shoulders feigning disinterest.

"You have to meet the press, darling." He bolsters his statement with a smile.

"Me!"

"Yes. Your attack and subsequent escape from the jaws of death made the front page. They are gathering outside Stone House to see you, not me."

I'm suddenly feeling rather uncomfortable. "How long have you known about this?"

"From the moment I arranged it." He's so nonchalant I could slap him.

I'm searching around in my bag for my panties. "And you didn't think I might prefer to meet the press wearing these?" I'm waving them in front of him, but only for second until I catch Lester's startled expression in the rear view mirror.

"I thought you might feel less constrained and more ... liberated without them." He's laughing, again.

I begin to laugh too. "You're becoming more like Ayden every day. This is definitely something he would do!"

"I'll take that as a compliment."

"You do that, but you still have a long way to go." I tuck the panties safely into my bag, fasten it up and let my mind wander. "Typical! I'm meeting the press and it's raining."

He tips his head to look out of my window. "Is it? I hadn't noticed."

At that very moment there is a break in the clouds. From out of the blue comes a streak of sunlight so bright and so warm that the droplets of rain evaporate off the glass. When I catch his eye, he says nothing, merely winks.

"Happy now?"

I'm shaking my head. "Euphoric."

"Anything else I can do for you?" he asks.

I take hold of his hand. "Keep hold of my hand. I don't want them to eat me alive."

He leans in and kisses my hair. "I wouldn't allow anyone to do that, darling. Consider this the preface to our adventure."

As the Rolls turns the corner we are confronted by at least 20 men and women with flashing cameras, shouting and scrambling to get to us. Lester steps from the car and waits for a signal to open the door.

He draws an invisible line under my mouth with his forefinger, and circles it beneath my chin; it's sensual and familiar. My first instinct is to say, "Don't!" But it feels too intimate, too much like Ayden's touch to show any displeasure. Instead I smile softly.

"Are you ready for your debut, Mrs. Stone?" he asks, squeezing my hand.

"No, but let's get it over with."

He taps on the glass and Lester opens the door. "Keep them away from Beth," he instructs. "I don't want them to manhandle her."

"Of course, Mr. Stone." He nods and holds back, leaving Ayden to face the mob while he protects me, creating a human shield against the pack of ravenous reporters. Hand in hand we mount the first step to the building. My jacket catches in the wind and I pull it tightly, refastening a button that had freed itself in the skirmish. The last thing I want is to be flashing my breasts in public.

One of the reporters stumbles backwards, still holding his camera. Ayden immediately picks me up and places me on the next step up, alert to the possible focus of the lens. For that I'm eternally grateful.

Having taken time to freshen up and compose myself, I march into the boardroom at Ayden's side. His strides are longer than mine and I have to quicken my steps to keep up. Thankfully, it's a short sprint to the top of the table. The gathering stands and begins to applaud; I'm not sure why.

He smiles wryly at the ovation. He can't have experienced many of those in his lifetime. "Please sit down. As Mark Twain once said, 'The reports of my death are greatly exaggerated.' I am very much alive."

The applause dies down.

Realising I have no seat he turns to Stephen. "I wonder if you would be so kind as to offer your seat to my wife?"

He was rude to me last time I was in here.

"I'm sure you want to make amends for the rudeness you exhibited the last time you met Beth."

Taken by surprise, Stephen rises, stuffs his papers under his left arm and pulls back the seat for me. "Mrs. Stone."

Taking care to hold onto my jacket I sit down, arranging myself into a comfortable position on Ayden's right. "Thank you, Stephen."

Along with the other Board members I watch him scuttle along to the far end of the enormous table. In less than a minute he has asserted his authority and no one in the room has the slightest doubt he's back with a vengeance. All I can do is offer an appreciative smile: so far so good.

He unbuttons his jacket and places his hands down on the polished table, scoping the room. I know why; he's picking up on thoughts and pairing names to faces. "So, here we are: home sweet home."

His opening gambit takes me by surprise, so much so I start to giggle. Taken aback, he turns to me, forcing me to conceal another giggle behind a smile.

Do you mind ...

I hear his words in my head and they are a sobering reminder that he is not, in fact, Ayden but merely an imposter.

Sorry.

His focus rests upon a thin-faced man of around 35 named, Lawrence Barber, who is shuffling papers. "Lawrence, I believe you have a couple of things to share with us today?"

Lawrence raises his head and clears his throat. "Yes, Ayden, I do. I've been keeping a close eye on operations in Seoul. We are having some issues with one of the single chip devices."

"What kind of issues, specifically?"

"Issues involving the STB functions, required to operate the standard video decoding circuitry."

"And is it something that can be rectified quickly?"

Lawrence is nodding. "I think so, but we've had to hold off on production until it's resolved."

"So how long are we talking? A couple of days?"

"I think so ..." He smiles nervously.

"Right. Get back to me tomorrow afternoon with an update. I want everything on line by Wednesday at the latest."

"Right."

He's getting into his stride.

You're doing great!

He reads my thoughts and turns to me to offer a cheeky smile. I feel my heart flutter and look away. He has no right smiling at me that way. I pour out a glass of water and sip it quietly, hoping he hasn't noticed.

If you're warm, why don't you remove your jacket?

Still sipping my water I look up to him with wide eyes.

You know why!

He smirks but carries on conversations with everyone in turn, reading their thoughts, tapping into their concerns and latching onto their secrets. He has an unfair advantage but it's working in our favour.

It occurs to me that there is one person missing.

Where's Jake?

He turns to Charlotte, sitting on the side line, dutifully taking notes. "Won't Jake be joining us?"

"He's on his way, Mr. Stone." She checks her watch. "The jet landed at Heathrow half an hour ago and he's en route."

"Thank you, Charlotte. Let's hope he arrives before we put the world to rights or he may be out of a job!" Ayden laughs at his own joke and so does his audience, sitting silently in awe of his business acumen and intellect.

There is a single person who has not spoken; a petite Asian lady sits silently, waiting to be selected. Her eyes are darting from left to right, seeming as if a single glance at Ayden will turn her to stone.

He directs a question at her and she is forced to do just that. "So, Miss Liu, what have you to share with us today?"

I watch as she takes a deep breath; Ayden is intimidating the hell out of her. I catch her eye and give her a smile; she smiles back, nervously.

"Mr. Stone, I have been undertaking a review of marketing and distribution strategies in the Pan Pacific Region and it is my belief that we are not focusing on ways to take advantage of growth opportunities. We need to leverage our brand and use data more effectively. The enabling technology is there but we are not building it into our business model."

The more she speaks the greater her confidence; she's young, smart and ambitious. Ayden would do well to let her continue with her proposal, but he's growing impatient.

Let her finish ...

He turns to me and smiles softly.

"Please continue, Miss Lui."

Feeling the heat rising in the room, he removes his jacket and makes a point of arranging it on the back of his chair. I hear her but I can't take my eyes off him. What is it about a fitted white shirt and a tie...

Are you assessing me, Beth?

Caught, I avert my eyes.

Or are you enjoying?

I find his words unsettling. It's getting so hot in here, even the men are wiggling their ties and undoing the top button on their shirts. I look across to Charlotte and she's fanning herself with her pad. I shake my head.

What have you done with the heating?

I get no reply. Instead, Ayden begins to walk around the table; he's nodding at Miss Lui's comments, taking it all in, refusing to look at me as I dissolve into a puddle of perspiration. He knows I cannot remove my jacket!

Bastard!

He conceals his amusement with his hand, leaving me to liquefy as, one after the other, the gentlemen remove their jackets.

As she brings her proposal to a close, he positions himself behind me. All eyes are on him, on me.

"So what do you think of that, Beth?" he asks, putting me the spot. What can I say? I was barely even listening. "I think Miss. Lui has given this a great deal of thought, and you should at least have a look at her proposal."

He kisses my head. "Quite right. I'll do just that."

Leaving me to stew, he heads over to the enormous plate glass window overlooking the Thames; it winds its way through London as far as the eye can see, cutting through the metropolis like a black anaconda.

He's positively regal in his stance; hands in his pockets, head held high; a perfect profile set against the clear blue sky. As hard as I try not to think of him with a craving that causes me to squirm in my seat, I can't help myself. My thoughts betray me as they form and leave me weak at the knees like a schoolgirl. I try to think of anything except him but I'm so overheated all I can do is lick my lips and content myself with another glass of water. Even my breathing is laboured and my panties are sticky with a combination of perspiration and arousal.

The door swings open and Jake enters carrying a Starbucks coffee and a leather documents case. Thankfully he brings a cool gust of air in with him. He places down the coffee and the case on the table. "What the hell! It's like a sauna in here. Is there something wrong with the heating or are we hatching chicks?" Immediately he loosens his tie and removes his jacket. It lands on a chair as he bounds over in Ayden's direction. His smile lights up the already sweltering room.

"Well, if it ain't Ayden Stone back from the dead!"

Without even acknowledging me he heads for the window. "You look awesome! No scars or anything. Did you have plastic surgery?"

Ayden is less animated. "No, just good skin, I suppose."

"No shit!" He reaches out to shake Ayden's hand and pulls him close so he can pat him on the back. "You nearly gave me a fucking heart attack," he whispers. He's continues to pat Ayden's arm. "So what did I miss? Have you been playing catch-up?"

If only he knew... more leading than catching-up here.

Ayden is unsure of how to act around Jake; I actually believe he's uncomfortable with his brotherly behaviour. Jake will be the first to notice a change.

You grew up together. He's the only man you're close to and you trust.

Ayden immediately becomes less abrasive. He pats Jake on the back. "We thought you weren't going to make it so we started without you."

"No worries. I've got Grace typing up my report. I dictated it on the flight back. Looks like you've got everything under control here."

He scans the room and his gaze rest on me. "Beth! I'm sorry. I didn't see you there."

As he comes over to me, I stand to greet him and in my excitement I forget to hold onto my jacket; the button comes undone and I approach him looking like I'm taking part in a wet T-shirt competition. It's only when he lowers his eyes and leaves them there, focusing on my sweat soaked blouse that I realise it. Thankfully, I have my back to the Board members.

He's grinning. "Did you get dressed in a hurry?" he asks, punching Ayden in the arm. "Looks like you two've started your honeymoon already. Up to your old tricks I see."

Crimson-faced, I quickly button up my jacket. I turn to Ayden preparing to be met by a grin but, instead, he is simply staring at me. There is not a trace of humour, merely an expression that I cannot fathom.

Ayden! Snap out of it!!

I take his arm and lead him back to his place at the head of the table. "We have some catching up to do," I remind Jake light-heartedly. "We're going out to lunch. You're welcome to join us."

Returning to the here and now, Ayden pulls back my seat for me and takes his place, leaving Jake to make the walk back to his seat.

"Before we close this meeting, is there anything else?" He scans the room and passes Stephen then sweeps back to him. "Yes Stephen ..."

He starts to mumble. "It's a delicate matter, Ayden, one that would be better discussed privately."

With the room cooling, Ayden reaches for his jacket. "Will it affect ASMI?" he asks impatiently.

Stephen is struggling to find the right words.

"Come on man, spit it out. Let's hear it."

"I'm afraid there seems to have been some confusion about the legality of your marriage to ... to Miss Parker."

Ayden and I look at each other in surprise. Then - with every other head in the room - we turn to face Stephen, and look back at Ayden as if we're watching the set point being played in a Wimbledon final.

Did you know?

Not until five minutes ago.

"That *is* disappointing news. And how do you propose we deal with this revelation, Stephen?"

All eyes are now on Stephen. Even Jake puts down his coffee; he's riveted to the spot.

"As I see it, we have three options." He clears his throat. "One. You leave things as they are and remain unwed. The Vegas ceremony will be invalid and thus annulled..."

All eyes turn to Ayden. "Two."

"Two. I arrange for the documents to be faxed over so you can read through and sign them. Thus legalising the marriage ..."

"And three?"

"Three. You make arrangements to be re-married here and you take it from there." His last word trails off and he sits down, visibly relieved to have communicated the bad news and managed to keep his job.

Ayden rubs his chin thoughtfully. "I see. We do seem to have a problem on our hands, don't we?" He turns to me. "What do you propose we do, Beth? How might we resolve our predicament? Will you be my wife in all respects, including name?"

What can I say to that? "I thought I was!"

"As did I, darling. You decide."

I'm shaking my head. When I look around the room, all eyes are on me. "I think we should sign on the dotted line, Ayden, and make it legal."

Straightening his jacket and fastening the button, he signals his agreement. "Then that's what we'll do." He looks back at Stephen. "Have the documents ready to be signed by lunchtime. We'll be leaving for our honeymoon tomorrow and we will do so as man and wife. Now, anything else?"

The gathering begins to disperse, with only Jake and I remaining seated!

Once the Board Members have left, Jake stands. "What the fuck! Didn't you two sign anything in Vegas?"

I try to explain, "No we didn't. The MI5 agents were so eager to get their hands on Ayden, we didn't have time."

Jake lowers his head, realising his accountability. "Yeah. Sorry. It was my fuck-up that caused that."

Tell him the truth!

Ayden reaches out to shake his hand. "No harm done."

"What?" I exclaim. "Tell him, Ayden. You can't let him think it was *all* his fault."

Jake looks repentant. "It's alright, Beth. No need to defend me I know I fucked-up."

"But you didn't." I take Ayden's arm. "Tell him, or I will."

I don't know what you want me to tell him?

It occurs to me that Ayden doesn't actually know and I've put him on the spot. I have to make a quick recovery. "I know how bad Ayden feels about this, so I'll tell you." I take hold of Jake's arm and lead him over to the enormous window. "You didn't fuck-up. It was a sting operation set up by MI5. It was arranged months ago and he couldn't get out of it. For the sake of making it look real, he had to string you along. He feels terrible about it."

Ayden sits poised and unruffled, massaging his chin the way he does when he's thinking things through.

Tell him you're sorry.

Jake turns to him. "Is this true? All this was going on and you didn't tell me? You let me feel like shit because I thought I'd let you down?"

"Yes, I'm afraid so. Sorry about that."

Jake begins to laugh. "You bastard!" His gaze shifts to me. "And did *you* know?"

I shake my head. "No. Not until I went over to see him in MI5's HQ." I have to diffuse this before it blows up in Ayden's face. "You think *you* were deceived and hung out to dry? I've ended up with a non-existent marriage because of it!"

Jake looks to Ayden. "You fooled us all, Ayd."

"I had no choice."

"I get that. Business is business right?"

I interrupt. "That's not how it was, Jake. It wasn't about business. It was about something more important than that. It was about the chips being intercepted and used for weaponry like rockets and missiles. That's why Ayden got involved."

Ayden defends himself, finally. "I should have told you but the fewer people who knew the more credible it was."

"Well, it worked."

"It did and the British Secret Services are working with the Saudi Arabian government to arrest and detain undesirables, as they call them."

"That's good news, I guess." He huffs away a thought. "So when were you going to tell me?"

"When the time was right," Ayden states.

Jake leans in and kisses me on my cheek. "You're a good person, Beth. I hope some of your goodness rubs off on our

Ayd here." He walks across the room, stopping to pat Ayden on the shoulder as he remains seated. "I'll go check on that report and meet you for lunch, right?

"I'll have Charlotte tell you where we're going."

He leaves the room in a dash and I can feel his disappointment wafting over us like a backdraft.

"What was that all about?" Ayden asks.

I stomp over to him. "It was about you not trusting your best friend."

"I don't see why ..."

I hold up my hand to quiet him. "You will."

***

D. I. Bowker is sitting in a plush waiting room on the top floor of the Stone Building. He's reading through notes and recalling yesterday's visit to Hatch End, feeling fascinated and benevolent; if ever there was a victim who needed his help it's Elise Richards. Contemptuously, he glances around at the white leather furniture, the accolades proudly displayed in gilded frames, the scented water. Before he can rationalise his disdain the door opens and a smart, mature lady moves towards him.

"Detective Inspector Bowker, please come with me. Mr. Stone will see you now."

He follows her along a brightly lit corridor decorated with photographs of capital cities; every one he recognises, none he's ever visited. He turns away and faces forward, refusing to be taken in by big business branding.

He enters the lion's den and sees Ayden Stone reclining in a high-backed leather chair that swivels left and right. He's dressed immaculately in a navy suit and tie. His features appear chiselled, his smile charming in the extreme. Behind him is the London skyline; familiar landmarks dwarfed by his monument to materialism: The Stone Building. Mack envisions King Canute, holding back the tides, and struggles to suppress a smile. Instead, he reshapes it into a polite greeting.

"Good afternoon, Mr. Stone," he says, reaching out to shake his hand. Thank you for seeing me. "I must say you're looking incredibly well after your date with death."

Mr. Stone gives him a wry smile and meets his handshake a little more forcefully. "Thank you Detective Inspector. It's amazing what they can do with modern medicine these days. Please take a seat."

Mack nods, incredulously. "I wouldn't know. I doubt you could get what you've had on the National Health though."

Mr. Stone will not be baited. "I'm sure it's universally available. No secret potions have been used." He laughs quietly. "What can I do for you? I have already been interviewed by one of your colleagues and I explained fully what happened."

"Yes you did and I thank you for that, but certain details have come to light in the past couple of days which I'd like clear up, if that's alright?" He's playing his cards close to his chest.

"Of course. Fire away."

"Can you confirm you knew Miss. Richards?" He's starting with the easy questions first.

"Yes, we were friends. She worked at the Estate Agents and was very helpful in the purchase of my home." Mr. Stone leans a little further back into his chair.

That's nothing he didn't already know. "And would you say you became close?"

"Close? Define close."

Mack recognises a smart arse when he meets one and realises Mr. Stone will not be easily pinned down. "By close, I mean were you engaged in sexual relations with Miss. Richards?"

"No I was not," Mr. Stone replies, indignantly. "She wasn't my type." He turns a photo of Elizabeth Stone around on his desk. "That's my type."

Mack recognises her as the small girl in the photograph, all grown up; an ugly duckling transformed into a swan. "Your wife is very beautiful, Mr. Stone, but you are newlyweds as I recall, after a whirlwind romance. It's the time before you met your charming wife I'm concerned with." He waits for an unhelpful response.

"I see. Then, once again, I would have to confess, Miss. Richards was not my type. I'm sure she was a very charming woman but we were only friends and I am still struggling to comprehend why she decided to hold a knife to my ribs and tried to kill us both. She was fixated on me for some reason. I feared for my life when she grabbed at the steering wheel."

Mack doesn't believe a word of it but three photographs do not make a case. "Yes, I can appreciate that. But what possessed her to consider suicide, do you think?"

Mr. Stone begins to turn left and right in his chair as if he hasn't a care in the world. "I was recently married, and all I can assume is that she felt betrayed in some way. Which, of course, was not the case."

Tiring of his farcical performance Mack opts for a more direct approach. "One possible scenario might be that she was blackmailing you, Mr. Stone. Was she?"

"Of course not. What a ridiculous idea," Mr. Stone scoffs. "What could she possible use to blackmail me? I have nothing to hide." He checks his watch.

"I just wondered if perhaps she had known you in the past."

Mr. Stone's brows arch in astonishment. "The past? What are you insinuating, that we were business partners of some sort?"

Mack won't be deterred. "Not necessarily ..."

"Well, what then?"

"I was merely enquiring as to the possibility that you might have known each other in a different capacity or at an earlier stage in your life when you were less ..." He struggles to find the right word; he wants to say *connected* or *rich* but some careful editing transposes it into, "... well known."

Mr. Stone looks around at the grandiosity of his office - the six TV screens, the artwork, the door leading to an en-suite bathroom and dressing room. He turns around and directs his accuser to the view. "I have been *well known* for some time Detective Inspector Bowker. How far back are you prepared to go?" he asks. Undaunted by his insinuation he turns to face him.

Recognising a veiled threat when he hears it, Mack prepares to back off. This is one battle he has neither the manpower nor the brainpower to win. He has been out-manoeuvred by a master. He feels out of his depth but more determined than ever to scratch away at the veneer of this man; to dig down deep with his bare hands if necessary, until he can look himself in the eye and say with confidence what happened in the past and why Elise Richards tried to sacrifice them both for the sake of a secret.

"Is there anything else I can help you with?" Mr. Stone asks, politely.

Mack stands and straightens trousers that have become creased while sitting. "No, nothing else. You've been very helpful, Mr. Stone. Thank you for your time," he says briskly.

"Not at all. I'll have Charlotte show you out." He presses a button under his desk and revolves in his chair. "I hope you've not parked too far away. It looks as though it's going to rain."

Mack doesn't bother answering, and leaves Mr. Stone's office without a backward glance. He makes the long descent to the lobby, steps out onto the pavement and closes his eyes, feeling the refreshing trickle of raindrops on his face. When he opens them the rain has stopped. He reads it as a good omen and crosses the road to where his car is parked, dodging professional looking people in designer suits who are talking on phones - doing deals with the Devil to make their next million. He wants no part of it. All he has is his sixth sense and a self-satisfied smile, and that's enough.

13

H aving stepped out of our business clothes we are relaxing in casual attire. I'm wearing a button-down khaki dress; he's dressed in black jeans and a pale blue T-shirt that accentuates the sapphire streaks in his eyes. Ayden is pouring champagne into two tall flutes. Ambient music is playing through the sound system in our home and we are celebrating the fact we are now officially man and wife, with the documents to prove it.

Bernie has prepared a meal for us. The aroma of onions and rich sauce is filling the lounge with memories of home cooking and we are relaxed in each other's company.

The table is set and the casserole is bubbling on the table. Thankfully the glass has been covered with a tablecloth, so no traces of my fingerprints remain; only the memory of a sexual encounter that has me squirming in my chair.

He sits across from me, poised and justifiably proud of his accomplishments today. He fooled everyone. For a moment even I believed him, but that was wishful thinking: I'm still caught up in this 'adventure.'

I stop eating to speak. "You're very quiet."

"I'm reviewing the day's events."

"Really? You did well, although turning the heating up was naughty of you."

He begins to laugh roguishly. "I was thinking about what your husband would do and that came to mind."

I'm laughing too. "I must have lost three pounds in perspiration. I've had to throw the blouse away and the suit will need dry cleaning – twice!"

"I enjoyed the experience although there were times when I had to suppress emotional responses."

"Such as ...?" I take a sip of wine.

"The way I felt when Jake looked at you."

"Well who's fault was it my blouse had become transparent? If I'd been wearing a bra there would have been nothing for him to look at. And, anyway, what did he mean when he said you were 'up to your old tricks?'"

He's shaking his head. "I don't know."

I think I do.

Silently, I put down the glass. "So how do you explain that feeling?"

"I haven't the faintest idea."

"I do; let's call it jealousy." I look away and return to the beef bourguignon.

"I've not experienced it before. You could be right." He nods, accepting the explanation.

"It's like I've said before; we humans feel everything, good *and* bad. That's what makes us what we are."

"I'm beginning to appreciate that. It would explain why I find myself in a permanent state of arousal." He just throws that out there.

My eyes widen at the thought. "You do?"

He places down his fork. "Yes."

I raise my eyes to his and the darkness of his irises makes me catch my breath. "I see that."

"You seem to have a profound effect upon this body. Some kind of intangible force of will draws me to you, sexually."

"Well, we *are* husband and wife." It's the only answer I can think of at the moment.

He is motionless. "Do you feel the same way about me?"

I take a sip of wine. "Yes. I want my husband so badly I could weep. I miss his soft words and his caress ..." I close my eyes. "The way he kisses me as if it's our last embrace and the feel of him inside me as though we're inseparable." I open my eyes. "So yes, I feel the same way." I pick up my fork and continue eating.

His hand reaches for mine across the table. "Let me make love to you, Beth."

I'm sniggering. "I would say yes, but I don't think you're capable of it. You've lived so long, taking and giving nothing in return, I'm not convinced you even know how to make love." I pat my lips with my napkin. "You rely on your tricks and demand that everything is just so ... with little regard for others. A good lover doesn't do that."

"Then I will learn how to love. You will teach me."

I smile at the absurdity of it. "See, there you go. Telling not asking."

"Have you finished eating?"

I nod my head.

"Give me your hand. I need to diffuse some of this sexual energy before I explode."

"If that's your idea of a pick-up line, it's not very good."

"Darling, I wouldn't know a pick-up line if it landed on my plate."

We walk hand in hand to the lift.

"They rarely land there, anyway."

"Then that's just as well."

Before we enter the lift I pull him back. "You promise there will be no hypnotic music or putting me in a trance?"

"I do."

"Cross your heart and hope to die?"

"Certainly not!"

I'm giggling. "It's only something we say ..."

"In that case I will object on the grounds that I have a vested interest." He kisses my hair. "Come to bed."

When we enter the master bedroom, I'm taken aback. There are crimson rose petals on the bed, candles on every surface and an ice bucket by the bed with an unopened bottle of champagne.

"When did you do this?" I ask curiously.

"Five minutes ago. Do you approve?"

"Yes, it's wonderful." I lift a handful of petals off the bed and hold them to my nose.

He's beaming. "If you consider today's events, this is our wedding night."

What an unsettling thought.

"Yes." I turn to face him, taking his beautiful face in my hands, preparing to do as I said I would; to give the performance of my life, to save the life of another. "I love you, Ayden."

"I love you more, Beth."

I'm momentarily wounded by his reply; although why should I be? He's been accessing Ayden's thoughts all day.

This is just one more to add to the long list of daily adjustments I'm having to make.

His nose brushes against mine as I tilt my face up to him like a sacrificial offering. There's no disguising his arousal; it's apparent in the deepest, darkest blue of his eyes and in the rigid mass pressing into my hip. We are physically attracted to one another, that's undeniable; but there's more. It's a pull, a yearning to touch and be touched.

I'm aching inside for him; I miss him, my body misses him.

We kiss.

He runs his tongue along my bottom lip, coating it in moisture. Sensing my need, he enters my mouth and I allow our tongues to dance and swirl to a sensual rhythm.

I throw back my head and shiver a little as his kisses tickle my throat and tease the skin beneath my ear. I make that noise I know Ayden loves to hear and suppress a whimper, knowing it will go unheard. But ... I dare not allow that thought to linger. I have to find the strength from somewhere to surrender myself and my body or ...

He murmurs into my neck, "Tell me what you need. I can give you anything."

I'm breathless and can't speak.

"Come on, Beth. Be bold, baby ..."

I gasp at those three words. There are no secrets between us now. He knows everything, sees everything, hears everything, feels everything.

He's becoming Ayden.

With that thought, I let go and throw myself at his mercy; I pull his T-shirt over his head so I can feel the warmth of his overheated body against mine. I pull him to me, dizzy with desire, and he spins us around until my back is against the wall. I am pinned with no means of escape but too entangled in a myriad of emotions to care.

When I pull back to catch my breath, I look into those depthless pools and see misty clouds of grey. Detecting a tenderness I haven't seen before from him; my fear dissipates. The nebulous hues are a reminder of the distance in time and space he has crossed to be here with me - to offer me this chance to love and be loved.

He speaks in a whisper,

And in Life's noisiest hour,
There whispers still the ceaseless Love of Thee,
The heart's Self-solace and soliloquy.

You mould my Hopes, you fashion me within;
And to the leading Love-throb in the Heart
Thro' all my Being, thro' my pulse's beat;
You lie in all my many Thoughts, like Light,
Like the fair light of Dawn, or summer Eve
On rippling Stream, or cloud-reflecting Lake.

And looking to the Heaven, that bends above you,
How oft! I bless the Lot that made me love you.

The Presence of Love
Samuel Taylor Coleridge

"I have travelled all over the universe to find you, Beth. Let me love you."

In this moment I realise how our lives have been inexplicably linked for decades; Death has found me wandering like a lost child so many times and now, as a woman, it has come to this one defining moment.

I can think of only one word. "Yes."

With dexterous hands, he leans back and unbuttons my dress; it falls from my arms and flutters to the carpet like falling leaves. I'm standing without shoes; flimsy underwear is all that lies between my modesty and my nakedness.

He lowers my hands from his chest to his hips and then places them on his belt, inviting me to relieve him of his trousers, all the time kissing and nibbling the skin beneath my ear.

I quickly unfasten the belt and release the buttons so the zipper comes down almost of its own accord. With my eyes closed I slide my hand down his jeans, over muscle and through pubic hair until I have him wrapped in one hand. He groans into my neck and the heat of his desire scorches my skin, urging me to tighten my grip and feel the pulse of a rigid cock rippling in my hand. He's dipping and shuddering, making the kind of noises that have me clenching and so aroused I can barely stand.

With steaming breath he whispers, "Show me how to love you, Beth."

With my free hand I move his hand to my left shoulder and ease down my bra strap. He follows through, left and right and leans into me to unclip it before it falls and dangles off my right wrist. I begin to pull out my hand.

"Leave it where it is," he says with a smile and then proceeds to snap the strap and toss it across the room. With it discarded, I am captured in candlelight. This is the first time he has seen my naked breasts. Before, there was only the glow of moonlight. Now there are shadows and the flickering light cast by 20 candles. I feel exposed and lower my head, embarrassed by his stare.

"Look at me!"

I raise my eyes to meet his. "Don't ever be shy about who you are. You are beauty personified. I have lived many lifetimes, travelled through space and time; read a thousand books and recited a hundred poems, but even I cannot find the words to describe you." He rests his palms on my breasts and strokes my nipples with the pad of his thumbs, making my body tremble.

"See how you respond? Your body recognises the touch of these hands and no other. These hands are the key to untold pleasures."

I throw my head back as I feel his erection growing, forcing its way through material, seeking freedom from containment. With both hands I lower his jeans and boxers, allowing it to spring free. When I see it, I gasp. It's bigger than I remembered, standing long and thick without support. I'm aroused further by its magnificence.

"Give me your hand."

I lift up my right hand. Enfolding it with his own, he places it around the skin coated rod of iron and begins to move my fingers and thumb up and down the length of it; rolling my thumb back and forth on the upward motion.

With a throaty voice he urges me to give him my other hand. I do.

He places it between my legs, his hand over mine, his firm fingers sliding between my own until they are wet and soaked.

With our hands moving rhythmically he begins to fuck my mouth with his tongue. He moans into me, stimulating me even more, and I gasp, caught up in a sexual frenzy that has us both teetering on the edge of an orgasmic high.

Like a woman possessed, I throw my head back and give in to the blistering heat of an orgasm that sears through my stomach muscles; it comes to rest in my groin with the force of an earth-shattering explosion.

I call out, "Ay-den" and struggle to remain standing, realising I still have him in my grasp. Without thinking, I fall to my knees and use both hands to pleasure him. When I look up, he's towering above me: an Adonis carved out of gleaming bronze, the perfect male specimen. I watch as the muscles on his chest rise and fall and his taut abdomen quivers under my instruction. His compliance gives me the confidence I need to do what I long to do; to take him in my mouth and rejoice in his gratification.

Even before I begin, he places his hands around his back and I know he's gripping his own wrists. Realising he has tapped into Ayden's thoughts causes me to wince, but only for a second. As I look at his stirring erection I'm reminded that this is my husband's body; I have known no other. With that singular thought I press on licking, tasting, sucking until my eyes begin to water and I can do it no longer. I fall back against the wall breathless and exhausted, marvelling at his stamina.

He lifts me from the floor and sweeps me up in his arms. As he places me down on the bed, I feel strong hands removing my panties. We lie together naked, bathed in candlelight on a bed of rose petals, and it feels perfectly natural. He reaches over and takes my face in his left palm.

"Thank you." His lips graze my forehead.

"For what?"

He traces the outline of my swollen lips with his thumb. "For trusting me."

"You promised not to hurt me," I remind him.

"Did I?"

"Yes."

I didn't imagine it, did I?

He smiles wickedly. "Then I must handle you with care, darling,"

"Please do." I look around at the candles and the shapes they are casting on the walls as they glow and deliver their flickering light. In a single movement he waves his right hand and a breeze extinguishes almost all of the candles. Only the two on either side of the bed remain. A smirk forms and I smile in response but say nothing.

In a move worthy of an escape artist I break free of his grip and scramble under the duvet.

"Are you hiding?" he asks.

I shake my head. "No I'm cold."

He draws back the duvet to join me and the rose petals fly high above the bed, then flutter down like a scattering of red confetti at a fairy-tale wedding.

"Come here. Let me keep you warm."

I snuggle into his chest. "Don't you want to start over? You didn't come."

He kisses my hair. "There's time enough for that ... not unless you want me to."

I raise my head, resting my chin on his chest, nestling in chest hair. "I don't want you to be in a permanent state of arousal." I can't help but giggle.

"I'm beginning to think that the most lovable part about you, darling, apart from your beauty, your intellect and your compassion - is your sense of humour." He kisses my nose. "You are truly adorable, and I will cherish the time we have together as a precious gift."

"You can be very sweet when you're not listening in to my thoughts, clicking your fingers or wafting your hands about." His chest is rumbling beneath my left ear.

"I do not waft. I command. There's a difference."

"I'll take your word for it."

"That would be wise."

I draw circles on his chest. "Tell me, did you turn off the rain today, or was it purely coincidental that the sun came out when it did?"

"There's no such thing as coincidence, Beth. Fate can be a cruel master or a gentle lover. I learned that long ago." He rests his hand on my hair.

"But how can that be when you do what you do? You change things."

"I can play with heating or engage with the elements - even suspend time - but destiny is too strong a force to control, even for me."

"So is that how you know where to be when you need to do your job?"

"Something like that; but time isn't a fixed thing for me. I can be gone a second and traverse a continent or witness a war and be back here in time to wake you. It's all relative."

Taken with his honesty, I crawl across him until we are eye to eye. "So what are you like when you're not Ayden?"

"Does it matter?"

"It matters to me."

"Very well." He thinks through his answer. "I am light."

"You're what?"

"I am a life force. I have no form as such."

"Shit!"

"Beth! Please."

"I'm sorry but that's not the answer I was expecting." I roll onto my back and gaze at the shapes on the ceiling. "So the only way you can interact is to take a human form like you have now?"

"Yes." He rolls onto his side to explain. "This doesn't change anything. I feel everything Ayden feels and love with the same intensity ..."

"But you're not Ayden," I announce a little too quickly.

"This is true."

"Don't say that. I know you're trying really hard to become him, for me, but it will take time for me to comprehend what's happened."

"Should I turn back time to the moment when you described the rose petals as red confetti at a fairy-tale wedding?"

I'm shaking my head. "No, I want to remember. You said you wouldn't lie to me. What would be the point of saying that if you just pretend we never had this conversation?"

"Because it would take us back to a time when you were more receptive to my advances, and less afraid of me."

"I'm not afraid of you."

Not much anyway ...

He hits me with a piercing stare. "*Not much* is too much, Beth."

His left cheek falls like a lead weight into the palm of my hand. "You called this an adventure and you weren't wrong. In a dictionary somewhere there will be a definition that reads: 'an unusual or exciting experience that involves taking risks.' That just about covers it. I'm risking everything for love. And, as long as we can both live with that' I think it will be an epic adventure, don't you?"

"I do indeed." He places a soft kiss on my lips. "Get some rest, we have a long day ahead of us tomorrow."

"We do?"

"Yes. We begin our honeymoon."

I turn over on my side and he wraps his body around mine until we are spooning. I feel the partial hardness of a fading erection against me. For some reason the thought of him enduring another night without release has me smiling into my pillow. As hard as I try to scatter my thoughts, they betray me, once again.

He whispers into my hair. "Try not to concern yourself with my gratification. I'm happy to defer until the morning."

I send him a message.

Stop listening in.

Stop sending out. Go to sleep.

"Goodnight, Ayden."

"Goodnight, Beth."

Pulled in the direction of the lounge by an intangible force, I don my bathrobe and tiptoe out of the bedroom. As I leave the room, I hear his even breathing and glance backwards, still in a state of disbelief.

My laptop boots up and I type in the password. Quickly I retrieve the digital scrapbook and consider my entry. Wanting to keep this record strictly private, I use the earphones from my iPod and shuffle through my selection of songs. I listen to Biffy Clyro singing *Many of Horror*. Unconsciously, I've managed to capture my thoughts in a song but dare not commit them to print. Instead I type:

NOVEMBER #2

"One half of me is yours, the other half yours,
Mine own, I would say; but if mine,
then yours. And so all yours."
William Shakespeare: The Merchant of Venice.

What a day! We made our first public appearance as man and wife only to find we were never actually married. Ha! All that planning of yours and our day was scuppered by MI5. Thankfully Stephen saved the day. (Consider the irony in that) We've signed the documents and we are married: it's official. It's only been 14 hours but already I feel different. Here's the photograph; I had Charlotte take it. You look as handsome as ever and me ... well, I was still trying to cool down after experiencing what could only be described as a heat wave in your Boardroom. Don't ask ...

Coming home today I realised just how far we've some in such a short time; but we have a lifetime of memories to share, Ayden, and this is only the beginning. Tonight, when we made love, it felt like we had truly found each other; two worlds colliding and not a single tear shed.

I love you, with all that I am and all I will ever be. I belong to you ... I love will you from this moment on, as I always have, for as long as we both shall live.

Yours, Beth X

I insert the photo from my SD card and paste a newspaper article about our arrival at the Stone Building. There we are hand in hand; Ayden a good six inches above me, oozing confidence and potent masculinity. He looks every bit the media mogul: not a trace of trickery, not a hair out of place.

I save the document and shut down; lock away my heart and put my camera back into my bag ready for the next photo opportunity. A faraway place awaits our arrival and I prepare myself mentally for the next chapter of this incredible 'adventure.'

***

Even though Mack has been working for the Metropolitan Police Service for over 20 years, he still relies on gut instinct. That's why he's hopeful that this latest clue in the Stone case will prove fruitful. He's at 11 Milton Avenue, the secondary residence of Mr. Rizler. Taking in the broken down cars and the smashed bus shelter, he makes his own prediction as to Mr. Rizler's lifestyle. Only today has he become aware of this address. CID has focused their attention on the Elm Gardens address after Mr. Stone's chauffeur recognised him as a resident, but further investigation has led him here.

Mr. Rizler's ground floor apartment looks as if it's been vandalised and used as a drug den. There's graffiti on the walls, and it smells of urine and sweat. Several hypodermic needles have been discarded and scattered about like deadly weapons on the carpet. Mack takes tentative steps towards the back of the apartment, noticing the smallest of details on the way; the brightly coloured squares of carpet around the edge of the room, the clean rectangle of wallpaper, the out-of-date computer smashed into pieces and the plastic bag half full of photographs. He squats and drags the torn pieces of black and white images out, noting how they have become yellowed and misty over time. He detects small pinpricks and surmises they must have once been part of a collage.

It takes him five minutes to sort them and one minute to recognise the girl in the picture. "Well, if it isn't Miss Parker." He shakes his head and gives himself an imaginary pat on the back.

Once again, he punches a number into his phone. "Sam, it's Mack again. I'm here at Rizler's place. It's a shit hole but there's a heap of stuff here that needs bagging and tagging. Get the team over here. Tell them to collect *all* the photographs." He pauses to listen. "I know the bastards dead but just humour me. This place has been trashed already and I don't want them coming back lighting a fire. There's important stuff here."

He turns off his phone and heads into the bedroom, kicking torn bedding, clothes and shoes aside. There's little for him to see, except a small black bag that most certainly didn't belong to the resident. He takes out a plastic bag from his pocket and drops it inside. His instincts tell him to gather evidence of his own before the powers that be decide to bury it, as they have every other single piece of information relating to this case.

He leaves with a sombre heart. All this death and deception is getting to him. He needs to get his head around it before it gets away from him; if not him, who else would pursue the truth?

For the rest of the day he digs. He starts with Dan Rizler, discovering all there is to know about him. He checks his bank balance and discovers he has over £10,000 in a savings account, with no next of kin to benefit from it. But the one thing he finds that makes him call out "Yes!" is his employment record. He has worked at Cambridge University for over ten years. A single thought occurs to him. 'What if he knew Miss Parker when she was there?' It's enough to have him playing the drums on his desk.

14

T here have been days when I have been awakened by sunlight, birdsong and a kiss, but this is a first for me. Ayden has his hand between my legs and his mouth at my breast. He is wrapping his tongue around a hardening nipple and I am responding to the push and pull of fingers and lips.

Instinctively, I arch my back and roll my body into his hand. His fingers slide through moist skin and enter me with minimal thrusting. All I can do is writhe and moan into the darkness.

Partially awake, I say, "Ayden," but he doesn't respond. It's apparent he's enjoying this as much as I am. I fist his hair and tug him from my swollen breasts. Gentle music is playing: it's Ed Sheeran singing *Kiss Me*, and I do. His mouth locks onto mine in a passionate kiss, deep and hard. When he raises himself from me I am gasping for breath and so aroused I would beg to be taken.

In a kind of judo roll he lifts me from the mattress and places me on top of him. My legs are spread on either side of his hips; I am wide open and the wetness between my legs is trickling from my body. I lean in to kiss him but he will not allow me; instead he holds onto my forearms and pushes me backwards onto his throbbing cock.

"Slide me inside your body, Beth. Watch me as I come inside you."

His words have me reaching backwards, one hand on his thigh and the other for the hard rod twitching beneath me. When I take hold, my breath catches. My fingers and thumb can scarcely grasp it, but I'm frantic with desire and I want to feel it inside me.

With little difficulty he lifts me and, with eyes locked, lowers me slowly onto him. Feeling the hard tip I brace myself and fan my hands across his pectoral muscles as I open my body to accommodate him. The tightness is exquisite; the feeling of overwhelming fullness unknown to me.

"Oh my God!" I call out feverishly, my eyes shut tight, my insides flexing to find room for this delicious invasion.

"Open your eyes."

I can't. I'm concentrating hard and holding myself off him, fearful my body will not be able to endure total penetration.

"Look at me!"

Startled by his command, I do. But my breathing is uneven and I'm panic-stricken, edging away.

"You can do this, Beth. This body belongs to you, remember? Relax."

With his gentle coaxing I calm, allow my breathing to ease and my heart rate to slow, slightly.

He softens his words with a smile. "That's it." His hands take hold of my hips tightly, then release. In a lifting motion he raises me up and down, slowly, painlessly, until the feeling of tightness fades and my body begins to mould around him.

His top lip twitches and he licks it, coating it in glossy wetness. A kind of snarling sound leaves his throat as I move of my own volition. I cannot tear my eyes away.

"You have all of me, Beth," he utters, tiny moans reverberating into the air, echoing my own. "Take this body and claim it."

With that thought in mind I begin to pick up the pace, to arch my back, to tighten my internal muscles and to begin the ride of my life. He removes his hands from my hips and allows me to canter towards my orgasm, swerving my body until the ridges of his cock are perfectly placed to stroke that illusive spot inside me.

Wide-eyed and almost delirious with unbridled passion I open my mouth to suck in more air. When I look at Ayden he is shimmering with perspiration, his eyes are an iridescent grey like the Milky Way.

With garbled words he cries, "I'm all yours, baby," and pulls me down hard onto him making me gasp and cry out. His orgasm tears through him, and the spark he has ignited in me catches fire as he detonates. I burn and burn with the intensity of an atomic wind that sweeps through me on its path of destruction; like that unstoppable wind, he roars as my body buckles around him and then it disperses, to become nothing more than a whisper.

Totally sapped of energy, I peel myself off him and roll over onto the cool side of the bed, still stunned by the intensity of our lovemaking.

Once the air settles, he turns to me and pushes back a strand of hair from my brow, "That was earth-shattering!"

"It was." I can't lie.

"Did I hurt you?" He inspects my body for any signs of bruising.

Feeling a little embarrassed, I reward his consideration with a smile. "No."

He reaches to the bottom of the bed and pulls up the duvet. "Then I'm learning." He kisses my forehead as you might a small child. "You're a good teacher. I will try to be the perfect pupil for you." Roughly, he tucks the cover around my neck. "Now go back to sleep for an hour before we have to prepare for our outing."

"Do you mean honeymoon?" I smile, lifting my chin out from under the cover.

"No. I mean outing. We will be attending Elise's funeral at 10 a.m." He kisses my nose and rolls away.

Funeral? What the hell ...

Feeling a little stiff and disoriented, I blink myself into wakefulness. It seems as if I have only slept for half an hour but, by the intensity of the sunlight, it must be 8 a.m. Surprisingly, Ayden is still next to me, sleeping. So as not to disturb him, I slither out of bed and tiptoe around to the bathroom but I'm pinned to the spot by the strangest sound. I turn to face him and watch his eyes flicker and his face contort into a grimace. He makes the noise again, only this time I hear it more clearly; it's like the muffled breath of a man having a nightmare.

I fall to my knees by the bed and do no more than stroke is hair. "Hush, hush." I whisper in his ear. With that he settles and the tension fades from his handsome features like watercolours on canvas. Quickly, I wipe my tears and hurry into the bathroom. I can't think clearly and must not allow myself to jump to conclusions. More important, I can't send out my thoughts.

By way of a distraction I dive into the power shower, not stopping to test the temperature. Thankfully it's pre-set and steaming hot, hot enough to wash away any trace of passionate lovemaking. The knock on the door makes me jump, and for some reason, I hurriedly reach for my bathrobe before the door opens.

Ayden enters naked; he's scratching his head and yawning. "You should have woken me," he says mid-yawn.

"I thought you were doing your other job," I reply, sweetly. "Anyway, why are you tired when you say you never sleep?"

"I don't, but your husband's body is feeling the after effects of strenuous lovemaking."

"Are you sure that's not you?" I waft past him. "Ayden didn't used to get worn out so easily."

He spins around as I pass. "Are you attempting to bait me, darling?" he asks, taking hold of my wrist.

"Of course not." I kiss his cheek." Merely stating a fact."

In a flash, he takes hold of both my wrists and wraps them behind me. I feel my back pressing against the doorframe.

The provocative scent of masculine essence and sex on his naked body causes me to shiver and, sensing my responsiveness, he draws his tongue along the soft skin beneath my chin. "Your perfume and your playfulness is a powerful aphrodisiac, Beth." He nuzzles into my wet hair and I feel the hardness of his erection though the soft bathrobe.

"I have neither the time nor the stamina to make love."

He whispers into my ear. "Who said anything about making love?" He takes hold of my earlobe between his teeth and gives it a gentle tug. "Right now I would like nothing more than to fuck you. Maybe then you would be less inclined to question my stamina."

His words cause me to widen my eyes and swallow deeply. "I don't question it," I reply, softly. "I fear it."

Instantly he releases my wrists and steps back. "Why?"

I lower my eyes. "You know why."

He's shaking his head. "No. I don't. Explain it to me. Wasn't I gentle with you, patient, attentive? Didn't I satisfy you sexually?"

"Yes. You were all those things," I confess, raising my eyes to his. "But you were holding back. There may come a time when you're unable to, and that's what scares me, especially when you talk of fucking me."

He's mystified by my logic and shaking his head. "I was using your husband's words. The thought of actually fucking you is abhorrent to me."

He moves away and turns on the shower. "How can I become your husband if you don't trust me?" he asks, checking his profile in the mirror.

"You can only become my husband by becoming more human and that's not something you can achieve overnight."

"Clearly that's the case."

I walk over to him and wrap my arms around his perfect body as I have done so many times before. "Don't be cross with me. Last night you were the perfect lover." I kiss the skin between his shoulder blades with soft lips. "And today you'll be the perfect husband." I release him. "Remember to wear a black tie with a black suit, it's customary at funerals."

Just as I reach the door he calls me back. "Beth ..."

I turn to face him.

"You're an exceptional teacher and I'm a fast learner. I'm enjoying every lesson."

He smiles at me in such a touching way I feel my heart breaking. I offer a grateful smile in return and leave. "Better not be late then or I may have to come up with a suitable punishment." I hear him laughing and it's enough to tip me over. I snatch at my clothes and toss a black dress onto the bed; I rifle through drawers for underwear, and throw a bra and panties carelessly on top of it, slam drawers shut, catching sight of myself in the mirror. Roughly, I wipe away my tears with my sleeve and step out of my bathrobe. I remind myself, "I am Mrs. Elizabeth Stone. I can do this."

For some reason we fall into an uncomfortable silence on the drive to the crematorium. I know this is something we have to do; I was the one who insisted upon it. But that was before I was confronted by the truth and I wanted closure for Ayden. It all seems a little irrelevant now. Thankfully, it's something that can be documented and discussed at a later date. Not only that, we can literally put her memory to rest once and for all.

We arrive at Chilterns Crematorium in Amersham after a thirty-minute journey. As we approach the gates, reporters begin ducking and diving around the car. Lester beeps his horn and ploughs through regardless.

A couple of cars are already parked; only one I recognise: A2MED1A. It's Jake's car. On seeing us arrive he comes over, opening the rear door for Ayden and I to climb out.

"You made it," he observes, nodding in my direction.

"Had no choice, Beth insisted," Ayden states, taking my left elbow. "Shall we go inside? Who's here?"

He walks at Ayden's side. "Her family, a couple of friends, work colleagues and that fucking cop. He's about as welcome as the clap around here."

"What's he expecting to do, commune with the dead?"

Jake sniggers. "He's just sniffing around."

We walk slowly into Hampden Chapel with five seats on each side and only the first three rows occupied; so few people for such a dynamic woman. Jake leads us to a seat on the left, I follow and Ayden sits nearest the aisle. I rest my hand over his on my lap, hoping to reassure us both that we can get through this together. It's such a sombre affair, as these things so often are.

Still unable to come to terms with my own loss, I reach in my bag for a tissue. I wipe my nose and listen to the words of farewell voiced so movingly by the minister.

"Are you okay?" Jake asks, giving my arm a squeeze.

"Yes." I force a flat smile in response.

"She brought this on herself you know. Ayd did good by her."

His reassuring words are well intended. "I know. I'm just thinking of what she went through as a child. No one deserves that."

He nods in agreement. "You're right."

I nudge Ayden to my right. "What do you want to do with these?" I open my bag and lift out the black pouch. He takes it off me and tips out the three marbles into his hand. They look so small and insignificant in his large palm.

"Nothing. Put them away."

"But ..."

"Put them away!" he whispers through gritted teeth.

I pull the string top together tightly and drop the pouch into my bag, knowing this will not be the last we hear of Elise Richards. Her legacy will live on long after her ashes have been scattered.

Solemn organ music begins and the coffin shakes slightly as Elise's body nears the flames; only her spirit lives on to pass over into that world beyond.

I look up to him and whisper, "Have you taken her soul?"

He nods. "Some time ago."

I'm thankful for that. We stand, bow our heads and turn to leave. From nowhere a distraught woman of around sixty launches herself at Ayden, her eyes wild.

"You bastard! You caused this." With an outstretched arm she slaps him across the face. The crack of her hand on his cheek echoes around the small chapel. "I hope you rot in hell for what you've done." With that she loses her balance; other family members take hold of her arms and lead her away.

Like the rest of the congregation, I'm stunned into silence. Ayden is rocked by her outburst and seems frozen to the spot as if carved out of ice.

Jake pushes me forward. "Take his arm. Let's get out of here! We shouldn't have come. He's been ambushed." He squeezes past me and storms off ahead. I see him signalling to Lester from the door to bring the car round to the entrance.

As I stand anxiously, waiting to flee the scene, out of the corner of my eye I spot D.I. Bowker approaching us.

He stretches out his hand to shake Ayden's. "Mr. Stone, Mrs. Stone. Good morning. Here for Miss. Richards's cremation I see."

Forgetting that Ayden hears his every thought, I speak first. "Yes. It was the least we could do."

"That's a very magnanimous gesture, Mrs. Stone."

He knows about Cambridge.

Shit!

Ayden confronts him. "What happened was shocking. She had her issues, but that said, her passing is tragic in the extreme."

Our Inspector isn't buying it. "Yes it is, Mr. Stone, particularly as you and she were so close." He sneers and turns away.

"As I have indicated previously, Detective Inspector, we were not *close*," Ayden says by way of a rebuttal "We had a friendship which she misinterpreted as something more meaningful."

Lester remains seated to make a quick getaway while Ayden opens the door for me. "As we are all aware, I was not responsible for Miss. Richards's death. She got into my vehicle with the sole purpose of ending both our lives. You have her note and her fingerprints all over the steering wheel as I recall."

"Yes. We do."

"In that case is there anything else I can help you with?"

He strokes his chin, making Ayden wait even though he knows precisely what he's thinking. "There is one thing."

Ayden sighs impatiently. "Yes?"

"Are you aware of Miss. Richards's association with Mr. Rizler?"

I lean back into my seat.

Shit!

Ayden shakes his head and sneers. "How could I be? We did not operate in the same social circles and, to my knowledge, Mr. Rizler had no interest in Media at a corporate level."

Even I flinch at his reply; it reeks of self-serving arrogance but it's a sure fire conversation stopper.

The Inspector slips his right hand into his pocket, preparing to leave. "I think we are both aware that his interests revolved around your wife, Mr. Stone, and had done so for some time."

"Of that we are in agreement. Anything else?"

"Not at the moment, thank you." The Inspector takes a step back, giving Ayden the space he needs to duck into the car but, before we can pull away, he taps on the glass, flips out a notepad and reads from it.

"Mrs. Stone, can you confirm that you were at Cambridge University between the years 2005 and 2008?"

Say yes, he knows.

"Yes. I can." I sweeten my reply with a smile. "I secured a First Class Degree in English Language and Literature there."

He smiles politely. "Well done. Thank you for your time. Do enjoy the rest of your day."

Immediately Ayden clicks the button to raise the glass and meets Lester's eye in the rear view mirror. Smoothly, we edge forward, leaving the mourners behind.

"That man continues to make a nuisance of himself," he says incensed by the Inspector's audacity. "Why must he persist in digging up the past?"

"Because he thinks there's something worth unearthing," I explain turning to count headstones upon which faceless names are inscribed. "He's trying to make a connection between me and Dan Rizler."

"Well he will have to keep looking. I won't have him dragging your name through the mud because some sociopathic misfit has been obsessing over you for the past seven years."

I wrap my right hand tightly around his arm. "But what about Elise? What if he traces you both back to Bright Hill?" I let out a weighty sigh as we approach the gates.

Ayden answers abruptly, "Then I'll deal with it." He calls out to Lester. "Stop at the gates."

I face him, horror stricken. "What are you doing?"

"You'll see. Trust me." He repositions his tie.

"I do, but don't you think it's best to get away from here as quickly as we can?"

"No. Already the press are wondering why we're here. If I don't give them something to print, they'll make it up. I can diffuse the situation with a simple statement."

My thumbnail finds its way to my mouth. "I'll stay in the car."

"You can't. We have to present a united front." He takes my hand and holds it to his lips for a second. "You see, darling, in warfare there are four approaches." He sticks out the fingers of his right hand and proceeds to count.

"One, to evade, which I cannot; two, to feign weakness, which I'm not prepared to do; three, to out-manoeuver, which I dare not do for obvious reasons; and four, to launch an attack when least expected. Hence the pre-emptive strike."

"Bloody hell, you have been thinking this through." I shake my head in disbelief. "Is this really necessary? Can't we just go home, finish packing and catch a flight to Hong Kong and begin our honeymoon?"

He shakes his head ruefully. "Only if you want your husband's integrity and your honour to be in disarray when we return. Our Detective Inspector Bowker is a like a dog with a bone. No matter how one might try to relieve him of it, he would rather bite your hand than let it go. Of that I have no doubt."

The car slows and the expectant reporters gather like vultures ready to tear us limb from limb. I take an energising breath. "Alright, what should I do?"

"Nothing. Stand at my side and be the beautiful woman you are. You need do no more than that to disarm them."

I smile confidently. "I can do that."

He kisses my cheek. "Ready?" I nod. "Good. Let me put us in the spotlight."

I swing my head to the left and see the clouds parting; a beam of light shines down, making me giggle. "That trick will never grow old."

"It's a classic. Take my hand." Ayden steps from the car and helps me do the same.

I feel the heat of the sun's rays on my face and I raise my chin to receive its blessing.

"Ladies and gentlemen, before we head off on our honeymoon I would like to make a brief statement." Cameras are rolling. "Elizabeth and I are here today to pay our respects to Elise Richards. As you will recall, she became very unstable a week or so ago and tried to take her own life and mine. Sadly, I could not keep control of the vehicle and we were both involved in a crash that proved to be fatal for Miss. Richards.

For the record, I was not romantically involved with Miss. Richards, but I think that due to emotional instability she found that hard to accept."

He pauses to take a breath. "We met just over a year ago when she assisted in the purchasing and remodelling of my home, having worked at the Estate Agency handling the listing. We became friends. Unfortunately, my relationship with Elizabeth seemed to put a strain on that friendship and she became highly unstable, to the point I became concerned about her mental health. Not wanting to prolong her suffering I terminated our friendship; and it is with much regret that I can look back and see how that added fuel to an already inflamed and unstable temperament. For some reason, Miss.

Richards's family seem to think I'm responsible in some way for her untimely death, but this is not the case. I became embroiled in her fantasy through no fault of my own and was drawn into a suicide pact over which I had little control.

Elizabeth and I would like nothing more than to start our honeymoon and to leave all this behind us. Our thoughts are with her family and friends at this time of sorrow and loss. Thank you for your patience."

With that he leads me back to the car and we are on our way in less than a minute. It's another three or four minutes before I speak. "You were very good."

"Thank you. Now they have something to report, it may stop them looking for more.

Feeling as if a great weight has been lifted from our shoulders I relax and lean onto his arm. Now I have only one question to ask before we arrive back home. "Why did that woman slap you?"

"She wrongly believed I was responsible for Elise's death. But I suppose a mother – or stepmother – will clutch at straws at moments like this." He turns to look at the clouds as they merge, filling the sun-drenched cavity he had opened up. "She wasn't privy to the facts."

"What was she thinking?"

"That I had abandoned Elise, cast her aside for you, which was not the case." He places a soft kiss on my head. "Your husband was not romantically involved with her; it was more of a fait accompli. She had her agenda and he was obligated to go along with it."

"That's what I thought. Did he love her?" I ask lifting my head to read his expression.

He pauses. "You ask me that?"

I nod, silent and pensive.

"He felt a great affection for her but not with the over-powering sexual intensity he feels for you; not that way. It was more ... familial than sexual."

I fall silent again.

"Does that put your mind at rest?" he asks softly.

"Yes." I fiddle with my rings and we sit in silence for the remainder for the journey.

15

I'm grateful for Bernie's help with the packing. Unbeknown to me she used to pack Ayden's case regularly and has made a point of ensuring his clothes are perfectly matched, as selected for him by his designer. If I'm honest, he could wear a boiler suit and make it look good. Unfortunately, I'm less blessed in that department and must rely on flattering clothes and accessories to complement my look.

Thanks to Celine's keen eye for detail and colour, my task is not so difficult. I leave Bernie to assemble handbags, shoes and everything seems to fall into place.

Ayden is missing, unwilling to participate in such menial tasks. He has a planet to plunder and no amount of pestering on my part will extricate him from his other job.

With the packing done, I make my way to the office down the hall. He's sitting in the plush leather chair with his back to me, wearing no more than a white shirt and suit pants. Pictures from our Roman holiday are appearing one after the other on the digital picture frame and I'm smiling more widely with each recollection.

"We had a lot of fun in Rome," I remark, positioning myself behind him. "Do you have a recollection of Miss Magnani?" I place my right hand on his shoulder close enough to allow the scent of his hair to waft over me. "She was your biggest fan, for a day." I snigger at the thought.

Concerned at not receiving a reply, I swivel the chair around. "Are you accessing that memory?"

Ayden cannot reply because he is 'sleeping.' I should have known by his regular breaths and the way his chest gently rises and falls. Taking a moment, I settle myself across his knee and wrap my arms around his neck. My nose fits perfectly under his chin.

As before, he makes a moaning sound and his eyes are flickering; he's being troubled by images that have him wincing as if in pain. I wrap my palm around his left cheek and nuzzle into his neck. "Hush, baby, I'm here." As before, he settles and I am left wondering what the hell's happening. Stifling tears, I thread my fingers through his hair and pull him in tight until my eyes close and I feel myself dozing.

Strong arms enfold me and I awake to the sensation of a heaving chest. I am not alone. I release my grip and sit upright. Ayden's hand is at my back keeping me balanced.

"I fell asleep," I confess, still feeling a little groggy. "You weren't here."

He shakes his head. "No, I was otherwise occupied."

I catch him glancing at the digital picture frame. "Those were taken in Rome."

"Mmm. I have a recollection of that." His mouth twitches at the memory.

"Why are you smirking?" I ask, curiously.

"I can recall architecture, food and much happiness, but by far the strongest image is of sexual encounters with you." His eyes find mine.

My eyes widen at the thought and I feel my cheeks beginning to glow. Out of embarrassment I giggle and look away.

A sexy smile forms, one I know so well. The skin around his eyes wrinkles, folds into tiny creases and stays that way until such time as the smile straightens into a pout. "My darling wife, I do believe you're blushing."

"Can you blame me?"

"Not at all, I'm close to blushing myself and I wasn't even there."

His declaration makes me laugh. "Then you shouldn't be such a voyeur."

He grins at my description. "How else will I be able to engage ..."

"Engage?" I interject. "Is that what you call it? Engaging in someone else's sexual liaisons?" I'm shaking my head and tutting like a school marm. "And by engage do you mean 'see' or 'experience'?"

He takes hold of my hand and places it on the bulging mass, straining against his zip. "You tell me."

I grasp his erection through the suit material, feeling ridges and sinews protruding through underwear and seams. Fearlessly I look into his eyes. "What are you thinking about? What's made you so hard?"

"Harder," he corrects. "I'm in a permanent state of arousal, remember? It takes an enormous amount of willpower on my part to control it." He folds his left hand around my face. "Your husband's virility is a force to be reckoned with. I have never experienced anything quite like this before."

"Perhaps you should take a cold shower?"

He raises a hopeful brow. "Perhaps I should spread you out on this desk? I can tell you're aroused. "

"This is true," I reply for my own amusement, feeling seriously tempted. "Why bother with the desk?"

"Why indeed when we have a comfortable bed a few yards down the hall." He raises an optimistic brow.

I play with a wayward curl on his forehead. "But we have a plane to catch..."

"Not for another three hours," he reminds me. "What do you have in mind?"

"I hadn't thought that far ahead," I lie.

As if to set the mood, the sun sets behind the winter clouds as they rush to collide and conspire. Subtle lamplight casts muted colours across the desk, softening the surface with a kaleidoscopic quilt, inviting me to lie upon it. At one and the same time I am at ease and empowered; passionate thoughts abound as a gentle glow rests upon Ayden's face. I am bewitched by his ethereal beauty. I have been so caught up in his sorcery I have become indifferent; only now am I in awe of his staggering masculinity. How could I ever consider letting him go?

"You've played your part to perfection so far." I swaddle his face in my palms. "How can I reward you?"

His mouth twitches a little on the right. "I seek only one gift."

Feeling bashful, I tilt my head and for some reason my thumb finds its way into my mouth. "Would that gift be - sex?"

I feel his fingers above my knee, slipping beneath the hem of my dress.

He shakes his head.

"What then?" I ask quizzically.

His face breaks into a tender smile "Your love, Beth."

The smoky hues appearing in his eyes are causing my breath to quicken. He takes my hand from my mouth and fixes it against his cheek, almost covering it with his own. Long, dark lashes sweep away any doubt I might have had that I wouldn't do *anything* to save this husband of mine.

I brush my lips against his, savouring the soft freshness of rejuvenated skin. My mouth invites him to taste me, to enter me, body and soul.

I unbutton his shirt to reveal flexing muscles and downy hair into which I weave my fingers. A moan of pleasure ripples against my lips and I press on with my audacious exploration, becoming more aware of his racing pulse.

This is the day I will cease to mourn. On this day, of all days, I will make it my sole purpose in life to celebrate love as a woman might, having been reprieved from execution for a crime she did not commit. I have been touched by Death several times, but only now do I understand the simplicity of my task; to love like today is the first day of forever ...

Ayden raises his eyelids having read my thoughts; the glistening iridescence of this universal truth radiates from his eyes like starlight, causing my palpating heart to soar. I smile softly, without fear or foreboding.

I can do this.

"I want to make love to you, Ayden," I whisper.

In a single movement he raises me off the chair and I'm swept along the corridor to our bedroom. Behind me lights are turned off: the lamp, even the spotlights overhead. It's as if I am leaving the darkness behind and heading into the light with him.

Once inside he places me down onto the bed. He closes the door and is confronted by the suit of armour; make-believe metal and chainmail. He cocks his head to the right and fingers the material.

I put his mind at rest. "It was Ayden's for Charlie's fancy dress party; he was busy with work and never got to wear it. Maybe you could wear it?"

Laughing, he turns to face me. "Do you mean now?"

I shake my head and mirror his laugher. "No, of course not, we can have a party after our honeymoon and you can wear it then."

"Mmm ... I could. And you could be my fair maiden."

"You could be my knight in shining armour?"

He gives me a wry smile. "I thought I already was ..."

All I can do is roll my eyes. "We'll see." I pat the duvet. "Come and lie next to me, Sir Lancelot."

He kicks off his shoes and slides across the bed. "Of course my darling, Guinevere."

"Bat Girl," I snigger."

"Who?"

"I was Bat Girl. We had fun that night with costumes. Check it out. I'll put some music on."

He falls onto his back, filtering through memories until he comes across the very scene. Music begins but he is undisturbed by it; he's transported back to that night before we left for Vegas, before he was taken away from me and I was almost taken from him. The music fills the empty space.

I place my hand on his chest where his shirt is now undone. I feel the thumping of a heart beneath flesh and watch his lungs inflate and deflate, expelling hot breath. He clenches the duvet almost tearing it into shreds.

He sees us.

He feels us.

He turns to me sharply. "Fuck, Beth!"

His response shocks me. "What? What did you see?"

"Everything. I felt everything." He pulls my mouth onto his fiercely.

I barely have time to catch my breath before I am flattened by his muscular torso. I buckle and fold into the mattress. Forceful hands, hard flesh and a devilish tongue lay siege to my body, causing my senses to stampede towards surrender.

I break free and come up for air, gasping, calling his name. "Ay-den!" It leaves my mouth in a garbled cry. But so frenzied is his assault upon my senses he cannot hear me. With his mouth on mine and unable to form words, I send out my thought as a plea for salvation.

Stop! You promised not to hurt me. Stop!

In a crescendo of movement and an agonising cry, he's catapulted into the closed door with an almighty thud. The suit of armour comes crashing down onto him.

Still gasping I sit up, resting my weight on my elbows while my heart rate slows, infinitesimally. Through lips still tingling from his onslaught I ask, "What the hell just happened?"

Like a man intoxicated by desire he shakes his head free of the chainmail and lascivious thoughts. When the sound of tumbling metal comes to an end he attempts to rediscover some semblance of normality.

Seeing him like this - this man who can sweep clouds from the sky and silence a room with the click of his fingers - sitting in a mound of silver vestments, breathless, is not a sight to be easily forgotten. I try to hold off on a giggle but I can't, even though I may suffer his wrath because of it. He sees the laughter in my eyes and, unwilling to endure the indignation of a less than stellar performance, offers a sigh.

"Your husband and his sex drive have me so turned-on I can't control myself." He tries to extricate himself from a mismatched tangle of shoulder pads and sleeves. "His memories of coitus with you are over-powering. I can't help myself ..."

I slither down from the bed and crawl over to him. "Oh we did enjoy our coitus," I state impishly.

He lifts my chin. "Did I hurt you?"

"No, but you scared me. I thought you were out of control. I had to shout my thoughts ..."

"Yes you did, and I apologise. I'll have to filter out some of these libidinous feelings I have for you or I will become ... overwhelmed."

I pull back an inch or two. "By 'overwhelmed' you mean out of control?"

"Perhaps."

"But I thought you were all powerful. You can control everything, except fate."

He shakes his head, struggling to rationalise his responses. "So did I. This is all very disconcerting."

"You know why that is, don't you?"

He tips his head pensively.

"It's because it's human nature and, because you're not human, you don't know how to harness it! This is what veneration feels like; what real love feels like." I take his face in my hands. "Don't stop feeling it, just enjoy it. It's not meant to be agonising."

He adjusts my position so I am straddling him. "How wise you are, Beth."

He's got it all wrong. "It's not about wisdom. It's about trust. I know what my husband feels for me. I feel the same way. We're two halves of one soul destined to be together in every sense of the word. It's like a cosmic union and not even death will part us." I take a breath, stunned by the clarity of my declaration. "Maybe we should prepare for our flight?" I attempt to twist my body away.

"Oh no, not so fast, missy. I've experienced enough to know your husband would not let this moment pass." He begins to unbutton my dress with steady hands. "If you think I'm going to let you evade me, you are very much mistaken."

The timbre of his voice and use of the word *missy* is enough to spark a visceral reaction in me. "What do you want to do?"

He peels my dress from my arms until I am sitting across him, wearing only black lingerie and an anticipative expression.

"To give you your wish."

"And that was?"

Quickly he removes his shirt and tosses it to one side, leaving it to land over the mound of metal and chainmail like a dusting of snow. "To make love to me."

Oh!

I fashion an untruth. "I'd forgotten."

He knows better. "Really?"

I have no answer to that. "No, but the moment has passed."

"It has?" With that, he rolls me over onto my back and arches his body into mine until I can feel the soft pile of the carpet against my skin and the weight of his body on mine.

"How do you expect me to fly for 13 hours with an erection like this?" He unbuckles his belt and pushes down his trousers. "You want me, don't you?" He licks his lips and waits for my reply.

Instinctively, I look down. What I see makes me draw breath and I avert my gaze, looking left and right, anywhere but there. "I ... do," I mutter.

"Then how would you like to make love to me?"

There's no going back.

He smirks in such a way every muscle below my waistline constricts and releases in a kind of internal spasm.

"I ... I want to take you to a place you haven't been before."

He tips his head like an attentive pupil. "I'm listening."

I reach out my hand for him to pull me up. As he does so, I push him backwards onto the carpet until I am lying on top of him like a human blanket. "Close your eyes."

He does.

I lift my iPod from the deck, scroll down to Shakira and press *Empire*. It starts softly but I know the music will build to a roaring crescendo as he sprints towards his riotous climax.

"Give me your hands." Obediently he holds them together as if praying and I reach behind me, open the drawer of the bedside cabinet, and lift out our set of handcuffs. I raise his arms above his head, sliding them under the lower half of the bed and attach the handcuffs around his left wrist. *Click.* He body stiffens. I ease the other of the handcuffs around the leg of the bed and attach his right hand until he is totally disarmed and at my mercy. *Click.*

Kissing the skin beneath his ear, I whisper, "Now this is what we're going to do. I'm going to make love to you because you are my husband and I adore you. Your body belongs to me now."

His breath catches. "I believe that to be true."

I prepare him for his sensual voyage of discovery by removing his trousers and boxers. In a matter of seconds he is lying naked and highly aroused on the carpet with his eyes closed, waiting, anticipating my touch. With the light of the bedside lamps he is clearly visible; every inch of him rippling and moving like taut, flesh-coloured fabric stretched over muscle. His eyes are closed but mine are free to roam, returning again and again to his impressive cock as it points upwards, dipping and rising as his abdomen undulates.

Quickly, I remove my bra and panties and stretch myself across his muscular torso claiming him in his entirety. "My husband could make me come with words; that was just one of his talents. Today you're going to experience exactly that."

His face is alight with expectation. "Let the lesson begin."

With my fingers outstretched, I descend his body, stopping along the way to kiss and nuzzle chest hair; to dip my nose into the curves of his abs and his hips. I begin ... "Your heart rate is increasing; you're having to take deep breaths to control your arousal and you want to be inside me ..."

He's breathing heavily, clearing his throat to construct a sentence. It leaves his mouth in a stutter. "I, I ... do, very much."

"Tell me how it feels to be desired, like this." I nip at his thigh and sooth the sting with a kiss.

"It feels ... like nothing else."

"Go back and feel what Ayden felt in my apartment. We are making love; he is coaxing me to come. Say the words..."

While he seeks out the moment, I clamber across him, rocking and grinding myself into him. My clitoris catches against hard flesh and I call out, "Ah!" forcing him to open his eyes.

What I see makes me pull back. His pupils are so dark they have bled into his irises like an oil slick. He begins to tug at the bed until the leg creaks and moves a couple of centimetres. The muscles in his forearm are contracting and I'm fearful he'll free himself.

"I want you," he growls with the intensity of a rabid animal. He raises himself on the carpet and arches his back in search of me.

"Ayden," I call out, "Look at me." I have his face in my hands. "Look at me and centre yourself. Absorb the feelings, don't fight them." I don't know what I'm saying but for the sake of self-preservation I have to say something. I can't afford to think of arrangements or adventures. All I must see is Ayden; to allow the desire diffusing through my bloodstream to enter the chambers of my heart and release itself through a display of erotic exultation. And, if that doesn't work, I'll just fuck him until he begs me to stop!

But look at him. I've fanned the flames of passion to such an extent I fear he is at the point of no return.

The music increases in volume and tempo, mirroring his agitated state of provocation.

"Don't play with fire, Beth," he snarls, reading my thoughts. "I need to be inside you, now!"

Hearing his words and watching how they escape through clenched teeth, reminds me of the intensity of our connection. Seeing him coming undone like this is affecting my own breathing; my heart is racing and I'm so moist he must be able to feel the wetness. Taking this bull by the horns I tease him further ...

"No. Not yet. I want to taste you ..." I run my hands across his abdomen, along his pectoral muscles and take hold of his shoulders; rocking forward, I follow the line of his jaw with my tongue and kiss the shadow of stubble forming there, spurred on by the groans emanating from somewhere deep inside his core.

"Do you want me to stop?" I ask breathlessly.

He struggles to say a single word. "No."

I descend slowly, ravenously, like a woman finding her appetite for a delicious meal laid out before her. "Tell me what you want."

In a husky voice I barely recognise he states, "You know."

I skirt along his pubic bone. "Tell me."

His body begins to quiver. "Tell you or show you?" he asks, causing me to lift my eyes to meet his. "Enough!"

As if in slow motion, the bed begins to move; it appears to be floating upwards off the floor just high enough for him to slide his hands beneath the leg supporting it. In one languid movement he frees his hands, still handcuffed, and the bed descends. My mouth falls open and my eyes widen out of trepidation.

He sits upright, outstretches his powerful hands and takes hold of my waist, keeping me in place. His hot hands inch upwards, the chain almost at breaking point. He finds my breasts and his thumbs rotate around my nipples in tiny circles until I am shaking with a heady cocktail of fear and anticipation.

"You asked me to tell you what I want," he says with a charcoal grey stare, so penetrating I fear that simply witnessing it will cause my palpating heart to explode. "Darling, I want to fuck you so hard and so deep, I can barely contain myself." He tips his head to the right. "Does that answer your question?"

All I can do is nod, feeling the power radiating from his hands as they take hold of my neck; his thumbs caressing my throat, feeling the movement of a hard swallow before easing their way to my face; the chain from the handcuff skimming my lips as he rests it there reminding me of who is really holding the reins. Inside I'm clenching, alarmed yet so aroused I'm starting to pant.

"What am I going to do with you?" he asks, shaking his head from left to right a split second before lifting his hands high above my head in a wraparound movement. His palms are wide against my back. "You said you wanted to make love to me. Well, here I am. All yours for the taking." He smiles in such a way, I realise this is just a game. He's being Ayden, exuding danger but using it to trigger my arousal. He really has been reading his thoughts.

I feel my body deflating, so rigid had I become with fear. I know now, Ayden's influence is so powerful that he won't allow him to hurt me. He might tease me mercilessly and scare me half to death, but he won't gain any pleasure from my pain.

"I think you're going to be a demanding pupil with your extra-terrestrial talents." I glance sideways to the bed. "I'll have to take you in hand." I lower my right hand to his impressive erection and take hold of it, feeling the sensation of the velvety soft skin that encases it. With his flattened palms, he arches me into him and finds my mouth; first with his moist tongue and then his lips. I feel his tongue touching mine as he deepens the kiss until it becomes a fiery fusion of extended sighs. With my free hand I grab at his hair, feeling the dampness of perspiration at its roots.

With my right hand I continue to run my fingers the length of his cock at a quickening pace; I feel it growing in my hands, thick and unyielding. Droplets of pre cum cover my fingers, making me moan into his mouth.

His hands descend and, at one and the same time, he grasps my buttocks, squeezing and lifting me aloft.

"I'm ready for you," I confess, resting both my hands on his shoulders.

"Are you sure?" he asks, smiling behind a kiss.

I descend onto him, not stopping to reply. "Ah!" I call out, feeling the sensation of something unfamiliar and imposing.

But, I'm so desperate to feel him inside me I push on regardless. I lower myself onto him, feeling a tingling sensation as sensitive tissue stretches to allow him access to my sex.

Fuck!

"Can you feel how hard I am for you?" he asks, beginning to rock my body forwards and backwards, coaxing me to feel the exquisite rub of ribbed flesh internally. "Slowly, I want to savour the tightness as you grip me."

I hold off, but my arousal is evident in my quickening breaths and feverish moans of pleasure.

A growl escapes from his throat. "Ah, the exquisite grasp of your body. You are something, Beth."

With us melded together, I hear a single click and know exactly what it is. His containment had been no more than a charade. He knew all along about the release catch.

His grip tightens on my buttocks. "Come on, Beth, show me what you can do with this delectable body of yours," he says, baiting me, his mouth switching between an involuntary pout and a roguish grin.

I slide both hands into his hair and pull his mouth onto mine. "You haven't the faintest idea what I'm capable of," I state plainly, claiming his mouth with my tongue. "Lie back while I fuck you!"

I push him backward, taking hold of his hands and slamming them down either side of his ears with our fingers entwined; the handcuffs dangling from his left hand like cheap jewellery.

I arch my back and reposition myself so our union becomes a slick assembly of moist flesh and matted hair.

"This is not the woman I married," he states, goading me on.

"That's because I am *not* the woman you married," I remind him, beginning to rock steadily up and down, gripping him like a gentle fist.

He closes his eyes.

"Look at me! Open your eyes and look at me," I call out. "You watch me come because that's what you want; to have me capitulate, to reveal my soul to you at that very moment. Now witness what I'm giving you and take delight in my surrender." I pull my internal muscles and squeeze him in a vice-like grip. I feel him shuddering at the sensation and reinforce my offensive with circular movements to stimulate nerve endings, and it works. He is groaning with pleasure; a deep growl vibrates in his throat, leaving his mouth like the final roar of a dying animal.

"Fuck!"

"You've been spending too much time in Ayden's head. Now you're even swearing like him," I announce, knowing my words will be lost in the heat of the moment.

I lift myself up and away from him until he is almost separate from my body then slide down again and again, taking him in one long thrust. I have to tighten my grip on his hands to displace the sensation of a simmering orgasm. I must close my eyes. With them closed I hear Ayden's voice.

I've let the genie out of the bottle ...

He's right, I don't recognise myself. With that declaration I dive into that endless sea headfirst, making ripples, hoping they will merge and form into a tidal wave that will remain unforgotten for a lifetime. I writhe onto him and lose myself, release his hands and succumb to the ecstatic embrace of carnal sex.

On opening my eyes, I see only Ayden. He's here; eyes dark like a cloudless sky at midnight; words reaching out to my very soul, his undying love touching my heart.

Be bold, baby.

Thinking only of him, I arch my back, press my body down hard and fuck him so ferociously he takes hold of my hips, trying to hold me off. The noises he makes are barely human; the roars of pure ecstasy are ricocheting off the walls. When I can take no more, I lean into him and graze his left ear with my mouth whispering, "It's time. Come for me, baby."

Immediately, I feel a jerking motion and a pulsating ejaculation so strong, it triggers a chain reaction in me. Whimpering, I shudder and moan my way through an earth-shaking, bone-rattling orgasm, the culmination of forty minutes of hot and hard sex.

Ten minutes later, still dizzy from our sexual exploits, we clamber from the floor a soaking mass of body fluids and perspiration. He seems stunned. I feel victorious. I think I know what's happening now ...

Wherever Ayden is, 'sleeping', he won't let go of life; he is holding on, fighting for his existence. If I can keep our love strong then we'll be able to endure anything – even this.

***

With one part of the puzzle partially solved, Mack leaves the confines of his stuffy side office for the slightly fresher air of Harrow town centre. Tuesday morning shoppers are seeking out parking spaces and delivery vans are holding up traffic; just another typical day in an English market town.

He strolls into the HSBC branch and makes for the smartly dressed bank clerk counting cheques behind a glass partition. Not immediately taken with his ordinariness, she becomes more animated when he introduces himself and quickly goes in search of the Bank Manager.

A suited gentleman appears from behind a side door and shakes Mack's hand. He's Mr. Taylor, the man in charge, just the person he's looking for. They seat themselves across a desk from each other, away from the prying eyes of employees and customers. What Mack has to say is private and has required a Court Order to access the information he needs to proceed with his investigation.

"Good morning, Detective Inspector Bowker," Mr. Taylor says, reading his card and placing it neatly on the desk in front of him. "What can I do for you? Are you here in a personal or professional capacity?"

Mack leans back into the chair, preparing himself for what he expects will be a lengthy conversation. "I'm here to have a look at the banking details of a Miss Elise Richards. She's a former customer of yours." He takes the Court Order out of his inside breast pocket. "I think you may want to take a look at this."

Mr. Taylor opens the document and reads through it; he's seen one before and the official jargon assures him of its legality. D.I. Bowker has come prepared.

"Thank you. May I ask why?"

"I can't say too much other than Miss. Richards is deceased, having been involved in a fatal traffic accident. There's a couple of points I'd like to clear up before releasing her funds to her family and their solicitor."

"I see. Well, everything seems to be in order. I'm sure we can accommodate you." He offers a perfunctory smile, cracks the knuckles on each hand, rests his fingers on the keyboard and focuses his attention on the computer screen in front of him. "Can you confirm Miss. Richards's home address, please?"

"4c The Oaks, Hatch End," Mack says not needing to consult his notes.

"Ah yes. Miss. Richards has two accounts with us: a current account for her everyday banking, and a savings account."

"Can you let me see last month's transactions, please?"

Mr. Taylor turns the screen around and Mack scrolls through. The only figure of any significance is a monthly payment made by her employer Taylor and Maine. She has a balance of £2,144; nothing out of the ordinary there. He turns the screen around. "And what about the savings account?"

"Ah ..."

"What's the '*ah*' for?" Mack enquires. "Has she got herself a nice little nest egg?"

The Manager nods. "You could say that. She has £50,000."

"Nice."

"Indeed. It's primarily due to the fact that she has been receiving a payment of £5,000 on the first of each month, going back for ... the past ten months."

With his interest piqued, Mack leans forward to rest his forearms on the desk; his sixth sense stimulated and prickling at the prospect of having stumbled across another part of the puzzle. "I'll need a print out of this, going back 12 months." He takes out his notepad, licks his right thumb and flicks over his notes until he comes to a clean page. "Okay, so tell me where the five grand is coming from each month."

Mr. Taylor, pauses, bites his lip and says nothing.

Mack takes it a bad sign. "Whenever you're ready..."

He prepares to break the bad news. "It would appear your Miss. Richards has a benefactor."

Mack's eyes widen. "A what!"

"A benefactor, an anonymous sponsor."

He's shaking his head. "That's a bit antiquated, isn't it? Who has a *benefactor* these days?"

"You'd be surprised," Mr. Taylor points out. "Some young people have wealthy parents who deposit a set amount into their account each month ..."

"Yeah, but Miss. Richards wasn't a kid and she didn't have parents who were rolling in it. He prepares to jot down notes like a bobby on the beat. "You'd better give me the name of this benefactor so I can go and have a chat with them. See what kind of relationship they have with the deceased." He waits, pen poised. Forced to question Mr. Taylor's hesitance, he asks, "I assume you *can* tell me their name. I don't want to have to come back here again with more legal paraphernalia."

"I'd be quite happy to tell you, Sir, but it's a sealed account. All I can tell you is that it is from a Swiss bank." He meets Mack's disbelieving stare with indifference.

"You can't tell me who's sending her the money? She could have been involved in some kind of money laundering scam for all you know."

Mr. Taylor rocks back in his chair; his nonchalance reminds Mack of a certain Mr. Stone.

"I can assure you there is nothing untoward going on here. The money has not been removed from the account in the ten months since the first payment went in. If large sums had been deducted, we would have investigated the account *and* Miss. Richards. It would appear she has a kindly sponsor." He reconsiders his observation and speculates further. "Either that or ..."

In no mood for his speculation, Mack asks. "Or what?"

"Or she had a business venture of some sort that guaranteed her an income each month. There will be a straight forward explanation; nothing requiring you to apply your detective skills, I'm sure." He laughs smugly.

Smart arse ...

"I think I've been doing this job long enough to know when something doesn't feel right, Mr. Taylor," Mack says, asserting his authority for the first time today. "I'll have the boys handling financial forensics to take a look. Maybe they will be able to do some digging."

Realising he may have overstepped the mark, Mr. Taylor steps down. "Of course. I'll have Miss. Richards's account details printed out for you."

"Right. Is that it then? There's nothing else?"

"I don't think so ... " He stops mid-sentence.

Mack waits to hear more.

"It would appear we are holding certain documents for Miss. Richards here at the bank."

Mack feels that prickling sensation again. "What kind of documents?"

"Deeds to her apartment in Hatch End, valuations for a collection of expensive jewellery, a Life Insurance Policy, and ... her Will."

Mack slumps back into the chair. "Now we're getting somewhere." He scratches at overnight stubble with his forefinger and thumb. "So, ballpark, what are we talking here?"

"Her assets are in the region of £476,500," Mr. Taylor declares, somewhat bewildered by the discovery.

The numbers appear on Mack's notepad like code. "That's one hell of a nest egg for someone working nine 'till five for an estate agent, don't you think?"

"I do indeed."

Mack exhales loudly, creating a tangible gust that hits the man across the table from him like a blast of bad news. "When can I take a look at the document?" he asks, preparing to leave the room.

Looking like a man perched on the edge of a cliff, Mr. Taylor replies. "Now is as good a time as any, I suppose."

"I couldn't agree more."

The two men leave the office, single file, one a little rough around the edges, the other smartly suited for the role, but only one has a spring in his step.

16

L ester has loaded the Rolls and we are airport bound. It's almost 10 p.m. and we're freshly showered and ready to embark upon the next chapter in our adventure.

We have spoken very little since clambering from the bedroom carpet, and yet it's as if an understanding has formed between us ... a kind of symbiosis. No matter how you look at it, we need each other; knowing that makes this tour of duty a little easier to bear.

Heathrow is humming with the sound of happy travellers leaping from taxis and mini-busses like lemmings. A familiar face is waiting to greet us; the suited brunette who took charge of our passports and luggage en route to Rome is offering a friendly smile. Unaccustomed to life's little pleasantries, Ayden holds out his hand for her to lead the way, assuming we will be bypassing the masses. He's a natural when it comes to pomposity, but money talks and he has plenty of it.

She attempts to make polite conversation. "Mr. and Mrs. Stone your jet is fuelled and ready. You have a slot for 11.15 p.m. May I take your passports? I will also make the necessary arrangements for your luggage."

He gives her a disinterested nod of recognition and, with his hand positioned at the base of my spine, gently ushers me towards our connecting limousine parked a couple of yards from the external door. As we leave the comfort of the heated VIP lounge, we are buffeted by a crosswind that takes hold of my hair, wrapping it around my face like a balaclava. With my vision impaired, I take hold of his jacket and fold myself into his chest. As naturally as breathing, he shelters me from the gust with his arm. In a disorderly tangle of hair and clothes I scramble onto the back seat.

"Where the hell did that come from? I feel like a scarecrow." I pull back my hair into a make-shift pony tail. "Couldn't you have done something about that wind?"

He leans across, attempting to flatten my hair with his left hand and sniggers. "So now you want me to use my *skills* to ensure your hair is kept neat and tidy?"

"Well wind is a natural element, isn't it?" I ask innocently.

"It is but far be it for me to intervene ad hoc."

"Ad hoc?" I huff. "This from someone who cancelled out the sound of people talking in a restaurant because they were a little noisy!"

"That's different."

I will not be deterred. "How? Do you mean that it's alright for you to use you special *skills* for yourself but not for me?"

"Not at all. Tell me what you want and, if I can, I will make it happen for you." He places a soft kiss on my forehead. "And who knows, it might be significantly more impressive than ensuring your hair remains unruffled." He tips up his head. "We're here. Are you ready?"

"What for? More wind?"

"No, for spending the night on the company jet. It's a 13 hour flight to Hong Kong."

I face him squarely. "I've been on the jet before."

The softest of smile brushes against his lips. "Ah, yes. I'd forgotten."

Keeping a firm grip on my coat, I step out of the car but there is no need. The wind has dropped and I do believe the night air is positively balmy. "You warmed things up a bit." I remark.

He shakes his head and chuckles. "Actually no, the heat is coming off the turbines." He points to the enormous aeroplane directly in front of us.

I open my mouth to speak and pause. "That's a *real* aeroplane! Where's the mini-jet?"

"I think Jake is making use of the mini-jet. Charlotte made all the arrangements and said something about it being a long-haul flight." He takes my right elbow. "Let's get on board before the wind starts up."

I kiss his cheek. "Something tells me that's highly unlikely."

Single file we ascend this Airbus ACJ319. Along the side is the familiar navy blue stripe and 'AS Media International'. The cabin crew are waiting at the top of the steps to greet us: a smartly dressed woman of around 30, wearing a navy blue suit and a smile; and an equally smart gentleman of a similar age holding a tray aloft with two glasses of champagne on it.

"Welcome aboard, Mr. and Mrs. Stone. I'm Tony and this is Sandy. It's our pleasure to be flying with you this evening."

I glance across to them and smile appreciatively. "Thank you. Happy to be here." I turn to my right and rock backwards, awestruck. "Whoa!"

It's more than I could have imagined: a sumptuous ivory interior; plush leather chairs facing each other, a dining table that seats six, perfectly set with glistening china and crystal wine glasses atop a crisp white tablecloth. Ambient lighting diffuses from a domed ceiling, drenching the whole space in a kind of unearthly glow. Seconds pass and still I'm rooted to the spot.

"May I show you to your cabin?" Sandy asks.

"Please do," I reply, reaching for the champagne flute. "I'll take this with me."

She's smiles warmly. "Of course."

Leaving the front lounge behind and bypassing the dining table we head towards the rear of the plane. To the left and right of me the walls are finished with highly polished wood, into which my effervescent drink reflects like a golden chalice.

Sandy slides back a door on the right. "This is your en-suite bedroom, Mrs. Stone."

To my utter amazement, she's right. There's a king sized bed; its opaque green sheets have a dusting of cherry coloured rose petals that perfectly match my blouse. It's too much to take in. I tip back the champagne flute, feeling its contents sizzle on my tongue and hold onto my thoughts, trying not to let them fly.

Thank you, Ayden.

This is what he had planned for us. Now an imposter has hijacked his body and his aeroplane; but I can't think about that now ... I step inside. "It's lovely."

She nods in agreement. "I'll have Tony bring your luggage in as soon as it arrives."

Leaving me to my daydream, she bows out. I ruffle the rose petals with my free hand, noticing how every burnished surface is reflected in the elongated mirror above the dressing table. Only one thing looks out of place: me. Without Ayden's radiance, I feel no more than a pale imitation of what a wife should be. Thankfully he isn't here to witness my woeful impersonation.

The man in question appears at the door. "This is impressive," he remarks, nodding approvingly. "I think we'll have a pleasant flight, don't you?"

I simply nod in agreement. One at a time I release the petals, allowing them to fall into a scented mound. When I hold my hand to my nose, the fragrance reminds me that they were once a perfect rose; and now, having become unattached, they're purely decorative. Having served their purpose, I brush them off the bed making a mental note of where they land, not wanting to step on them as I leave the room.

I wrap my right hand around his arm. "Show me the rest of this awesome aircraft."

After the tour, Tony spoils us with a selection of canapés and decaffeinated coffee while Sandy turns down the bed and readies our cabin for the night. When we retire, the flat screen TV is on, bedside lamps are lit and anyone walking into this perfect space could be fooled into thinking they were on terra firma - not above the clouds travelling at 500 miles an hour.

I dive onto the bed, face first. "My God! This is life in the fast lane for sure."

He pulls his sweater over his head and yawns. His chin and then his mouth appear from beneath the collar with an exaggerated "Ah ..."

Seeing how weary he is I scamper up and help him remove it. His eyes are screwed up tight and he's obviously exhausted.

"I think you need to get yourself washed and into bed. We can watch TV for a while and fall asleep. It's 1.30 a.m."

He enfolds my face in his powerful hands, caressing it, until it becomes no more than a tiny bud. "That sounds like a good idea. You have worn this body out, my darling." He smirks, planting a soft kiss on my forehead. "I won't be a moment."

I watch him head for the en-suite bathroom. "Don't rush. I'm not going anywhere."

With him out of the way, I open my laptop, checking to see if I have access to the internet. It takes a minute, giving me time to strip out of my clothes and hang them up in the wardrobe. My nightdress is cool on my skin and the silken material floats over my curves like a sheet of fine tissue paper.

"Yes!" I utter. I have internet access! When he is 'sleeping,' I'll make my next entry in my digital scrapbook, away from prying eyes. I take a moment to return to the world I once knew, needing no more than our first-ever photograph together as a conduit.

Ayden returns to our honeymoon suite in the sky, wearing boxers and a radiant smile. His provocative fragrance finds its way across the room and rouses an already restless heart. Even though it's an opulent space it is, nevertheless, confinement of sorts. What I have experienced over the past five days is monumental, unbelievable, but my secret. He's pretending to read the newspaper and says nothing at all, other than, "Your turn."

With my nightly routine out of the way I slither under the softest of sheets and rest my head beneath his right arm with my cheek pressed against his deliciously scented chest hair.

"Do you want to sleep, or can we talk?" I ask shyly.

He wraps his right arm around me and folds his fingers together, resting them on my lower back. "We can talk until you fall asleep." He sighs contentedly. "Do you want to talk about anything in particular?"

I stretch my arm across his abdomen, feeling the need for intimacy after our sexual escapade earlier. "I may have trouble sleeping. I'm not a good flier."

"I didn't know that. You hide your fear well." He kisses my hair and tightens his grip around me. "You have nothing to fear. You're perfectly safe."

"How can you be sure?" There's that familiar rumble beneath my ear.

"You ask me that?

"Sorry," I snigger. "I didn't think that through."

"Do you think I would be here if this flight was doomed?"

I place a soft kiss on a flexing pectoral muscle. "I suppose not. What would happen to you if something untoward happened?"

"Nothing, I would move on."

Troubled by his nonchalance, I raise my head to see the flickering hues in his eyes. "To where?"

"Anywhere, everywhere, it's of no consequence to me."

I settle back down. "I don't think I'll ever get my head around this. You said you're light, right? Aren't you the light people speak of during near-death experiences?"

"He nods. "I'm part of it."

"But isn't that supposed to lead to the gateway to heaven?"

"You really are in a talkative mood." He's shaking his head. "What would you like me to say? I take departing souls by the hand and lead them to the light or the flames depending on how they have lived their lives?"

I shrug my left shoulder into the crook of his arm. "Don't they go to heaven or hell??"

Meeting my gaze squarely, he explains. "It's not that clear cut. They wait to be selected."

I feel my face folding into a frown. "Selected? So you're telling me the souls of the departed are sitting around in an enormous waiting room in the sky?"

He smiles broadly and it's so contagious I match it. "It's not so much a waiting room as a ... a two-star hotel."

My eyes widen at the thought. "Oh no! And is that where Ayden is?"

"At the moment, yes."

"Shit!" I sit up until I have both arms folded across his chest. "He'll be a pain in the arse; complaining, sending food back, asking to see the manager." I giggle at the absurdity of it.

"It's a brief stay for most. They move on and find eternal rest while others ... do not." He smiles resignedly.

"It's all very biblical."

He thinks through his response. "This is true."

Those three words crucify me but I swallow hard and carry on. "Can't any of the 'hotel' guests come back?"

"Not if their earthly forms have been ... dealt with."

I'm quick to interject. "By 'dealt with' you mean buried or cremated?"

"I do."

"So is that why you're occupying Ayden's body, to keep him in transit up there and alive down here?"

He nods and presents a tight-lipped smile.

"Why haven't you explained this to me before?"

I feel his hand caressing my hair. "Because, darling, you weren't ready to hear it."

I nod in agreement then face him squarely "And you think I am now?"

"You've rationalised what's happened and can process the information. Before, you would have broken down and run away screaming."

I lighten the mood. "I'm not a screamer."

He taps my nose. "I didn't mean it literally."

"So you have seen thousands and thousands of people pass over. Do you remember them all?"

"Not all, but I do have my favourites. Some I was unhappy to become acquainted with, in a professional capacity."

"You make it sound as if you cared."

"It's still possible to collect a soul and to care. There have been incredible thinkers, warriors, artists, inventors, philanthropists and poets who I have come to admire long after their departure from this earth."

"Anyone I might have heard of ..."

"There are so many." He arches a brow. "Mr. Shakespeare was an outrageously bad actor but a wordsmith of the highest order."

"You knew him?" I ask incredulously.

"To say I knew him would be an exaggeration. I did meet him several times and, of course, I was with him at the end."

"So you can recite a sonnet then?"

"Several ... would you like me to regale you with my recital skills?" He's grinning.

"Why of course ..."

He clears his throat:

"Shall I compare thee to a summer's day?
Thou art more lovely and more temperate.
Rough winds do shake the darling buds of May,
And summer's lease hath all too short a date.
Sometime too hot the eye of heaven shines,
And often is his gold complexion dimmed;

And every fair from fair sometime declines,
By chance, or nature's changing course, untrimmed;
But thy eternal summer shall not fade,
Nor lose possession of that fair thou ow'st,
Nor shall death brag thou wand'rest in his shade,
When in eternal lines to Time thou grow'st ..."

I look away and he stops reciting. Realising there's something wrong, he stretches forward and gently kisses my forehead. It's a paternal gesture that moves me to tears; tears for the loved ones I have lost and the lover who recited that very poem on our very first meeting. I pull my arms in close and snuggle into him for warmth and comfort.

"Why are you saddened by it?" he asks quietly.

"I was teaching that poem when Ayden found me."

"I see."

"You wouldn't have known."

He pulls up the sheet around me and rests his chin on top of my head. But for the hum of the turbines there is only the sound of our breathing. I fight to contain my thoughts, not to send them out or to share them. I want to suffer in silence. His chest rises and falls in even breaths against my cheek.

"Ayden," I whisper.

"Yes," he answers. "I'm still here."

"You're very quiet."

"I'm scrolling through," he says as if it's a perfectly natural thing to do. "I need to know everything if I'm to be the husband you deserve and that means going back to ..." He pauses. "Back to school."

"It seems the logical place to start."

"It does indeed. I should have done this days ago," he confesses.

Leaving him to his flashbacks I begin to snooze, thinking only of Hong Kong nights and sun soaked days spent stretched out on golden sand; a veritable feast of sweet and sour moments. My eyelids begin to flutter...

I am roused from my slumber by the shocking realisation that I'm not in my own bed. The steady rumbling of this fragile piece of metal forcing its way through turbulent air is enough to wake me with a start. Ayden is sleeping next to me and so princely is he in his majestic pose, I dare not wake him. I peel myself from his heated skin and move slowly from the bed to the bathroom, using the glow from the mirror as a guiding light. The bathrobe is fluffy against my skin, keeping me snug as I tip-toe over to my laptop that's quietly hibernating on the table by the window. I lift up the shutter and look out at the night sky, wrapping my hands around my face and touching the glass with my nose, but all I see is a blanket of blackness dotted with stars.

Refusing to dwell on my screensaver, I open the scrapbook page.

November #3

"Such is my love, to thee I so belong,
That for thy right myself will bear all wrong."
William Shakespeare: Sonnet 88

Today has been one of those days when my emotions have been thrown this way and that. It started with Elise's funeral this morning. Jake met us at the crematorium and we sat through a service interrupted by her mother's mournful cries. Before we could leave she vented some of her anger on you; it was uncalled for and your cheek took the brunt of her despair. I'm sorry you had to experience that, Ayden. No one knows the lengths you've gone to protecting Elise as a child and as a grown woman.

Being the media savvy man you are, you suggested we meet the press. (Video below) Now they have something to write about. I'm not sure Bowker will be deterred quite as easily; he seems to have it in for both of us.

We had fun with your Lancelot costume this afternoon!! (Laughing) The handcuffs fit quite nicely around your wrists ...

I stop typing to dust away tears; they formed silently, leaving me with damp cheeks. Once again I slip in the earphones and play back his announcement to the press. He's every inch the man I married, confident and cultured. His refined English accent transcends the realms of the ordinary, hypnotising me, taking me back to happier days.

I'm astounded by my performance too. I actually look as if I belong by his side; I appear confident and poised in my role. We actually complement each other in a dark and dainty kind of way. I listen to Katy Be and feel somewhat reassured as she sings, I'm *Crying For No Reason*.

I return to my entry.

Right now we're on our way to Hong Kong in your enormous jet. Yes, you know, the one you didn't tell me about. (Tutting!) I think I might just have it refuelled and spend the rest of my life in it, up here in the clouds, alone with you.
You're making my every dream come true, Ayden, and not a day goes by when I don't thank my lucky stars for you. We belong to each other, baby. I love you so much.
Yours, Beth. X

I save and shutdown; return to bed and fold my body into Ayden's, dragging his lifeless left arm across me like a seatbelt. I hold onto it for dear life, close my watery eyes to shut out the memories and prepare for a hard landing.

***

Under the glare of fluorescent lights, D.I. Bowker is inspecting the contents of a safety deposit box belonging to Elise Richards. Mr. Taylor stands quietly overseeing his inspection, curious as to the actual contents.

As described in her file there is a large brown envelope; inside it are documents pertaining to the purchase of her apartment in Hatch End. There is nothing strange about that: the name of the vendor is documented and Miss. Richards is named as the buyer. What strikes Mack as odd is the fact there is no reference to a mortgage. From the legal document pertaining to the transaction, it appears that the property was paid for in cash. The purchase price was £465,000.

Mack is writing down information in shorthand, but even the smallest letters and figures can't diminish the impact of this discovery.

Next he flips through four valuations for two rings, a bracelet and a necklace amounting to £11,000. Once again, this is a significant amount of money for a woman of her standing.

Keeping his thoughts to himself he takes out the envelope upon which is typed:

THE LAST WILL AND TESTAMENT OF ELISE RICHARDS

He holds it up against the light, spying the formal print of letter headed stationery but returns it to the box, preparing to leave it to the scrutiny of her family's solicitor. Just as he's about to close the lid, he notices a two small white envelopes. Feeling a flurry of excitement, he lifts out the first between his finger and thumb, turns it over and reads the name written upon it;

Mr. Ayden Stone.
MOD ASMI

The envelope sits on the metal table like a sheet of ice, its contents a mystery but its addressee well-known to Mackenzie Bowker.

Finally he delves into the bottom of the empty box and lifts out an envelope that is not new and not sealed. As he lifts it out, the contents fall. He picks up the formal looking document, dismissing the suggestion that he might be acting inappropriately. What he sees surprises him. Saying nothing, he jots down some names and the date of Miss. Richards's adoption sixteen years ago, when she was fourteen years old and her maiden name was Kilbride.

He prepares to close the lid on her past but something small and easy to miss catches his eye. He chases it around the bottom of the metal case with fat fingers, flips it up and lifts it out between his finger and thumb. It's an SD card in a small transparent case, not much bigger than a postage stamp.

"I'll take these two items and make sure they get to the right people," he assures his witness, holding up the SD card and the envelope addresses to Mr. Stone. Once they are nestled snugly against the notebook in his breast pocket, he reaches out to shake Mr. Taylor's hand. "I'll pass on the information I've uncovered today to the family's solicitor. They'll be in touch in due course, no doubt."

"I'm sure they will, Detective. Good luck with your enquiries. I'm sure you'll get to the bottom of this sordid affair."

Mack will not allow him to speak disparagingly of the dead. "There's nothing sordid about love, Mr. Taylor," he declares. "Not when it results in the tragic death of a troubled young woman. Thank you for your cooperation. Good day."

17

We weave our way through a web of flashing lights and masonry, crossing intersections and bridges as if on a magical mystery tour. Hong Kong harbour is a myriad of buildings vying for position on the skyline. I have never seen anything like it.

I turn away from Ayden and edge across the leather seat in the limousine to get a closer look. "Ayden look! It's spectacular!"

He's nodding, taken with my enthusiasm. "Wait until we reach our hotel. You'll have a better view from there."

It's almost midnight here but I feel as if I have just awakened; how will I ever sleep?

We arrive at our destination. I step from the car, feeling miniscule and insignificant beneath the International Commerce Building. The gold lettering across the entrance catches my eye: The Ritz Carlton. I turn to look out across the bay in one long, drawn out sweep, taking in the panorama, saying nothing.

He reaches for my hand. "Shall we go inside?"

Excitedly, I nod and take his hand, tilting my head to take in the magnificence of this wondrous building.

As if he has done it a hundred times before, he hands a business card to the petite young lady in a back suit who comes to greet us. She reads it, checks him out and immediately responds. "Mr. and Mrs. Stone, please come this way; the Presidential Suite has been prepared for you."

I tug at his hand. "Presidential Suite?"

"Why not? It's all tax deductible," he states, shrugging his shoulders. "I told Charlotte the highest and the most expensive suite there is, and ..." He holds out his right hand for me to enter the lift. "This is it."

In the confined space of the lift, I stand on my tiptoes and whisper, "But why ..."

He pushes back my hair and nuzzles into my right ear. The sensation of his hot breath on my skin makes me feel a twinge of something sensual. I can't help myself; I tip my head into him and sway a little.

"Because I can, darling," he mutters a split second before placing a soft kiss beneath my ear.

All I can do is lick the lip-gloss from my lips, maintain my equilibrium, and watch the blue luminous buttons click through the floors. We stop at 117.

The key card slides into the slot and the green light releases the door but I'm totally unprepared for what I see.

"Welcome to the Presidential Suite Mr. and Mrs. Stone," our escort announces, opening the door into Wonderland. If ever there was a time to feel small and overwhelmed, that time is now. I take my time moving forward, feigning indifference when all I want to do is scream, take my camera and start clicking away.

On my left is a huge dining table in mahogany and reflected in it is an enormous chandelier, simply hanging there like a billowing cloud of light. On my right is the lounge, decorated in rich ebony shades; beneath my feet is a beautifully crafted floor, the colour of a sandy beach daubed with streaks of the bluest ocean. But all that pales into insignificance once I become aware of the view. Victoria Harbour is visible through the enormous glass windows. My jaw drops. I cannot speak.

"Beth ... Beth!"

Somewhere behind me Ayden is calling my name but I'm so transfixed I can't tear myself away. I feel his presence behind me and take in his provocative scent.

"Let's take a look around." His hand slips into mine and he lifts it to his mouth. "The view will still be here in five minutes time."

Hand in hand we continue to explore an unpretentious bedroom with a king sized bed and sofas in a kind of muted grey; the walls are adorned with mother of pearl inlay. Gorgeous.

Next we make our way to the bathroom where a sunken, square bath takes pride of place; turquoise bubbles cling to the far wall, ready to burst. Luxury toiletries wait to be sampled on the vanity unit, a compendium of polished wooden surfaces with gold trim.

All I can do is shake my head. "Ayden, this is too much."

"There's more," he says, arching a brow.

"I feel as if I've fallen into a treasure chest; the ornaments, the furniture … everything."

I follow him into the fully equipped office, past a sauna, into another en-suite bedroom and a kitchen.

"We can have a private dinner for two prepared right here then sit and watch the sunrise. What do you think?"

Is he after my approval?

"I think it's all very beautiful but much too extravagant. I don't need to experience all this to feel loved." I turn and make my way to the lounge, back to my view.

In a matter of seconds he's behind me. He turns me around to face him, trying unsuccessfully to conceal his disapproval. "You may not need to experience all of this because you have the rest of your life to do it. I do not." Stalling, he brushes away an invisible strand of hair from my cheek and takes a moment to regulate the tenor of his voice. "I choose to do this, first because I can and second because I choose to experience it with you. Is that so difficult for you to understand?"

He's seeking validation.

"Last night while you were sleeping and we were airborne, I went back to school; to the theatre, to Rome, and all those private places in between. I discovered many things, not the least of which was your love of music and of your desire to fly; to escape the confines of your daily life and to soar…" He tips his head to the right, contemplating his next sentence. "We will reach great heights together, my darling. Just you wait and see."

Bewitched by his sincerity I gaze longingly into his eyes; the midnight sky is besieged by slivers of colour and lights reflecting the landscape. It seems as if the man behind those eyes is lost in that myriad of colour.

"I'm sorry. I didn't understand the reason for us coming here." I take his face in my hands and brush away the lines forming above his cheekbones with my thumbs. "I didn't mean to sound unappreciative; I can't begin to imagine the things you've seen and done in your lifetime." I tilt up my head until our noses are touching and place the softest of kisses on his lips. "Tell me why we're here."

He inhales deeply, raises his eyes to the ceiling and returns his focus to me. Sensing the shift in mood, he clicks his fingers and light gradually returns to the room, filling the glass wall with a mirror image of the furnishings and us. "Do you want the sugar-coated version or the truth?"

I take a couple of seconds to consider my answer. "The truth. *Always* the truth," I assert curiously.

"Very well. This is the highest hotel in the world; it provides us with a vantage point to look down upon humanity in all its glory, in comfort. It's also a reputable hotel where I have stayed several times."

I move away from the window and sit on the sofa. "I know that."

"Yes, but what you don't know is my secondary reason for being here. Funds from ASMI are being embezzled. It would be remiss of me to discover that and not to do something about it."

No way!

He has me riveted to the spot. "What does that mean exactly?"

"It means someone in a position of trust is misappropriating funds."

"You mean stealing from the company?"

He's nodding. "That's what I just said."

"How do you know?" I ask eager to hear every sordid detail.

He sits down next to me, lifts up his right leg and rests it on his left knee seeming totally at home in this palace in the sky. "Purely by accident. When we were in the boardroom I read Mr. Cheung's thoughts and tucked behind the things he wanted to tell me, were things he assumed I knew nothing about."

"Have you told Jake?"

"No," he answers sharply.

"Why not?

"Because he may be masterminding it," he states coolly.

I am almost too shocked to speak. "What ... what? Jake wouldn't steal from the company. He just wouldn't." I fall back onto the cushion, trying to take it all in.

"He just returned from negotiating a manufacturing agreement over here and it seems very odd that he didn't pick up on some irregularities."

I offer some kind of excuse for Jake's ineptitude. "Maybe they were hidden from him. He doesn't speak Chinese."

He's laughing at me. "I believe negotiations are carried out in English, Beth. Jake's inability to speak the indigenous language is irrelevant."

I give him an indignant stare, "Well, I wasn't aware of that."

He leans across to stroke my hair like a wayward child in need of reassurance. "No you weren't, darling. But I wouldn't be so eager to lend Jake your support just yet."

"Maybe you're right. How will you sort it out?" I ask, not doubting for a moment he will.

"I plan on calling a meeting tomorrow to ascertain who is responsible. "

"And do you think they'll just come out and spill the beans."

He shakes his head disconsolately. "No, I will have to listen to their thoughts. Unwittingly, they will tell me what I need to know."

I stand and straighten out my skirt. "And what about Jake?"

"He will too," he states calmly. "All this will be sorted out before we leave for Australia in two days time." His eyes follow me around the room. "Where are you going?"

"To change for dinner. If this room and the view is anything to go by, the food must be spectacularly good."

He concurs. "It is."

I leave the room with his words ringing in my ears and the possibility of Jake's betrayal still invading my thoughts. This is not the way I saw my honeymoon playing out.

Like a moving shadow Ayden appears at the bedroom door, holding a hotel brochure.

"There's a fashionable bar upstairs," he remarks reading from the text. "It called Ozone Bar of all things. Would you like to pay it a visit?"

I'm taken by surprise that he would even make the suggestion. "Sure. I can't believe there's an upstairs."

He smiles broadly. "Apparently, there is."

"Give me a couple of minutes to change and I'll be right out." I'm grinning. "Aren't you going to change?"

"Into what?"

"A shirt and some dress pants," I suggest, busying myself with my case.

He shrugs his shoulder. "Is that necessary?"

For some reason my hand finds its way to my hip. "It's not necessary. I just thought you might like to ... dress up."

"Ah." Is all he says.

"But you don't have to. It's up to you ... but I am."

He moves over to me, pulls me close and places a soft kiss on my head. "Then so shall I, darling. I will follow your lead." He leaves the room. "But first I'll ring ahead and organise a table."

"Good idea." With him out of the way, I select a smart dress by Jasper Conran; it has a black grid print and the tailored fit adds just the right amount of sophistication for this kind of outing. While he dresses, I slot my iPod into the dock and select *Skyscraper* by Demi Lovato. The song might well have been written for me.

In the throes of an animated striptease, he returns, flinging his sweater down onto the bed on his way to the bathroom. To save time I select one of his made-to-measure shirts in white, a tie to complement my dress and lay it out on the bed. I pick up his sweater and begin pulling out the sleeves, only to be captured unawares by the scent of his cologne. Obsession rouses my senses. Instinctively I bundle up the collar between my hands and hold it to my nose. With my eyes closed I picture him by my side, above me, all around me. My reaction is so profound I have to turn my head away to seek out less evocative air. I fold it up neatly and place it in one of the drawers nearest the bed. The sound of approaching footsteps breaks the spell.

Still reeling from the potency of his scent, I gather my bag and lip-gloss. When I raise my head, he's unbuttoning his casual black shirt, exposing a little more chest hair and muscle with each button he releases.

Don't look …

I offer a brief smile and scoot past him, redirecting my eyes and my thoughts to less suggestive images as I pass. I'm in the bathroom, standing with both hands gripping either side of the sink, trying to compose myself. All this talk of Titanic moments, tantalising smells and treachery has my nerves jangling to the beat of a racing heart. I clip up my hair and tidy my make-up, daub my lips with a lush pink layer of gloss and take a deep breath.

When I return to the bedroom he's dressed and ready. Before I can contain my first thought, I let it fly.

My God you're such a handsome man.

He is about to say "Thank you …"

I watch as his tongue slides out between his teeth and how he rethinks his response. Instead he licks his lips and winks. It's more than I can stand. In a dithering mess I snap my clutch shut and head toward the door, hoping to steady my trembling hands en route. "Let's go."

He knows.

"Stop!"

I flinch and my breath hitches. He takes my clutch from my hand and throws it onto the sofa. I hear it land with a thud.

His breath caresses my neck. "You won't be needing that."

I find my voice from somewhere. "It has my camera in it. I want to take some …"

" … No need. I will paint you a picture with words."

"But I …"

"Hush! Just do as you're told. Two hands on the door and less of the fucking back-chat," he says, lifting the hem of my dress until it settles around my hips, exposing my lingerie.

Ayden …

With my hair up he has free access to my neck and takes full advantage. The tension in my body is palpable; it's a kind of quivering helplessness.

He nuzzles beneath my ear and, not wanting to lift my palms from the door, I arch into him. He responds by lifting my dress higher and pulling me towards him, firmly, holding on to my hips. I feel a rigid mass of muscle against my lower back and throw back my head, visualising it unleashed and formidable against me, inside me. A muffled moan leaves my mouth.

The lights dim to a twilight glow with a single click of his fingers. He prepares to speak. "Last night I lay awake listening to you breathe while I relived every fucking moment. In my conscious state I undressed you and possessed you. I pleasured myself while you slept."

No!

His right hand skates across my buttocks and slides between my legs. His fingers arch and fold to assess the extent of my arousal.

"I hunger for your touch, Beth. Like a starving man I have circled this earth in search of sustenance and I have found it with you. I must have you now, or I will surely die."

His words resonate; all I can hear is Ayden. He's back from the dead.

My recollections fade, and I'm back in the present with a jolt. His left hand snakes across my body, ascends and comes to rest on my right breast. With impatient fingers he eases back the fabric at my neckline and slips inside, stroking my collar bone and gently squeezing my right breast. Anchored, front and rear, I can't move. All I can do is succumb to the sensation of being claimed.

His nose tickles my neck and his tongue licks at my ear.

"Where did you learn to do this?" I ask, feverish with need.

"I learned from the best. All I had to do was look and listen."

"To memories?"

"No, my darling. To you."

Me?

The burning sensation I have come to crave is building. I'm tipping forward into his caress and rocking into his hand; sparks are flaring around my groin and I'm moaning into the space between my head and the door.

"Close your eyes," he instructs, his voice circling around us like a satellite. "Don't be afraid."

I do as he asks. "I'm not."

"Good girl," he reassures, the final vowel leaving his lips in a gust of hot air. "Open," he says.

I gasp. Now my hands are pressed against the glass window, the view obscured by the steam exhaled from my lungs.

"Tell me what you see."

While I try to verbalise my thoughts he is lowering my panties with both hands, falling to his knees. I feel the lacy material against my ankles.

"Lift."

I step out of them, right foot first, wobbling on my black Louboutins. How bizarre I must look outstretched against this enormous window like a human kiss reaching for the moon. To steady myself I take hold of the window frame with my right hand and plant my heels down onto the wooden floor. I'm not going anywhere.

I feel his breath on my neck a split second before he speaks. "Look closely. Can you see what I see?" he asks quietly. "The world is laid out at your feet. Every flickering light is an artificial star. This is the nearest you will ever get to my world. I brought you here to share it with you."

Superimposed on the magnificent vista we stand together, reflected in the glass like gods. I watch as he takes hold of my hands and separates them until we are united in a flying position.

"Doesn't this count as a Titanic moment?"

I stare into the glass, wide-eyed, unable to answer. All I can do is contain my emotions and nod.

"The first of so many for you and I." He sniffs at my hair and pushes his nose into the sensitive spot beneath my ear. "Welcome to my world, Beth."

I close my eyes and lean backwards into his rock-solid body. I feel his mouth curving into a satisfied smile. He has me where he wants me; craving his touch like a drug. It's getting so I want - no, I need - my daily fix of Ayden Stone.

He lowers my arms and rotates me until we are face to face. His hands descend and he squeezes my buttocks as if kneading dough. He begins to swerve his hips like a dancer, creating pleats in my dress with his inflexible erection. This is a man on a mission to get me hot and wet and ready.

Mission accomplished.

His two-handed grip on me tightens and the friction against my groin is enough to start a fire. I bury my hands in his hair and claim his mouth, thrusting my tongue between his teeth and teasing him until our tongues are no more than a tangle of taste buds.

In one frenzied movement he tears open my dress like tissue paper from a present and strips it from my shoulders. My bra is quick to follow. I stand before him naked, panting, aching. As I reach out to remove his tie, he takes a step back, then another until he is out of reach.

"Let me look at you," he says through fractured breaths. "You are beautiful." Roughly he removes his tie and rips off his shirt. "Take my hand so that I may claim your body and your heart as mine." He holds out his hand.

Without a second thought I take hold of it and follow his lead into the bedroom. On entering I gasp. Once again he has astounded me with his magic. The room is wall-to-wall white with flowers and ruby red rose petals. The hypnotic blend of fragrances from roses, lilies and orchids has my head in a whirl.

"It's like the garden of Eden," I mutter, not really expecting him to hear.

"Then I will be your Adam and you can be my Eve," he says, pleasantly surprised by my observation. "Lie down. I want to taste you."

Oh my God!

Momentarily, he stills as if trying to get a hold onto a flickering memory. All it takes is a click of his fingers and there is music. The sultry tones of Lifehouse singing *Everything* only make me want him more. Having discovered the perfect background to our lovemaking, he pins me to the mattress with a smile so devilishly sexy it has me squirming; a lather of creamy wetness gathers between my legs. I raise my head off the sheets to watch him undress as I have done so many times before.

My naked Adonis closes the distance between us, places his hands on my knees and parts them. "Tonight we will both give in to temptation," he says, licking his lips. "And there is nothing more tempting than you, my darling." With his hips he nudges my knees further apart and covers my body with his.

My face fits into a single hand; his thumb grasps my chin while his left hand covers my breast, preparing a hardening nipple for his mouth. His descent is leisurely and agonising; I'm arching my back to hurry him along, but he will not be rushed.

My patience is rewarded. He takes hold of my right hand and sucks on my fingers, pushing them in and out, simulating our sexual coupling. I begin to moan more out of need than desire. His free right hand circles my pubic bone, splaying out so his thumb can follow the natural curve of my body. His thumb rests on my clitoris and stimulates it with gentle brush strokes, flicking it just enough to have me opening my mouth to make rapturous sounds that no one but my husband should ever hear.

"This is all I think about, being inside you like this." He takes hold of my knees and bends my legs until my feet are resting on the bed. Instinctively I move my hands to cover myself, but pause at the sight of black curls tumbling and coming to rest between my legs. Holding me in place, he enters me with shallow thrusts and swirls that make my body convulse. With anticipation building I fist his hair, writhing to the rhythm of Al Green's sweet rendition of *Simply Beautiful*.

"You're so wet," he moans.

Shifting position he raises me off the bed until I am forced to rest my thighs on his broad shoulders, held in place by his firm hands. He growls against my sex and the vibrations off his lips send an electric shock through my body. Using only the tip of his tongue he takes me to the point of no return and I lose myself in the ecstatic haze of an orgasm. It's a toe-curling, sheet- ripping sensation that has me calling out like a woman possessed.

"Ah, Ay-den!"

Before I can catch my breath he is over me. "I can't keep my hands off of you," he says, taking hold of my wrists and positioning my hands either side of my head. "I want to bury myself inside you," he growls.

My pulse remains unnaturally fast, making me pant and shiver at the prospect of being held down and taken forcefully. My fantasy lover meets my post orgasmic gaze and I witness the depth of his desire. I see the grey vastness of the cosmos in his eyes and, for fear of falling into it, I close mine.

"Don't look away," he commands.

But I must. My body yearns for his touch but my rational mind still refuses to accept him as my beloved.

"Tell me you don't want me," he implores. "Tell me ..." In one languid movement he slides into me. "This is my home, Beth; remember? You belong to me. Say it." The rocking, in and out movement has me lifting off the bed; I'm trying to free my hands but I cannot. He's gyrating his hips and leaning, fucking me with his cock and his tongue and it's all I can do to stop my heart from exploding.

He tightens his grip on my wrists and picks up the pace, groaning with each penetrating thrust. I watch his expression changing, becoming darker; a seductive smile is replaced by a hard unyielding stare. I screw my eyes shut and allow my body to ride the wave of passion dragging me down, deeper. That endless sea begins to swallow me up ...

"Beth ... Beth ..."

Hearing my name whispered so softly, I open my eyes. What I see causes my inside to clinch and tighten. Gone are the grey tints of the universe I have come to expect; instead I'm looking up and into a midnight sky sprinkled with flecks of starlight.

"Ayden," I whisper, letting go, not wanting to look away. "Stay with me." I begin to grind my body against his until our movements are synchronised.

Knowing I'm close he coaxes me with his words and a smile. "Come on, Beth, let me hear you."

His wish is my command.

With the promise of his return I come loudly, panting and screaming my way through an orgasm that brings me close to unconsciousness. My internal clenching grips him with the force of an unyielding fist and triggers his climax. He flattens his body against mine and grunts into my neck like an animal caught in a trap. Gradually, he settles.

Once he releases my wrists I wrap my arms around him and calm him with soft words while salty tears sting my eyes. Breaking the bond, he raises himself and rolls to the side. His head rests on his right palm. I stare at the ceiling too afraid to face him for fear of coming face to face with this great pretender once again.

"You were on fire," he says, removing a few strands of hair from my cheek. "I've not experienced that level of intensity before."

I feel my heart sinking but turn to face him, remembering to scatter my thoughts into a thousand pieces. Only one remains ...

Ayden is alive.

***

Troubled by vivid dreams Mack climbs out of his crumpled bed at 4 a.m. The previous day's findings have added fuel to his already raging bonfire of determination. His lounge carpet has become an expanse of white. The four files he has collated are assembled like ice packs; as the bonfire burns, so they begin to melt and merge. They have yet to meld but Mack reassures himself that it's only a matter of time until they do.

Laced with whiskey, his thoughts wander. What he needs is a time machine to take him back twenty years or more; to that time when three young children meant everything to each other. He reaches for the faded photograph he removed from Elise's apartment and takes a lingering look, wondering what brought them together. He returns it to her file and spots the SD card. Now seems as good a time as any to see what's on it.

He moves over to the dining table, boots up his laptop and waits, arms folded, pensive. His eyes widen and he gasps. It's a video of a woman tied up, being whipped. It's Elise. Feeling uneasy witnessing this sadomasochistic sex act, he's actually nauseous. 'To each his own,' he thinks. 'But what the hell ...?'

Reluctantly, he dispels the notion that this is Elise Richards being violently whipped and sexually exploited. First because he needs to view it objectively and second, she seems to be enjoying it. Undaunted, he looks for clues; the man with the whip is muscular, tall, dark haired. The voice is that of an Englishman; well spoken, firm, authoritative. One name comes to mind - Ayden Stone.

He shuts down the laptop and returns the SD card to its plastic case. What an insignificant strongbox for such an important file; one that could make or break a reputation with a single glance.

A decision is made and he christens it with a sanctifying mouthful or whiskey. He will spend the day in the office, finish typing up reports on a couple of cases he had resolved and then he'd devote himself to doing some old-fashioned digging; except most of it will be done via the internet and the phone. The first point of contact will be the adoption agency handling the Richards case, or rather that of a fourteen year old girl named Elise Kilbride.

He places down the SD card by her file and turns to leave. The light bulb above his head flickers and he smiles. "I know Elise, don't worry. I won't stop until I get to the bottom of this." Instantly the flickering stops and becomes a streak of bright light; it seems to come from the bulb then flares and fills the room with a radiant glow. In the blink of an eye, it's gone.

"Night, Elise."

Mack turns off the light and makes his way upstairs to bed. 'It's a cruel world.' He thinks. 'Kilbride. That name shouldn't be too hard to trace.'

18

I have no idea what time it is or how long I've slept but I still feel groggy. The bedside clock reads 10.00 a.m. That can't be right!

I reach over to my watch on the bedside cabinet and it's 3 a.m. A person could become very disoriented with this time zone business. Thank goodness we were able to sleep on the flight over.

Ayden has long since departed, and on his pillow lies a single white orchid with a note. I read it and hold the fragile flower to my nose, allowing the delicate fragrance to fill my nostrils and the rest of my body with a powerful stimulant that reminds me of last night's impassioned lovemaking.

Morning, Beth,

You were dead to the world so I let you sleep. I've a 9 a.m. meeting but will be back around lunchtime. We'll make our way upstairs for lunch.

By upstairs he means to the Ozone Bar, I assume.

Thank you for a wonderful evening...

Please don't leave the hotel alone! If you want to go out for any reason, please call me, and I'll make arrangements for you to have an escort. We both know what happened last time you wandered off alone!

I love you.

A X

All the flowers from the previous night have been removed except for a single vase, full to the brim with delicate white lilies. Normality, of sorts, has been restored.

After a quick shower, a strong cup of coffee and two delicious Danish pastries, I'm ready to start my day. With no more than a fluffy bathrobe around me I boot up my laptop. Our first picture pops up, precipitating the inevitable pangs of guilt and remorse. I access my digital scrapbook; it's taking shape. Pages are filling up with newspaper articles, photographs of us and press releases. The music I've added pulls at my heartstrings, but it's truly a reflection of how I feel. I have to confess my undying love somehow amid all this pretence.

November #4

"Doubt thou the stars are fire;
Doubt that the sun doth move;
Doubt truth to be a liar;
But never doubt I love."
William Shakespeare: Hamlet.

Well, baby, we arrived at this wonderful hotel, The Ritz Carlton Hong Kong just before midnight local time. It's such a magnificent suite. You spoil me, Ayden. Being eight hours ahead, our bodies were operating on UK time and we were, (how should I put this delicately?) Still full of energy... (Laughing)

We got all dressed up and made it as far as the door before you did what you do best; seduced the hell out of me. Mr. Stone, you are such a naughty man, but I do adore you ...

For a brief moment, I stop and compose myself. I have to believe Ayden will remember the time we've spent together or, at least have the faintest memory. If not ...

I can't contemplate that now. I busy myself uploading a picture off my phone that Ayden took of us on the plane, and a stock photo of the hotel. The music I attach is a personal favourite. Lifehouse sings *From Where You Are*.

Before I can type another word, I have to take a breath - and hold back my tears before they cascade onto my keyboard like raindrops.

Even when we're a room apart I miss you, Ayden. Wherever you are, I feel you reaching out to me, touching my heart. Last night we made love and the universe was ours while we were bonded together in the heat of passion. Nothing will keep us apart.
Yours, Beth X

I save the document and reach for my phone. I text a quick note to Charlie and snap a couple of photos: the lounge and the bathroom; just enough to impress. Knowing she's tucked up in bed I don't bother waiting for a reply. I move on to my third task, to text Sylvia, Ayden's adoptive mother.

Thinking carefully about what I'm texting I begin:

Hi, Sylvia, Ayden's in a meeting but we wanted to let you know we're enjoying our honeymoon. Hong Kong is a spectacular city! We're about to take in the sights tonight before leaving for the Great Barrier Reef tomorrow. Would you do me a favour? Please have Patrick scan & email Ayden's Birth Certificate to song.birdBP@hotmail.co.uk We'll speak soon. Beth x

With all my jobs completed, I focus on my appearance. What does one wear to a lunch in the Ozone Bar? Smart casual, I think.

By 11.30 a.m. I'm ready to go. My black Calvin Klein Blazer looks smart over my Pepe Jeans and white blouse. I slip on my black ankle boots, tie a scarf to my bag and fill it with my camera, purse, phone and basic make-up. Who knows where this simple lunch date will lead.

The TV is on the business channel. There's a live news report on foreign investment, unilateralism and trade wars. A gathering of business types are leaving a high rise building in the financial district and stopping to address the media as they exit. I spot Ayden and reach for the handset to turn up the sound.

Surely he's not going to meet the press? He *is* ...!

Instinctively, I stand. My thumbnail hits my teeth and I move towards the enormous screen, as if that will make the slightest difference to the way he carries himself.

I needn't have worried. Seeming totally self-possessed, he delivers a statement looking perfectly poised and regal in his signature suit; he's flawlessly disguised. After waiting for silence, he breaks the news like a raconteur spinning a yarn so adeptly you would easily believe he had done it a thousand times before. I'm so taken with him, I actually find myself applauding.

Before departing, he finds the camera lens and looks into it – at me! A sexy smile forms and I find myself smiling back as if sharing an intimate secret that no one else is aware of. He winks and I'm so startled I jerk backwards into the coffee table. Thankfully I manage to steady myself, by which time the report has ended.

By way of a final touch, I dab my lips with a little gloss and head for the door. A midday text stops me in my tracks.

I'm on my way back to the hotel. See you on the roof! A X

I quickly reply:

See you there. B X

It's a short ride in the lift one floor up. Unfortunately, it's crowded with tourists and the mishmash of languages and perfume has my head in a spin. The narrow corridor to the bar is bustling with bodies coming and going like a dual carriageway. Cheerful voices and music set the tone and prepare me for the shock and awe of a world-class view.

At first there is only sky and the promise of high-rise buildings with a panoramic view that stretches all the way across the harbour, as far as Victoria Peak. The swirling blanket of white foam widens and there is little to witness, except the smile from the smart bartender as I pass. I head for the window and claim two high-backed stools with a small marble table between. It isn't until I feel the wind in my hair I realise it has an open roof; wearing my blazer was a good idea.

I envision what there is to see beneath the smoky ribbon wrapping itself around the building; last night we saw only lights and today only rainclouds. I feel cheated.

Five minutes pass, then ten; I check my watch. Perched up on this high backed stool I pretend to peruse the cocktail menu when really I'm thinking through the events of the past six days. I find myself lost in thought; my chin on my upturned palm, and my head in the clouds ...

I really don't know what to make of these circumstances in which I find myself. My 'husband' and I have an understanding of sorts and, with every new day, I'm beginning to feel a little more comfortable in his company and in his arms. I suspect it's not because of any grandiose ideas about omnipotence or spirituality but the simple fact that he is becoming more like Ayden; in each new situation and conversation there are flashes of him. When we made love in Stone Heath, I saw flickers of the man I love - I know I did; shimmering hues of sapphire gazed back at me through the miasma of a distant universe. And last night! I heard Ayden's voice as real as if we were back in my apartment all those weeks ago ... the breathless whisper of a man experiencing unadulterated rapture. I saw the love in his eyes and was so desperate to hold onto him but ...

Out of the blue, it hits me: maybe that's the way to keep his spirit alive, not only in my memory but within a body seized by an imposter. Is it the physical act of making love or a heightened emotional state that sparks him into life? I have no way of knowing.

"What do you have no way of knowing?" asks Ayden, appearing through the horde of noisy tourists. He pulls me to him for a soft kiss.

"Whether this mist will clear," I reply, reminding myself to shatter my thoughts before they wing their way to this mind reader extraordinaire.

He attempts to seat himself on the high-backed stool, opposite me, but he's obviously unhappy with the setup. With his feet on the foot rest, his knees project forward, so much we are a metre or more apart. His leather-soled shoes slip off the footrest, frustrating him further. He huffs and stands. "We can't sit here."

I'm too busy looking out of the window to be distracted by his cantankerous comments. "Can't we just enjoy the view?"

He raises a brow. "View? What view?

He has a point.

"Maybe it will clear later?" I suggest returning to the drinks menu.

"I think it might be a good idea to clear it now." He takes my hand, helps me to climb down from my perch, and escorts me to a vacant space where we are able to gaze out onto the sea of swirling mist unobstructed.

I feel his lips against my right ear.

"Blow."

Looking startled I turn to face him. "Here?"

He smiles mischievously. "Yes."

I glance about the bar, now full to overflowing with cheerful customers and tourists with iPhones and video cameras held high. "In front of all these people?"

"They won't know what you're doing," he explains.

Wide-eyed I shake my head. "The minute I unzip your trousers, I think they'll work it out."

He throws back his head and fills our little space with raucous laughter. "My darling, you are adorable."

I have no idea what's about to happen and attempt to return to our stools before they're claimed.

He circles my waist with his arm. "I meant for you to blow out there." He tips his head towards the window.

"Why would I do that?" I ask.

"To disperse the clouds, of course. Go ahead."

I'm frowning and constructing a look of utter disbelief. "You want me to blow at a plate glass window?"

"Why not? Let's see what happens." His wink tells me this is going to be a lot of fun, now we've cleared up the initial misunderstanding.

I look around before tipping my body forward, purse my lips and blow.

"Harder."

Feeling foolish, I do as he orders; I lean back to set myself for the task and blow hard like a child extinguishing candles on a birthday cake. Before my eyes a small crack appears in the clouds; it opens up and widens, making me laugh. I blow harder, encouraged by his boyish smile. In a matter of minutes the curtain between two worlds clears completely. We are looking out towards Hong Kong Harbour and can even pick out the towering peek of Mount Austin in the distance.

He slips a hand in a pocket and whispers into my ear. "Now that's what I call a view."

"Me too. That trick will never grow old," I remark, propping myself up against him, relishing the skyline.

"I like to think of it as a crowd pleaser," he teases, looking at the people now beginning to converge around the windows.

"Well, you've certainly pleased this crowd *and* me." I kiss his cheek and wipe away the evidence with my fingertips. "And what's your next trick going to be?"

He scans the room. Our stools have been taken and we appear to have nowhere to sit. "Getting us a table. Wait here. I'll sort something out."

I'm just about to say, "Never mind ..." but he's gone. Finding myself alone, once again, I return my attention to the spectacular view and smile as I replay the miraculous event over in my mind. I'm still smiling when he returns, looking decidedly pleased with himself.

"Get your bag." He takes my hand and we follow a waiter to a small table that has a reserved sign on it. "We'll be more comfortable here."

Less than a minute after we're seated, a fleet of staff appear, carrying two trays and what looks like a heavy-duty ice-bucket and a stand.

"Thank you," he says, pointing at the table and issuing instructions in flawless Chinese. The servers disperse, leaving the head waiter with the unenviable task of popping the cork. He does so with minimal fuss and pours from the bottle of Krug Grande Cuvée.

"Champagne? What's the occasion?" I reach out for a toast.

"We're on honeymoon - isn't that occasion enough?" The skin around his eyes wrinkles as he smiles and so does mine.

"Of course it is. Cheers." The delicious elixir tickles my tongue then slips down my throat like liquid gold. "It's delicious." I reach out for a cracker. "What's this?" I ask, placing a napkin across my lap.

"That's sushi and that's caviar." He seems disinterested.

I place a couple of morsels on my plate. "I thought you didn't know about food."

"I don't. One of the waiters walked past me with that. I asked what it was and then told him to bring it to us with the most expensive item on the menu. It was an easy selection to make." He sits back into the cushioned sofa.

"Aren't you going to have anything to eat? God knows it must have cost a fortune."

He shakes his head distractedly and checks his watch. "I can't stay."

I return a cracker to the plate before it reaches my mouth. "You can't stay where? In this bar?"

"I need to go and check something out..."

"Didn't you discover the identity of your embezzler at the meeting this morning?"

"No."

"It wasn't Jake then?"

"He wasn't there. He said he had to check out one of the manufacturing units."

I shrug my shoulders and continue eating. "In that case he probably did. So where do you have to go now?"

"I plan on paying an unscheduled visit to the same unit." He checks his watch again.

"Please stop checking your watch." Disappointment is written all over my face. "Why did you order all this if you knew we wouldn't have time to eat it?"

"Just because *I* have to leave doesn't mean *you* can't enjoy it."

"On my own? Up here in the clouds?!"

He chortles. "Of course not. I've arranged for you to have a companion."

I take a long sip of champagne, put down my glass and top it up. "Some honeymoon this is turning out to be," I huff, despairing of his lack of consideration.

"Would you prefer I renege on my duties?" he asks, pinning me in place with a disparaging stare. "To allow ASMI to suffer the indignation of a court case whereby the guilty party is sought out by investigators and prosecuted in the full glare of the media?"

I'm shaking my head. "Of course not."

He stands and fastens his jacket. "Then, I have to go and sort it out."

I inspect him from his knees to the top of his head, not stopping to take in the cut of his trousers or the way his jacket clings to his muscular body like a second skin, but revering everything most sacrosanct in the male form. I find myself licking my lips, coating my tongue in lip-gloss at the merest thought of him - and last night.

He clears his throat, walks around the table, eases back a couple of strands of hair from my left ear and speaks softly. "You know how hard it is for me to keep this revving libido under control as it is without you coveting me with your eyes."

"I wasn't," I lie. "Stop reading my thoughts" I'm giggling.

He licks my earlobe and continues. "I don't have to read your thoughts. Your eyes betray your every desire." He stands upright and adjusts his trousers as best he can to conceal the bulge that just happens to be at my eye level. "Now look what you've done." He grins and shakes his head. "You're a terrible flirt, Mrs. Stone."

"You're a horny bastard, Mr. Stone," I reply, trying unsuccessfully to hold back a broad smile.

"This is true," he answers as naturally as breathing. Something or someone catches his eye over by the bar. "Your companion is here."

Companion?

Jake appears, catching the eye of every female en route. When he and Ayden combine forces the body heat in the room tends to increase a couple of degrees; I know mine has.

"Well if it isn't Mr. and Mrs. Stone enjoying an afternoon snack." He winks at me and pats Ayden on the back. "So, you have me baby-minding now?" he asks, sitting down and kissing my cheek. "Hi, Beth. You look as lovely as ever."

"Thanks, but I don't need baby minding," I huff indignantly.

Jake is about to place a cracker in his mouth but stops before it reaches his lips. "There's approximately one and a half million people over there on Hong Kong Island. Take it from me, you'll need a minder." He taps my knee. "Stick with me, baby, you're in safe hands."

I glance up at Ayden, who has adopted a look of unaccustomed concern. It would appear he's thinking twice about leaving me in Jake's *safe* hands.

Jake continues to dig into the caviar. "How long you gonna be, Ayd?" he asks between mouthfuls.

"A couple of hours. I'm hoping it won't take longer than that to check out a couple of things." He looks over to me apologetically.

I offer a sympathetic smile. "Go. We'll be fine."

"Right." He leans into me and kisses me softly. As he pulls away I see a furrowed brow and a flicker of something grievous in his eyes; an uncertainty I haven't witnessed before. I have no time to speculate why before he leaves and I'm left with my handsome companion.

"So, how's the honeymoon going so far?" Jakes asks, patting his mouth with a napkin and throwing back a glass of expensive champagne.

"It's not exactly what I'd envisaged but I know Ayden won't settle until this problem is sorted out."

Now why did I say that?

He's on it in a flash. "Problem?"

"Yes, nothing major." I displace my interest and focus on the selection of food. "This is rather extravagant."

"Yes it is, but he can afford it." Jake reminds me.

I say nothing and pop a piece of sushi into my mouth.

Jake lounges back on the sofa, his arms outstretched in an overly casual pose. "After we've finished up here do you wanna go into the city? You can do some shopping or something..."

"Yes. That sounds like fun. But only if you don't mind."

"No. I don't mind. You've come a long way to stay cooped up in this tower like some damsel in distress. The least I can do is come rescue you for a couple of hours." He laughs out loud and I do the same.

"I don't need rescuing, Jake - but thanks for the thought."

He nods his head. "I believe you. You've been through a lot."

"I'm fine. Look! Not a scar to speak of." For some reason I turn my hands over.

He smirks. "I can see that." He places his empty glass on the table. "Ayden loves you, you know."

What a surprising thing to say.

I can't conceal my astonishment. "I know ..."

"But that doesn't stop him being a fucking pain in the arse sometimes."

I'm laughing at his directness.

"The thing is, Beth, he listens to you. I'm not saying you can change him overnight, but he'll get there. He's been flying solo for a long time."

I reach for his hand and give it a squeeze. "Thank you. I think we've both been living the single life for some years."

He's shaking his head. "He's had that fucking Elise to contend with and you had that psycho bastard on your heels. It's about time you had some R and R."

"Yes, but things are a lot quieter now, although Charlie will claim I'm neglecting her. She's in Brussels on business at the moment, so I suppose we both have things going on in our lives."

He's genuinely interested. "Good for her. She's a real fire starter." He tips his head to the side and smirks.

His comment makes me laugh. "I'll tell her you said that. She'll be thrilled."

He tops up our glasses. "I bet." His attention shifts to something else. "I try to take a break from all this when I can." He raises his glass to in the direction of Hong Kong Island. "It can get kinda intense, you know what I mean? It's what I do but not who I am."

"Yes. I know what you mean." I look away then back again. "Then who are you?" I ask, holding him in place with a wide, blue-eyed stare.

He extends his right hand. "I'm Jake Harrison, Mrs. Stone. Pleased to meet you."

Playing along I shake his hand, noticing how he holds my fingers for a couple of seconds longer than is necessary. "So, Jake Harrison, what are your plans for the future?"

"To make as much money as I can, as fast as I can, and to get out. Maybe buy a ranch and breed horses."

His declaration takes me by surprise. "Oh! Not to have your own business?"

"Been there. Worked the 18 hour days, had the ulcers. Thanks but no thanks." He folds his arms then rests his chin upon an upturned palm.

"Horses?"

"Yeah. Sounds crazy, right?"

"No." I'm smiling at a distant memory. "I used to ride when I was younger. I can see the attraction."

He's suddenly animated. "You ride?"

"I did. Although I'd need a much bigger horse these days." The connection between us is palpable.

"I wouldn't worry about that. You're perfect as you are."

I hear the compliment and, for the hell of it, decide to run with it. If I can get him to lighten up, who knows, he might shed some light on the illegal dealings involving ASMI. "Thanks. It's always nice to get a compliment."

He's quick to interject. "If you were mine, I'd shower you with them."

I shake my head at the thought. "Shower?"

He's a little embarrassed. "Not sure where that came from."

"From the heavens," I declare humorously, suspecting Ayden is watching from above.

He nods his head and smiles boyishly. "Yeah. Heaven sent." He takes a sip of Champagne. "Ayd's a lucky guy." He reaches for my hand. "Ready for some retail therapy?"

"Always!"

We gather our possessions, he checks his phone and asks the bartender to arrange for a car to be waiting 119 floors below. His easy, confident swagger is a visible contrast to Ayden's upright, self-righteous stance. Ayden exudes power and authority whereas Jake steals it artfully right from under your nose.

It's a long way down. Our descent is punctuated with friendly smiles and we mentally count the numbers on the neon blue panel to the right of the door. It seems an awfully small space even though there are only the two of us. Out of nowhere Jake hits the stop button and we come to a standstill. I turn to him for some kind of explanation.

He clears his throat. "I have to ask you something."

I think I know what's coming ...

"Have you noticed anything kinda strange about Ayden? I can't put my finger on it but he just seems different somehow."

I fabricate a look of surprise. "What do you mean?"

"Not sure. It's just a feeling, I guess. Nothing obvious but ... something." He frowns and waits for my reply.

All I can do is look into his worried eyes and shake my head. "Really?"

"You haven't noticed anything ... different?"

Oh, you have no idea ...

"He's a little stressed about this manufacturing problem but maybe you can help him with that." I watch for any signs of anxiety.

He leans back against the mirrored wall. "Something tells me the shit is about to hit the fan again. Only this time it might stick." He's shaking his head and, to worry me further, he runs his hand over his hair as a visual gauge of his unease.

"Why? What's happening? Can you tell me?" I touch his arm tenderly.

He begins to speak ... the alarm sounds, the lift jerks into life and we begin to descend.

Damn!

"I'll tell you in the car."

We compose ourselves. We don't want anyone thinking we were doing anything other than talking while the lift was at a standstill.

Outside, the limousine is waiting and the doorman recognises Jake instantly. We climb inside and head out in the direction of Pacific Place. It comes highly recommended, apparently.

I'm eager to get back on track with our conversation. "So, you were saying about the shit and the fan ..."

"I may be speaking out of line here but Ayd seems so distant I'm not even sure he wants to hear this from me ... or anyone else, for that matter."

I turn side-on to face him. "I'm sure he does, Jake."

"It's as if he's seeing me for the first time. And the way he looks at you - watching how you move and how the words leave your mouth. Crazy shit like that." He turns away, taking a moment to calm down.

"Jake. You know what happened with Elise, right?"

He nods. "It was my car!"

"I know, that couldn't be helped."

"I'm not bothered about that. I can't believe he got out alive. It was scrapped."

"He was very lucky, thank God." I hold my hand to my chest to stress the point. "Everyone thinks he bounced back, but it hit him hard. Not just because of the connection they had as children, but because of what he almost lost: his life. It's business as usual, and I understand that, but he's still finding his way back. We both are."

I feel his arm around my shoulder and a tight one-handed squeeze "I know, Beth. I get it now."

"I think he'll feel so much better once he's able to put this Hong Kong business behind him and we can stretch out on a beach and watch the world go by."

He's shaking his head and laughing. "And you seriously think he'll be able to do that, do you?"

"I can live in hope." I smile broadly.

"I wish you nothing but the best. You know that, right? But don't be surprised if you have to put your beach party on hold."

"Why would we do that?"

"Just a hunch."

"What kind of hunch?"

"The kind of hunch that tells me someone is trying to pull the wool over our eyes." He reaches into his pocket and pulls out a small pen drive. "See this? On it are two sets of accounts; one set we're privy to, and the other the Kowloon plant keeps under wraps. Take one from the other and you're left with a whole lot of shit to explain."

I'm aghast. "Does Ayden know?"

"I think he suspects something. Why the hell would he take a trip out there today and leave me to play minder? He must have a good reason."

I smile knowingly. "Is that where you were this morning? He said you weren't at the meeting."

"Yeah, I paid a guy to get the information out so we'd have proof. Maybe catch these bastards in the act before they embezzle any more money from ASMI." He slips the pen drive back into his pocket.

"Are you sure it's safe in your pocket? What if you lose it?" I ask.

"I won't. Besides I've already uploaded it to my laptop. This was for Ayd."

I rub my hand the length of his bicep. "You're a good friend, Jake. Ayden's lucky to have you looking out for him."

"Sure. Just doing my job," he murmurs.

"Even so. You go the extra mile for him."

"What else would I do; we're like brothers, right?" He means every word.

"Yes. You are." All I can do is nod in agreement.

If he only knew ...

"That's why I can't get my head around what's going on with him. He looks at me like I'm an employee he just hired this morning."

I feel for him. "The crash was so traumatic, Jake, especially after what happened to me. It's been rough for him. Give him time to come around." I kiss his cheek.

His face breaks out into a wide smile. "You're right. Brains and beauty. You have it all, Beth."

I roll my eyes and fall back onto the seat. "I don't know about that."

Pacific Place nestles in the southern part of the island between polished towers, stretching into the clear blue sky like metallic stalactites. It offers one of those shopping experiences you read about but never get to experience. Yet, here I am with a handsome escort and a Visa card with no limit!

He seems to know where we're going and I'm happy to follow. We make our way up to level three, passing by gleaming shop fronts and pillars that seem to stretch up to the very top of the building. All I can do is marvel at the opulence of it all. We come to a double-fronted boutique and he stops. Reaching out, he beckons me inside. It's Chanel.

First I'm drawn to the make-up; a beautifully presented assistant applies colours to my hand then wipes them off with a moist tissue. I move on to the perfume, then the bags, then the hats, all the time checking to see if Jake is still around. There's no sign of impatient pacing; he's content to check his iPhone and to look up occasionally to acknowledge my gleeful smile.

I try on hats and he joins me to make suggestions, laughing and shaking his head. It's a 'no' to the one with the floppy brim but the beret is a winner! This is fun.

For the next hour I try on clothes. I wander out of the dressing room posing and twirling in bare feet. Jake sends one of the assistants off on a mission for matching heels to finish off the look and applauds when the outfit is complete.

From the corner of my eye I notice a young assistant who is eyeing me with derision; I feel a twinge of embarrassment and watch as she wrings her hands, seemingly incensed by my self-indulgence. How strange.

I undress in the cubicle, hanging up a ridiculously expensive evening dress the colour of ripe strawberries with an unusual neckline and a structured bodice. Standing only in my underwear I stop to take a mental snapshot of the moment. For the past two hours I've felt like my old self, laughing and giggling at the silliest of things. Jake has seen to it that I haven't been rushed or abandoned; he's been the perfect minder and companion.

It's been over 30 minutes since I last thought of Ayden and I'm shocked by my own admission. But, then again, it's not him I'm forgetting, it's a pale imitation: a husband who's becoming less of a stranger every day. In a split second, my joy melts away like a snowflake on a windowsill, leaving only a glistening droplet as proof it ever existed.

Realising that puts everything in perspective. I blot a tear from the corner of my eye and pack away my things. Having taken some time to dress, I make my way over to the counter. All my purchases have been wrapped and deposited in half a dozen stylish bags and Jake is handing over his card. I can't let him do that.

"Here. Take my Visa card," I call out. "You don't have to pay for them."

He puts his card back into his wallet. "Too late." He picks up the bags and moves towards the door, offering the obliging shop assistant a wink as she opens the door, clearly sorry to see him leave.

I catch hold of his arm. "Seriously Jake, you must let me give you the money for my clothes. I don't expect you to mind me and pay for my shopping too."

He won't hear of it. "No way. Let's call it a belated wedding present." He manhandles the bags. "Do you want to grab a drink or head back?"

"I think we should head back. We've been out for hours." From somewhere above our heads there is the sound of thunder; it rumbles across the skylights and echoes around the concourse like a train approaching a station. Shoppers are scattering. "What's happening?"

He shrugs his shoulders and frowns, unable to offer an answer. "I don't know. I'll ask." He approaches a young girl and asks her, "What's going on?"

Using animated gestures, she explains that a very bad storm is coming and people are being evacuated from the mall before the skylights break or the roads become too flooded to get home.

"Fuck!" Jakes says. "I'll ring the limo guy to come pick us up where he dropped us off." I take three of the bags to lighten his load and free up his right hand.

As we leave Pacific Place a chilling wind takes me in its grasp, stealing the breath from my lungs; it blows from the ocean in gusts. Rain falls vertically in sheets, creating a seemingly impenetrable wall through which we must dash, hand in hand, in the direction of the limousine; bags flapping, hair flying.

Jake squints and pushes me onto the back seat, resting his hand on my head to prevent me from catching it on the frame. "What the fuck! We're gonna get drenched."

I duck inside, grappling with shopping bags and laughing. "My clothes are sticking to me." I tug at the lapels on my blazer. "These raindrops are like bullets!" He shakes his head and the water flicks across my face, forcing me to hold up my hands and giggle. "Stop! Stop!"

He scrapes his hands across his face and over his hair, which I notice has grown an inch or so since I last saw him.

"Sorry." He grins, gives the driver instructions and we begin our return journey downhill, back to the hotel.

I smear the window with my fingertips as it fogs over, checking out the chaotic conduct of unwitting shoppers as they scurry along the pavement, doused by great waves of rainwater created by cars like ours. When I look skyward there is the rumble of more thunder, threatening to puncture the rolling clouds inflated with rain. In view of earlier events, I wonder … is this the work of a tempestuous husband? One so enraged with anger he has caused the sky to erupt so violently we must return to the hotel before the roads are flooded? Surely not!

***

Fuelled by caffeine and corned beef sandwiches, Mack spent most of Wednesday with his head down cross-referencing dates, people and places. When he did lift his eyes it was only to scroll through a computer screen or to pick up the telephone. He amassed information from multiple sources, contacted social services, university administrators, an adoption agency and the Manager of a Children's Residential Care Home, a pleasant sounding woman called Winifred Osoba. She agreed to speak with him about one of her former dependants, Elise Kilbride.

It is with that meeting in mind he selects a shirt and a pair of trousers from his limited selection. Since being widowed a year ago, he has bought very few clothes. He doesn't see the need to 'dress-up,' but today is the exception; he may even wear something from his 'Sunday best' collection.

His Sat Nav states the 56-mile Journey to Hove will take around one hour fifteen minutes, but, with the traffic and road works on the M25, it turns into an exercise in perseverance. The excursion takes two hours and concludes with a formal announcement, "You have reached your destination."

He looks left and right at the neat row of gardens fronting semi-detached properties, and edges further towards the dead end. There, camouflaged behind naked branches is the sign for Bright Hill.

He steps from his car, straightens himself up, and presses the intercom. He's expected. The gate clicks open and he pushes it back, making rarely used hinges grind against one another. The undignified squeaking stops and the lock snaps shut behind him. With the enormous Victorian building in his sights, he takes out Elise's photograph and holds it up to eyelevel, moving his head left and right and back again to make comparisons. He's come to the right place.

He's welcomed into the building by a plump woman of around fifty with wild hair and a paintbrush wedged behind her right ear; her cheeks are emblazoned with coloured paint which gives her the look of a tribal elder. She escorts him upstairs, giving him time to look about the impressive hallway at the stained glass, the ornate tiling and the wide stairway. He's making mental notes. 'It's well maintained and well resourced. Children will be safe and well cared for here.'

As they ascend, she asks him about his journey, how far he's come and how bad the traffic was on the M25. It's all very perfunctory. Mack answers politely and is as relieved as she is to reach the office where the grown-ups are based.

The office is bustling with activity. The young lady nearest the door offers him tea or coffee while the other members of staff look on suspiciously, refusing to make eye-contact for some reason. Again, he makes a mental note, but before he can jot down his observation on paper a rotund black woman breezes in wearing a crimson smock dress and red shoes. She's not at all like the woman he visualised her over the phone. His mouth twitches in response to a private thought.

More like Mother Christmas than the mistress of the house.

Unlike the other members of staff she offers him her hand; she engages him with her smile and scrutinises him with eyes the colour of dark chocolate. Once inside her office she directs him over to the window, where a small group of young children can be seen playing on freshly painted climbing equipment.

"Just look at the little mites," she says. "They're having so much fun it'll be a terrible struggle for Margaret to get them back indoors." She directs him to a high backed chair on the other side of her desk. "So, Detective Inspector Bowker, what can we do for you?"

He takes out his notepad and begins to flick back pages, licking his thumb a couple of times to ease the process. "I'm investigating the tragic death of Miss Elise Richards or, as you might know her, Elise Kilbride. She was a ward of this institution some 22 years ago."

Mrs. Osoba appears to expand and folds herself into her high-backed office chair like a bread mix in a baking tin, spreading out until every possible inch is filled with *her*. Her smock dress plumes up around her stomach like dough rising; she flattens it down with both hands and covers the desk top with her broad arms. "I see. How did she die?" she asks unswervingly.

"She was involved in a car crash." Mack watches for her reaction.

Her eyes widen yet she manages to refashion her response into something less expressive. She lowers her chin to speak. "How dreadful."

"Yes it was." He consults his notes. "May I ask how long you've worked here?"

As is her way, she becomes animated and throws back her hands feigning embarrassment. "If I tell you that then you'll be able to guess my age," she states laughing a little too forcefully. "I've been here for over twenty years."

"Ah yes. Almost 22 years, in fact," Mack adds, flicking over to the next page. "So you'll remember Elise then?" he asks.

She's shaking her head. "Detective Inspector ..."

"Mack ..."

She starts over. "Mack ... there have been more children here in those 22 years than you can possibly imagine. You can't seriously expect me to remember every single child?"

He offers a flat smile. "Of course not. But I think you may have a recollection of her even though she was only here for a matter of months; more so because she was associated with another of your residents here, Ayden Stone. You must have a recollection of him, surely, especially as he's gone on to make quite a name for himself?"

Her face flinches defensively. "Yes, he has, but I can't see how that has anything to do with Elise."

He prepares to test her memory with a dramatic statement of fact. "Actually it has a lot to do with this investigation. Mr. Stone was driving the car that careened off the motorway, resulting in her death."

It appears as if the air has been sucked from the room. Mrs. Osoba's façade crumbles at the mention of his name; she is struck dumb by the possibility of him being injured or worse.

Mack seizes the advantage. "You'll be pleased to know he survived unscathed, more or less." he reassures her. "You do have a recollection of them, then?" He senses his digging is about to pay off and he's on the verge of striking gold.

She regains her equilibrium and folds her chubby fingers into a tower on her desk. "Mack, I don't know why you're here or what your intentions are but there is no wrong-doing here. For as long as I've been here, the children under our care have been well looked after. Their emotional, physical, educational and spiritual needs have been addressed. Some of our charges have gone on to do wonderful things, like Mr. Stone; others have not." She casts a loving eye across the collages dotted around the room and the smiling faces of children of every size, colour and creed. Speaking softly she avows, "We have done our best."

Mack places his notebook on her desk and leans forward until they are eye to eye. "I'm not here to stir up trouble. I'm here to find out why a woman took a knife to someone she loved in the front seat of a sports car and then tried to kill them both by grabbing the wheel. That's all."

"And what makes you think I can shed light on something as dreadful as that?"

He lifts out the photographic evidence, places it on her desk and turns it around so she can see the three children clearly. He taps it on the corner with his finger. "This," he states.

The severity of her stare is diluted by her tears. Clearly moved by the picture of them she lifts it between her finger and thumb so she can resurrect the memory of them with her eyes. "They were inseparable. Saffir was heartbroken when Frannie left. I started working here a month after this picture was taken but he told me *all* about her. Kept her memory alive until it became a kind of fairy-tale he would tell himself at bedtime. He kept a picture of them under his pillow and every night made the same promise." She glances at Mack but looks right through him, all the way to that very moment. "To find her, to rescue her."

Mack senses his cue. "Well, he kept his promise. He found her. In fact he flew her off to Las Vegas and married her."

Mrs. Osoba is shaking her head. "Always was a determined little boy. Knew what he wanted and went all out to get it. But Beth's not merely an acquisition to him. He loves her, always has and always will. And that's the end of it." She hands him back the photograph.

"Thank you." He slips it into his jacket pocket, secretly thanking her for more than the simple return of a photograph. "That makes sense. I got this photograph from Elise's apartment and there was a note addressed to 'S'. I assume she was calling him Saffir." He receives an affirmative nod. "What I don't understand is why he was so taken with Beth - then

Frances - when Elise was here all the time. Weren't they close?"

"I wasn't here to witness how close they were but Saffir did speak to me about Frannie." She laughs and heaves herself out of the chair to stand by the window. "He loved to talk about her, how sweet she was, how she made him laugh; but mostly, how he saw himself as her protector." She folds her arms, preparing to elaborate. "You see, all he knew was to fight for the ones he loved. There was his mother. She was forced to give him up. He had two names but he chose to keep the one that reminded him of her, even though that meant defending it every day. He fought Elise's battles for her too, not that she needed him to, but he did it anyway. Then Frannie came along." She sighs and the hot air from her lungs creates a fleeting cloud across the glass. "I would love to have seen them together; living out their childish fantasies, acting out fairy-tales as children do when they have no concept of reality or of the *real* monsters out there."

She returns to her seat and perches on the edge of it so she might lean forward to make her point quietly but forcefully. "The monsters came for Elise one night in the guise of two male members of staff who worked the night shift. They had been abusing her sexually for some time and, once it was discovered, I'm ashamed to say, it was hushed up and Elise was transferred to a different establishment. I was new here and no one mentioned a thing, except Saffir."

Having listened patiently, Mack is eager to wrap up all the loose ends. "Do you think anything happened that might make it possible for Elise to blackmail him?"

She is horrified. "Blackmail him? Of course not! Why do you ask?"

"It was just a thought. She had a substantial payment going into her account each month. I wondered if the money was coming from him."

She's quick to come to his rescue. "It might be coming *from* him but it won't have anything to do with blackmail. He'll see it as a way of taking care of her as you might a sister or those you love." She glances around her office until her eyes come to rest on her top-of-the-line laptop.

"Is that why this place is so well furnished, the grounds so well-tended and your staff are so suspicious of my intentions?"

She laughs out loud. "No. It's because we all love him dearly. He's the Patron Saint of Bright Hill."

"Is he now?" Mack isn't convinced.

"So don't bother digging, looking for dirt, Mack, because there is none. Ayden and Beth are beautiful people, inside and out. They've come through hell and high water to make it this far and I send them my blessing every single day. After that terrible incident in her school, no one could doubt they're meant for each other. He deserves nothing but respect. Even you must concede that?" She reaches for Mack's hand.

He raises himself from his chair and leans across to her to shake it. "I'll take your word for that Mrs. Osoba ..."

" ...Winnie, everyone calls me Winnie."

He smiles briefly, leaving only a smirk in its place. "I imagine they would," he says amicably. "Thank you for helping me piece together some of my puzzle, Winnie. I'll leave you to get back to your children."

She flounces over to the door like a crimson tide of scented perfume: the fragrance from a hundred freesias fills his nostrils.

"Thank you, Mack. I'll come down with you. Margaret may need a hand."

The stairs creak as they descend. The sound of children's voices and laughter fills the hallway as they march single file into the art room. A blond haired girl of around eight years of age comes skipping past him, humming a tune; he can't help but smile and think of Elise and how different her life might have been.

The drive back takes another two hours. Mack passes the time by listening to Radio 4 extra, distracted by the retelling of a novel right up until the point where someone dies. Twenty minutes in, he swaps the drama for something more cheerful: Sports Round-up.

By the time he reaches the Bromley turn off he knows all there is to know about transfer fees and goal differences. More importantly, he returns knowing a lot more about Elise Richards and, of course, the mercurial Mr. Stone.

19

W e leave the limousine protected by the canopy and enter the hotel looking rather dishevelled but unscathed.

"Do you want to have a glass of brandy to warm you up?" Jake asks, taking hold of my bags.

I shake my head. "No thanks. I think I need to get out of these wet clothes before I catch pneumonia."

"OK," he says with smile.

We move together in the direction of the lifts. First lift number one then the second to the 118th floor. I turn to Jake. "Are you on this floor?"

"No. One below. Don't want to see you struggle with all these fancy bags." He smiles softly and his eyes fix on mine for a split second longer than I'm comfortable with.

"Thanks. I don't know what time Ayden will be back. What are you doing for dinner? Would you like to join us?" I fiddle in my purse for my key card.

"I don't think so ... If he's got any sense, he'll keep you all to himself tonight." He tips his head and his mouth falls naturally into a kind of suggestive smirk.

I lower my eyes modestly. "Maybe ..."

The door to the Presidential Suite opens with a single push and I tumble inside. Laughing, we exchange shopping bags. He kisses me on my cheek and walks away.

From down the corridor he calls out. "Be good!"

Still chuckling, I close the door with my foot. When I turn around Ayden is standing there, looking like he's been carved out of some kind of ancient stone; gaunt and sour-faced.

Saying nothing, he turns and walks toward the enormous window. He stands tall, looking out into the curtain of swirling mist; thunder roars and zigzags of lightening shiver from the heavens above. Even the building appears to be swaying. I feel as if we're on the brink of something monumental, like the prelude to the great flood.

"Ayden?" I call quietly. "When did you get back?" He doesn't answer. I drop my bags and approach him, touching his left arm at the elbow.

He spins around and I gasp. The dazzling beauty of the man I love has been replaced by an anxious visage that is both engaging and terrifying in its transformation. He has the pallor of an aging man; his skin has lost its natural glow and his eyes reflect the leaden, grey sky.

"What's happened? Is it ASMI?"

He looks through the glass into the wrathful sky.

"Talk to me. Better still, just listen." I grasp the lapels on his jacket and turn him to face me. "I can guess why you're so upset. I saw you watching me at the boutique. That was you, wasn't it?"

He says nothing but stands rigid and unrecognisable, air leaving his lungs in a kind of seething snort.

"You set the whole thing up to amuse yourself, to feel the pangs of jealousy you felt back home and you knew Jake would play his part beautifully. If this is the case then why are you so upset? The streets are flooded, people are frightened, injured, maybe dying because of your tantrum." I turn to my right and begin to walk away but, as before I cannot; some kind of invisible force has me pinned to the spot.

"So this is what you do when things go awry - lash out, show your true colours?" I lower my head and consider my words very carefully. "You said you wanted to feel, to know love in its many forms. So what do you think this is? Name the emotion that has you wound up so tightly."

He closes his eyes and when he opens them I see an open sea swimming in tears. "I don't know. Jealously?"

"No, it's more than that. You know how that feels; it's a nagging ache, a disappointment that comes and goes. This is actual pain." I glance over at the clouds, rolling and tumbling in the wind. "Call off the thunder and lightning, Ayden. People are getting hurt."

I wrap my hands around his face, reaching up to place a soft kiss on his lips. "Stop this now." I lower my hands, slide them inside his jacket, around his back and hold on tight. His heart is racing against my ear and his chest still heaving.

Outside the storm begins to ease. The storm clouds are thinning and there are streaks of light; it isn't blue but a kind of off-white that promises better days.

He takes hold of my shoulders and pushes me away from him. "These feelings I'm having are alien to me. I'm struggling to give them a name."

"I know." I take hold of his right hand and position it on his heart, resting mine on top of it to keep it in place. "You know what this is?"

"Of course I do. It's the heart: a cone shaped, muscular organ made up of four chambers that pumps blood received from the veins into the arteries, thereby maintaining the flow of blood through the entire circulatory system."

His answer makes me laugh. "And there I was thinking you didn't have a sense of humour." My eyes are glistening with adoration.

He's smiling. "That's not the answer you were after, is it?"

"No. I was highlighting the fact that you're alive; a living, breathing, feeling entity. A human being."

He pulls me in close and presses his lips against my hair.

"Fear."

I look up into his eyes; opaque windows to a tortured soul. "What?"

"Fear. That's what I was feeling. I had a panic attack of some sort; a surge of adrenalin that I simply had to dissipate. It resulted in the storm."

"So you didn't create it to get me back here?"

He tips his head and nods in the direction of the pane of glass now clearing after the deluge. "There was that."

"What were you afraid of?"

He's lost in thought. "I'm not sure. It was a visceral response over which I had little control."

I'm trying to make sense of it. "You mean like arousal?"

"Yes, although I seem to have that under control now."

I press my body against his. "I think you might not be at that point just yet."

"That's because of your proximity," he explains.

"Is it? And what if I do this and get even closer? Are you still in control?" I lower my right hand and place it between his legs; slowly I raise it until his zip is against my thumb.

"Is this a test of some sort?" he asks, clearing his throat.

"No, not a test; a reminder that you have nothing to fear." Standing on my tiptoes I'm able to nibble his chin, to drag my tongue across his bottom lip, tasting but holding off on an actual kiss.

"But it was apparent you like Jake. You were laughing; no, you were giggling and enjoying his company." Instinctively, his hands take hold of my waist, pulling apart my jacket, pinning me to him, climbing my body with eager hands.

I whisper into his ear. "I do like Jake. He's like chocolate. He can be very sweet; but that doesn't mean I want chocolate all the time. It's just something you fancy now and again as an accompaniment to something more substantial. But you … you're so much more … an element and not a piece of confectionery. You're like oxygen to me. I need you to breathe."

Unable to hold back, he raises me off the ground, taking my legs and wrapping me around his body like a human vice.

"Is this your way of telling me I'm forgiven?" he asks, covering my mouth with his.

Breathless, I answer, "Yes, forgiven - and that I love you." I pull his mouth onto mine, taking hold of his hair in both hands and holding him in place. "I've missed you, Ayden."

"And I you, Beth."

With silent music we waltz over to the doorway. The bedroom is only ten yards away but I grab hold of the doorframe before we can pass through it. "Here. I want you here."

He looks around, gaining his bearings, sizing up the wall. He lowers me until my feet touch the floor and begins to remove his jacket.

"No. Leave it on. I can picture what you look like underneath." I begin unfastening his belt, then the buttons on his trousers, eager to feel him in my hands.

He's fiddling with my jeans, pulling out my blouse in handfuls and letting it drift over my derriere like foam on ocean waves. An involuntary moan leaves my throat when he pushes down my jeans and my panties in a single, forceful movement.

I wrestle with a stubborn zip and wriggle his impressive cock out of his trousers; his boxers catch over it, making it necessary for me to gently free it from the folds.

He sanctifies our union with passionate kisses so deep and urgent I can barely catch my breath. My face is encased in his hands. I feel desired and loved. When I open my eyes he is staring ahead, a boyish smile manifests, and I am once again reunited with the man I adore.

I want to say so much but only one word leaves my lips in breathy exhalation. "Ayden."

Without a word of warning I'm being lifted. The interior wall hits my back with a thud. A hard, unyielding cock seeks me out as I balance on taut forearms. I'm clawing at his hair and sucking on his tongue as our breaths dissolve into rapturous moans of delight.

Words hiss from his mouth in a garbled cry. "I have always wanted you like this. To take you is the sweetest thing, Beth. I may be elemental but you give me life."

In a single thrust he enters me, swallowing up my moans as the sweet agony of his penetration has me convulsing. Slowly he rocks, back and forth, widening the gap, making the outward movement infinitesimally longer each time until he is ready, once again, to slide into me in one stomach-clenching thrust.

He growls with contentment. "Look at me, Beth."

I open my eyes and see my husband's features. All my senses combined serve only to seduce me into total submission.

Through heated breath he whispers, "I love you. You belong to me."

I grip him internally. His mouth twitches and his hips jerk forward in response. I smile and reply, "I love you more, and you belong to me." I crush him once again and seal my mouth against his, swallowing up the garbled sounds of pleasure emanating from his throat as he thrusts deeply, grinding his hips against mine, grappling with my buttocks. He's unbridled and I'm his for the taking.

I close my eyes and allow my head to fall backward. Our orgasms converge and build until they become a searing bonfire of ecstatic flames so intense I fear we will melt like altar candles.

The flames subside. He has me in his powerful embrace and I can do no more than revel in his magnificence. It hits me like a bolt of lightning: he will always catch me, I will never fall; he will always love me and keep me safe forever. What more can I ask for?

I wished for a prince and have been blessed with an angel.

***

The highlight of Mack's day was when he made the discovery that Elise Richards was the last person to speak to Dan Rizler. His understudy, D.C. Sheridan emailed him the list of calls just after lunchtime, at that moment when he was beginning to feel his four-part premise was a figment of his imagination. He just can't fathom why a man plotting to rape and kidnap an innocent young woman would bother ringing an estate agent.

After he kicks his shoes off; relieves the after-dinner glass of its golden liquid and sits himself down in his favourite chair, he is ready to face what amounts to another square peg to slot into a round hole. In the time it takes him to read through the list of calls, he's convinced he's made a discovery: Elise Richards and Dan Rizler became friends after the rental agreement was signed for the Elm Gardens apartment. But *why*?

It's as if a light bulb goes on behind his eyes! He grins and shakes his head. "You both had a vested interest. Well I never!"

Of course, he knows it's purely hypothetical, but that doesn't stop him from digging out a roll of wallpaper from under the stairs and stretching it out ready for pasting over his dining table. Instead of paste he uses felt pens, and, instead of broad strokes, he scratches away, decorating the sheet with circles, arrows and lines that lead onto other lines and circles. After an hour spent scribbling, he has what looks like a complex network of connections. On the page there are four names and they are all linked to one another directly or by association.

All he needs now is proof.

***

In a room starved of light, I'm being roused from my sleep. "What time is it?"

"It's time to get up, darling. Get dressed. Wrap up warm and wear comfortable shoes."

I'm rubbing my eyes, still half asleep. "Where's the fire?"

He laughs, switches on the bedside lamp and hands me a cup of tea. "There's no fire. There's something I want to show you."

"It's 6.15 a.m. Can't it wait until the sun comes up?" I ask mid-yawn.

"No." He folds his arms and taps his foot impatiently.

"Do I have time to shower?"

"No need. We won't be gone long." He hands me my bathrobe. "Now be a good girl and get some clothes on, or else."

"Or else what?" I call out.

"Or else you'll miss it."

I do as I'm told; slipping on clean underwear, my jeans and a sweater. In less than ten minutes I'm dressed.

He hands me my jacket. "You might want to tie back your hair."

I grab a clip from my bag and scrape it back into a rough ponytail. "Are you sure I don't have to look my best?"

He reaches out for my hand and pulls me to him until out noses are touching. "You always look your best, because you are the best. Now take a deep breath and close your eyes. Don't open them until I say so. Alright?"

I haven't the slightest idea what his surprise is, but he's so insistent I'm happy to go along with it.

"Are your eyes closed?"

I nod.

"Good. Hold tight." He wraps his arms around me until I am no more than a small bundle of flesh and bones encased in something much more durable.

I feel kind of woozy and respond with a shudder to a gust of air crossing my face. From somewhere there is the sound of nature, of birds and of wind brushing against leaves.

He releases his grip, encouraging me to stand upright, his hands on my forearms. "Open your eyes," he urges.

What I'm confronted by causes me to lean back and gasp. "What the hell!"

He laughs softly. "Don't worry. You're perfectly safe. We're here to see the sunrise over the Tianmen Mountain Range."

I reach out to hold onto his arm. "How did we get here?"

He smiles softly. "I brought us here so we could see the sunrise together. It will rise in four minutes."

"And you're sure about that are you? Not five or ten ..."

He shakes his head and pulls me to him. We are standing side by side. Instinctively I enfold him in my arms and feel an unimaginable intimacy brewing between us.

"All I can see are shadows but I sense we're high up." He nods and rests his chin on my hair. To my left a luminescent glow appears; dawn approaches from the east and peeps over one distant peak, then another and another, flooding the sky with light. "Oh my God!" I declare, tears forming and overflowing until they're drizzling down my cheeks. My mouth falls open with the marvel of it all. Before us is the world in all its splendour; rivers, peaks, clouds and the sun-drenched sky; every element assembled to create this monumental canvas of natural wonders. And here we stand, on a walkway clinging to a mountain. I tear my eyes away from the view and look down and scream out loud.

"Argh!" I bury my face in his chest, but that familiar rumble of laugher reassures me I am in the safest of hands.

"Don't be scared. Look." He eases me away from his body and we look down together at the glass, metre-wide walkway. "It's the best way I could think of to show you my world, Beth. This is Heaven's Gate Mountain. Aptly named, I think." He takes hold of my hand and presses it against his lips. With his right arm he presents a wide arc. "You see?"

There are more things in heaven and earth, Beth,
Than are dreamt of in your philosophy."

I snigger at his quote from Hamlet. "I see that now." I reach up and kiss his cheek. "Thank you for sharing this with me. It's an experience that will stay with me forever. I just wish I'd brought my camera, although I doubt any picture I take will do it justice."

He slides his hand into the pocket of his jeans. "I thought you might need this." He hands me my camera.

I smile appreciatively. "Thank you. You think of everything."

He senses his cue. "Not everything. I didn't think that our arrangement would be so hard on you. I assumed too much and yet you have given me your time and your love." He lifts up my chin and I'm held spellbound; the early morning sunlight has exposed the flashes of cerulean in his eyes and I can't help but be bewitched by their luminosity.

"I intend to make this adventure of ours truly memorable for us both, Beth. Beginning today." I feel his lips against mine in a soft kiss that communicates sincerity and love.

How could I not fall in love with this unique individual who personifies all that is most heavenly and handsome in this world?

He takes my hand and we begin our Skywalk. He points out peaks and follows the line of the S shaped road with his forefinger; he disperses clouds below us that threaten to ruin the view and points me in the direction of the rising sun so I might feel its heat on my face. I'm overwhelmed by his knowledge and his powers and his willingness to forsake all else for me.

Before we leave I edge him forward in front of me. From behind I lift up his arms into flying position. "This is our Titanic moment, Ayden. The best so far."

He takes hold of my hands and wraps them around his body. "Yes it is, and just the start of many. You'll see. Close your eyes, baby."

With his words ringing in my ears I do as he asks. In that split second I feel a little woozy, as before, and the wind brushing against my face.

"Open your eyes."

I should be surprised, but I'm not. He turns around and faces me, looking even more handsome than I had imagined him to be. "That's one hell of a trick."

He grins broadly. "I like to think it's one of my better ones."

Impulsively, I slide my hands around his neck, jump up and wrap my legs around his waist. "Let's go back to bed and dream of more adventures."

He hoists me up into a comfortable position. "Let's not."

I'm being carried to my bed and all I can do is giggle. "You're insatiable, Mr. Stone."

"This is true, Mrs. Stone," he declares, throwing me over his shoulder and smacking me softly on my right cheek, making me squeal. "Now let's see if we can turn those giggles into moans."

Oh my ...

20

B reakfast is served on the dining table; I delve into an array of hot and cold dishes with a heavy helping of contentment. Sharing the memories of last night's wall sex and this morning's playful romp, we're glancing furtively at each other, smiling when we catch each other's eye.

I'm able to face each day with a profound sense of weightlessness; it's as if a burden has been lifted from my shoulders. I'm free to take life as it comes and approach each new adventure with a greater sense of purpose and dedication.

I catch Ayden discretely checking his watch. "Do you need to be somewhere?"

"Unfortunately yes, but only for an hour. I gave our three guilty offenders 24 hours to repay what they had embezzled before taking it to a higher authority," he states, pushing back his chair and throwing down his napkin.

"A higher authority you say? And who would that be, God Almighty?" I smirk, finding my comment amusing.

He places one hand in his trouser pocket and the other on my hair. His lips brush against my forehead. "Are you ridiculing my choice of phrasing, dear wife?"

"I wouldn't dare," I mutter, raising my eyes to catch the humour sparkling in his eyes.

"I will be one hour and then we'll decide what to do. We can go sight-seeing or take the jet to our honeymoon destination. Let me know what you'd prefer so I can have them prepare for the flight." He moves towards the door.

Before he leaves, I say what needs to be said. "Remember to include Jake in your business transactions. He has something to give you that may prove useful."

He glances back. "And what might that be?"

"It's a pen drive with the actual and reported figures from your three dishonest employees," I announce.

"Is it indeed? In that case I'll give him a call."

"That's why he wasn't at the meeting," I call out. "He was gathering evidence together for you."

He leaves without replying and I'm left alone in this palatial suite to muse over recent events. But this is not the time to ponder. In the limited time I have I must take care of a number of things.

My iPhone indicates I have a couple of texts to reply to.

Charlie's comments about Belgian men and cheese make me chuckle and her late night selfies remind me of just how much of a firecracker she is. What a lifeline she has been all these years.

Once my laptop has booted up I go straight to email and give thanks when I see Patrick's response. He has attached a copy of Ayden's Birth Certificate and it opens straight away. Naturally it's slightly out of focus, but the names that matter can be easily read.

Saffir Ayden Pierre - Isabel Françoise Pierre

I can't believe I haven't asked him when his birthday is. Now September 7th will be forever etched in my brain. I jot down all the details on letterhead stationery conveniently laid out on the bureau; I hope these dates and names will be all the information I need to move forward with my plan.

I finish of my glass of orange juice and wait for my digital scrapbook to load. I'm scrolling through, barely able to recognise the entries. They're light-hearted and playful, exuding love - and yet, if you read between the lines, it's possible to detect my inner sadness. Regardless, I have to press on. Ayden must remember these days if and when he returns to me and this record of time spent in foreign lands will serve as a memory aid. I listen to Katy Perry and *I'm Thinking of You* ...

NOVEMBER #5

"I would not wish any companion in the world but you."
William Shakespeare: The Tempest.

Aren't you the clever one! You solved the crime and saved the day! The embezzlers have been exposed, but you paid the price with your time and volunteered Jake to be my minder. It was a selfless act. I made him endure a session of clothes shopping and bag carrying and we were soaked in the rain so ... quite an eventful day for us both.

When I got back you were waiting for me. We haven't been apart for days and I needed to hear your voice and feel your hands on my body, the way I always do. We didn't make it to the bedroom. There's a lot to be said for wall sex! (Blushing)

Today you arranged a sightseeing trip to The Tianmen National Park where we watched the sun rise over mountain tops from a glass walkway perched precariously on the side of Heaven's Gate Mountain. I loved every minute of it, Ayden. Thank you. These things we share are so precious to me...

I stop. My fingers are frozen and my hands begin to shake so violently I think I may hurt myself. I slam them down on my thighs and inhale - deeply, slowly and hold each breath until I feel able to release it. Before I can stop myself, words spew out like blood from a severed artery;

... every day I think of what we had and what I may never experience again with you. I know I promised to always take care of you and I'm trying so hard to do that, Ayden, but you just don't know...

He has me cornered. He seduces me with your words and your smile and yesterday he brought the heavens down upon me because I laughed when he wasn't there. Now he knows my body; he touches me with your hands, and it's the familiar heat from your body that makes me burn.

I must be everything he wants me to be; to do everything he wants me to do if I'm to have any hope of seeing you again.

You know I would do anything to save you. My betrayal is guiltless. If I must sell my soul to the devil to save you, I will. We will be reunited, baby; if not in this world then in the next - because I can't live this lie indefinitely. I have to know we'll meet again for my life to have any meaning.

So be strong. I'll look for you in those heated moments when our two worlds collide; when we are locked together, inseparable, for ever. Please forgive me ...

Yours, Beth ...

I come to my senses and snap out of my moment of defeatism. Confounded by the sincerity of my confession I read it through as if stumbling across it for the first time. I'm reminded of the person I have become; I am the archetypal princess, imprisoned in a tower; surrounded by wealth and luxury beyond her wildest dreams and yet finding little joy in this gilded cage. But I have to wonder: is this where I belong? I am guilty of many crimes, some too shameful to name.

Remorse thrums through my body like the remnants of a thunderstorm. Yesterday's storm has dispersed and I must see to it my internal tempest does the same. I have thirty minutes to rediscover my game face or everything I have done will have been for nothing. I let the music play while placing the cursor on the last letter of my confession, and hit delete until every single word has been removed. Only I know what secrets were revealed on that blank page and it has to stay that way.

Feeling in need of some sunshine I forgo the sightseeing tour even though I know there is much to be seen and experienced. Ayden comes to this part of the world so often I can come with him any time. Having left Jake to handle things we vacated our hotel room and make the midday dash to Hong Kong International airport.

By my watch we're three hours into our seven and a half hour flight to Cairns, Australia, home of the Great Barrier Reef and our next honeymoon destination. Our estimated arrival time is 8 p.m. giving us time enough to transfer via helicopter to Bederra Island.

Feeling very proud of himself, he is skimming through pages on his iPad, showing me where we're going. I'm close to tears: it's paradise found.

He's sitting across from me in one of the plush leather chairs on the mini-jet. He's dressed down for the occasion in dark blue jeans; his sky blue shirt complements his skin tone and does wonders for his eyes.

If the Heaven's Gate Mountain was the crown in a fine array of priceless experiences, the Great Barrier Reef is set to be another jewel in that crown. As we approach for landing all I see is a blanket of midnight blue illuminated by the dazzling light of the moon. It's stunning.

A brief 30-minute helicopter ride later, we reach our destination. This tropical island beach resort is a cross between Shangri-La and a scene from Robinson Crusoe. I struggle to find the words to describe this overwhelming feeling of escapism.

Who does this?

"So what do you think? Do you like what you've seen so far?" he asks, taking hold of my hand and giving it a gentle tug.

"No," I answer, casting my eyes to the heavens and closing them to take in the fragrance of wild flowers and pure sea air. "I love it."

"That's the response I was aiming for." He offers me the widest smile; I can't help but mirror it and continue on my merry way to our villa.

Unpacking takes no time at all. Ayden sits out on the deck wearing khaki cut-offs and a body-hugging V-neck T-shirt in pale green. I've slipped into a pair of denim shorts and a pink crop top. Out on the horizon a lonesome ship catches my eye, but only momentarily; I return to him, drawn to his captivating presence and, from behind, throw my arms around his neck.

He reaches up to me and takes a handful of hair. "Come and sit here next to me."

I circle the sofa and sit on his left side, our thighs touching, his arm around my shoulders, pulling me in close.

Giddy with excitement I speak first. "I can't wait to see what it's like in daylight, can you?"

"I'm afraid you will have to wait, unless ..."

Knowing what's coming next I rest my palm on his pectoral muscles. "Please, no show- boating tonight. Let's just have a night with no storms or whistle-stop tours of mountain ranges. There are snacks in the fridge and a selection of drinks. Let me get you something." I prepare to stand. "What would you like?

He takes hold of my hand and caresses it with his lips. "Only you, Beth."

"You already have me," I reassure him. Positioning myself across his lap, I pull up my knees so I can fold myself into his body. "We'll have the best of times here, Ayden."

"We will indeed." With nature behind us, sea in front and the carefree whisper of the evening breeze, we put the pressures of the urban jungle behind us and focus on each other.

"You want to name this feeling?" I ask, having timed my moment to perfection.

Before answering he inhales deeply, allowing the air in his lungs to escape in one long, stress-free wheeze. "Contentment."

He can't see my face but he must sense I'm smiling. "Good word. I feel the same way. This is one box I can quite happily tick off thanks to you."

He's shaking his head. "I'm afraid I can't take the credit for this, Beth. The villa, the transport – everything was already booked. I have simply been following a pre-existing plan."

I raise my head from his chest. "This wasn't your idea?"

"No. It was arranged over a week ago. I am simply allowing fate to determine the proceedings." He strokes my hair while speaking.

"I can't believe all this was planned." I push away from him, resting my right hand on his shoulder. "So what's next on the itinerary?"

"Now that would be telling, my darling. What kind of adventure would this be if every chapter was laid out for all to see?"

Having been alerted to this startling news, I press him further. "But I thought you had to get back to ASMI..."

"Not at all. Everything has been taken care of," he assures me confidently. "Now that Hong Kong debacle has been resolved, I'm all yours." He grazes my cheek with his thumb and brushes across my chin with the pad, finding the crevice beneath my mouth. Our eyes are locked together, held fast by an invisible force; with every reassuring word I'm being drawn closer to him. Unable to look away, I close my eyes and fall into his embrace. He wraps his arms around me protectively and I feel the warmth of a heat shield diffusing through my body.

"We're all that matters. Time will stand still and I will be yours ..."

"... for ever!" I exclaim, to his delight.

"Yes," he sniggers. "That can be arranged."

I hear his subtle declaration but better judgement tells me to move on. Now is not the time to discuss matters of such magnitude. Feeling my movement, he releases his grip.

I sit bolt upright. "Have you ever been skinny-dipping?"

He smiles, and it's a wide toothy grin reminiscent of our Roman holiday. It hits me hard and, somewhere deep down inside I feel the pointed edge of a knife piercing my soul. Concealing my wound, I forge ahead. I'd do anything to see that look again on my husband's face.

"No, I can't say I have." He licks his lips. "But it sounds like something I might enjoy."

I clamber up from his knee. "I've never done it before either, so it'll be a first for us both."

"Even better."

Hand in hand we stroll down to the water's edge; the sand still retains some of the day's heat and cushions our feet as we near the rippling waves, gingerly dipping in toes and ankles. I release my hand and unbutton my shorts, push them down with my panties and toss them up the beach. I pull my crop top up over my head and throw it in the same direction. He stands before me utterly mesmerised.

"What are you doing?" he asks, looking about him furtively.

"I'm skinny-dipping." I turn towards the ocean and begin to take a tentative step into the rippling tide.

"You are?"

I glance back at him over my shoulder. "Yes ...You said you wanted to."

"That's before I realised what it was!"

I'm beginning to feel very foolish standing with water up to my shins wearing no more than a smile; a smile that is quickly fading. "Why didn't you ask me what it was?"

"Because you assumed I knew."

Tiring of the conversation I continue to stride forward until the water is above my knees. "If you're scared of being seen you can always block out the moon." I start to giggle, realising how ridiculous that would sound to any normal person. I turn to face him and watch him mumble something inaudible, drag his T-shirt over his head and step out of his cut-offs. "Be careful. You don't want anyone to see your sexy body," I call out, laughing as the water tickles my waist.

He comes marching towards me. "I don't give a fuck about anyone seeing me. I don't want some voyeur getting an eye-full of you." He pulls me to him forcefully. "I don't want to share you with anyone. Not even your silhouette." His lips find mine and I wrap my arms around his neck instinctively.

"No one's here," I reassure him, tearing my mouth away from his long enough to catch my breath. I feel the hard prod of an erection against my hip and respond by lowering my hand to caress it. It appears to be buoyant, floating into my hand of its own accord; and I find it so amusing it makes me giggle.

"I love that sound, but I haven't the faintest idea why you're making it," he declares, grinning so excitedly I can see the laugher in his eyes reflecting, caught by the moonlight.

"It's because I'm in love with you and you make me happy," I reply not stopping to think through my answer.

He leans back, taking my words to heart. A smile forms slowly and a moment of intimacy ensues. "I love you more, Beth. Making you happy is my dearest wish." He slides both hands around my cheeks and into my hair. The dampness of his palms cools my heated skin and I am reminded of the lengths to which my lover will go to keep me safe and satisfied. I jump up and wrap my legs around his waist and, forgetting myself, kiss him with the fervour of a woman craving intimacy and love.

With long strides, he takes us deeper into the ocean. The water undulates and rises as far as my breasts, then my shoulders, but all I can feel is him: a powerful presence entering me and moving back and forth to the rhythm of a breaking surf.

I pull away from his suffocating kiss and lean backwards into the inky blackness, staring up at a midnight sky encrusted with stars. Slowly he gyrates his hips and begins to spin me around until the water takes hold of my hair and I am swallowed up by the sea.

"See, feel and be part of the universe. Give yourself to me," he commands, claiming all of creation.

The authority with which he speaks captures my imagination; his words touch my primeval being and I arch into him, drowning in lust. I cry out until his name becomes lost to the wind. Only his guttural moan remains, sending shock waves ocean-deep, proclaiming our love.

The endless sea that stretches out before us suddenly surges; waves come crashing over our heads and I am lifted from the foam coughing and spluttering. Once we reach the beach, Ayden lays me down, peeling strands of saturated hair from my face.

"You're alright, Beth. Clear the sea water from your throat and breathe normally." He sits back on his thighs and pulls my head across his knees. "You're going to be alright. It's not your time."

I look up and see the face of the man I love; there are worry lines around his eyes and his brow is furrowed with concern. I try to speak but liquid dribbles from my mouth as I continue to clear my throat of sea water.

He slips his arms beneath me and lifts me to him in an almighty heave. "Hold tight, let's get you into bed."

Suddenly, feeling bone tired, I rest my head against his chest, becoming aware of the beating of a heart over-dosed on adrenalin. I have no idea what just happened; but, whatever it was, it nearly killed me. If it hadn't been for his quick thinking and brute strength I don't know what would have become of me.

I will remember this night, and I will remember his intrepid rescue with gratitude.

***

Mack anxiously waits for the Manager at Taylor and Main Estate Agents to open the door. He taps the glass with impatient knuckles and is greeted by a young blond lady wearing a painted smile and high heels.

"Sorry to keep you waiting," she says, flipping round an open sign. "Come in and take a seat by my desk."

He follows her to one of two desks by the display of rental properties, imagining Dan Rizler doing the exact same thing not so long ago. As soon as he flashes his badge she goes in search of the Manager, promising to be back "in a flash."

To pass the time, Mack eyes the properties on offer, matching monthly rent to square footage and locality. He tears himself away when he hears voices approaching.

"Detective Inspector Bowker, good morning. I'm Trisha Hargreaves, the Manager. I assume this is about Elise?"

He nods. "Yes, it is."

"Please come into my office." She outstretches her right arm. "Can I get you a cup of coffee or tea?"

"No thank you." He's not one for coffee mornings.

The door closes and, away from prying eyes and ears, Mack begins his subtle interrogation. "How long had Elise Richards worked here?"

Trisha reaches for her folder of 'Employees,' only stopping when she comes to the letter R. "Yes, here it is." She points at the document. "Elise has been working for us in one capacity or another for ten years. She was a valued employee and a friend. I will miss her. In fact, I can't believe she's gone. What a terrible way to go, so ..."

Before she gets into her stride, Mack interrupts. "Yes it was."

"Have you arrested the man who was driving the car? Was he drunk?"

Feeling the sting of her questions Mack deflects. "No and no. We're still investigating. In fact, we believe it may have been a tragic accident."

"You can say that again," she gushes. "We were only having a drink the night before."

His lets her ramble on.

"It was Marie's 21st birthday." She points to the door and he assumes she means the blond on reception. "We headed over to the wine bar down the road for a couple of drinks.

Usually Elise doesn't bother, but this time she agreed to come along. She said she could do with a drink."

He interjects, "Did she say why or what was wrong?"

"No, she tended to keep herself to herself and we knew better than to pry. If she got wind that you were showing an interest, she'd clam up. I'm not sure why." She smiles amicably.

"Was she seeing someone?"

"Not seriously. She had been out with one of our customers a couple of times but she wasn't into him, if you know what I mean. They were just friends." She shrugs her shoulders.

"Do you know his name?" Mack has his pen poised.

"Dan Rizler. She arranged for him to rent the third floor apartment at Elm Gardens. He was having trouble with a flat mate or something and was in a hurry to move in. She handled the paperwork and he bought her a drink. That's how they became friends."

Mack puts down his pen so he might give her his full attention. "How many times did she see him?"

"Two or three times, I think. She didn't tell me, but she brought a case to work so she could change clothes; that's how I knew."

Mack prepares to commend her on her vigilance. "That was very observant of you."

She flicks her hair back behind her ears and prepares to regale him with more observations. "I like to keep my eyes open." She smiles and he offers her one in return as encouragement. "I do recall a funny thing that happened while we were having a drink, though."

"Funny how?" he asks, giving her the opportunity to enlighten him.

"Not funny ha-ha, but funny in a strange way." She holds back, feeling a little embarrassed. "At least I thought so."

"Please ... I'd love to hear." He sits back and folds his arms, signalling his interest.

As if about to tell a story, she leans forward, places her elbows on the table and begins gesturing. "It was about 9 o'clock and we'd had a couple of drinks. The guys from the other branches had come over and there was about eight of us. We were having such a laugh. Even Elise was beginning to thaw. She'd had a couple of glasses of wine and well ... you know ..."

Mack nods.

"We were just messing around when this young guy comes over. He had one of those containers, you know, the ones they use to collect for the homeless or for the RSPCA? He was collecting for the RSPCC. He came over to our table and Mike, from the Kensington office, who's a bit of a smart arse asked him what he was collecting for." She laughs at the memory. "The young guy said "for children" and Mike said. "In that case you can bugger off. I won't be having any ..." She continues laughing but noticing Mack's disapproving look, clears her throat, straightens her blouse and picks up where she left off.

"Anyway, Elise grabs her bag and says she's leaving. We all say goodbye, but on the way out I notice she took £20 out of her purse, folded it into a small square like she's doing origami, and slipped it into the container. I jumped up and went over to her - you know, to say goodbye properly, and I heard the young guy say, "Thank you. You're not like them." And she answered, "No, I'm not. I'm much worse." With that she left; and that was the last time I saw her."

Mack sits in quiet contemplation; he bites his lip and looks her in the eye, hoping to extract every minute detail. "How did she look when she said it?"

She shrugs her shoulders. "Serious."

"Okay." He flips the cover over his non-existent notes, stands and offers her his hand, checking her name plate on her desk. "Thank you, Miss. Hargreaves; you've been very helpful."

"Is that all? I'm not sure I have, but thank you. Elise was not much of a socialiser but she was reliable and a hard worker. There was talk of her having her own branch in a year or so and she was voted employee of the month twice last year." She bows her head and taps on her file. "She'll be missed."

Mack makes his way to the door. "I'm sure she will. Goodbye."

In the time he's been inside the noise on the high street has increased to a crescendo of urban sounds. Speed-walking he makes it back to his car in record time and slumps into the driver's seat feeling stunned by what he's heard. By her own admission Elise was guilty of many shameful things. Now he strongly suspects that one of them involved sanctioning the kidnapping and rape of Elizabeth Stone, by Mr. Rizler.

21

November #6

"I love thee, I love but thee with a love that shall not die.
Till the sun grows cold And the stars grow old."
William Shakespeare.

Saturday

While you're checking emails, I'm sipping coffee on the deck, trying to find my bearings. You chose this villa for us knowing I would love it, and I do. I've been taking photos all morning and here they are. There are a couple of us I set on the timer, but most are pictures of this tropical haven.

Listening to Temper Trap, I am singing along experiencing such a *Sweet Disposition*. I add the collage of photos to the scrapbook page with a couple of captions. Each photo has been lovingly taken, capturing the unique interior, the polished flooring, the luxury furniture and accessories and especially the vaulted ceiling. I include a couple of pictures of Ayden raising a mug of coffee and another looking utterly gorgeous as he climbs out of the pool, drenched and glistening.

I attach several snapshots of the view from the deck, having recorded it through the lens of an Olympus camera, but even it cannot capture the magnificence of this tropical setting. No photo can adequately reproduce the way the sunlight streams through the palm trees; the creaking of a hammock as it rocks to and fro in the warm breeze. It can't record the sound of birdsong, crickets and the sea as it laps against the shore. All this and more is Mother Nature's dawn chorus lovingly christening the start of each new day. What a sight to behold. What an experience to cherish, for ever.

You've made our honeymoon simply wonderful, Ayden. I feel so blessed to have your love. Last night when we made love in the ocean, it was as if the moon and stars came together to create a magical backdrop. I love you more with every passing day. This is just the beginning, baby. We are making memories to last a lifetime.

Yours, Beth. X

Hearing Ayden approaching I remove my headphones, save and shut down. We're going scuba diving today and having not done it before, I'm apprehensive, particularly after last night's near catastrophe. My highly skilled companion assures me I will be perfectly safe, and I believe him.

November #7

"I will have poetry in my life. And adventure.
And love. Love, above all....
Not the artful, postures of love, but love that
over-throws life."
Shakespeare in Love."

Sunday

Yesterday we went scuba diving and saw coral of every imaginable colour. It's hard to believe that something so insignificant can become so impressive. A line of surf rose out of the ocean and we began our dive beneath the foam. There are countless species of fish and I swear we saw every one of them. You were

right to persuade me to scuba dive, Ayden. You held my hand and we did it together. I've never experienced anything like it. The fish were exquisitely beautiful. My favourite were the angel fish, the manta rays, and that sea turtle we saw that seemed to be smiling. (Laughing)

As you promised, you're getting me to experience everything, and for that I'm eternally grateful. What adventures we are having! No one could be happier than me right now and here's the photo evidence to prove it.

I love you more than life itself.

Yours, Beth X

Sunday begins with a leisurely a walk through the rain forest; leaves are weighted down with dew, and the much-needed moisture appears to be rising from the forest floor in a transparent sheet of light. Our guide, Lucas, points out the birds and the butterflies, plants and wildlife and I feel as if I have been transported to another world. All this talk of adventures rings true; all I can do is take hold of Ayden's hand and look on, awestruck.

We join some other guests for lunch but Ayden can't keep his eyes or his hands off of me. He offers me food from his fork, wipes away breadcrumbs from my lips and stops mid-mouthful to stroke my hair. He smiles at me so adoringly it brings tears to my eyes. I feel truly loved.

There are moments now when I forget who he *really* is – I've become so caught up in this charade. No man could love me more; I doubt even my husband could be more consumed by our love affair.

November #8

"All days are nights to see till I see thee,
And nights bright days when dreams do show
thee me."
Shakespeare: Sonnet 43.

Monday

Yesterday was the third day of our honeymoon and with every new day comes a new experience. We rose with the sun and watched it cast its spell over the reef, then took a walk through the rainforest. Lunch was spent with the other guests but we were terrible company! As usual, we only had eyes for each other. You insisted I wear a hat and apply plenty of sunscreen. You take such good care of me, baby.

Later on, you had the owners organise a boat to take us over to our own, private island for a dinner date like no other. The turquoise sea was simply stunning and then there was the sunset. The sky was ablaze with light; nature's magical medley of colours so bright I wished the day would never end. It was another perfect day. Thank you. You make <u>every</u> day so special. You're the man of my dreams, baby, and I love you more with every passing day. Enjoy the photos I have included.

Yours, Beth X

The days have been passing so quickly! I've been sending some photos to Charlie so she can share this unforgettable experience with me. Yesterday we had a lazy day on the beach and I snorkelled for the first time. I got to actually cook a meal and we spent the evening curled up on the deck bed, watching the sun go down and sipping champagne; listening to John Legend and getting *So High*. It was another glorious day in paradise.

Today is Tuesday, our last day here, I listen to Damien Rice singing Cannonball, while gathering bits and pieces together to pack, anything I won't need for the next 24 hours. Tomorrow we will take the helicopter to Cairns, and then the company jet home. It would be so tempting to say 'let's stay here another couple of days,' but with each new day Ayden is being torn between business commitments and his desire to please me. Even though I know he would not refuse me, I simply can't put him in a position where he has to decide. After all, he *is* Ayden Stone.

Tonight we are going somewhere special. He won't say where but I'm going to wear the stunning red dress Jake bought for me in Hong Kong. I may never have a more fitting occasion.

This week we have been inseparable. I could not have asked for a more attentive husband. The adventure he promised has been delivered tenfold. Accepting his presence was difficult at first, but now telling the two men apart is virtually impossible. Some mornings I wake up and imagine this has not happened; that Ayden has been here all the time. Then, out of the blue, he demonstrates his unearthly powers and we're right back where we started. I know he suppresses them to appear human and he is at home here surrounded on all sides by the elements. We have basked in sunlight, dived into the ocean, walked through a rain forest, captured the wind in our sails, and he has excelled in everything. While he has circled the globe and Ayden had slept, I have relived the events of our honeymoon in glorious colour through a digital scrapbook. But how long can this continue?

With each passing day, my husband of old is fading like an old black and white photograph, so overpowering is his stand-in. He doesn't merely look the part, he possesses all that is most endearing in my husband; his sense of humour, his memories, his sexual prowess, his undying love for me. Loving him has not been an arduous task.

I hear voices coming from the next room. Ayden is sitting bare-chested, talking loudly and laughing; that alone reassures me it isn't a business call. I wander over and place my hand on his shoulder, noticing Jake up close on the screen. They are using Skype to catch up on business and personal news.

I lean in within camera range and smile happily. "Hello Jake. What's the weather like in Hong Kong?"

"Hello beautiful. I wouldn't know. I'm back in the UK and it's pretty grim over here. I see your tan's coming along nicely." He raises a roguish brow.

Realising I'm wearing only my bikini I pull back, feeling a twinge of embarrassment or something more pleasurable in response to his words.

Ayden offers a retort, "Don't you be worrying yourself with thoughts about my wife's sun tan, Jake. You can leave that to me, thank you."

Jake roars with laugher. "Yes, Sir. And what about those awesome dresses?" Jake asks taking no notice. "Are you getting to wear them, Beth?" He winks.

I sit across Ayden's knee and pull his arm over me to conceal a little more skin. "Actually I am. There's photo evidence."

"Very pleased to hear it. And what about the Reef? Been out on it much or has your husband locked you away for a couple of days?"

"No he hasn't. In fact, we're going out on a catamaran today, but we've snorkelled, and scuba-dived, and been swimming in the sea. It's simply wonderful; the villa, the beach, the entire location couldn't be more beautiful. It's the perfect honeymoon destination."

"Awesome! I'll let you get back to the fish then." He's about to sign off. "Oh, by the way, I've asked Charlie to come with me to some fund-raising event this week. I'm sure she'll give you the low-down." He gives me a wink that hints at something wicked.

I chuckle and roll my eyes. "I'm sure she will. Just be nice, Jake; I don't want to come back to a heartbroken friend."

He shakes his head. "Oh ye of little faith." He sniggers and looks directly into the camera; I feel myself blushing, knowing he's inspecting my body.

Ayden has heard enough. "Anything else we can help you with Jake?" he asks dismissively. "Maybe a tour or the villa with Beth? "

"Nah, I'm not one for tours. I'm more of an outdoorsy kinda guy, but thanks for the offer."

Ayden pulls me close. "In that case we'll let you get back to your grim weather while we go and check out the view. He turns his laptop and points it in the direction of the sea. "Later, Jake."

"Awesome! Later you two."

Still positioned across his lap I turn to face my handsome husband. "Don't get jealous and cause a tidal wave, Ayden. He's only teasing. He knows what you're like." I caress his lips with mine.

"I realise that. But I don't like the way he looks at you, as if he would lick the sweat from your body if you asked him to," he says, becoming restless beneath me.

"That would never happen." I take his face in my hands. "One, because I wouldn't let him, and two, because I don't sweat, I perspire... and only when we're making love."

He grins at my reply. "I stand corrected."

"You do indeed." All this talk of perspiration and lovemaking is enough to disturb the peace. The proximity of his body and the way his eyes are flickering with a kind of frenzied excitement does something to me. I lick my lips and mail him my thoughts first class, knowing they'll reach their destination in seconds.

"You look at me like that, Beth, and even I won't be able to hold back," he says, his face morphing into a sensual smile. "All this sun and sea air has me feeling even more alive." His right hand tightens around my waist and edges upward; fingertips caress flesh and an exploratory thumb slips beneath the thin triangle of blue material covering my left breast. I move in to kiss him but he leans backwards out of reach.

"No. You'll have to settle for my hands, darling. Our lips mustn't touch. I want to see the way your lips swell and your mouth opens to gasp when I make you come."

His words excite me further.

With eyes still locked, he skilfully unties the bow at my nape, letting my bikini top slide from my breasts and flip over onto my abdomen. In a single movement the remaining bow beneath my shoulder blades is untangled and I am left in no more than bikini bottoms, which are now sodden and uncomfortable.

A low-throated growl announces his pleasure as he pumps and squeezes each breast in turn, his head dipping to feed and suckle like a new-born. I knot my fingers into his hair and yield to his sexual charisma, feeling the warmth of blossoming arousal, hearing my own moans of pleasure.

With acrobatic grace he tips me backwards, steadying me with a firm hand against my neck; with nothing to hold onto I let my arms fall to the floor, feeling weightless and secure. A familiar hand moves towards my bikini bottoms and slides under the fabric; it's warm and reassuring against my moist flesh. He arches his fingers, finding more space, and massages a swollen clitoris with the pad of his hand. "Now tell me, was this what you had in mind when you looked at me that way? To have my fingers here?" He moves toward my vagina, now soaked and ready for penetration.

"Yes," I pant.

"Or maybe here?" He inserts two fingers and pushes them inside until his hand is pressed up against me.

"Y ... es," I answer, breathless with want, aching with need.

"Then your wish is my command." Once again he finds my breasts and sucks hard, drawing my nipples deep into his mouth, causing me to whimper and moan.

"You're so wet for me, baby," he pants. "Come onto my fingers so I can watch you give yourself to me."

His grip tightens on my neck as he bends his finger into position and strokes me internally; his thumb massages my clitoris in small circles as I writhe into his hand and whimper like a woman experiencing sweet agony.

"I feel you tightening, you're close. Look at me."

With a single hand he raises my head and our eyes meet. Through my ecstatic haze I see the intensity of his arousal and the pleasure he experiences from my surrender. That triggers my own.

"That's it, hard and deep. Feel it, Beth."

I do.

I stretch out my legs, toes clenching, back arching. My entire body spasms and I throw back my head as the raging heat of an orgasm rips through me. My groin throbs with the flames that spread like wildfire through each clenching muscle as he continues to grind away at my insides with expert fingers.

"That's my girl."

I'm way past screaming and can only offer a kind of animalistic growl so deeply felt it's barely audible. When I'm able to speak, I call out his name, "Ayden!" and close my eyes to contain my tears. I am lying across his knees utterly sated and delirious with desire; too weak to even raise myself. All I can do is lift my arms and be hoisted into a sitting position. The smile on my face must be priceless.

"There you are," he says, smirking. "Are you feeling more like yourself now?"

"I'm not sure who I am when you do such weird and wonderful things to my body, Ayden," I reply softly, holding onto his shoulder with my left hand to steady myself.

"I do?"

My smile broadens. "Don't go fishing for compliments not when you have such a smug look on your face. You know exactly what you do to me." I kiss him chastely.

"Yes. I do, but as much as I would like to, I can't take the credit for that. I believe this face and these hands have a universal appeal. And, besides that, you're a very responsive woman...

"... with little self-control..."

He laughs quietly to himself. "I won't argue with that; but watching you lose control ranks up there with one of the most erotic events I have ever witnessed."

I can't conceal my surprise. "You rank them?"

He arches a brow. "Not as such, but I do have my favourites, it has to be said."

"Do I feature in any of them?" I ask curious to hear more.

"You feature in all of them, darling," he declares, caressing my left arm with his fingertips.

"I do?"

"Yes. Being inside your body is my idea of heaven on earth, Beth."

"Mine too. I miss us not being ... together."

"My delight comes from experiencing your surrender and your willingness to trust me."

"I do. I felt as if I was floating ... even flying."

"That's because you were. Angels are meant to fly, my darling, and you are an angel. You are unique in composition: beauty and innocence coalesced, a perfect specimen in form and substance.

I melt into his arms; our naked bodies amalgamate into one perfect bundle of sensuality. "Thank you. You make me feel so special. I will miss you so desperately when you go."

"I may go, but I will never leave you. Your safety is assured."

I loop a stray curl around my forefinger and play with his hair. "I have a proposition for you?"

His face is alight with humour and curiosity. "Do you? I'm intrigued."

"Alright we have an hour before we have to leave for our trip, and now that I have come down to earth, I propose to make love to you."

His mouth twitches as he tries unsuccessfully to suppress a coy smile. "Sounds promising."

"We can make love right here or I'll fuck you with my mouth." I raise my head feigning confidence. "Your choice."

"How long do I have to decide?" he asks playfully.

"Ten seconds ..."

"Very well."

While he strokes his chin pretending to be wrestling with his dilemma, I fold back the fingers of my right hand and then my left, counting the seconds.

"Time's up!"

"Both," he whispers.

"Well ... I'm not sure," I answer, shaking my head. "I think you may be taking advantage of my angelic nature."

He tips his head to the left, accepting his transgression. "You could be right."

Making a big deal out of my magnanimity, I shrug my shoulders. "But, seeing as we're on our honeymoon and I love you more than life itself then, I suppose, I could ..."

He's laughing and I'm rocking on his knee. "Said in true angelic fashion." He pulls my mouth onto his and tangles his hands into my hair. "You are truly adorable, Beth. I can't wait to be inside you."

Those words leave his mouth like a barrage of bullets. I've heard them before. When they were first said I was swept away, but know I'm caught in the crossfire. Ayden raises my chin; and I rediscover my smile and camouflage my sadness. This is a battle I cannot win and, resignedly, I fall to my knees.

We have showered and dressed for our outing and Ayden is drying his hair. I busy myself collecting various travel items for a day spent at sea in the midday sun and quickly slip on a pair of deck shoes. His laptop is still where he left it, facing the plate glass window. I saunter over to it and prepare to close the lid. On the screen there is an empty room - an office. When I check to see who is still on the other end of the Skype connection I gasp. It's Jake.

During our love making, we were still connected minus visuals but with sound. I hold my hand to my mouth, feeling my cheeks heating but, as the rosiness fades so does my embarrassment. Instead I'm gripped by fear. Listening into our ecstatic moans is bad enough but what did Ayden say, and what did I say? Did we reveal our deepest, darkest secret?

I hear Ayden approaching and close down the laptop, slam the lid down and head for the deck, my heart beating through my T-shirt.

He takes my arm. "All set?"

"Yes," I reply light-heartedly.

He picks up on my nervous smile. "Everything okay?"

I nod. "I'll tell you now ... I get seasick on long boat rides, especially when it gets rough."

He takes hold of my hand and kisses my fingers. "Don't worry. I'll see to it that the ocean remains like glass for you. Nothing and no one will ruin our day."

I think something and someone already has...

I stand on my tiptoes and kiss his cheek. "Thank you."

***

Mack is driving home from work, feeling like he has misread the entire situation. It's as if he has bestowed goodness upon Elise; goodness that simply was not there. Since finding out about her likely collaboration with Mr. Rizler, the world has become just a little murkier. The darkness that pervaded her childhood seems to have stayed with her like a stain on her heart.

He had been quick to pass judgement on Mr. Stone and to cast Elise in the role of the helpless victim, but now he's having second thoughts.

Maybe I was wrong...

The sound of his phone ringing breaks his moment of introspection. He rummages through his pocket and grapples with it before it rings off, answers and puts it on speaker.

"Mack, it's Phil at the morgue. You asked me to give you a call when we'd finished the autopsy."

He recognises the Pathologist's voice straight away. "Yeah, so how's it going, Doc? Any surprises?"

He sniggers. "Maybe? Depends what you call a surprise."

"Okay, fire away. What did Miss. Richards die of?"

"Well, that's an easy one. She had a fatal cervical spine injury at craniocervical junction C_1..."

"Whoa! Hold on there, Doc. Give me that again in plain English."

"In simple terms, her neck was broken. The car was hit side-on sending it into a spin, causing a whiplash effect and, as she wasn't wearing a seat belt, she was catapulted through the windscreen. She has facial injuries, cerebral contusions and multiple micro-haemorrhages."

"Alright, I get the picture. Are you saying, there was no way she could have survived the accident, even if help arrived sooner?" He has to know.

"No. And even if by some miracle she survived the crash, she would have been paralysed from the neck down and sustained some pretty gruesome facial injuries."

Mack indicates and pulls up in his drive. "Thanks Doctor Phil. That's straightforward enough. Send your report through the usual channels and we'll close the case. I appreciate you letting me know ..."

Phil is quick to point out, "There was one thing ..."

Mack pulls out the car keys and waits to hear more. "Is this the surprise you were telling me about?"

"I think it might be." He pauses. "I checked her next of kin and she has a mother listed but no children."

"That's because she didn't have any," Mack states.

"That's odd because she has a caesarean scar."

Mack sits up in his seat. "A what?"

"You know, a caesarean scar? She must have given birth."

"Now that *is* a surprise." He frowns and taps his chin with his car key. "I suppose she could have had a kid. She was married at sixteen, but divorced the guy at 22. Since then..."

Phil jumps in, "No! This is an old scar."

"How old?"

"I'd say around sixteen years by the type of cut and the scar tissue, maybe more." He sounds certain.

Mack is shaking his head. "I tell you, the more I hear about this woman the more I'm convinced she's a bloody mystery. She has more secrets than the KGB."

Phil sniggers. "She must have been a looker in her day. She has a good bone structure.".

"You've not taken a liking to her, have you?" Mack asks laughing softly.

"No but I can tell by the scars across her chest and her back that she's had it rough."

"Scars? What scars?" Mack asks, sounding shocked, but reminded of the video he watched.

"Some were recent but most of them were old, consistent with her being beaten. Maybe she was into some kind of sex games. Looks that way. But that wasn't my brief. All I'm concerned with is cause of death. No need to drag her name through the mud. But I tell you Mack, the press would have a field day with this one."

Considering who was driving the vehicle, Mack agrees wholeheartedly. "I can imagine." He lets out a deafening sigh. "Thanks, Phil. I owe you one."

"It's on the house. See you, Mack."

"Ha! That's what they all say, and then I get an enormous bill at the end of the month. Bye Phil." Mack is laughing but it's sour laughter. What he's learned is messing with his detective's mind.

What happened to the baby and why was she adopted the same year?

***

Still tingling from a mixture of salt water and sun on my skin, I wriggle into my red Chanel evening dress. We have both acquired a healthy glow, thanks to days resting outdoors and hours spent out on the ocean today on a catamaran. Little make-up is required; tinted moisturiser, a dash of mascara and matching lip-gloss is all I need. I place my platinum and sapphire bracelet in the safe and lock it away as I have done everything I value most in my life. My most precious of possessions are safely tucked away out of reach, but not out of mind.

My heels clip-clop noisily on the wooden floor and announce my arrival seconds before I actually appear. Outside on the deck photographic equipment has been assembled and inside Ayden is chatting with a familiar young gentleman. He looks so distinguished in his dinner suit and bow tie. He dressed before I could return to our bedroom and I'm unprepared for this vision of masculine beauty. He winks and gives me the kind of smile that tells me I look good, causing me to smile appreciatively in return. For a second or two I'm gripped by the memory of another time and place; a terrace in Rome, beneath the stars, bewitched by poetry and beloved by the man of my dreams: my prince. Where is he now, I wonder? Why, he's six yards in front of me.

Ayden reaches out a hand. "And here's the lady in question," he says proudly.

I acknowledge Josh's presence. "Hello Josh. What brings you to this part of the world?"

"A long-haul flight and a boat ride, Mrs. Stone," he says smiling. "This place is amazing. You two are living like castaways; well sort of ..." He scans the room, taking in its unique style and beauty. "This is an awesome place."

"Yes it is. " I take hold of Ayden's arm. "So where do you want us, Josh?"

"I'd like a couple of you in here and then some outside, if that's okay."

"Sure. You're the expert, you just tell us what to do."

Josh places down his beer and positions us on the sofa, then snaps another photo of us standing by the doorway. He makes his way outside and we follow.

Ayden unfolds my hand from his arm and holds it against his lips. "Beth, you look ravishing."

I raise my brows. "I do?" His eyes seem to have that scintillating sparkle I have come to adore. "This is one of the dresses Jake bought for me in Hong Kong. Glad you approve."

With my hair wrapped up into a neat chignon he is able to nuzzle my ear. "I don't approve of the fact he bought it for you but I do approve of the dress. Remind me to reimburse him."

I pick up the dress to step out onto the deck. "No need, it was a belated wedding present."

"It was?" he remarks, smirking even before his next comment leaves his lips. "And what did I get?"

I hold my head high and floor him with my most seductive of look. "You get to unzip me out of it later."

He sniggers. "In that case, I'm indebted to him for his thoughtful gift. " He slides a hand in place against the small of my back. "Remind me to thank him when we get back."

All I can do is laugh softly. Josh has everything organised. His camera buzzes and clicks. We shift position: we stand, we sit, we laugh; we look longingly into each other's eyes; we kiss, and it all feels very organic, instinctive. These photographs will be the cherry on the top of what has been the sweetest of subterfuges.

"I'll call the desk and have someone help you load your stuff into the boat," Ayden announces, scooting back inside.

Josh turns to me to speak. "I think you'll be pleased with the photographs, Mrs. Stone. You make a very handsome couple."

Feeling a little embarrassed I offer an amiable smile. "Thank you. I loved the ones you did for our engagement and the wedding."

"Thanks. You make my job easy." He slams a large equipment case shut. "I was wondering If you could give me a couple of quotes to go with the pictures ... like what word you'd use to describe your honeymoon."

Taken aback I stop to think through my answer. Only one word comes to mind. I turn to face him squarely. "Magical," I announce confidently.

He grins once again. "That's a great word."

I reach out to shake his hand. "I think so. Would you mind taking some of the villa?"

"Already did while you were getting ready. Mr. Stone thought you'd like to have them as a reminder of the time you spent here."

"Yes, that's right...I would." Unsettled by his response I move inside, leaving him to assemble his equipment to be loaded onto the boat waiting on the jetty. Ayden is returning from his office and I have to quickly steady my nerves. The thought of these photos becoming my only memento of our time here troubles me. Surely, I'll have my husband to share the recollections with, won't I?

22

We wave Josh off and return to the comfort of the villa, my mind still in turmoil. I tuck carefree strands of hair that were captured by the sea breeze behind my ears and turn to face Ayden, scattering my thoughts before he has time to piece together the cluster of uncertainties taking root there. He hands me a champagne flute and fills it with our favourite golden liquid, but before it touches my lips he proposes a toast.

"To our memorable days and unforgettable nights," he says, claiming the words as his own.

Sensing my hesitation he asks, "You don't like me using *those* words do you?"

They're only words ...

"I don't mind. Every day of our honeymoon has been memorable and every night has been unforgettable." I raise my glass. "I'm happy to celebrate those occasions. We have memories that will stay with us both for ever."

He smiles softly. "This is true. And we're about to experience one more." He takes the glass from my hand, places it on the coffee table and passes me my clutch. "Come." Taking my hand he leads me out onto the deck, allowing the delicate fragrance of wild flowers and the sea to work its magic; I close my eyes to absorb nature's heady scent and feel Ayden's arms enfolding me.

He whispers into my left ear. "Keep your eyes closed, Beth. I have a surprise for you."

I do as he asks and feel a little faint. The familiar gust of air on my face reassures me that this is something we have done before and I can't help but feel exhilarated at the prospect of being transported to another place.

Even before I open my eyes I'm aware of unfamiliar sounds. The sea has been replaced by the sound of voices, and the chill of the night air prompts the appearance of goose-bumps on my skin.

He releases me from his embrace. "You can open your eyes."

When I do as he says, I see him standing before me, his hands resting on my bare shoulders. His eyes are luminous, alive with desire and amusement; he's a man with a plan that he seems to have been devising for some time. Now that it has come to fruition, he looks mighty pleased with himself.

"Where are we?" I ask, unable to tear my eyes away from his.

"You tell me." He turns me around.

I gasp, knowing exactly where we are: it's Sydney Harbour. "Oh my God! I've always wanted to come here," I confess, sliding my hand around his waist. "How did you know?"

He wraps his arm around my shoulder and pulls me to him. "I didn't. It was a wild guess."

I'm trembling with excitement. "Well, you guessed right." I tip up my head and kiss his cheek. "Thank you."

"Don't thank me yet, you haven't seen the opera." He checks his watch and takes my hand. "Come on we'd better get inside."

Like a pair of young lovers we appear out of the shadows and mount the steps leading to the foyer. I lift the hem of my dress to try and keep up as he leads the way. "Have you been here before?" I ask, becoming increasingly breathless.

He swerves left then right, finding a passage through the crowd. "Yes, but I haven't seen Madame Butterfly here."

"I've not seen it either," I reply, pulling him to a dead stop. "Wow! There's the bridge." To my left is the iconic Harbour Bridge, an enormous stretch of steel with an arc of zigzag metal above it. Boats are passing beneath it, dispersing the lights reflected in the water. "It's so much bigger than I imagined it to be. "

"Yes, it's quite a landmark," Ayden agrees. "We'll take a closer look after the opera."

I nod and begin the trek again, dodging tourists - ladies in summer dresses, men in formal evening wear but none as handsome as my impatient escort.

We mount more steps and keep going, higher and higher until I tumble onto him breathless, barely able to speak. "Why couldn't you have us magically appear in our seats? That would have saved us so much time and energy," I ask, fanning my face with my clutch.

"Is that a serious question?" he asks, raising a thoughtful brow. "How would it be if we just *appeared?* That would take some explaining." He shakes his head. "It's not far now." He takes my hand. "We really must work on your physical fitness."

I release my hand. "There's nothing wrong with my physical fitness. I'm only human, unlike others I might mention who seem to act as if flying around the planet is a walk in the park."

He's laughing. "Perhaps we should have taken the lift?"

"What?" I cry. "There's a lift and you've had me climb two enormous flights of stairs?"

"They can hardly be classed as enormous," he maintains, slipping our tickets out of his inside breast pocket and showing them to a smartly dressed staff member positioned by a door way. The concert hall is right behind him.

Once inside the theatre, I start at my left, rotating my head clockwise, taking in the ornate wooden panelling and the cathedral configuration. The vaulted ceiling, the tiered seating, and the opulence gives me the overwhelming feeling of being somewhere exceptionally beautiful. I slide my fingers through his.

"This place is amazing," I declare, edging closer to our seats on Platform E, numbers one and two, overlooking the stage.

"I knew you'd love it," he says, seeing my joy mounting and revealing itself as a broad smile. "I think you'll love this opera too."

We take our seats. He calls an employee over and asks her to bring him a programme. Ten minutes later she returns; he rewards her with a generous tip and a smile.

I scan through the pages, commenting on costumes, looking down at the stage and marvelling at the wonder of it all. Thirty minutes ago we were standing by the ocean having our photographs taken, and now look where we are.

He catches me staring at him. "Are you assessing me, Mrs. Stone?" he asks, taking me by surprise.

Without a second thought, I answer, "Not assessing Mr. Stone, enjoying. Always enjoying." Before I can rethink my instinctive behaviour the lights dim, the orchestra finishes tuning their instruments and an expectant silence follows.

The first of three acts begins with muted lighting. Two women are huddled together under a tree, surrounded by cherry blossoms. Puccini's haunting melodies rise to the vaulted ceiling and resonate off the rafters that enclose this colossal space; melodic voices tear at the heartstrings. In the three hours that follow, every emotion is laid bare for the delectation of a grateful audience.

As the final act draws to a close I grip Ayden's arm, knowing what's coming but wishing for a less tragic resolution. Surrounded by scarlet rose petals, Butterfly, the abandoned bride, bids a sorrowful farewell to her son and takes her own life. The lights fade to black and the music dies away until there is only the hushed sound of snivelling.

I turn to him, my eyes glossy with tears. I've been so moved by the experience, I can barely speak. He respects my need for time to arrange my thoughts before we show our appreciation for the magnificent performance with applause while the cast hold hands and bow repeatedly.

Taking our time, we leave the theatre hand in hand. Many of the guests have found their voices and are speaking enthusiastically about the set and the music. I'm still processing what I've seen and heard in this chapter of our unbelievable adventure. There's little left to experience, surely.

We took a leisurely stroll around the harbour. I felt over-dressed and Ayden removed his tie, draping it loosely around his open collar. Now we're sitting by the window in Aria Restaurant, having enjoyed roasted Holmbrae duck breast with black figs and macadamia nuts. I'm spooning Valrhona caramélia chocolate into his mouth, and he's sharing his coconut ice-cream. Madame Butterfly's tragic demise has been forgotten and I fear the Clare Valley 1996 Aberfeldy Shiraz that he took so long selecting is making me tipsy.

The picture-postcard view across the harbour holds my attention and it takes a gentle squeeze from Ayden's hand

across the table to remind me that this is real, I am here and
...

"You're lost in thought," he remarks. "Anything you want
to share?"

"Since when did you need my permission to know what
I'm thinking?" I ask, made bold by the wine.

He gives my hand another squeeze. "Since you learned
how to shut me out."

I laugh to conceal my embarrassment. "I didn't know I
could do that."

He reaches for his wallet. "You can do many things, my
darling, most of which you're blissfully unaware of." He
signals for the waiter to bring the bill.

"Really? Like what?" I rest my chin on my right palm and
wait, wide-eyed, to hear more.

"Let's pay the bill, return home and discuss this further,"
he says, smiling seductively at the prospect of us being alone. I
reach into my clutch for lip-gloss and take out my camera. The
waiter offers to take our photo and we gaze into the camera,
but the harbour is a blur behind us.

Standing outside the restaurant, I have the waiter taking
several shots of us with the iconic backdrop. I take a couple of
snaps myself and Ayden pulls me close for the classic arm-
outstretched shot I have come to love. All I can do is take one
last look, wrap myself around him and close my eyes.

"Let's go home."

***

Mackenzie Bowker has spent the best part of a week
investigating a road traffic accident and he has a heap of
information to write up, but before he does, he has scheduled
a meeting with his superior officer, Chief Inspector Malcom
Royle. They have been colleagues and friends for nearly
twenty years, and there has always been a bond of trust
between them. Mack will not be happy until he has discovered
every detail of the crash. and if that means unearthing secrets
that have remained buried for decades so be it.

He straightens his tie and enters the Chief's office. It's
located on the sunny side of the building and the Chief is little
more than a silhouette sitting behind a desk in a high backed

chair. Mack doesn't wait to be asked to sit, he simply drops into a chair and begins ...

"How's the wife Malc, is she still breeding Shih Tzus?"

"Course she is! Obsessed with the little buggers. We've had an extension built to keep them out of the bloody house," the Chief replies, shaking his head.

"Could be worse. They could be Great Danes." Mack laughs at his own joke.

"I suppose so." He laughs and leans forward. "So are we going to talk about dogs or is there something more important you'd like to discuss? Word is you've been putting in some hours with this Richards case."

"Yeah. It's had more twists and turns than Brands Hatch." He takes out his notebook.

The Chief is chuckling. "Don't tell me you're still using bloody notebooks! What happened to your iPad?"

"I couldn't be bothered with all that finger pointing. By the time I'd set it up I'd forgotten what I wanted to write. These books have everything I need in them." He licks his thumb and turns back to the start of his investigation.

"OK, let's have it!"

Mack clears his throat, readying himself for what he knows will be a long winded explanation. "Well, I became curious when I discovered Miss. Richards was connected to Dan Rizler. Remember ... that guy who attacked Mrs. Stone in the school ..."

The chief nods and purses his lips unsure of what's coming next.

"Turns out Mr. Stone, who was driving the car, had known both his wife and Miss. Richards for a couple of decades, and he ..."

The chief holds up his right hand. "Hold on. I thought forensics and the crash investigators had proven she tried to kill them both. She had a knife and she took the wheel ..."

"Yes, she did but ..."

"So why the fuck are you dragging Ayden Stone into this? He's the victim, right?"

Mack is surprised by the adjustment in his demeanour. "Yes ... but ..."

"There's no 'but's' about it. Have you found out anything to suggest that anyone other than two dead, crazy bastards were responsible for bringing about their own deaths?"

Mack backs off. "No."

"Then the job's finished. No harm done. Mrs. Stone lives to fight another day, and Ayden Stone gets to keep his throne and remains king of the castle."

What?

Mack sits back in his chair, dumbstruck, sucker punched by police politics. He folds over the front cover of his note book and arranges his thoughts. "So, I'm done. We can all rest safe in our beds at night knowing they're both six feet under. The fact that Elise Richards was repeatedly raped as a child, and Rizler attacked and probably assaulted untold numbers of female students is no concern of mine, right?"

"I didn't say that, Mack." He takes a breath. "Look, there are people who would rather this whole thing just went away. You know what I mean?"

Nodding listlessly, Mack stands and turns to leave. He takes hold of the door handle, but stops before he turns it, spinning around to face the Chief. "The Elise Richards's of this world are still out there. No one is reading them bedtime stories. Someone recently told me that the *real monsters* are out there. Looks like there's one in here, too."

Throwing the door wide open he leaves, making his way down the corridor and back to his corner office on the sunless side of the building, feeling dispirited and deflated. He calls out insolently, "See you around, *Sir.*"

***

In the blink of an eye we're back at our temporary home on our island paradise. I open my eyes to see scented tea lights arranged around the decking area and a fancy bottle of something expensive-looking chilling in an ice bucket. It couldn't be more romantic.

"Did you arrange this?" I ask, standing to one side, looking out to sea.

"Yes. I instructed the staff to have everything ready for our return. It's our last night here and I wanted it to be ...

unforgettable." He sniggers, remembering my disapproval of the word. "But I still have a couple of things up my sleeve."

I take hold of his hand. "I'm not sure I can take much more tonight. I'm suffering from surprise overload."

"Then perhaps you should sit down ... but before you do, let me look at you." He edges away from me to the sofa, removing his jacket and tossing it to one side. He reaches for his shoes and unties the laces, removes his socks and places them together to the left of the chair. Unselfconsciously, he spreads himself out, adopting a familiar pose; arms stretched out across the cushions and his right leg crossed over his left knee. I don't think he has ever looked more handsome.

"Ayden ..."

"Just stand, Beth. Please ..."

I do, unsure of what to do with my hands or how to position my feet. He rotates his finger on his right hand indicating I should turn around. I'm smiling, feeling a little self-conscious but taking great delight in the pleasure he's experiencing by simply looking at me. Adoration is a powerful aphrodisiac.

"Seen enough?" I enquire, realising I have my thumb nail in my mouth. "I'm getting a backache standing here in these heels."

He smirks. "Wait one moment. There's something missing."

I look down at my dress; then, as I raise my head, I feel something tumbling gentle down from above. From somewhere up in the clouds red rose petals are falling, caressing my bare shoulders, fluttering over my nose, and gathering at my feet until I'm standing in a circle of of them. I turn my face skyward, enjoying the scented veil of nature's bounty as it covers my face and hair.

On hearing Ayden's voice I turn to face him.

"O my Luve is like a red, red rose
That's newly sprung in June;
O my Luve is like the melody
That's sweetly played in tune.

So fair art thou, my bonnie lass,

So deep in luve am I;
And I will luve thee still, my dear,
Till a' the seas gang dry.

Till a' the seas gang dry, my dear,
And the rocks melt wi' the sun;
I will love thee still, my dear,
While the sands o' life shall run.

And fare thee weel, my only luve!
And fare thee weel awhile!
And I will come again, my luve,
Though it were ten thousand mile."

All I can do is applaud. "That's one hell of a trick," I announce, taking his hand and stepping clear of the scattering circle of red. "Robert Burns captured the moment beautifully. Thank you for reciting it."

"My pleasure. Take off your shoes."

I kick them off and stand next to him, significantly shorter. "Where are we going?"

"You'll see..."

And I do. On the beach is a four poster bed with white voile curtains tied back at the corners. "Wow! When did that arrive?" I ask, lifting my dress with my free hand.

"I had the staff bring it down to the beach while we were at the theatre. I could have ... arranged it but it would have caused a few unwanted questions. Shall we go and get comfortable?"

"Yes. I'd like that."

The sand has still retained some of the day's heat and it's soft between my toes. When we reach the bed I notice a glass hurricane jar with a scented pillar candle and an ice bucket waiting for us at the base. Inside is a large bottle of Perrier, sitting beside two crystal tumblers.

I can't conceal my surprise. "What! No champagne?" I ask, crawling up on the bed.

"I think we've had enough, don't you? And, besides, you'll need a clear head to appreciate what I have to say." He smirks, leaving me in no doubt about that.

I make myself comfortable on the bed; my head nestles into the soft pillow; the fingers of my left hand are entwined with Ayden's. "What a wonderful surprise. I've never seen so many stars." I stare up at the millions of pinpricks twinkling like sequins on a gown.

"You're not alone in that respect. Most people's lives at so cluttered with light and self-absorption, they seldom look up."

I give his hand a squeeze. "Most people could never afford to come to a place like this."

"This is true. But this sky is not the property of the rich and famous, it's a universal. One has only to look up to see it."

I snigger at the simplicity of his answer. "In that case *I* must have been too self-absorbed to look up and see it, just like everyone else."

He's smiling and shaking his head. "You were no such thing, darling. You were too busy looking down, hiding yourself away. That's an entirely different matter."

"I suppose so but I've seen it now, thanks to you. Which star are *you,* by the way?" I ask playfully."

"Always the brightest one right above your head, of course," he says plainly.

"In that case, I'll make a point of looking up."

"Then this has been a worthwhile journey," he chortles. "What is it you say? Your future is written in the stars?"

I'm nodding. "Yes, ... but wasn't it Shakespeare who said, *'It is not in the stars to hold our destiny but in ourselves'?*"

He snickers at my suggestion. "Perhaps ... our futures might already be taking shape up there. Who knows?"

He pulls me to him and I place my hand on his chest, feeling its heat against my palm. "I think you do," I whisper.

"In that case, why don't you wish upon a star, the way you used to when you were a child?"

What?

I raise my chin to watch him speak. "How do you know I did that?" I ask curiously.

"Because I watched you."

"When I was a child?"

"Yes."

I feel my brows elevating. "All the time?"

He leans up to kiss my forehead. "Of course not. I was drawn to your sadness and there were moments when you were understandably distressed. It aggrieved me that I couldn't comfort you." His hand tightens on my shoulder.

"I had my family around me in the early days but they left me, one after the other." Just saying those words causes my throat to constrict.

"They did nothing of the sort, Beth. Your grandmother was elderly; she had a good life."

"And my mother?"

He takes a thoughtful breath. "Your mother was terminally ill, darling. Even I couldn't help her."

Help her?

I sit up, place my forearm on his chest and face him wide-eyed like an animal caught in a searchlight. "You knew my mother?"

"I did. Our paths crossed on several occasions. I was taken with her bravery and moved by her determination to hold on as long as she could – for you."

I cover my trembling lips with my hand.

"I'm sorry, Beth. I didn't intend to upset you." He enfolds me in his arms, keeping the night air out and my sense of unimaginable loss inside. "You can cry. Don't feel you have to be brave on my behalf." He buries his lips in my hair. "Losing a loved one is a terrible thing. Losing a mother must be unspeakably painful."

I sit up, wipe away my tears with a napkin and turn to him. "What did she say to you?"

"Do you really want to know?"

I nod in reply and focus on his handsome face.

"Alright then, but, as you know she wasn't completely lucid at the end; morphine is a powerful analgesic. In the week before her passing we talked several times."

My eyes widen. "You did? What did you talk about?" I wipe my nose and sit up on my knees, rapt.

"About you. Her wish for you, her love for you and ..."

"And ..."

"And the promise she asked me to make to watch over you." He cups my face in his hand. "I could have done so much more but ..."

I pull his palm to my lips. "You did enough. I'm alive aren't I? There were times I thought I would die and it was only your intervention that kept me alive. I'm sure of that."

I press my full weight onto his pectorals and cover his lips with mine. "Thank you. You kept your promise."

His kisses me lovingly, but there is little passion. I pull back.

"What's wrong?"

"I can't explain further without giving you something." He reaches into his trouser pocket. "You must close your eyes. Think of your mother and make a silent wish, and only then, open your eyes." He holds my attention with an unwavering stare.

"Alright, but I don't need ..."

He places a finger over my lips. "Wish, my darling."

I close my eyes and do exactly that. I wish for my mother to be happy wherever she is; to have found my father and to be proud of me and ... there is one other thing.

I open my eyes slowly, not knowing what to expect. He is sitting bolt upright. His left hand rests on my bare shoulder and his other is turned upright into a closed fist. I gaze into his eyes and see a softness there that comforts me.

"Did you wish?" he asks in a half whisper.

I smile. "Yes. I wished."

"Open my hand." He directs me to his right hand, now resting on my knees.

As I peel back his fingers, I feel a kind of giddy excitement. I've had gifts before but I suspect this will be the gift to outdo everything else. I'm expecting a piece of heaven or a falling star but what I see is much more precious.

"Oh! Ayden!" I cry, recognising it instantly. "It's my mother's engagement ring. Where on earth did you find it?" Scarcely believing my eyes, I hold it up to the light. It is worth so little in actual money compared to my other jewellery but that doesn't detract from its exquisite beauty. "Thank you. It's what I wished for." I place it on my finger and throw my arms around his neck, peppering his cheeks and chin with kisses. "You're so wonderful."

He's grinning and trying to hold me off. "No. You have it all wrong. You have no idea just how wonderful you are." He takes hold of my face in his palms to make the point. "I want to give you everything."

I caress his face and brush a curl from his forehead. "You do, Ayden."

I settle onto his chest and hold up my right hand still disbelieving I have my mother's ring on my finger. Feeling curious, I ask, "Can I ask you where you found it?"

"It was concealed in Mr. Rizler's bag. I simply relieved him of it so it could be returned to its rightful owner."

"Well, thank you. It makes me so happy to see it on my finger. I think my mum will be smiling down on us."

"I think so too. Now let me pour you a celebratory drink and we'll prepare for the show." He reaches for the Perrier, turning the bottle around to face me. "I believe it's a very good year. Would Madame care to taste it first?"

He's arching his brow, making me giggle. "No thanks. I've had that vintage before. Just pour."

"Very well." We raise our glasses.

"To unforgettable nights."

"Absolutely! I'll drink to that."

Still overjoyed, I sip my water, finding it really refreshing after the earlier wine with our meal. Picking up on his declaration I ask, "What show? Surely we're not going back to Sydney?"

"Not tonight. The show is about to begin. I think we should take our seats."

I look around, unable to see further than a couple of feet from the bed. "What seats?"

"Right here." He takes my glass and pats the bed suggestively.

I have no idea what's coming next so settle myself.

"Lean back," he says, pointing at the pillow and look up.

"What am I looking for, exactly?" I ask, scanning the sky for U.F.O's

"You'll know it when you see it."

Like a prowling cat he crawls up the bed and positions himself next to me. He takes my left hand and presses my knuckles against his lips. "See anything?"

"Nope." Just then I spot a shooting star. "Did you see that? I snatch my hand from his mouth and point to the west. "Over there! I think it was a shooting star!"

He seems disinterested and folds his hands behind his head. When I look again, his eyes are closed and his mouth is shaped into a sexy, 'I know something you don't know' kind of smile.

All I can do is lie back, fold my arms and look out across the sea. And then they appear. I gasp, full of wonder. "What's that?" I grab his arm and shake him awake. "Look, there are lights in the sky. More and more of them. What are they? Ayden, look!"

He feigns boredom. "What did you see?"

"If you open your eyes you'll be able to tell me. Take a look." With each new second the sky is coming alive. Miniature explosions are flooding the clouds with light. Shooting stars are falling from the sky; some kind of red-tailed comet is speeding across the horizon. "This is it, isn't it? This is the show. Oh my God! It's spectacular." I grab his hand and hold it to my breast, encasing it in my hot palms. "It's truly magical; nature's firework display just for us. How amazing is this?"

"This is just a small glimpse of the universe. There's a whole galaxy of stars and planets out there."

I turn to him, my eyes awash with glossy tears. I'm overwhelmed by the night's events. For as long as I live, I will never forget this night. I flop back onto the bed, spent of all emotion. "All that's happened tonight has been like a dream, Ayden. I don't know what to say other than ... thank you."

"We had a lot of fun. It was my pleasure to watch you; how moved you were by the opera, how you were tipsy over dinner, your joy with the rose petals and your childlike excitement as you witnessed the meteor shower." He turns on his side to face me until our noses are touching, cradling my face in his hand. "What a delight you are, Beth."

"You made it so special,. I just happened to be here," I confess.

He will have none of it. "That's simply not true. All this magic pales into insignificance compared to you." He rubs across my bottom lip with a gentle thumb. "I am seen as a blinding light by some, yet *you* are the light people are drawn to; you have an aura of goodness around you, Beth. You wear it like a mantle. You always have."

"Only you can see it," I say, smiling. "But thank you for saying so."

He runs his hand across my shoulders and down my right arm, coming to rest on my newly-ringed finger. "This is one of many gifts I can give you ..."

I interrupt before he can finish, "I don't want any more gifts..."

"I know, but you do want a child, don't you?" He sweetens his question with a kiss.

A child?

"I do, but ..."

He kisses me again. "Hush. There will be no buts tonight, my darling. I have spent too many millennia taking care of the dead. Is it too much to ask to be given this one opportunity to procreate?"

His choice of words makes me giggle. "Is that another one of your pick-up lines?" The humour glistening in his eyes has me laughing into his chest.

"I do so love to hear your laughter, darling Beth. I will miss it dearly."

He moves down the bed, holding out his hands to help me disembark as if leaving a shipwreck. As he prepares to speak he looks into my eyes into my very soul. "Let me make love to you. We have spoken of worlds colliding. Now the time has come for me to show you what can happen when the forces of heaven and earth come together."

Wrapped up in one another, we walk barefoot back to the villa.

"You just love talking dirty, don't you?" I tease.

"Is that a serious question?" he asks, burying his nose in my hair.

"No."

His grip tightens around me. "I thought not."

23

I nside the villa, there's an air of silent expectation. The sound of the sea is behind us; the gentle lapping of waves against the shore is barely audible. I break the silence with some music. In the bedroom I scroll through the iPod deck until I find something fitting to the occasion. Lana Del Ray speaks of a *Burning Desire*. The rhythm of the music is complemented by the humming sound coming from the ceiling fan as it disperses the heat and creates a welcome draft that catches wisps of my hair, giving me the dishevelled look of someone who lost her innocence on that short stroll from the beach.

Into the bedroom steps the man of my dreams. In the candlelight, I see his shirt is unbuttoned and his tie discarded. As he stands across from me on the other side of the bed I feel my body responding to his overpowering presence. My chest heaves. I feel edgy and impatient, aching for my husband's touch. He might well *be* Ayden for the way he carries himself in and out of the bedroom. He has everyone fooled; even me at times. He fills the space with his aura and his authority transcends the ordinary. No man has looked more determined in purpose. He means to have me, his way, or not at all.

I shudder at the prospect of being taken and yet, the gratification that comes from being so prized excites me more. I draw my tongue across my lower lip in anticipation. "How do you want me?" I ask, removing my earrings and placing them onto the bedside table.

His mouth twitches on the right. "How? Willing," he replies, causing me to glance away for fear my pupils will belie my indifference.

"I couldn't want you more, even if we'd been apart a month or a year. Come here. I have a wedding present to unwrap." As I walk around the bed he's unbuttoning his cuffs and beginning to undo his shirt.

I take hold of his hands to still them. "Let me." Still keeping eye contact I undo every button, fold back his shirt and claim what is mine; flexing pectorals covered in a downy layer of hair just begging to be stroked. I lay my palms flat, allowing his masculine essence to seep through to my fingertips like an electric current, urged on by my heavy breathing and a stifled moan. But there is no time for that. Before any power is bestowed up me I am turned about.

"You are a vision in this dress, Beth," he murmurs, close to my ear. "But some visions are real and others are figments of the imagination. Which are you?" He takes hold of my zip and lowers it, slowly until it reaches my lower back. He slips his right hand into the open dress and slides it around my abdomen, pulling me into him tightly into him until l I feel the fullness of his erection against my derrière.

He slips his other hand inside and cups my breasts, causing me to whimper as I'm held fast, imagining all kinds of sensual scenarios.

He whispers into my right ear, "Are you ready for me?"

"Yes," I answer nervously.

He licks my earlobe and nips at it before continuing his interrogation. "Are you sure? Because for what I have in mind, you must be very, very wet."

Fuck!

I rotate my neck backward and sideways into him. "Yes. I'm ready for you, Ayden." Just saying his name causes my abdomen muscles to tighten. This is the man I know and love. This magnetism we have is undeniably sexual but it begins with words; words that tempt, tease and prepare me for sex. I have missed these words.

With me still facing away from him, he removes the dress from my body as if freeing a sweet from a wrapper. "Step," he orders. "Again." With feather-light fingertips he strokes my calves and thighs; climbs to my waist and position me against his hard torso. "Tell me, Beth. Do you want to play?"

Just the thought of it causes my back to straighten and every hair to stand on end. An instinctive "Yes," leaves my lips.

"Me too. Turn around."

I rotate on the spot and find his eyes with mine, augmenting our connection. "What do you want to play?"

"Mmm ... so many games to choose from but only one comes to mind." He reaches behind him and opens the bedside drawer. "You brought these, so I assume they come highly recommended."

My eyes widen as I see the length of cord, the blindfold and ... the G spot massager.

He passes them from hand to hand. "I think we can dispense with this." He throws the rope to one side. "But these I like."

Is he reading my mind?

The thought of the massager causes me to bite my lip; it's been a while since Ayden used it on me and, as I recall, it was one of the most stimulating experiences of my life.

He places the massager on the pillow and refocuses his attention on me. "Tonight I'm going to take you to a place you've never been; to heaven and back. Are you ready?"

I nod. "Yes, I'm ready."

He kisses me softly, tempts me with a moist tongue and pulls away. With my eyes closed I feel the blindfold sliding over my hair and resting over my eyes. He takes hold of my hands as if we're going on a long journey. "Now close your eyes and trust me."

"I do."

His grip tightens on my fingers. "Take my hands, these are yours to use. Show me."

Feeling a little hesitant I grapple with his fingers and lift his hands until he has my face enveloped in his warm embrace. Needing no further encouragement, his lips find mine. Held in place I respond, focusing on the moistness of his kiss and the sounds emanating from his throat. His hands move into my hair, removing the clip, scooping it up in handfuls as his kiss deepens. My head begins to spin as he begins his masterful possession of my body one inch at a time.

My bra is removed. He takes each hardening nipple in his mouth and sucks hard, lengthening it, forcing me to gasp and sway.

"You're perfect, Beth. To taste you isn't enough. I have to have you. Lie down."

I'm falling backwards onto the bed; his hands take hold of mine to break my fall and I lie in breathless anticipation. To my right I hear the hum of the massager and take hold of the sheets, gathering them up in my fists, knowing what's coming. The bed sinks on my right and I sense he's facing me, examining my body, memorising every curve. The vibrator tickles my collar bone, making me wriggle and smile.

"Is this pleasurable?" he asks.

"It tickles."

"Tickles? Oh I think we can do better than that," he says, lowering his vibrating hand to my breasts. "Still tickles?"

I'm not smiling now. "Not so much."

"And now?" He rests the massager on my panties and proceeds to move it up and down in slow sweeps.

The teasing movement make we writhe and cause my hands to twist the bedding in response. "It doesn't tickle ..."

"No?"

"It makes me want to come," I moan and raise myself to increase the pressure.

"Then you shall."

He moves from the bed and pulls off my panties in one long tug that ends with them flying off my toes as if jet-propelled. Feeling exposed, I pull my knees together; I'm aroused but still bashful. I turn my head away. Throughout our adventure I have played every game but this one is a stretch too far. I see vanilla sheets, I hear my husband's words, "I'm going to use this on you ... this will be intense and I want you to try to absorb the feeling to make it last." How can I make it last when he's not here ...

"Beth," he whispers. "I can't love you if you hide from me." He kneels up and pushes back my blindfold. He sighs. "We have been intimate before. I have *known* you and yet you still don't trust me?"

I see the disappointment in his eyes and it saddens me. "I trust you, Ayden. I want you." Without hesitation I reach over to him, releasing his belt and undoing the clasp on his trousers, knowing the extent of his arousal even before I lower the zip. With careful handling I release an impressive erection from the confines of his boxers and take it in my left hand. He leans backwards, using his hands to support himself and thrusts his hips forward. Impulsively, I arch my body around him and take him in my mouth.

Taken by surprise he throws back his head and growls with primeval satisfaction. I feel his body heat rising; his cock is pulsating and swelling in response as I pull him deeper and suck harder. He's losing all self-control.

"Fuck, Beth!" he calls out. "This body is yours. Take it!"

His words are so achingly familiar that salt water fills my eyes and flows like guilty tears onto the sheets. I press on until he begins to tremble, taking him to the back of my throat, coaxed by his words.

"Yes! Right there. Suck me hard, baby."

Only when his hands take hold of my hair do I ease off, slightly.

"Stop! You're making me come ..."

But I will not be deterred. I move into a more comfortable position, taking hold of his thighs and attacking him with greater confidence and determination.

"Beth!" he calls out, realising my intention. "Beth!" Without warning, he shoves me off him and clambers over my body. With trembling knees he forces my legs open and thrusts into me in one forceful movement.

His urgency catches me unaware, making me scream with sweet agony and with the urgency of his penetration. I take hold of his shoulders, pushing him off and then pulling him back to me a second later, rocking to the rhythm of his forward and backward movements.

Realising his selfishness, he eases off and finds my ear. "I'm sorry if I caused you pain." His breath coats my throat in hot gusts while his kisses remind me of the bond we have established. I pushed him too far.

"You didn't hurt me," I whisper. "I was ready for you."

He leans up on his elbows and gazes adoringly into my eyes. "Is that true? Are you ready, for *me*?" He continues to glide in and out with the precision of a human metronome, each thrust deeper than the last, each languid lunge driving home a single message: you belong to me.

"I've been waiting for you all my life," I state, pulling his mouth to mine to swallow up my confession.

"And I for you Frances, Elizabeth Parker. I'm here, darling, and I can give you everything."

I hear the words but I can't process them; his power possesses my body, my mind and my soul ... I have no-place to hide.

He fixes me with a piercing stare. "Look into my eyes. See what I see: the power of heaven and earth and creation. Come with me."

I can't look away. I feel my knees buckling, my legs folding to allow him to thrust more deeply. I feel his physical presence over me, his raw, covetous hunger consuming me.

Conquered and claimed I stare into oblivion and, amid those saintly orbs of the darkest sapphire I see a thousand stars so bright and so bewitching I can't look away. The gravitational pull of the universe lures me in. I begin to feel lightheaded and drawn to the light. My body hums with orgasmic sensations, and his guttural roars of passion resonate, creating a crescendo of ecstatic fervour unparalleled in the known universe.

As he nears the abyss I draw him deeper rejoicing in his omnipotence, letting go. All I can do is call out his name over and over, "Ayden, Ayden..."

As if responding to my coaxing, he comes inside me with a ferocious out-pouring of liquid fire. He yells, "Fuck!" His face contorts, my mouth opens and we combust as our worlds collide, exploding into a million stars.

As our bodies spasm and shiver I close my eyes and silently weep, hearing three words as they escape his throat in a strangled cry, "Choose me, Beth."

I feel my jaw moving but I have no words to convey my thoughts. What can I say?

Regaining my sanity I look around the room. The candles are out, the covers on the bed have been tossed aside, furniture has been overturned. The room looks as if a powerful force of nature had just appeared and left.

That's a fair assessment of what just happened here.

I've left Ayden sleeping, peacefully. Feeling both physically and emotionally exhausted. I'm seated out on the deck with a glass of orange juice on one side and my camera, phone and laptop on the other. I dread opening it. I know what awaits me on my desktop; two people in love who

278 . Sydney Jamesson

believed they had their lives ahead of them. What is to become of them now?

I brace myself and boot up, avoiding Ayden's eyes and directing my thoughts to my digital scrapbook. So much has happened I scarcely know where to begin, but I have to put it down so there will be no gaps in my husbnd's memory and our honeymoon will not become my solitary recollection. I'm listening to Jason Mraz who reminds me that *I won't give up.* Using the lyrics I channel my thoughts.

November #9

"Eternity was in our lips and eyes,
Bliss in our brows' bent; none our
parts so poor
But was a race of heaven."
Shakespeare: Antony and Cleopatra.

If I live to see one hundred, Ayden, I will never forget the time we've spent here. You have seen to it that our honeymoon has been the best of times and never let it be said that you don't know how to show a lady a good time (Laughing)

Today we posed for Josh and you flew us to Sydney for a spectacular production of Madame Butterfly. I cried, as you knew I would; and we left the Opera House in silent reverie. It was a beautiful occasion. Thank you.

The restaurant overlooking the harbour was the perfect setting for dinner. We shared desserts and laughed until all the wine was gone and I ...

I want to write, until it was time to take some photos and leave, but as I'm so overcome with emotion, it's impossible to fabricate happiness after what's happened. I take a couple of gulps of chilled orange juice to settle myself enough to tell one of the most shameful lies I have ever been guilty of.

Forgive me, Ayden. I have lost my way but I will always find my way back to you ...

The photos we had taken will go straight into the album, as will the programme and a stack of other mementos I have collected.

When we arrived back on our island paradise you had arranged for a bed to be set up on the beach. We laid back and counted stars. The sky was the colour of your come-to-bed eyes and ... that's exactly what I did. (Blushing)

The night ended perfectly with soft music and the sound of our orgasmic cries; and no one could ask for more. You held me in your arms until our hearts slowed and I fell asleep, blissfully happy.

I wipe away a tear with my cuff.

Never has any woman felt more loved and grateful for so much. You are my life. I may travel the world or look to the heavens once in a while, but you'll be the only man I'll ever love. My heart and my soul belongs to you, baby.

Yours, Beth. X

I attach two of my favourite photos of us and one of the Opera House, captured so beautifully with the bridge in the background. I send two photos to Charlie with a brief message

Hi Char, last day here. We managed to squeeze in a night at the opera in Sydney. Flying home later today. Can't wait to see you. Looking forward to hearing your news. Love B.X

Before I'm able to return to the comfort of our bed, something moving on the deck catches my eye. It's the circle of red rose petals, now broken and scattered. Feeling utterly despondent. I stomp on them, kick them left and right, then watch the way they are caught by the breeze and carried up and away ... to be forever lost on the wind. I know how they feel ...

***

It isn't as if he hasn't had years to work it out, but Mack still believes the worst thing about being a detective is discovering secrets and then being ordered to keep them. Tormented by his own sense of morality he's left work early, vowing never to return. It's a temporary state of mind, but he meant it when he said it.

He fills up a kettle with water and watches Judy in the back garden, hoping that being home will somehow soften the blow and ease his conscience. After all, what can *he* do?

He pierces the cellophane covering of a microwave meal described as '*a delicious mixture of spices from the Orient fused with rich meat flavours.*' He's not fooled by the fancy packaging or the manipulation of language and prepares to be disappointed. His words leave his mouth like a volley of rubber bullets, "It's all bullshit!"

Five minutes pass slowly. With nothing better to do, he watches the countdown, wondering what he's going to do with all the information he has in his head and in those notepads his Chief was so quick to ridicule. The bell sounds, announcing that dinner is served. He's just about to lift out the carton when he hears a noise coming from the lounge; something crashing or smashing.

He calls out, "Judy! Come out of there. Damn dog!" The heat of the carton burns his fingers, causing him to yell and rush over to the tap. The cold water stings but it lessens the sensation of burning flesh. His eyes move from his fingers, to his meal and then to the garden where Judy is still sniffing around. He checks the back door. It's closed.

Somewhat curious, he leaves his steaming lamb in black bean sauce, strolls down the hall and into the lounge. The files are as he left them, spread around the floor like stepping stones. The wallpaper is still draped over his dining table like a mediaeval banquette. All seems intact until ... he spots a picture frame upside down on the carpet; it had been on the television set. Now, Kate, his daughter, is in pieces. The picture is intact but the glass is shattered, no more than a collection of slivers of sharp glass.

He looks around the room for any signs of a disturbance, but there are none. Only one piece of information he accumulated in his investigation is out of place; the envelope addressed to

Ayden Stone
MOD ASMI

It's apart from the other sheets and photos and sitting on his favourite chair. He didn't put it there. Taking a couple of steps towards it, he feels the hairs prickling on his neck as if some-one just opened a window to let in some air. The skin on his hands is covered in goose-bumps but he isn't cold; even his breathing is a little strained. He has the strangest feeling he is not alone in the house.

He looks at the hallway, preparing to leave, and sees Judy sitting less than a foot away from the threshold. She's looking at Mack, but something behind him appears to be holding her attention. She whines noisily and leaves, leaving Mack to fend for himself.

He rolls his eyes and shoves his hands in his pockets in an attempt to warm them. He's in no mood for tricks; he's been mind-fucked once today and isn't about to go through that again.

He turns, slowly ...

Nothing and no one is there, except for one solitary object; a marble on the carpet. It isn't particularly striking or beautiful, yet when Mack holds it close to his eyes to inspect it he sees the richest streaks of cocoa brown. Within the sunburnt hues there is the suggestion of chocolate and of sweetness. He grips it tightly in his right palm and holds the letter in his left hand like the scales of justice.

"Thank you, Elise," he whispers. "It's a fair exchange. I'll see to it that he gets it."

In less than a minute the temperature rises, his breathing becomes less laboured and his mood changes for the better. With this simple gift comes all the gratification he needs for a job well done. Overcome with joy, he smiles with pride and begins to place the shards of glass onto a plain piece of paper.

With no harm done, he places the photo back onto of the television and for the first time he actually sees his daughter in all her beauty. He caresses her face with a fat finger and checks his watch. 'Is it too late to give her a call?' he wonders.

While he waits for her to answer her phone he recalls a quote by Benjamin Disraeli that seems fitting at this moment in time, "*Justice is truth in action.*"

He knows what he has to do but for now ..."Hello love, it's your dad. I was thinking about you and I just thought ..."

***

In no hurry to leave, we wrapped souvenirs, packed away our clothes and waited on the deck for the chopper to arrive. As with every other day, the midday sun shone brightly and the turquoise sea reflected in Ayden's eyes as if he were an extension of it.

The flight to Cairns was brief and exciting. Helicopters have a way of bringing you close to nature. Maybe it's the way you see the world laid out in front of you - a coverlet of cool blue, a carpet of green and then the man-made world of bricks and mortar. We came back to reality with a bump.

The company jet was waiting on the runway, stocked and ready to whisk us back to Hong Kong in less than eight hours. I marvelled at how organised my life had become, thanks to my handsome husband and his highly dedicated and efficient secretary. Where would we without Charlotte?

From the moment we awoke Ayden has been attending to my every need. While I prepared fresh fruit for breakfast he took care of the bedroom, righting furniture, clearing clothes from the floor and generally straightening things out. He didn't volunteer an explanation and I haven't asked for one. I've put two and two together; his strong emotions prompt a surge of energy and can quite easily whip up a storm. Nothing strange about that ... he catches me smirking.

"And would you like to share that thought?" he asks with a sideways nod.

"No." I smile back at him and return to my Kindle. With only two hours remaining of this leg of our flight, the time seems right to direct the conversation my way. Here goes.

"Ayden...?"

He looks up from his iPad. "Yes, Beth."

I place my Kindle on my knee. "Do you keep a list of people you have ... you know, taken?"

He frowns and shakes his head. "What kind of list?"

"You know. Names, ages, dates of birth. Things like that."

"Not as such."

"Okay." I have his full attention with my innocent enquiry.

He changes seats and positions himself in front of me. "Why do you ask?"

"I just wondered if you'd be able to tell me if someone was alive or dead? That's all."

He reaches out and takes my hand. "Of course. I'd be happy to."

I reach for my bag and take out the letter head stationery from the Ritz Carlton, opening it on my lap. There are two names written there; Saffir Ayden Pierre and Isabel Françoise Pierre. I turn the paper around so he can see both names.

At first he is surprised; his eyes widen. "I assume you mean Madame Pierre?"

"Yes. Is she alive?"

He releases my hand and leans back in his chair, probably going back through decades, looking for her name. "There was a woman of that name in 2012 but she was 82, and another in 1074 who was 59, neither of which were the right age."

I feel a flurry of excitement. "So she's alive."

"Not necessarily. She would most likely have married and changed her name." He offers a flat smile. "Although ..."

I'm leaning forward, eager to hear more. "Although what?"

He's massaging his chin with his thumb, contemplating possibilities. "Although I could go back and check..."

"You could?" There's no disguising the surprise on my voice.

"Yes. But it could take some time..."

I'm quick to interject. "We have time. Will you at least try?" I reach out for his hand.

"Would it make you happy?" he asks, looking a little too earnest.

I'm nodding. "It would make me very happy."

He kisses my cheek and moves to a chair on the other side of the aircraft, taking a pen and pad with him.

I return to my Kindle, not really following any of the words on the screen. Gabriel Emerson is celebrating Christmas and dealing with an old flame, but I'm merely skimming paragraphs; he deserves more of my attention another time when I can concentrate. As I listen to Alexis Jordan singing, The Air That I Breathe, I inhale every word like a powerful fragrance laced with love. If I can get one thing out of this adventure, this is it. What can I give to the man who has everything? Only this.

I stop pretending to read so I can watch him at work, eyes closed, hands on his thighs, sweeping through time and space in search of a woman called Isabel Françoise Pierre, who gave birth to a beautiful baby boy over 32 years ago.

All I can do is wait.

Thirty four minutes later he's touching my hand, I've dozed off and wake with a start. "Oh! How did you do?"

He hands me my piece of paper with a list of new names and places on it. "I had to trace her back to the day she gave her baby up for adoption."

I can't help but respond. "Oh Ayden, I'm sorry. I mean ... if you were Ayden I would be sorry. Oh, what the hell, you know what I mean."

He leans across, takes my hand and pulls me over to him until I'm sitting across his knee, running my finger over a chiselled cheekbone and into his hair. "You're amazing, you know. You have so much goodness in you."

He takes my hand and plans a noisy kiss in my palm. "Everything I have become is down to you. You are a gifted teacher, my darling, and I will miss you." He brushes back my hair with his free hand. "I have spent most of my life in the company of the dead or the dying. You have brought light into a dark and lonely existence."

"Don't say that." I pull him to my breast. "I will worry about you when you leave."

He laughs quietly and shakes his head, pushing me backwards into a sitting position. "When I leave ..."

"Yes. " I make myself comfortable. "Let's not speak about it now. We have months together to think about that."

He smiles half-heartedly and returns to his seat, turns off his iPad and leans back into the headrest.

I reach into my bag for a tissue and blow my nose as discretely as possible. Out of the window I see an unfamiliar, urban landscape, reminding me that I am so far from home. Now my happiness rests in the lap of the gods.

We had no need to disembark at Hong Kong; the aircraft was refuelled and within forty minutes we were airborne again and en route to Heathrow. Our two cabin crew members, Tony and Sandy have prepared dinner and are cheerfully setting up as we dress for dinner in our cabin. I freshen up and apply a little mascara and lip-gloss to match my pale blue smock dress; Ayden slips into a casual white shirt that complements his tan. He selects a tie and debates whether to break with tradition and eat dinner minus a jacket.

Accustomed as I have become to faking a smile, this is a feat worthy of an Oscar. I drink more than I should, and play around with my Veal Scallopini crêpe Suzette, even though the meal is perfectly delicious. My thoughtful husband had the bar stocked months ago so our palates are treated to the finest wines. We end with coffee and a glass of 1993 Bas-Armagnac, which we're taking to our cabin as a nightcap.

I'm tipsy and Ayden is amused. I kick off my shoes and crawl onto the bed, propping my chin in my right palm, listening to *Holding Onto Heaven* by Foxes. He is saying nothing but his wry smile says it all. Sitting with his back to me, he removes his shoes and hums along. Meanwhile, I'm contemplating every possible scenario and coming up with the same terrifying conclusion. He's not bringing my soul mate back.

With nothing to lose I crawl over to him and wrap my arm around his shoulders from behind. I bury my head in the crook of his neck and whisper softly, "I love you, Ayden"

He bends back his arm and cradles my head in his right hand. Into my ear he says the four words I have longed to hear. "I love you more."

As I sob quietly, tears fall from my chin and splash onto his trousers in heavy droplets, dampening his thighs.

He turns into me and kisses away my tears. "Hush, baby, don't cry." He blots away the remaining tears and damp patches with his tie. "Come, let's get you ready for bed. I think you may have overdone the Tempranillo." He cleans up smeared mascara with his thumbs and takes my face in his hands.

I rest my hand on his. "Make love to me."

He's shaking his head, slowly. "I can't. Not here and not when you're like this."

I can't conceal my disappointment. "Ayden would."

He brushes my lips with his. "But I'm not Ayden, darling."

What a fearful reminder. When I look into his eyes, the starlight of the previous night has departed. I'm looking into the eyes of the boy I fell in love with over 22 years ago, my husband. I see myself reflected in that endless Caribbean Sea, and despite his assertion, I am reassured.

He's still here and there's still hope.

For what will probably be my last entry I boot up my laptop and leave him sleeping. My tears have dried and I've made a decision to make our remaining time together a pleasurable one. I have a feeling my destiny will be determined by the events of the past 11 days. Maybe I could have behaved differently. Could I have loved more convincingly, given more and missed Ayden less? I don't think so.

I'm scrolling through my digital scrapbook, hovering over photographs, lingering over lines of text wishing I'd said more.

NOVEMBER #10
"Hear my soul speak:
The very instant that I saw you, did
My heart fly to your service."
William Shakespeare: The Tempest.

We're almost home, Ayden.
 Usually honeymooners feel unhappy about returning to the humdrum of daily life after having such a romantic time gazing into each other's eyes, but I feel no sadness. We have been to heaven and back this past week; reached for the sky and touched the

bottom of the ocean; travelled from west to east and beyond ... but, for all of the excitement in discovering new places, together, there's no place like home.

You reminded me not so long ago that we'd both been lost souls, wandering in circles, opening doors that lead nowhere, but no more. We've come home; found that place we had been searching for and that place is in each other's arms.

You live inside me, Ayden, not as a memory but as a living, breathing piece of me. My heart is yours to keep and, when the time comes for me to leave this earth, it's your name I will be whispering.

Yours for ever, Beth X

To this final entry I attach *our* photo, my screensaver and, through tears I promised myself I would no longer shed, I reach out and stroke his face. The memory of that night makes me smile.

Goodnight my beautiful prince.

24

W hile waiting for our bags to be offloaded and taken through to passport control Ayden calls Lester. There are rumblings of displeasure, which make me wonder what we're walking into.

I give Lester the warmest smile I can muster. "Hello, Lester. How are things back at the ranch?"

He opens the door of the Rolls and waits for me to step inside. "The ranch is much as you left it, Mrs. Stone." Not one for humour, he forces a smile.

Ayden gives him a cursory nod and slips in beside me. I reach over and take his hand. "What's wrong?"

He looks puzzled. "Why, nothing," he replies sandwiching his other hand over mine.

"I don't mean with us. I mean generally." I'm focusing on his face, looking for clues. There are none.

He kisses my cheek as you might a small child who needs reassurance. "Nothing I can't handle."

I pull my hand free and turn from him. "That's not an answer. I'm not a child. I don't need protecting. If it's about us, I want to know." I look out into the 4 a.m. mist and gloom of our capital city and see myself reflected. My arms are folded and I'm pouting in a very childlike manner. When I turn to face him, looking up through mascaraed lashes, I see he's smirking.

"Beth, I will never become tired of your antics." He wraps his arm about my shoulder and clears his throat to speak. "Our D. I. Bowker has been making a nuisance of himself this past week, and has arranged to come to our home later to speak with us."

"Why? What does he know?" I ask.

"Everything," he states casually. "He's been very diligent in his investigation."

I'm shocked by his reply. "Everything! And you knew?"

"Of course. He seems to be a man of good moral standing and I assumed he would come to me with any matters arising out of his investigation."

"And you didn't think to tell me?" I enquire indignantly.

"Why would I? There was nothing you could do 10,000 miles away."

I can see his point. "Well, I know that, but it's a good idea to talk these things through, even with someone like me."

He tightens his grip on my shoulder. "Someone like you would be the *only* person I'd discuss this with. You know that, so don't pout or I'll have to kiss you to turn it into smile."

"Is that a promise?" I smile into his chest.

He laughs and plants a kiss on my hair. "Yes, it is." He lifts me away from him. "We're here."

Tea seems the best way to celebrate our homecoming. Ayden attends to emails and other correspondence in his study downstairs, and I'm left alone with my thoughts. Watching the kettle come to the boil, I count the seconds, wasting time, trying not to address the simple matter of my husband's return. I suspect a decision has been made already. There is nothing I can do to persuade or alter what amounts to a date with destiny.

With no need of sleep I descend to the 1st floor carrying two teas and a plate of biscuits, trying to replicate normality. Before entering Ayden's office I pause, hearing the harsh tones of a man used to exuding power and authority with every syllable, but concealing it behind a façade of civility.

"It's unfortunate you feel that way. You should come straight here when you land so we can sort things out. I appreciate that, but I would suggest you don't do anything you might regret, Jake."

Jake?

I take a step backwards, reeling at the mention of his name. With the call concluded, I push open the door with my foot. "I made tea," I say, smiling. "Where should I put it?"

For the first time since our adventure began, Ayden is pacing, rubbing the back of his neck with his right hand. He points to a small coaster on his desk. "Thank you."

I reach for his arm. "What's happened with Jake? Is it business?"

He's shaking his head. "No. It's pleasure."

I rest on the edge of his desk. "Can you tell me?"

"Yes, as *you* seem to have caused this predicament." His eyes flash in my direction; it might be the effect of the rising sun peeping through the blind or it might be suppressed rage. I have no way of knowing.

"What did *I* do?"

Surely he can't still be jealous?

Thankfully, he stops pacing and sits in his swivel chair. He takes a sip of his tea then plants it down noisily, making me jump. When he lifts his head and his eyes meet mine, I see he has calmed a little, but the cerulean shimmer I love most of all is absent. He takes a breath. "You've been communicating with Charlie haven't you?"

Shit!

I nod. "Yes. Why would I not? She's like a sister to me ... I ..."

"You've been sending her photographs haven't you?"

Unsure of his line of questioning I continue. "Yes, that's what you do on your honeymoon. I wanted her to see what a wonderful time we were having. There's nothing wrong with that."

His head falls, as if he understands for the first time what's happened. "You sent her photographs of Hong Kong?" I nod in reply. "You sent her photographs of Heaven's Gate Mountain too?"

"Yes, so what?"

"Do you know how far Heaven's Gate Mountain is from Hong Kong?" he asks.

"I have no idea," I admit, still without a clue.

"It's a six hour flight." He begins to swivel in his chair; left then right, left then right. "Jake had my itinerary. He knew we didn't have 12 hours free to go sightseeing."

The penny drops. "Oh crap."

He laughs and reaches for his tea. "Oh crap indeed. It gets worse." Purposely making me wait he sips his tea. "So on to our honeymoon destination we go and ..." He stops, held steadfast by my open-mouth. I am utterly captivated. "And, *you* tell me what happened next."

I wrap both hands around my mug and relay the details of our excursions and activities. It's not until I reach our last night, I raise my wide eyes to his. "We went to the Sydney Opera House."

"We did, and what an enjoyable evening we had." He smiles, teasing me shamelessly. "I believe you sent her a photograph of us posing in front of said Opera House."

Embarrassed by my stupid mistakes, all I can do is nod. "I didn't realise. I'm sorry. How long is the flight to Sydney from Baderra Island, anyway?"

"Not too long, only around four hours with the transfer to the mainland, but there is the return flight to consider."

I shrug my shoulders. "Well that's not too bad then."

"It wouldn't be except for the fact that we spoke to Jake in the morning and you sent photos of us out on a catamaran for most of the day."

All I can do is sip my tea quietly and wait for a solution to occur to me. Five minutes later, I'm still waiting. "What did you tell Jake? He must wonder what the hell's going on."

He does. Particularly as no flights were going out to the Tienman Mountains because of bad weather ..."

"Bad weather you caused!" I state briskly.

"Precisely."

I remove my thumbnail from my teeth to speak. "So what will you tell him when he gets here?"

His broad shoulders rise and fall. "I haven't decided yet."

"You can't tell him the truth!" I declare, placing down my cup and standing to straighten my dress. "He won't believe you."

"This is true."

We both laugh at his reflexive response.

I take a chance and launch an emotive question in his direction. Licking my lips I begin, "What if you weren't here when he arrived? You wouldn't have any explaining to do. I could come up with some kind of plausible explanation, I'm sure."

"Are you attempting to negotiate with me, Mrs. Stone?" he asks, finding my attempt to introduce an exchange of power quite amusing.

"No, just trying to find a solution that suits everyone." I pick up my mug and prepare to leave. "Have you finished with your tea?"

"Not quite. Do I have time to finish it?" he enquires, making light of my negotiating skills.

I simply shake my head and walk away. "Yes, you have all the time in the world, Ayden."

My life has become a merry-go-round of bad decisions and an affair of the heart that has my head in a spin. If I don't find some way to decelerate, this adventure will turn into a tragedy very quickly.

Now we have a relay of guests to contend with. First on the list is Detective Inspector Bowker at 9 a.m. I've been left in the dark and Ayden's single declaration about him knowing "everything" has done little to calm my nerves. With ten minutes to myself I boot up my laptop, intending to scroll through photographs, deleting those incriminating reminders of unearthly powers and impossible excursions!

I open up the digital scrapbook, looking for lines to delete, then the buzzer sounds by the lift, making me jump several inches high, signalling the arrival of our interrogator. I move my laptop to the kitchen counter, watch the lift descend and check my appearance. I'm not sure why I'm so nervous; we've done nothing wrong.

I feel a surge of adrenalin as the lift glides to a halt. D.I Bowker steps out first. A worn out man of around 40, he looks as if he has aged somewhat since I met him for the first time at my apartment.

I move over to greet him. "Detective Inspector Bowker, how nice to see you again. Please take a seat. May I take your coat?" He removes his rain coat and I slip away to the guest bedroom and fold it over a hanger that conveniently hooks over the bedroom door.

When I return, Ayden is playing host and pouring coffee.

"You've got one hell of a place here," he comments, allowing his eyes to skate around the room, taking everything in.

"Yes, I've travelled quite a bit and picked up some ornaments along the way," Ayden replies, handing him a porcelain mug of tea. I push a coaster in his direction and take my cup.

"You're both looking tanned and rested after your honeymoon, I see. Where did you go?"

"Thank you," I respond, smiling. "We went to Hong Kong and then onto The Great Barrier Reef. It was an amazing experience."

"I can imagine." He smiles cordially, knowing just how unlikely that is.

Ayden sits next to me and strikes a familiar king of the castle pose; arm outstretched, right leg crossed over his left. "So, what can we do for you, Detective Inspector?"

He takes out three small notepads, places two on the coffee table and begins flicking through what looks the oldest of the three. All we can see are scribbles but he seems to know what he's written down.

"Ah, yes. There are a few things I would like to go through with you if I may, Mr. Stone; that is if you wouldn't ..."

Before he can finish his sentence Ayden holds up his right hand and our guest pauses as if frozen in time.

"What's the matter?" I ask, turning sharply to face him.

"The ring. Take off the ring. He'll recognise it and then find it missing from the items listed as belonging to Mr. Rizler." He reaches out his hand. "Give it to me for safe keeping."

I wriggle it from the third finger of my right hand. Before handing it to him I offer a thankful smile. "That was very clever of you to remember it, Ayden. Thank you."

"I didn't. He did." He slips it into his breast pocket and taps it lightly. "It's well hidden now. Shall we continue?"

"Yes." I turn to our guest.

"... mind answering a couple of questions." He finishes his sentence and I look on sweetly, glancing at him and over to Ayden, so composed and quietly confident in a god-like way. Nothing fazes him; no one will ever be more powerful or a better protector. I will always be safe with him. I wonder if he's reading my thoughts ...

Are you reading my thoughts, Mr. Stone?

I turn away and reach for my coffee, establishing myself as mere decoration. No questions are directed at me. I have become a steadfast wifely figure who stands by her husband through hell and high water. Is that me?

Yes, that's you.

I hear Ayden's words in my head. Yet when I look at him he is conversing with our guest.

You're reading my thoughts?

Only when you want me to.

I want you to now. I love you. I love you for everything you've done and for every experience you have allowed us to share and I will be for ever indebted to you for your kindness.

Ayden doesn't reply.

"Excuse us for a moment, would you? I need to speak with my wife about something." He takes my hand and we pace quickly down the corridor into the guest bedroom. Once inside the room he pins me against the wall with his body and seals his mouth over mine, holding my chin in place with firm hands. I have to respond. I reach for his hair, drawing him to me until our bodies are a flammable fusion of flesh and blood. Breathless, he breaks away and shakes his head to clear his mind of libidinous thoughts.

"Don't share your thoughts with me, Beth. Not those kinds of thoughts. I need to read *his*. When you say those things I can't concentrate."

"I'm sorry. I just was sat there watching you and I felt that way."

He rearranges my hair. "Look. This guy means business. He won't back off and I don't want to give him the wrong impression. "I must keep my mind on him, not you, baby ... later, but not now. Do you understand?"

I understand those three little words better than he knows but give nothing away. I simply nod, remove the gloss from his lips with my forefinger and straighten his shirt and tie. "There you are, all handsome and tidy again."

He runs his thumb along my bottom lip, removing gloss that he been spread below it, grips my hand firmly and presses it against his lips. "Let's face the music."

When we return, D. I. Bowker is helping himself to another cup of coffee. "I hope it's okay." He holds his mug aloft.

"Of course. We had some unfinished business to attend to concerning purchases we made in Hong Kong. Please continue." Ayden returns to the sofa, pursing his lips between his finger and thumb, feeling the texture of my gloss. He looks sideways at me but I look away. I have no intention of becoming a distraction again.

"So, where were we?" He consults his scribbles. "Am I right in thinking you and Miss. Richards knew each other prior to the purchase of this house?"

I'm startled by his directness. He knows something.

Ayden is quick to put him right. "Yes, as I'm sure you've already worked out, we were both orphans and we spent time together at Bright Hill, a children's residential home in Hove."

What?

"Yes, I have a note of that. But she was there for only a short period of time. Can you tell me why? There is no record of her being adopted until years later, as far as I can see." He flips over another page.

"She was moved because she was being sexually abused by two men at Bright Hill. They caused a commotion one night which drew attention to them, but I believe they pursued her to her new home and continued to rape her for some time after."

I hold my right hand to my mouth.

Why are you telling him this?

He already knows.

"I'm sorry to hear that." Indicating his disgust, he purses his lips and shakes his head. "And may I ask how you came upon this information, Mr. Stone?"

Ayden prefaces his response with a laboured sigh. "She told me before the car crashed. She became very distressed. As a child, she thought I would come and rescue her, but I was too young and I couldn't find her; not even later on when I employed the services of a private investigator. We didn't meet again until I came to buy this house."

"Mmm ... and how does Mrs. Stone fit into all of this?" He fixes an unnerving eye on me.

Me?

With the softest of caresses, Ayden reaches over to stroke my hair. "Beth came with her father to Bright Hill. He was doing volunteer work, painting and decorating, that kind of thing. While she was there I took care of her; we became inseparable. I fell in love with her. In fact I never stopped loving her." His words fall from his mouth like petals that float softly through the air and settle silently around us. I close my eyes and picture my beautiful boy.

He clears his throat and explains further, "Our paths crossed by chance one day when I went to her school to give a speech to students. I recognised her instantly - and the rest is history, as they say."

D. I. Bowker's mouth twitches. "So you were childhood sweethearts?"

"We were," Ayden confesses. "Do you find that amusing?"

He shakes his head as if he's been caught sniggering during a sermon. "Not at all. My wife and I were childhood sweethearts. We met at junior school and were never parted ... until a year ago, that is. She died of breast cancer."

I lean over and place a compassionate hand on his knee. "My mother did too."

He bows his head, as if acknowledging her passing with a moment's silence. "It was a sad day, but we have a daughter and she has all her mother's qualities. So I have been blessed in that respect."

"That *is* a blessing," I agree, nodding and offering a comforting smile.

He closes one small notepad and opens another. "Now to you Mrs. Stone. Tell me about you and Mr. Rizler at Cambridge. He must have given you quite a scare to force you to change your name and to hide yourself away for all those years..."

He knows everything!

I nod in agreement, as this seems to be our day for confessions, I prepare to explain. "He tried to rape me in my final year at Cambridge. He and two other men grabbed me one night in a car park and they only stopped because a man came out to walk his dog. A light came on, they ran away and forgot about it. But not Mr. Rizler. He had my possessions and found out where I lived. He called and even broke into my room once. I'm sure he stole a couple of things. Underwear most likely."

"I see. So when you had the break-in at Elm Gardens, it was him?"

"Yes," I admit, regretfully.

"But you didn't tell me at the time, even though I had my suspicions you knew the assailant. Why was that?"

I should say because Ayden told me not to but I won't. "I didn't want my past to come back to haunt me. Ayden and I had become very close and this sort of thing would have sullied his reputation and mine. Besides, I thought that would be the end of it. I was wrong of course." I scoff at my naïveté.

"Yes you were. He had been looking for you for some time. There were pictures of you going back to your university days. He had them pinned up on his wall like a shrine. He only tore them down when he became deranged and desperate. He took chances. Thankfully, Mr. Stone was on hand to rescue you."

I reach for Ayden's hand. "Yes ... he was."

Seeming unconvinced about something he scratches at the stubble on his chin with his fingertips and takes a noisy slurp of tea.

"Is there anything else we can help you with?" Ayden asks, prompting him to share his thoughts with both of us.

"Yes. Two things. What do you know of Miss. Richards's involvement with Mr. Rizler?"

The question stumps us: we're shrugging shoulders and shaking our heads.

"We had no idea they knew each other," I confess. "Did they?"

"Yes. From telephone records and further investigations, it would appear they were in cahoots with one another: quite the team, in fact." He seems pleased with himself. Maybe it's his choice of words or the fact he thinks he's actually telling us something we don't know.

"We had no idea," Ayden says, sounding rather unconvincing.

"Well, it is becoming clearer the deeper I dig but, I suspect she was using Mr. Rizler to – if you would excuse me Mrs. Stone – to get rid of you."

"My God!"

"She had her sights on you, Mr. Stone, and did not respond well to your rejection." He places down notebook number two on his knees. "That would explain her behaviour when she discovered you were married to your childhood sweetheart, I think."

I interrupt him with a question. "How did she know? Ayden was careful never to mention it for that very reason."

"I visited her apartment and saw photographs scattered on the floor. She had pieced it together. One photograph was of you as children, one of you taken by Mr. Rizler and one torn from the newspaper article announcing your engagement. I suspect it was this discovery that subsequently resulted in her being an inebriated passenger in Mr. Harrison's car."

"She took the wheel," Ayden asserts. "There was nothing I could do."

D.I. Bowker takes a breath and eyes Ayden reflectively, preparing to make some kind of declaration. "But you did manage to take control of the car after she was seen leaning across and grappling with the wheel. It was the car that appeared to slow then pick-up speed that sent you spinning and careening down the embankment. You were in no way responsible for the death of Elise Richards. Eye witnesses and forensic evidence has proven that beyond a doubt."

Feigning relief, Ayden bows his head.

I reach for his hand. "You couldn't save her, Ayden."

"I believe she's correct, Mr. Stone. We have apprehended the driver of the vehicle responsible for her death, but he claims to have no recollection of the collision. Once again, we have forensic evidence that would suggest otherwise, but a far as you're concerned, the case is closed."

"Thank God!" I exclaim, clutching my breast with my free hand.

With that case solved, he focuses his attention on me. "And the same goes for you, Mrs. Stone. After looking into your case very thoroughly, I have come to the conclusion that Mr. Rizler came with intentions of raping and killing you that day in your classroom or even taking you to Elm Gardens where he had equipment assembled two floors above your apartment."

For the second time I cover my mouth. "Just the thought of him being that close terrifies me. I can't believe there are people like that out there."

He gives me a solemn look of condolence. "I'm afraid so. The world is populated by monsters it seems, Mrs. Stone." All three notebooks are stuffed into his breast pocket, creating an unsightly bulge, but he's not a man to waste time picking out clothes, fussing over shoe polish or matching ties. As Ayden pointed out, 'he means business.'

"Now all that remains is for me to write this up formally and to trace the two male employees at Bright Hill 22 years ago. That shouldn't be too difficult." The sofa creaks as he stands. "I think that's everything ..." He pauses, realising something significant.

"Did you forget something?" I ask, tipping my head and waiting for his reply.

"Only this." He pulls a folded envelope out of his other breast pocket.

"What is it?" Ayden asks, as if he doesn't know.

"It's a letter addressed to you from Miss. Richards. It was in her safe deposit box at the bank." He fastens his jacket and prepares to leave. "I believe she wanted you to have it."

Utterly perplexed, Ayden takes it. "Thank you. Do you know what's inside?"

D. I. Bowker faces him head-on until they are positioned like two book ends on either side of the coffee table. He seems to be thinking through his reply. "I have no idea, Mr. Stone." He mitigates what appears to be a lie with a smile. "I'll forward a copy of my reports to your solicitor for your information. If there's anything I've missed or you want to add, please feel free to call me on this number." He slides a card across the glass topped coffee table.

I scoot off to fetch his raincoat and, when I return, Ayden is showing him out.

"Don't forget this." I fold it over his arm."

"Thank you." He reaches for my hand. "Mrs. Stone, it was a pleasure meeting you. May you have many trouble-free years ahead."

I chuckle quietly, noticing the gentleness lurking behind his fierce stare. "I hope so and I hope we'll meet again under happier circumstances."

"I hope so too. Good morning to you."

I watch them get into the lift and descend. My head is crammed with information; there's so much I didn't know, and so much I was blissfully unaware of.

When Ayden steps from the lift he is positively radiant. "Well, that went better than I expected."

"You said he was a man of good moral standing. He is."

He's grinning. "Did I say that?"

"You did." I gather up the mugs and float past him.

He appears behind me. "Is there anything you want to ask me? Anything he left out that you're curious about?"

I continue to rinse out the cups. There *is* one thing. I turn to face him directly. "Did you know about all that? Mr. Rizler and his fixation with me? That I was in danger of being found?"

"I watched over you after your attack, Beth. You were never in danger. Until ..." he thinks carefully about his choice of words.

"Until?"

"Until you were reunited with ... me." He lifts a playful brow.

I huff at the thought. "By *you*, you mean Ayden? How so?"

He answers with a nod. "As I explained before, I can't control destiny, only interfere with it temporarily. You were bound to come together sooner or later."

I give him a puzzled look. "So we could have met before we did at my school? You interfered and saw to it that we didn't?" I throw down the tea-towel. "What gave you the right to do that?"

"I have no need of *rights*. It was my choice."

He doesn't understand. "You had no right to choose whether or not we should meet!"

He's becoming irritated. "Beth, your fate was inextricably linked with Ayden Stone and Elise Richards and, by association, Dan Rizler. If I hadn't intervened he would have gotten to you earlier. I wasn't prepared to let that happen.".

"So when should we have met?" I snap at him.

"I don't recall." He turns to leave.

I grab his arm. "That's a lie. You recall everything."

"Why do you want to know? What does it matter?" he asks angrily.

I can't conceal my disappointment. "It matters to me!"

"Why?"

I call out, "Because I spent all those years alone, waiting, when we could have been together!"

He turns to face me, removes my hand from his arm and places two strong hands on my shoulders in an attempt to calm me. "Look, your honesty and your goodness makes you vulnerable. Those kind of qualities endeared people to you but you were bound to suffer as a consequence. You've spent your whole life putting other before yourself; your mother, your father, your friends and your husband. You've forgone so much for them and for love. When will you learn to hold back, to see this cruel world through my eyes, and to find strength from weakness?"

I shake my head. "Never! I may be a sorry excuse for a human being but I won't change and become contemptuous like you. If I see goodness, it's because it's there. I don't imagine it. I won't change. Not even for you." I shake free of his arms and walk away. He doesn't attempt to call me back.

I fall down onto the enormous bed, bury my head in my hands and cry for all the nights spent in the arms of a stranger, and for the safe return of the only man I have ever loved. I'm brought back to reality by the sound of footsteps.

Ayden appears in the doorway. "Jake is parking. Go and tidy yourself while I greet him." He kisses my moist cheek and leaves in a hurry. "We'll need to present a united front to deal with this."

He's right. Thankfully our luggage has been left here and I have access to an array of cosmetics. I cleanse my face and splash it with cold water. A cold compress removes the redness from my eyes and a decent foundation covers a multitude of blemishes. My tan gives my face a healthy glow and I can disguise the rest. In ten minutes I am transformed. I slip on a pair of jeans and a red sweater, throw a scarf around my neck and head for the lift.

When I step into the lounge mistrust is thick in the air. The two of them are sitting across from each other, barely speaking and engaging in what resembles a staring contest.

I breeze into the room. "So, what did I miss?" Jake rises and comes across the room to greet me. "Hello, beautiful. Nice to see you got yourself an even tan." He kisses my cheek.

I giggle at his suggestion. "Yes we both had fun in the sun. Can I get you a drink? "

"No, thanks. We are sampling something from the wine cellar, apparently." Jake gives me a wink and nods in Ayden's direction.

"I might join you." I reach for the bottle of Chateau Le Pin Pomerol 1999. "Looks expensive."

"It is," Ayden calls out. "Bring the bottle over, Beth, and join us."

I do just that and sit next to him. He takes my hand, warms my knuckles with a kiss and returns them to me. I'm sitting prim and proper, waiting for the bomb to go off. Taking the initiative, I light the fuse.

"So how did your date go with Charlie?" I ask, cheerfully. "I haven't heard from her yet."

Jake grins and raises his glass. "No news is good news, right?"

I raise my glass. "That's what they say." Ayden is bringing nothing to the conversation other than a winning smile. I suspect he's reading Jake's thoughts in preparation for his onslaught.

"Charlie was showing me some pictures you sent her, holiday snaps, that kind of thing. You both looked great, but ..."

Here it comes ...

"...what I don't get is how you covered so many miles in such a short time. You wanna explain that to me?"

"Sure." Ayden puts down his glass. "I had them photo-shopped."

Jake throws back his wine. "Fuck me! Why would you do that? It was your honeymoon."

Ayden draws him in. "Public relations. Once word gets out we secretly went to the mountains and Sydney Opera House, businesses will be clamouring to get a piece of us."

Piece of us?

I turn to face him, surprised by his line of defence.

"Josh is putting a piece together for us. It'll go out to four magazines next week. Some photos have already been leaked."

Ayden stops speaking and reaches for the bottle of wine. "This is worth every penny," he declares, topping up our glasses.

Jake isn't convinced. "And when did you decide to go all Posh and Becks? I thought you wanted to remain in the background, Ayd? That's the way you've always played it; quiet but fucking deadly."

Ayden reaches for my hand and slips it between his until it's concealed by masculine fingers. Only his wedding ring remains visible in the neat bundle. "Since I had this beautiful wife to show off."

Jake throws me a wink. "I won't argue with that. And what about you, Beth? Are you happy to be the Belle of the ball?"

I construct my lie. "Why not? I got to wear that red dress you bought me, didn't I?"

He laughs out loud. "Now that's a picture I would pay to see." He turns to Ayden. "Although I'd have to fold the page back on your side, Ayd. Wouldn't want you ruining a good picture now would we?"

Ayden isn't amused. Why would he be? He doesn't feel the brotherly bond they have established over 20 years.

I take a long sip. "Would you prefer if I left the room so you two could talk about me privately?"

Sensing my embarrassment or prompted by jealousy, Ayden redirects the conversation. "No, we've finished, darling. You won't be the topic of any further conversations with Jake today."

With the wine taking effect, Jake sniggers. "What's with the *darling?* Who the fuck says that these days?"

Ayden takes offense. "*I* do apparently."

"You've been watching too many black and whites. Either that or you're getting old, Ayd."

Picking up the empty bottle, Ayden stands and glares at it. "Unfortunately, you're wrong on both counts, Jake."

Jake, leans back on the sofa. "Aren't we opening another bottle to celebrate?"

"To celebrate what, exactly?" asks Ayden.

"You getting the girl you always wanted." He stands and raises his glass. "Let's drink to that. They say a girl has to kiss a lot of frogs before she finds her prince, but our Beth here is the exception. I raise my glass to you, *darling.*" He throws back the remnants of his wine in two noisy gulps.

Before things get out of hand I intervene by taking Jake's arm and leading him over to the lift. "You're in no state to drive. Let me get Lester to drive you home."

He's laughing. "I've had two glasses of wine, Beth. I'm fine. I think it's Ayd who needs to loosen up." He spins around to face him. "You've got a Board meeting at 9 a.m. tomorrow. The honeymoon's over my friend. It's business as usual from now on."

Seeing the sense in his words, Ayden nods his head and winks. "Don't start without me," he orders, semi-seriously.

Jake smiles, relieved to witness his return. "I wouldn't think of it. It's good to have you back." He raises my hand to his mouth and plants a noisy kiss on it. "No need to come down. I can find my own way out."

Feeling forsaken I watch him descend, waving behind frosted glass. With his departure leaves any sense of reality. I feel an ominous conversation brewing up here in adventure land.

25

I stood facing the lift for longer than I should have. I must have looked like a prisoner planning an escape. Now Ayden is opening another bottle of vintage wine and pouring out two large glasses, but something tells me, the alcohol will not be sufficient to deaden the pain of what he's about to divulge.

Taking a glass from his hand I sit next to him, responding to a silent invitation. Outside, the midday sun is trying its hardest to shine but the winter storm clouds are gathering and there's the threat of more rain. They make for a sombre sight.

"Do the storm clouds bother you?" Ayden asks, reading my thoughts.

I offer a flat smile. "Not especially. I'd forgotten how dark it is here. We've been spoilt by all that tropical sunshine."

"Yes. It was beautiful."

He takes my glass from me and places it next to his on the coffee table, leaving the wine to reflect in the glass beneath. I feel a strong left arm about my shoulders pulling me close and respond by kicking off my shoes and snuggling next to him.

"It's time," he says, so softly it's barely a whisper.

I place my hand over his heart. "It was never going to be six months was it?"

He shakes his head sluggishly. "No."

"And have you made a decision?" I ask as my heart begins to race.

"I have." He folds his right arm across my body, wrapping me so tightly in his embrace I can hardly breathe. The heat of his heaving chest radiates from his core and causes my cheek to glow. "I can't let you go, Beth."

Unsure of what that means, I lean back, taking his sculptured face in my left hand. "I don't understand."

"I owe you a great debt of gratitude for what you have taught me in the time we have been together." He releases his grip and I watch him speak, using words that are reflective and considered. "I came here a mere shell of a man, lost to the world. I had been around death for so long, and it took you to show me the beauty of life. You have taught me what it is to love and how an existence is of no consequence without it. Every emotion you have introduced me to I have named and can identify as one might stars in the sky. I have witnessed that ripple we spoke of on an endless sea and watched as it has become a wave of consciousness, ebbing and flowing like the tide. Such is the impression have you made on me, but I cannot stay one more night."

"Where will you go?" I ask softly.

He forces a smile. "Anywhere. There is much to be done and still so many things to see. The universe is vast and infinite."

"I can imagine."

He strokes my hair, lovingly feeling the texture of every strand. "You've had merely a glimpse of it. Wouldn't you like to see more?"

I'm not sure where this conversation is going but I detect an insidious inflection that's causing me to perspire. "One day perhaps. Right now I'm just happy to be home." I look into the eyes of the man I love for some kind of sign, but all I see is myself reflected in shimmering cerulean orbs. "You're not bringing him back are you?" I ask, feeling an ache so deep in my heart I think it might break my body in two.

He asks me squarely, "Is that what you want?"

I wipe away a stray tear. "I want ... I want the man I married to live his life to the fullest, with me. Yes."

"And do you value *his* life more than your own?" he asks, tenderness fading from his eyes like smoke caught in a draft.

"I value our love and everything I have done has been for that. Haven't I done what you've asked of me? You asked for the impossible and I gave you my love and my body and ..."

"This is true," he says, mocking the memory of the man he's impersonating. "But I want *more*."

"What more can I give?" I ask, intimidated by the menacing nature of his demand. "When did you decide this?"

"When I fell in love with you." He caresses my cheek and finds my lips with his.

I can't respond. I'm numb with fear. I seek out his eyes with mine. "But I thought you said you couldn't stay. That you had to leave."

"I do."

Disappointed and saddened I turn away. "I see it now. You have wooed me with your omnipotence and it has been wondrous, I confess. But there's more to you than meets the eye." I see him for what he is. "You said you never lied but even *that* was a lie. You falling in love with me is a lie."

He's shaking his head.

Still defiant, I continue, "I'm a fool to ever have trusted you. Underneath that handsome exterior is a soulless bastard."

He floors me with a fierce stare. "Careful, Beth."

"I thought you were an angel, a messenger from God, a guardian offering protection but you're nothing of the sort. You're the Dark Prince. Everything you have done has been out of selfishness with no regard for my feelings. All pretence."

He pushes me away from him. "That's not true," he calls out. "I have given you everything."

"It wasn't yours to give!" I cry to the heavens above. "This house, the clothes you wear, the business. They're all Ayden's. Even me." Through streaming tears I laugh scornfully. "You've stolen everything but now there's nothing left to steal. You can't hurt me. You've already stolen what matters most to me: my husband and my heart. You bastard! You made me fall for you!"

I stand and try to leave but he holds up his hand and I can't move.

"Wait! I can give you more, Beth," he implores. "More than material possessions; more than the moon and the stars; I can offer you eternity. We'll have new adventures and live forever!" He stops shouting and modulates his voice until it becomes almost muted. "You're a born fighter. I have watched you battle your way through grief and disappointment; loneliness and despair. You can do this."

I bow my head seeking atonement for my sins. "I don't think you realise what you're asking me to do. What do you expect me to say?"

He stands inches away, tipping up my chin with his forefinger. "That you choose me, my darling." He moves away to the side, leaving me motionless and shattered. Set against the backdrop of a darkening sky he stands tall and proud, sipping wine while I picture the pieces of my broken heart falling about me like rose petals.

I muster every ounce of strength I have and channel it into my voice. "What do you want from me?"

Turing slowly until his profile transposes into a handsome visage, he declares. "Your life, Beth."

I stifle a horrified gasp and tilt up my chin. "What's my motivation?" I ask, holding onto my husband's memory like a lifeline.

"What motivation do you need?" he asks fiendishly.

"You must promise me you'll bring Ayden back and that he'll be healthy and allowed to live a long life."

"I can do that," he says without a moment's hesitation. "Anything else?"

I stretch out my hand. "You have to give me my mother's ring back and allow me time to say goodbye to those I love."

"Of course." He reaches into his inside pocket and retrieves my ring. In four paces he is beside me again. "Here, let me put it on for you." He holds out my right hand and slides the ring down onto my third finger like a mock engagement.

I sneer and turn away but, feeling his body moving into mine, I turn to face him. "If I ask you something, will you answer me truthfully?"

He eyes me curiously. "I will."

"Did you cause Elise's death by crashing into the car after it had been brought under control?"

He sniggers. "You are as astute as you are beautiful. *That* was a minor detail our Detective Inspector regretfully brought to your attention."

I can't conceal my disgust. "But why?"

"It was only a matter of time until I came for Elise. I arrived early and seized the opportunity to *rescue* your husband." He takes hold of my hand. "I could never have gotten this close to you any other way." He runs his thumb over my wedding ring.

"But you said Ayden was dead," I state anxiously.

"No," he asserts, steadying his nerve. "I said your husband was *close* to death when I arrived. That's not quite the same thing."

My heart leaps. Tears prick my eyes. "So he's not dead?"

"As I have said many times, he is merely *sleeping.*"

That news causes a colossal wave of joy to sweep through me. If I can do nothing else I can guarantee Ayden will get to live the life he deserves. I reach down to my wine and take two large slugs in the hope they will give me the courage I need to see this adventure through to its bitter end.

"There's something I have to do." I carry my wine over to the kitchen counter and place it there next to my laptop patiently waiting to be woken from its sleep. I tap in my password and close my eyes, unable to face my husband at such a mournful time. I click on my digital scrapbook and begin to type my farewell note.

Ayden,
I have added this special song. I hope you like it. I know I've sent you many before but this means so much to me. The words spell out how I feel ...

I attach *Hurt* by Christina Aguilera in the hope I might be forgiven for sending him away when all he wanted to do was love me.

I'm not sure when you'll get to read through our honeymoon scrapbook but I mean every ...

Just as I'm about to press the next key I hear my phone ringing. I make a dash for my bag by the sofa and reach for it before it stops. I smile seeing it's Charlie. She must be itching to tell me about her night with Jake. I press receive to take her call.

"Hi Char."

"Hey, Beth. When did you get back?" She sounds as if she's eating something.

"This morning early, but we slept on the plane. I suppose the jet lag will hit me in a couple of hours. How are you?"

"Yeah. It'll take you a couple of days to get over it, hon. I'm good. I've just stepped out of my office to stretch my legs and get some lunch. I was wondering if Ayden heard from Jake." She's dying to tell me all about their night out.

I watch Ayden move from the sofa towards the kitchen in search of more wine.

"Yes, Jake came round earlier. He seemed in a very good mood. Did you have anything to do with that?" I'm feigning cheerful laughter and covering my mouth to conceal my misery. I want to say, *I have to leave and I love you, don't grieve for me; please tell Ayden I love him more than life itself and I'm sorry, but* ... instead I wipe the tears from my eyes and listen as she regales her night of passion. I punctuate her ecstatic tale with. "wow" and "no way" and turn to see Ayden standing by the counter scrolling through my most private of thoughts so tenderly composed to my one and only love.

"Oh God!" I call out, instinctively. "Look Char, can I call you back? I've left the bath running. I'll speak to you later." I'm about to end the call and think better of it. "Charlie, Charlie..."

"I'm still here, hon. Shit! I just dropped mayo on my skirt."

I stand and move towards Ayden. "I just want to say thanks for everything, you know, for being the best sister ever. That's all. Love ya."

"You too hon. Call me back when the fire brigade leaves." She's laughing down the line.

With her laugher still ringing in my ears I end the call. I speak softly. "Ayden..."

He continues reading and merely holds up his right hand to silence me.

I reach out for the laptop but he moves it away, leaving me no alternative other than to plead with him. I beseech him, "Please don't read any more ..."

He turns to face me. I watch as his expression darkens; the accommodating smile of ten minutes ago has been replaced by a hard, unyielding stare. I swallow hard, stunned by his transformation. I've seen this wrathful face before.

His temper flares and catches alight like a forest fire; his body tenses, his eyes flash with so much ferocity I take a step back.

Dear God no!

"You have been keeping a diary, I see."

He might have delivered his question through a punch for the damage he's inflicted on me. "I had to. I didn't want my husband to return to me having no recollection of our marriage or our honeymoon." Still reeling, I feel a single tear fall from my right eye and trickle to my chin before I have time to catch it.

"You said if and when he returns he may not remember me, the times we've had or, worse still, his love for me. I couldn't risk that. I had to let him know what our honeymoon meant to me and what we'd experienced was real. Not a dream or a figment of his imagination. Being no more than a ghost would have been too much to bear."

In slow motion, he closes the lid of the laptop, still keeping his eyes on me. "So the time we've had together meant nothing to you? You have been playing a part and nothing more?"

I tip my head to one side so he might see the sincerity with which I speak. "That's not true."

Unimpressed by my claim, he snatches the bottle of wine off the counter and brushes past me without so much as a sideways glance. "You reneged on our arrangement."

The impact of his chilling declaration is profound. I reach for his arm but my attempt to hold onto him is useless; he's too strong and too fast. I have to spin around to see where he's going. "No. I didn't."

Deep in thought, he wipes the sticky residue forming at the corners of his mouth with his forefinger and thumb and positions himself by the floor to ceiling window. Behind him the plummeting darkness casts a sinister shadow over the city, mirroring his mood and my deepening despair.

"You have been toying with me, Mrs. Stone." he sniggers sardonically, disbelieving that I, a mere human might have fooled him.

All I can do is approach him contritely and state my case. "No ..."

A lascivious sneer forms slowly, causing me to squirm in my chair. "Did you think I could be duped so easily?"

I don't bother looking in his direction, I sit awkwardly, fixing my eyes on a single spot on the table and focusing on it. "It wasn't like that. You have to let me explain."

"There is nothing to be explained, other than your duplicity. Have you any idea how much self-discipline I have had to exhibit to appease you?" His brow furrows as he prepares to elucidate. "Did you think I was unaware or your late night trysts? I knew you kept a diary of sorts, but I have not been privy to it until now."

I frown and ask, "Then, if you knew, why are you making such a big deal about it?"

"Because, my darling, by your own admission, a meaningful relationship is based on trust, is it not?"

"Yes ..."

"Then how can you explain what you have done? You have betrayed a trust. "*God has given you one face and you make yourself another.*"

I'm smirking at the suggestion. "You think?"

"I do."

I raise my head and hit him with a contemptuous stare. "We're here talking about trust and you're quoting Hamlet. Let me tell you a thing or two about trust." With dogged determination I prepare to enlighten him. "In what seems like a lifetime ago I married the only man I have ever loved. He was taken from me on our wedding day and yet, when we were reunited, our bond was stronger than ever. He has lived in my dreams and my subconscious for most of my life. He's a prince among men. You came along and stepped into his shoes demanding lessons in love in exchange for his safe return. That's when we began our adventure; an adventure based on trust."

I stand fearlessly and approach him, having to look up at him to make eye-contact. "But let's come clean; lay our cards on the table. Once you 'rescued' Ayden, trust went out the window." I wave my hand in the direction of the enormous glass pane to make a point. "This charade has been a test of my ability to please you, to be yours in every sense of the word; to break my spirit before you initiated your plan to steal it, as you have everything else I hold dear." I pause, gauging his reaction as his handsome features reflect in the glass. "I thought it was about saving Ayden's life but it's not. It has never been about that, has it? It's been about my death; sacrificing myself for him to be yours for ever."

He raises his chin, acknowledging my accurate assessment of the state of play but offers no defence. Instead he tips his head assuming I still have more to say. He's right.

"You have masked your true nature beautifully except for that one night when I saw you for the dark angel you are, devoid of goodness and compassion. You bewitched me, left me covered in bites; battered and bruised, requiring your magic to heal me." I laugh at myself, sardonically. "And still I went along with it, allowing you to access the most intimate of Ayden's memories, encouraging you to transform yourself into him. For that I will never forgive myself."

Feeling suddenly chilled to the bone, I fold my arms about my body and massage lifeless arms that have become goose-pimpled and icy to the touch. "I have betrayed my husband, but worse still I have betrayed myself and become the one thing I hate most – a fraud. If I were to end my life I might be able to redeem myself; to find absolution for my sins."

"That would be your choice," he interjects.

My eyes flare. "What other choice do I have?"

"To remain here..."

"As a widow?" I scoff. "That's not a choice. I would rather live in purgatory than remain here alone."

"You need not. You've had a glimpse of my world. It would not be torturous."

He reaches out to me but I reject his advance and turn away. I see myself reflected in the glass. I don't like what I see. My features have become harsh, unyielding and unrecognisable.

"I would never hurt you, Beth. Not now that I know what it is to feel your soft caress, to hear your laughter and to experience the consummation of love so profoundly beautiful it touches even my dark soul. If I didn't love you I would not be listening to you and I would not be offering you several lifetimes spent in the arms of someone who can hold back tides, direct the wind, ignite your passion, turn back time and move heaven and earth ... for you."

"It's too much. I can't live in a world overflowing with superlatives. The honeymoon is over." I turn about, having made my decision. "I'm leaving."

With dark eyes narrowing to a squint, he takes my arm. "Superlatives, in what sense?"

I shake free of his arm. "It's only now I realise how your pride has governed every decision you've made. You've poached Ayden's memories and bettered them by seeking out the highest, the biggest, brightest, deepest, longest ..." I pause to take breath. "Nothing you have done has come from the heart. You've turned it into a dick measuring contest, and even went all out to win that too! Why did you do that?"

His chest inflates. I anticipate those three tell-tale words to fly from his mouth. And they do.

"Because I can!" he yells in a thunderous roar that has me recoiling.

With trembling hands I pick up my bag and throw it over my shoulder, casting an eye over the envelope waiting to be opened on the coffee table. I throw down my bag and tear it open.

"Aren't you going to read this?" I call out, holding it out to him timidly.

He shrugs his shoulder, disinterested and detached from a woman who had her life taken so fiendishly.

"You said you wanted lessons in love. Then let this be my last one." I clear my throat and begin to read the final words of Elise Richards:

Dear Ayden,

You reading this can only mean one thing. I am dead or dying.

I've written this letter hoping you'll do a couple of things for me that I've not had the courage to do for myself. You're a man of your word and, even though we have become distant, I know you loved me once; not as much as I loved you, but what little love you have shown me has been more than anything I could hope for or deserve.

Firstly, you must promise me you'll follow through with my wishes, even though they might cause you embarrassment. I'm not doing it for that reason, you know that. This is my last chance to make amends for my sins and to make others accountable for theirs.

Attached are the names and addresses of the two men who followed me to my new home when I was taken away from Bright Hill. They continued to rape me, every month, sometimes more. They'd come to collect me, pretending to be family members and no questions were asked, no one wondered why I cried myself to sleep when I returned, and no one cared. It went on for four years until I became a little old for their taste and they moved on to younger girls. I was relieved but hated myself for saying nothing. But I had no one to tell, all I could do was wait for you.

You never came.

When I was fourteen I met a boy who was nice to me. Ralph's mother was ill and he came to stay for three months. We fooled around. I became pregnant. He left and went back to his mum. I hid my pregnancy until I was eight months along but started haemorrhaging and they took me to hospital. I was petrified. The pain was like nothing I'd ever felt before.

After four hours of labour I gave up and they delivered my baby boy by caesarean section. (I've included as many details as I can about the time and place.)

I named him Saffir after you. I don't know his real name because they took him away from me but I did get to see him. He was beautiful, Ayden. Every wish I'd ever made came true with him; he had beautiful blue eyes and a mop of black hair. I wished so hard for that. I've been waiting for the day when he comes looking for me. He'll be sixteen soon and I'm praying his parents have taken good care of him and have not been cruel with their description of me. I didn't want to let him go but I was about to be adopted and they said I couldn't keep him. I was so desperate to finally have a home I agreed. But I did love him. The eight months he was inside me I loved him with every beat of my heart. He's the one thing in my life I got right.

I need you to find him, Ayden, and to help him make his way in the world. His father was smart and funny and he'll be the same. He may not be the perfect son but someone like you could put him on the right track. I don't expect you to shower him with gifts or anything so I've signed the apartment and all my expensive jewellery over to you in my will. I haven't touched the monthly allowance you've been sending me so I could give my adoptive mother £5,000 to help with her debts, and give the rest to Saffir. Maybe you can help him set up a business or show him how to use the money wisely or for good. He's the same age you were when you were starting out, so you'll know what's best.

I understand if you don't want to get involved. All I ask is that you try to find him, and tell him something nice about me. I'm afraid all he will hear are bad things once my past catches up with me. Tell him I tried to be good but somehow I seemed to attract the bad.

I hope you remember me with fondness and think of me now and again. The times we've spent together have been the happiest days of my life. My mind has been twisted by the shadows that used to come for me and I know I asked you to do some shameful things. I'm sorry.

I'm hoping you'll remember the fun times we had together a lifetime ago and help me. You are the only person I have ever loved, and the only one I would trust with the welfare of my son.

Please be my friend, Ayden.

All my love,

Elise Richards (Kilbride)

Wiping the tears from my woeful eyes, I take an invigorating breath and prepare to face my once lover-turned-nemesis. "That's one hell of a lesson. " I fold up the letter and slip it back into its envelop. "So, can you name it?"

"Name what?"

"The emotion?" I reach for a tissue and wait.

He turns away and stands face to face with his reflection. "No."

All I can do is sneer. "I have taught you nothing." I pick up my bag. "Then I'll tell you. What you *should* be feeling, shall I?" I don't bother waiting for a reply. "Compassion."

I turn to face him, head bowed, stopping only when I see a vision. Outside, the clouds have been chased away and the full moon hangs low and bright in the sky. It may well be staged but, from where I'm standing and his position by the window, his head is arced by a circle of white light. I cover my mouth with my hand to stifle my mournful sobs.

"Beth, it pains me to see you so distressed." He holds out his hand.

I won't take it.

"What if I said I could tell you what your future holds, would you want to know?"

He piques my interest with that possibility. "Is this another one of your tricks?"

"No. I have come to the conclusion that my *tricks,* as you call them, have no relevance at this point. There is little I can say or do to persuade you that my intentions are honourable."

Honourable?

"You have made it perfectly clear what your intentions are, and honourable is not the word I would use, quite frankly." I grab another tissue out of my bag. "But go ahead. This I've got to hear."

He directs me to the sofa. We are sitting opposite each other like chess players anticipating each other's moves and trying to think ahead before giving anything away. He glances to his left side, seeming to scroll forward.

My tears are beginning to dry and my cheeks are smarting from the tidal wave of salt water they have endured. I'm sitting, waiting, wringing out the paper tissue between my hands, trying to convince myself that everything he says will be a lie laced with selfishness and jealousy. Maybe I should just leave now while I have the willpower?

His eyes meet mine. "You will continue on your fateful path and continue to love and live the life you imagined ..."

My body sags. I was fearful of his prediction but now I'm elated ...

"... for several years at least. You will not be able to give Ayden a child and his dream of having a family will not be fulfilled."

No!

"You will grow apart. After five years he will begin to spend more time at the office; he will work late, have an affair – or two - and you will begin to drink." He faces me squarely. "Champagne mostly. You'll start to lose your looks and your beauty will fade. He will not see you the same way he does now."

I fall back into the sofa. Feeling utterly desolate I close my eyes, allowing my head to fall, with neither the strength nor desire to lift it from its penitent position.

He continues to chronicle my life, recounting it like one might a Victorian novel. "When you are thirty five your husband will demand a divorce. You will become a wealthy woman but your nights will be spent alone." He pauses, no doubt giving me time to absorb his poisonous prediction. "Your husband will return to his previous lifestyle and you will be able to follow it in the news, in magazines and on the TV but you will be on the outside looking in."

I raise my head and fix him with a scornful stare. "Are you finished?"

"Not quite." Taking his time he folds his hands on his thighs, glances about the room and resumes his tortuous prophecy. "Several bad business decisions and a technical flaw will bring about a fall in share price for ASMI and several millions of pounds in revenue will be lost as a result. With returns on investment floundering, units will be sold to reduce company debts. A cost saving initiative will be introduced, resulting in the closing of Far Eastern units and ..."

I'm holding up my hands. "Enough! Why are you telling me all this? I don't care whether my husband has two hundred or two million pounds in the bank. That's never mattered to me."

"But it has mattered to him," he states, plainly. "As his business loses favour so does he. Three days before his forty second birthday he is found beaten and robbed outside a London night club."

All I can do is shake my head. "You're a liar. That's not how this story ends. This is some elaborate creation you're concocting to make me feel as if I have no choice but to be with you. You're suggesting my staying with Ayden would lead to his downfall and his death?" I snatch my bag from the sofa. "Why would you say such terrible things?"

He shrugs his shoulders. "Because that's what I see."

"You have it all wrong. All you see is what *you* want to see. You want us to fail." I will not allow him to see me cry. I have shed enough tears to fill an ocean. No more.

"You act as if love is a kind of condition; something for which there is no cure. Love is not that. Love is that which remains once you realise you could not love another person more; so deeply, sincerely and unconditionally. That's what love is. That's what we have." I sniff and raise my chin boldly. "When I look in your direction I'm drawn to you because you have the face of an angel, but you're *not* Ayden." I stand, pulling down my sweater and, for the first time, tower over him. "You can't scare me with talk of divorce and death. All that does is remind me of how desperate you are; that someone of such high-standing would stoop so low to get what he knows is not his to steal." I launch my final assault through a single thought, using words from Ms. Bronte's I know he will recognise and understand.

Your presence is a moral poison that would contaminate the most virtuous.

Not stopping to hear more he stands and regains some of his status through his height. Through eyes swamped in tears I witness him in his sorrowful subterfuge and read it as a sign. I approach him, take his face in my trembling hands, close my eyes and taste his lips. Overcome by drowsiness I open my eyes languidly to be greeted by glossy, sea green eyes.

"I love you," he murmurs.

Through swollen lips I force a smile and whisper adoringly, "I love you more."

The garage door jerks into motion. In ten long seconds it creates a crack wide enough for a boisterous Boxster to slip through.

After heading west for fifteen minutes I indicate and join the M4 when, without warning, the radio begins to play. I know the song and understand the message. Christina Perri is singing *A Thousand Years*. Regardless of which button I press it continues to play until the final orchestral note, every chord ripping at my heartstrings.

With open road ahead, I put my foot down and cruise at 80 miles an hour, flicking through lanes and overtaking with ease. It's ironic how reassuring it feels to be encapsulated in this sweet little car after the confinement of my Belgravia home. This cockpit is womblike, the air thick with memories and Ayden's cologne.

As the plummeting darkness swallows up the rural landscape I'm sniffing back tears, pressing buttons in search of headlights and wipers to clear away noisy raindrops that are rattling against the glass like bullets. Every new volley is a reminder of the battle raging in my mind and the conflicting emotions I'm harbouring.

The motorway stretches out before me, a road leading me nowhere punctuated by the soundtrack to our love affair. *The story of us* plays out one song at a time. I fast forward to transatlantic tunes that closed the miles between us.

One after another the tracks play out, bringing with them a heart-breaking series of flashbacks. Every song sparks a memory, every memory fuels more tears until the cars in front are no more than smudges on the windscreen. J-Lo reminds me of a time when I was eating cereal and thinking *I'm into you,* Hoobastank explains *The Reason* for your devotion. We're *Feeling Good* and dancing on our terrace in Rome thanks to Michael Bublé. And it's all too much.

I search for less meaningful songs but there are none; each recollection of images leaves me with only one conclusion: *You're all I have.*

I turn off Stone Patrol and search for something less emotionally charged on the radio. Florence Welsh sings about *Sweet Nothings* and I mouth the words! She reaches the chorus. I'm hitting the accelerator. I'm gripping the wheel as if my life depends on it. The world on all sides is a blur. I turn up the volume, feeling every word as if they are my own. Like a proclamation to God Almighty they voice my utter desolation, and bring me closer to the ultimate sacrifice; to do the hardest thing I will ever have to do: to forfeit my life for the sake of another. To atone for my sins I prepare to give my soul and all that I am: *everything*.

The music builds to a resounding crescendo. I fortify myself with a deep breath that might well be my last, and hit the accelerator. Glancing down I watch the dial edge past 100. Only when I raise my eyes to the open road do I spot the approaching neon sign above the motorway flashing wildly with an unequivocal command.

STOP BETH! STOP BETH! STOP BETH!

I can't believe my eyes. Even now he tries to intervene, to decide my fate - but I will not be manipulated a moment longer. This is my decision to make.

Once again above my head the sign reads:

BETH! SLOW DOWN!

Defiantly, I increase my speed. Out of the corner of my eyes I see a single blinding light coming up behind me; it's filling my rear view mirror. I'm being pursued.

Death is seeking me out, but I won't be caught so easily. With all hope lost, I apply more pressure to the accelerator and watch the finger move on the speedometer past 120. Other cars appear to be parked as I fly past them on the outside lane like a shooting star. Through a voice strangled by tears I call out, "Everything I've done, I've done for love, Ayden. Please forgive me."

Unexpectedly, the rain clears from the windscreen; I see an opening in the grey curtain of clouds obscuring the horizon. The dial begins to wind backwards like the hands on a clock turning back time. Even though the accelerator pedal is flat against the floor, I'm slowing down. Fearful of being caught I check my rear view mirror but all I see are paired headlights .

In a blind panic I have travelled 40 miles from home, crossing junctions and flyovers with no destination in mind. I have no idea where I am.

I signal and pull over onto the hard shoulder to park up. My nerves are frayed; my emotions are swirling. Like a drowning woman having made it back to shore, I gasp for air and wipe the salt water from my eyes.

Overcome with fatigue, I slump back in the seat and feel myself dozing, rocked to sleep by the jerking movement of turbulent air created by passing cars. A mechanised lullaby lulls me into a false sense of security and, before I fade into oblivion, I hear Ayden's thoughts in my head.

It's time to say goodbye, my darling. You have taught me so much in the brief time we have spent together. I have learned, first hand, the true meaning of self-sacrifice and there is no purer form of love than this in heaven and earth. Yours, for ever. Your dark prince.

26

I' m stirred from my unconscious state by a recurring sound; it's mechanical, not human, more like a beep than a bang, but rhythmic - almost like the beating of a heart. I'm leaning forward; my head is resting on my left forearm.

With my eyes closed I'm willing myself to go back to sleep, having realised the noise I can hear is a heart monitor. I'm alive. The finer points of the deal I made with my paramour come back to haunt me.

If I'm alive, Ayden is dead.

That realisation causes my body to sag; treacherous tears roll onto my arms like a bleeding heart, and I weep for the love I have lost and for the loneliness I must endure. I will pay the price for my adultery in the days and months and years I will spend mourning my loss.

How will I survive this?

Now my imagination is playing tricks on me. I feel someone stroking my hair, but still fearful, I close my eyes tightly, shutting out light, willing the fantasy to be real but terrified it's not. I say a silent prayer, repeating over and over; please let it be a dream. Please let it be a dream. Please ...

I raise my head and turn to my left, slowly, and what I see causes me to gasp so deeply I catch my breath. I take Ayden's hand from my hair and hold it to my lips, christening it with my tears. I have to remind myself to take a breath.

"You're alive!"

He wipes away my tears with his thumb. "I think so." He winks and I cry harder. "Don't cry. I'm all right. I was only sleeping." His smile forms slowly, his eyes glisten with love and I reach out to l him.

"Careful, you don't want to hurt yourself." He points to a box of tissues on the bedside cabinet. "Dry your tears, Beth. It kills me to see you like this."

I grab a couple of tissues and blow my nose noisily. My unladylike behaviour causes him to raise a brow. Feeling facial pain, he reaches for his cheek and touches the pad concealing an injury likely to cause a scar.

"Don't worry about that. It's nothing," I reassure him, standing to pass him a glass of water. "Here, you must be thirsty."

He sips it slowly and hands me back the glass. "I had the weirdest dream."

I respond without thinking. "Me too."

"I was in this room waiting for you. Every time you were nearby I would call to you but you didn't hear me, and I couldn't make myself heard. It was like I was half asleep. I must have been waiting for you to wake me with a kiss," He smiles broadly, forcing the skin to crinkle around his eyes; it folds into tiny creases like lifelines marking his reawakening.

I reach out with a hand, close enough to feel the warmth radiating from his body. "I can do that." Dragging the line from the intravenous drip with me I stand and position both of my trembling hands around his face as a mother would a small child; I close my eyes and place a soft kiss upon his lips. When I open them, all I can see is an ocean of love; a Caribbean sea with splashes of emerald.

A sob sticks in my throat. "I'm so sorry I sent you away. I didn't mean any of those things I said."

He cups my face with both hands. "I know, baby. You were just doing what you always do; putting *me* first."

"I didn't want you to settle for someone who couldn't give you all you've ever wanted."

He takes a handful of my hair. "Don't start that again. *You're* all I've ever wanted."

Unable to hold back my tears I let them fall. "I love you so much, Ayden. I thought I'd lost you."

He sniggers. "Now that's just crazy. It would take more than a blind date with Death to take me away from you." Sensing my sadness he raises my chin with his forefinger. "So, tell me about *your* dream." He pats away my residual tears with a tissue.

I rest my chin on an upturned palm, only inches from his face. "Oh, I dreamed we were together on honeymoon. We were in Hong Kong and then we went to the Great Barrier Reef. We swam in the ocean and spent most of our time counting stars and making love."

He's rolling his eyes. "Sounds to me like you got the better deal. I just couldn't wake up, but I felt you were close by.

I'm nodding my head. "I was."

He takes hold of my right hand and holds my palm against his lips. "I felt your presence. I might not have ever awakened if I hadn't." He caresses my fingers, stopping only when he sees the ring.

I see it too. As hard as I try to conceal my horror I cannot. A strangled whimper escapes my mouth before I have time to mask it. A stunned silence ensues.

Ayden breaks it. "What's the matter?" he asks, troubled at my sudden outburst. "Come here. I'm not going anywhere, Beth." He pulls my head into his neck. "I didn't mean to frighten you."

Regaining some strength of mind, I wipe away my tears. "You didn't. I visualised how different things might have turned out, that's all."

"I think someone was looking out for me. When Elise took the wheel I had visions of it turning out badly, but I've too much to live for to go like that. I have you."

I'm smiling and crying but these are not tears of sadness, fear or regret; they're tears of joy. Somewhere out there in the night sky is a blinding light and in that light there is goodness and compassion. Now I know the truth. I have been loved by an angel. I hold onto his hand, fearing he may be snatched away from me again. "I have you, Ayden. We have the rest of our lives to look forward to but we have to make things right."

He's baffled by my assertion. "What things?"

"Everything. We need to get in touch with D.I. Bowker and explain what's been happening. He has a good heart." I release my grip, run my fingers under my eyes and pull myself together. I have to put my adventure behind me and face each new day with thankfulness. I stand and straighten his bedding. "But now's not the time to talk about that, there will be time enough ..."

Unexpectedly, the door opens behind me. Seeing me standing, Charlie lets out a deafening squeal. "No!" She rushes to my side. "You shouldn't be moving around like this."

I reach for her arm. "I'm okay. Look who's awake."

Having been too preoccupied with my welfare, she hadn't bothered to look over at Ayden. When she sees him she bursts into tears. "You stupid bastard! You had her scared out of her wits!"

It's not the response either of us are expecting and we begin to laugh.

"It's good to see you too, Charlie," he announces. "Will you get the nurse so she can turn off this damn machine and I can hold my wife?"

Charlie wraps her arms around my neck. "He's only been away for five minutes and already he's giving bloody orders," she declares, leaving the room in a hurry. "I'll be right back, Mr. Stone."

I push back the wheelchair with my foot to make room for the nurse.

Ayden notices. "You came in a wheelchair?" he asks. "Hadn't you better sit down?"

Feeling better than I have for a long, long time I shake my head from left to right. "I feel great. Don't worry about me. I've had ages to heal. It's your turn to be *my* patient."

If only you knew the immensity of my love. There has never been a day when I haven't been willing to lay down my life for you. Now I can sleep at night, knowing you'll be here when I open my eyes. No longer a wish or a dream, only you.

Unaware of my thoughts, he smirks sexily. "I'll have you know, I can be *very* demanding, Nurse Stone," he sniggers.

I drop my right hand by the bed, concealing my precious new ring. "I do hope so, Mr. Stone," I state, feeling something maternal stirring inside me. "I plan on being around for a very long time; for ever in fact."

27

A yden appears from the lift and comes bounding across our rooftop terrace like a man returning home from battle. The make-believe metal encasing his Sir Lancelot costume is rattling as he walks, adding to his comedic performance; my husband has been reborn with a joie de vivre that even I could never have imagined. He's making me giggle, and so powerful is his presence I am bowled over by it. The light-hearted ambiance is set against the incongruent backdrop of a Latin beat. Pink Martini plays *Let's Never Stop Falling in Love,* proclaiming our joy for all to hear.

He takes my hands and I am swirling; a Star Wars princess all dressed in white, wrapped up in the arms of the only man she has ever loved. That's me.

The music dies. Exhausted I fall backwards onto the sofa bed, my view of the sky obscured by my knight in shining armour, no less noble for his impending state of undress.

"I thought they'd never leave. I can't wait to get this stuff off." Ayden's fiddling with buckles and creating an untidy pile of bits and pieces, letting them fall noisily by his feet.

"Do you need any help?" I ask, amusement glistening I my eyes.

"No. You just lie back, birthday girl and sip your water. Give me a minute ... I'll be right with you." He gives me a playful wink and continues to disrobe punctuating, his mediaeval striptease with profanities.

I use the time to unclip my hair; the Princess Leia buns I fashioned for my birthday party seem superfluous now, but better a white robe than a leather bodice and Bat Girl boots ... hardly suitable attire for a mother to be.

He flops down next to me, dressed in what amounts to an undergarment made of chainmail. It clings to his muscular frame and I can't help but leer; his chest is heaving and his biceps are flexing.

He catches me looking. "I know I look ridiculous but I'd rather be here looking like this than another minute away from you getting changed. I've had to share you with everyone tonight." He slides his arm across my shoulders.

I fold into him, avoiding the herringbone pattern of the material that stretches all the way up to his chin. "Thanks for the birthday party. This house has never been so full of people and music." I brush back a curl from his forehead and stroke the small scar on his right cheek ... that perfect imperfection I love so much. "I know you're not one for dressing up."

He sniggers. "At least I looked half decent. What was Jake thinking coming as Superman?"

My head rocks on his chest as he chuckles, forcing me to place my hand upon it to steady myself. Wanting to see him in this gloriously happy state, I arch my body away from his and rest my chin on my palm. "It was a little obscene, wasn't it? There aren't many men who can pull off a look like that."

"Well, I think we've established that Jake isn't one of them." He laughs loudly and pulls the material from his throat after almost choking.

Our happiness rings out into the night and I fall backwards laughing, recalling Jake dancing with Charlie. What good friends they have become.

Still harbouring a gleeful expression he turns to face me; I sense his eyes on me and feel his forefinger following the line of my nose, my lips, my chin. Turning to meet his adoring gaze I ask, "After all this time, are you still assessing me, Mr. Stone?"

He's shaking his head and holding me spellbound with a shimmering stare. "No. Always enjoying, Mrs. Stone, especially now you're beginning to blossom." He kisses my cheek and places his right hand on my stomach. "All that we've been through has brought us to this point. I can't recall a time when I was ever this happy."

"Me either. We're the luckiest people in the world, Ayden." Enjoying the intimacy, I weave my fingers through his hair. "Once we meet your mother tomorrow and are introduced to your extended family we'll have everything we've ever wanted."

Softly he kisses my nose. "What a wonder you are, Beth. You never did tell me how you found her."

"I told you; through a good friend." I turn from him, ending the conversation, and look skyward at the brightest star directly above my head. "We need never wish for anything more."

His grip tightens on my shoulder. "This is true."

From out of the midnight sky appears a streak of light. "Look, Ayden. A shooting star! Maybe you get to make a wish, after all."

His mouth closes to a slant. "No need. I have everything I want, darling."

Special thanks you go to my awesome TouchStone family for helping to make this dream become a reality. They have been my best friends, Beta readers and a constant source of encouragement and support.

Love you guys, Paula, Jenn, Julie and Steph.

Songs featured in the soundtrack to ***TouchStone for ever*** will be available as a CD. They are the perfect accompaniment to

The Story of Us.

Twitter:@SydneyJamesson, @TouchStoneFans, @ElizabethP1984,@AydenStone, @CharlieM_TSFP

Facebook: https://www.facebook.com/Sydney-Jamesson

Website: http://sydneyjamesson.com/

Amazon: http://viewBook.at/B00CW6FNXU

9297847R00188

Printed in Great Britain
by Amazon.co.uk, Ltd.,
Marston Gate.